Praise for Sarah Price

"There are many books I have read that have touched my heart in a special way, but once in a lifetime you find that very special story that keeps you thinking long after you've read it, wondering what the characters were doing and wishing you were living that tale. For me, this is it. Sarah Price has taken two wonderful yet very different characters and woven their lives together in such a way that the reader is left breathless and wanting so much more. Alejandro and Amanda are characters you will never forget. Their struggles, their differences, their love in spite of all the obstacles . . . well . . . this series will make you a Sarah Price fan forever. Fresh. Different. Wonderful! I highly recommend!" —Sue Laitinen, book reviewer for DestinationAmish.com

"Fans of Sarah Price's Plain Fame series will not be disappointed. Amanda and Alejandro continue to delight." —Nicole Deese, Kindle bestselling author of the Letting Go series and *A Cliché Christmas*

"*Plain Again* proves that some series just get better with each book, which I didn't think was possible!" —Gina McBride, reader

"As someone who appreciates a good romance, *Plain Again* captured my heart and my imagination. Just when I think Sarah Price has written her best book ever, she surprises me and does it again! This is a must-read for anyone who has followed Amanda and Alejandro's love story from the very beginning or for any reader, frankly, who wishes to get carried away by love." —Erin Brady, Kindle bestselling author of *The Shopping Swap* and *The Twelve-Step Plan*

Plain Again

The Amish Classic Series

First Impressions (Realms)
The Matchmaker (Realms)
Second Chances (Realms)

For a complete listing of books, please visit the author's website at www.sarahpriceauthor.com.

Plain Again

Book Three of the Plain Fame Series

Sarah Price

Waterfall
PRESS

Text copyright © 2015 Price Publishing, LLC

Published by Waterfall Press, Grand Haven, MI

www.brilliancepublishing.com

Amazon, the Amazon logo, and Waterfall Press are trademarks of Amazon.com, Inc., or its affiliates.

ISBN-13: 9781503945401

ISBN-10: 1503945405

Cover design by Kerri Resnick

Printed in the United States of America

In Plain Fame, *I dedicated the book to the singers, performers, artists, authors, and entertainers who give so much of themselves for our own enjoyment.*

In Plain Change, *I dedicated the book to all of the people who adore the stars who entertain us.*

As for this book, I'd like to dedicate it to the people who support the entertainers: their family, friends, fans, and staff. It's not easy keeping up with them, but our support and encouragement motivates them to continue.

Without us, they'd be lost.

And, of course, this entire series is dedicated to my favorite "worldwide" entertainer, un chico de Cuba, the inspiration behind Alejandro and this work.

You know who you are!

<3

About the Vocabulary

The Amish speak Pennsylvania Dutch (also called Amish German or Amish Dutch). This is a verbal language with variations in spelling among communities throughout the United States. For example, in some regions, a grandfather is *grossdaadi*, while in other regions he is known as *grossdawdi*. Some dialects refer to the mother as *mamm* or *maem*, and others simply as *mother* or *mammi*.

In addition, there are words and expressions, such as *mayhaps*, or the use of the word *then* at the end of sentences, and, my favorite, *for sure and certain*, that are not necessarily from the Pennsylvania Dutch language/dialect but are unique to the Amish.

The use of these words comes from my own experience living among the Amish in Lancaster County, Pennsylvania.

Foreword

Many of my readers have written to me, telling me how they have fallen in love with Amanda and Alejandro. Perhaps more compelling is the number of women who wrote that they are completely enamored of Alejandro and asked how on earth did I come up with the idea intertwining a young, innocent Amish girl from Pennsylvania with a man from Cuba born into poverty only to rise to international superstar status.

Well, I have a confession to make. Since this is the third book in the series, I feel that the time is right to share something with my readers.

Approximately two years ago, I was watching television, something I do not normally indulge in. I call television a "time waster." When other authors ask me how I can be such a prolific author, the answer is simple: I don't waste time. However, on this particular evening, yielding to yet another capricious demand from my dear children, I happened to watch with them one of those talent reality shows (I forget which one). In between contestants, a performer came out to sing a song that I had never heard before.

As I listened and watched, the world seemed to stand still. The one singer was an attractive young man wearing a white suit and black shirt. He was bald and wore sunglasses. The way he danced, the way he moved, the way he played to the audience completely intrigued me. Charisma and character simply oozed from this Latino performer, one that I had never heard of nor seen prior to that evening. As soon as the program ended, I went to my computer and searched Google for his name.

From that moment, the seed was planted. The more I learned about this international Latino entertainer and how he rose from his humble beginnings to something akin to a world-renowned role model, how much he gives back to the community, how gracefully he treats his fans, the more I began to see him as the perfect character for a future book. But how could I possibly reconcile the life of such an international superstar with that of a plain Amish girl? How would their worlds meet? Would their respective cultures clash and collide? Was it even possible? What could be a plausible outcome?

And so the challenge was set.

I began to imagine life on the road, the downside of fame, and the loneliness of never truly knowing which person to trust. It began to make sense. Paparazzi stalk the stars just like tourists stalk the Amish. Reality shows about the Amish describe this amazing culture and fascinating religion in an unfavorable light just like gossip magazines love to expose the worst side of superstars. There are indeed similarities between these two so apparently different worlds.

That was how this story was born.

It took me longer than anticipated to write this third book of the series. For that, I apologize. Two things happened . . . both on the same day: At nine in the morning, I found out that I had breast cancer, and exactly twelve hours later, I finally met the artist who inspired this story, at nine in the evening. Needless to say, at least for the day, the joy of the latter completely overshadowed the apprehension about the former!

The meeting was brief and I handed him the first two books in the series. He proved to be a gentleman true to his reputation, worthy to have become such an inspiration to so many people across the globe. I will never forget what he said. He looked at the books, he looked at me, and then he put his hands on my shoulders and those blue eyes locked into mine as he said, "Wow. You are truly an amazing woman! That deserves a big hug."

And a great hug indeed it was, much to my ever-patient husband's chagrin!

So, dear reader, that is the true story behind the fictional story that so many have waited for so long to continue reading. I apologize for the delay. After I came down from cloud nine and started to finish this book, those pesky medical tests, four surgeries, and chemotherapy got in the way. And then a deadline from my publisher for another book popped up. Forgive me for the delay, but I do hope you enjoy the result.

After all, Alejandro belongs to all of us.

    <3
    Sarah Price

Prologue

The sun was setting over the horizon just behind the barn. Amanda lifted her head from the cow that she was milking, her eyes wandering to the open door as she paused, watching the sun dip below the tree line, the sky quickly changing from reds and oranges to gray and dark blue. Two birds flew past the doorway and disappeared toward the trees. Time to hunker down in the nest or birdhouses, wherever it was that they slept, she thought. In the distance, she could hear the familiar sound of a horse's hooves and the whirling hum of buggy wheels approach down on the road beyond her parents' farm.

She knew that it was almost six o'clock, perhaps just a few moments before, as the sun was setting earlier and earlier each day. The milking was almost finished and she would head into the house for a light supper with her *mamm*. It would be quiet in the house, the silence almost deafening as she sat in the rocking chair afterward, crocheting a blanket while her *mamm* read the Bible. By eight o'clock, they would both retire to their respective rooms: Mamm to the bedroom under the stairs and Amanda to the one next door, in the *grossdaadihaus*.

But, for now, she merely stared at the setting sun while her mind took her far away to the big city where she imagined that she was standing backstage with Alejandro as he prepared to meet his VIP guests in the special lounge. In her mind's eye, she could see him standing alone, wearing a fresh, clean black suit with cuff links at his wrists and a black tie around his neck. His shoes were buffed and shone, reflecting the light that was overhead. And, as always, he wore his sunglasses. She smiled as she imagined his expression when he paused before entering the room where the fans were waiting, a half smile spreading on his face and a quick adjustment to his suit jacket and tie. There would be a mischievous gleam in his eye, the look that always told her he was ready to make the transition from Alejandro to Viper.

The cow lifted her hind leg and stomped the ground, reminding Amanda that she was not standing backstage with Alejandro or waiting in the lounge for the VIP guests. No. She was at her parents' farm, milking the cows and tending to the chores while her mother took care of her father, who was still in the hospital. Sighing, she looked away from the sunset, feeling as if the darkness that started to fill the sky were closing in around her heart. She dipped her head and turned her attention back to the chore at hand, knowing that each day spent apart from Alejandro meant it would be one day closer to rejoining him.

He stood behind the black curtain, his hands behind his back and his head bent down as he waited for his cue. It had been a long few days with live performances on morning news shows, interviews on television, and appearances on late-night talk shows. Yet, despite his busy schedule and the constant crowds, he felt alone, as if some part of him was missing. He found himself constantly glancing at his cell phone, hoping for a voice mail or a text message from Amanda. When he only saw messages from various members of his team, he felt as though a hole were opening inside his heart.

Earlier that evening, he had sent her a text before he began to prepare for the show and the VIP Meet and Greet. It had been close to six o'clock and he knew that she would be out in the dairy, milking the cows before retiring to the house. He didn't know when she would get the message. By the time he would be able to check his own phone again, it would be well after midnight and she would have gone to bed hours earlier. When she would awaken in the morning, he would have most likely just gone to bed.

Their schedules were not conducive to anything more than texts and occasional quick phone calls.

Now, it was nighttime. Almost ten o'clock and that meant only one thing: the concert was starting. The music blasted, the lights glared, and the crowds roared as they waited for him. He wore a black shirt, black slacks, and black shoes. With his large sunglasses on, he made a formidable image standing there, his broad shoulders hunched over slightly as he waited, quietly praying as he always did before the show. No one bothered him. They knew that this was his time to reflect, absorb, and transform.

When he heard the fireworks explode from the front of the stage, the crowd shouting in surprise, he burst through the curtain and leapt onto the stage, microphone in one hand and his other fist pumping into the air. Lifting the microphone to his mouth, he tossed his head back and yelled, the crowd responding with a roar of cheers and screams.

Showtime.

Chapter One

Thinking of you and missing you.
Daed doing better.
Enjoy your day and call later if you
can.
<3
A.

The knock at the door surprised Amanda. She wasn't expecting anyone, especially since Mamm had left for the hospital already and the rest of the community had been avoiding the Beiler farm; now that the paparazzi had discovered that Viper's wife had returned to her plain roots, it had taken only three days for word to spread. And then, the privacy and peace that she had anticipated on her parents' farm quickly disappeared as the media descended again upon their farm in Lititz, Pennsylvania.

Amanda had no idea of how it had happened. Who could have possibly known? How had they learned about her *daed's* condition? How had they known that Amanda was there while Viper was on tour? But, by now, she knew that it was exactly what the media did for a living: discover things that others wished were kept secret. And the successful ones were quite good at it. They could ferret out information from even the most secretive members of Alejandro's entourage. Or, more likely, from the peripheral people who were involved in his life.

For the first few days after Alejandro had left her at the farm, Amanda had spent time with her *mamm* at Daed's bedside at the hospital. It was an unfamiliar and sterile environment with strange noises and smells. The nurses and doctors had seemed pleasant enough to Amanda and her *mamm*, but she knew that more than one person who worked at the hospital had done a double take when they realized who she was.

A few were brazen enough to outright question her. "Are you . . . ?" However, they never seemed to finish the question when they asked it.

As Alejandro had trained her, she merely smiled and greeted people who stared while remaining distant and reserved. After all, her entire attention was focused on Daed, making certain that he was properly tended to during his hospital stay.

On the second day, he had begun to awaken. He had blinked his eyes several times, trying to place where he was and what had happened. And then, his eyes found Amanda, sitting in the chair by the bedside. His eyes had sparkled, and he tried to greet her. But he wasn't able to speak, at least not very coherently yet. He had moments of clarity and a speech therapist was working with him every day. The doctors had seemed hopeful that he had not suffered brain damage and would fully recover. From his reactions, eye movements, and hand gestures, it appeared that the doctors were correct.

It was just a few days later when someone must have recognized her while visiting another patient at the hospital. A stolen photo posted on social media began the firestorm. And before Amanda knew it, she was greeted at the hospital with crowds of photographers, waiting for her arrival. For some reason, it had taken her by surprise that the paparazzi were there, eager for stolen photos of her and her *mamm*. But she wasn't taken by surprise when they returned to the farm and began to camp outside of the driveway, eager for more photos of Amanda when she would return in the evening. Amanda knew all too well that anytime she stepped outside of the house, her picture was being snapped with telephoto lenses and sent over the airwaves to the media for distribution to the public.

This time, however, Amanda knew better. She knew how to handle the paparazzi. Alejandro had taught her well. During the day, she continued to go about her chores as usual. With the police once again positioned at the end of the driveway in order to hinder the photographers from trespassing, she had some degree of isolation. Yet she knew that, in the predawn hours, the photographers snapped her picture as she walked from the house to the barn, her head down and covered with a simple black knit head scarf since the weather was turning cold. She was able to shut the barn doors before turning to the task at hand: the morning milking. When she turned out the cows, she knew that the paparazzi were stealing her photograph from the road with their long telescopic lenses. This time, she didn't care. Her image would be sold to websites and gossip newspapers. There was nothing she could do about it, and truth be told, she really had no choice as she was determined to help her family.

"How can you get used to that?" her *mamm* had asked earlier, a look of disgust on her face, as she waited for the driver to pick her up for the twenty-minute drive to the hospital.

Amanda hadn't known how to explain it to her mother. Living it was the only way to understand it. So, rather than try, Amanda gave a weak smile and simply shrugged her shoulders. "Guess you just do, after a while."

"Is that what it was really like?" her *mamm* had asked, a curious look on her face. "Traveling with him?"

For a moment, Amanda had shut her eyes and a whirlwind of memories flashed through her mind: Philadelphia, Los Angeles, Las

Vegas, Miami. After she had opened her eyes, she simply looked at her mother and smiled. "There were moments like that, I reckon," she replied. "But, for the most part, there's a lot of isolation from it. It becomes . . . white noise, I suppose."

Her mother had frowned, not familiar with that term. "White noise?"

"Background noise. Like the sound of a buggy driving down the hill. After a while, you just stop noticing the sound unless you are listening for it."

Now, however, there was someone knocking at the door. That was a noise that Amanda noticed, all right. No one came to visit the Beiler farm, not with the nosy photographers stationed outside of the farm, waiting for the million-dollar snapshot of Amanda Diaz, the Amish-born wife of Viper, international sensation and superstar.

Cautiously, she peeked through the glass, surprised to see a man standing there. From the way he was dressed, she could tell he was a local man and most likely a farmer. While he certainly wasn't Amish, she thought he might be a Mennonite. Cracking the door open, she kept her foot at its bottom and glanced over to make certain the police were still there. One of them was watching for her and waved his hand. Clearly, they had vetted the visitor.

"Yes?" she asked timidly.

"Mrs. Diaz?" the man responded, plucking his hat from his head and holding it in his hands. He was nervous and shuffled on his feet, avoiding direct eye contact.

It felt strange to have someone call her Mrs. Diaz. Among the Amish, such formalities were never used. While on the road with Alejandro, she had been known as Viper's wife or simply as Amanda. No one ever referenced either of them by using Alejandro's last name. In fact, most people always called him by his stage name. She often doubted that the greater part of his fans even knew his Christian name.

"*Ja?*" She remained blocking the door, just as a precaution.

The man glanced over his shoulder toward the barn as he said, "Your husband hired me to help with the farmwork."

"My husband hired you?"

The man nodded and glanced toward the barn. "With your father being in the hospital, Mr. Diaz asked me to step in with the barn chores so you can tend to your *daed*."

Amanda frowned. *Daed?* That was a word used by the Amish. Yet, clearly, this man was not Amish. "What's your name?"

"Harvey," he responded. "Harvey Alderfer."

Alderfer? The last name was definitely Mennonite. Yet she wondered why Alejandro hadn't told her about hiring him. That worried her. Still, if the police had let him through, certainly it was safe enough to let him muck the dairy barn while she tried to sort this out with Alejandro. It would be just like him to do something so thoughtful, she realized with a warmth building inside her chest. Only Alejandro would think to hire help for the manual labor around the farm.

"Ja vell," she said, gesturing toward the large building that housed the cows. "You could get started with the mucking, I reckon, while I contact my husband to find out about what, exactly, he has arranged."

The man seemed satisfied by her answer and tipped his hat in her direction as he backed away from the door. She watched as the willowy stranger hurried down the porch stairs and wandered over toward the barn, his shoulders slightly hunched over and his hands in his pockets. Despite having lived in the area her entire life, she did not recognize the man, but she sure recognized his disposition: Mennonite.

Amanda made certain to lock the door after she shut it, and then, chewing on her lower lip, she hurried over to the place where she kept her cell phone. It was nearly eleven in the morning. She knew that Alejandro had a performance scheduled for the previous night and had to make an appearance at an after-party, but certainly by now he would be awake, she thought. Hesitantly, she pressed the button to dial his number. She disliked using the phone and, even more so, did not want to disturb him. She never knew whom he might be meeting with or what he was doing. But she certainly needed to find out about this man, this Harvey Alderfer, who had just shown up on her doorstep.

He answered on the third ring, his voice cheerful as he greeted her. "Princesa! You must have been reading my mind!"

"I was?" she said lightly, smiling as she clutched the phone to her ear and turned to look out the window. Her eyes scanned the empty fields, but her heart raced. "And what exactly was on your mind, Alejandro?"

She heard him move, a shuffling sound that was muffled. With a low voice, he replied, "You, *mi amor*. Always you. And if you knew about what, you'd blush."

She couldn't help herself and caught herself laughing. "I think I am blushing, even without knowing."

"I only have a few minutes, Princesa. I am headed to a lunch reception," he said, his voice thick with regret. "But I trust you are calling because the hired man showed up, *sí*?"

"Sí," she said back, her eyes sparkling just from the sound of his voice.

He laughed as he always did when she tried to speak Spanish to him. "I simply can't have my wife doing all of that farmwork now, can I?"

"I have done it for many years," she pointed out, still smiling to herself.

It had been almost a week, and she missed Alejandro more than anything in her life. Yet she knew that sacrifices had to be made. Life was greater than just her. And, at this time, her parents needed her at the farm. To not be there would risk her sister's upcoming marriage to her beau in Ohio. If Amanda had been selfish and continued traveling with Alejandro, Anna would have felt compelled to return home and help rather than marry her young gentleman friend. Having already lost one prospect, Anna certainly could not risk losing another. At least, that was Amanda's perception of the situation and the main reason she had stayed behind on the family farm while Alejandro toured on the East Coast.

"Ah," he breathed, his voice deep and full of emotion. "But now you *are* my wife," he said solemnly. "And, despite the distance, I must continue to take care of you, *sí?*"

"*Sí,*" she whispered back, feeling an intense sense of loss. She had not realized how much she had grown to depend on Alejandro, on his love and support. Now that he was gone, she knew that she had become far more attached to him than she had even imagined. Loving him was just one part of the equation; counting on him was another. "*Sí,* you will always take care of me, Alejandro."

She heard him catch his breath at her words and he swallowed, fighting his own emotion that continued to swell in his chest. "And your father, Amanda. How is he? Has he returned home from the hospital?"

"Next week," she said softly into the phone. "He'll be home next week." That's what the doctor had told her *mamm* just the day before. It was news that Mamm had been most excited to share with her *dochder* when she had returned home from the hospital last evening. Yet Amanda knew that coming home was a long way from being back to normal. She wasn't certain how things would work themselves out. It all depended on his recovery.

"We must talk, Princesa," Alejandro said, a sense of foreboding in his voice. "What to do with the farm in order to help your parents."

A sigh escaped her lips. She didn't need to hear the words to know exactly what Alejandro meant. Her father certainly could no longer handle the farm, not alone. Without a son to take over, there was no one to inherit it. Not now anyway, with Amanda married to an Englische international superstar and her sister, Anna, getting married to a farmer in Ohio. Clearly, her parents' farm would have to be sold and her parents settled into a smaller home, one that her *daed* could handle. But that was definitely not something he nor his family were looking forward to, having lived on their farm for the greater part of their lives.

"*Ja,*" she admitted. "I know. Decisions I don't want to make today, that's for sure and certain."

"Now, Princesa," he said, a noise in the background distracting him for just a second. She could hear voices and laughter. "I must say good-bye for now. I am needed to greet some people for this luncheon." She sensed the dread in his voice. She knew how taxing these events were on his energy level. Yet he had taught her how necessary they were for maintaining his image and fan base. "I shall contact you later, *sí?*"

"*Sí,*" she said softly, wishing more than anything that she could be beside him. He had affirmed to her more than a dozen times how much her presence had soothed him, giving him the energy and motivation to face the crowds with a smiling face. She could sense that now this energy was forced as he faced endless streams of fans and reporters and sponsors, all of whom had no idea about the true essence of the man they knew as "Viper."

Outside, at the barn's entrance, she stood in the shadow of the doorway, her eyes adjusting to the darkness for just a brief moment. The pungent smell of the cows mixed with hay and manure accosted her nose. For some, it could have been a distasteful odor. But for Amanda, it was comforting, a smell that reminded her of her youth on the farm.

Growing up Amish had taught her a great deal about life and faith and family. Even though she loved her husband and wanted nothing more than to be beside him as he traveled the world and entertained his fans, she was secretly glad to be home with her parents, even for just a short while. Oh, she missed Alejandro . . . his teasing, his laughter, his attentiveness. But breathing in the strong scent of the barn made her realize that, indeed, there was no place like home.

As she walked down the hallway toward the dairy aisle, she could hear the scraping of a shovel against the concrete: the hired man was mucking the dairy. She made her way toward the noise, careful to step over loose manure. Her old black sneakers felt comfortable on her feet, but she realized that she was too aware of how clunky and unattractive they were. Pride and vanity, she thought and quickly chastised herself. Yet she was torn. Her new life with Alejandro conflicted so sharply with her old lifestyle on the farm. How had she changed so much in such a short period of time?

"Harvey?" she called out when she approached the tall man in order to avoid startling him. "How are you making out, then?"

Leaning against the shovel, he looked at her. "Just fine," he replied. "Been working farms for years. Nothing different here."

His tone was dry, his expression emotionless. The weathered look on his face told the story of years of laboring in the sun, tilling the soil and battling the elements. Amanda had seen that look before, among many of the Amish in her community. It dawned on her how much older the Amish, and in this case the Mennonite, farmers looked, both men and women. Unlike in Alejandro's world where the youthful appearance of the face meant more than anything else, the Amish focused more on living well off the land rather than looking well in the world.

"You live nearby, *ja?*"

He nodded his head. "Just north of Ephrata," he said.

"Well, that's not too far, I reckon!" she replied. "How did my husband find you, if I may ask?"

"Not certain of that," Harvey admitted. He paused and glanced around at the barn. "Lots of work to do, Mrs. Diaz," he said. The use of her last name startled her. Most Amish and Mennonites did not call one another by their surnames. That was definitely an Englische method of addressing others. There was something different about this

Harvey. He was a Mennonite farmer, so she wondered why he had called her by her last name.

"It's just Amanda," she said. "I'll make certain to have some coffee for you, then." With a slight smile, she turned and walked out of the dairy, pulling her black shawl tighter as she exited the barn and braved the cold to return to the house.

Inside, she looked around. Everything felt and looked smaller to her. And darker, too, she realized, giving it some thought. It no longer felt like home, yet everything about it spoke of her upbringing: the sofa in the kitchen where she had crocheted many a blanket, the kitchen counter where her *mamm* had taught her how to make bread and cheese, the table where they had enjoyed many a dinner and supper with her sister and younger brother. It had been a lively, happy kitchen until her brother had died. Then, the house had been shrouded in a cloak of sorrow and darkness. Until, she realized, Alejandro had arrived.

With a sigh, she fought the longing in her heart. She couldn't deny how much she missed Alejandro: his soft words, his attentiveness, his teasing, his love. Yet she knew that it was a big relief to both of her parents that she was there, helping to take care of the farm while her *mamm* took care of her *daed*. Just the other day, she had received a letter from Anna, a short note expressing her gratitude for Amanda's returning to the farm while she prepared for her wedding in just another week. She had promised that she would return home with her new husband as soon as they were married.

Married, Amanda thought. She would feel such relief when her sister was finally married to her beau, Jonas Wheeler. If the newly married couple traveled back to Pennsylvania, it would present the perfect opportunity for Amanda to rejoin Alejandro, at least until Anna and Jonas would return to Ohio.

And then what? That was the question that she kept asking herself.

Over and over again, she had made a mental list of options for her parents. Moving them to Pinecraft in Florida, a wonderful community of Amish, where the weather was nice all year long; this was definitely one suggestion she wanted to offer her parents. The other was selling the farm and moving them to a smaller, more contemporary house on the outskirts of the church district. Many older Amish couples did that when they had no children to take over the farm. And young Amish couples were always in need of farms, so there would be no shortage of offers on their property.

Of course, there was always that last option, that spark of hope buried deep within her heart that, perhaps, she might be able to stay on the farm, stay with Alejandro. He had been so happy on the farm during the summer, and he knew how to manage the dairy. It wouldn't take much for him to be able to handle the farm chores, especially if he could afford hired help. Yet she knew that she couldn't ask him that. His leaving the Englische world had never been part of their arrangement. It would be most unfair to extend such a request. He had a life, a career—one that he loved—at least while she was by his side. No, she realized, her staying on the farm was not an option, after all.

Amanda took a deep breath and buried her face in her hands, fighting the tears that threatened to spill from her eyes. If only Aaron had not died, she thought, but then realized that, had her brother lived, she never would have gone to Ohio last summer, and subsequently, she never would have met Alejandro. The thin thread of life that had spun itself from that one single event had changed everything, making her realize the interconnected nature of each moment in every individual's time spent living in this world.

That was the moment when the tears fell.

Chapter Two

Getting ready to go onstage, Princesa.
It's not the same without you.
I imagine you are sleeping already.
Sueñas con los ángeles, mi amor.
V.

No sooner did he step offstage at the Fillmore Detroit than the security detail surrounded him and led him through the back of the arena and down a dark corridor. People passed him, some hurrying without so much as a second glance, while others were walking about at a more leisurely pace. A few of them paused, with a raised hand, to congratulate Alejandro on yet one more outstanding performance.

Security was impatient for him to continue down the corridor, holding his one elbow as the guards led him through the people. Every second was needed to escort him away from the arena as quickly as possible. Indeed, at the end of the corridor, two black SUVs with tinted windows were parked, escorted by two police cars in front and one behind them.

Alejandro took the bottle of water that one of the staff members handed to him as he slipped into the first car. Moments later, Mike, his business manager, jumped into the seat next to him. Someone shut the door and hit the side of the window twice, indicating that the driver should leave.

The lights of the police escort began to flash, and the vehicles moved up the ramp toward the exit. Alejandro settled into his seat and took a long swig from the chilled bottle. It had been a good show, but he was already thinking ahead to the next location. One show down, he told himself. One day closer to Amanda.

As usual, there already was a crowd of people at the gated security booth at the top of the exit. No matter how quickly he would leave the arenas, there were always fans waiting, holding signs in the air and screaming for him. He never could understand how they knew where the location was for the arena's secured exit, although he felt certain that the Internet provided a lot of information for the most persistent fans. They were willing to leave the concert early to stake their claim to a spot near the exit in hopes that they would see him. Most of the time, he would roll down his window and wave, rewarding their tireless loyalty. Tonight, however, he didn't feel like it.

"Sold out again, Alex."

Alejandro nodded as he lifted the water bottle to his lips. He couldn't help but notice the pride in his manager's voice as he shared the good news about the show. "How are the other cities looking?" he asked, but without much concern. He already knew the answer before his business manager responded.

"Good, good," Mike replied as he flipped through several pieces of paper that he had pulled from his briefcase. "And of the South American countries . . . Brazil is your most popular by far. They've asked if you can add another date in São Paulo."

Alejandro let his head fall back, resting against the headrest, and sighed. He waved his hand. "Sure, whatever," he mumbled. "Might as well if we are already there, no?" Out of the corner of his eye, he looked at Mike. "But make certain that there are some open days, sí? I want to show Amanda the country."

There was a moment of silence and more papers ruffling. The noise sounded loud in the quiet of the car. Outside the SUV, the lights of the highway glowed orange, and the farther the vehicle traveled, the more Alejandro felt himself unwind. Within a few hours, he would be in Chicago, where he was scheduled to perform a Friday night concert, and then, once again, he'd fly overnight to the next destination: St. Paul. By Sunday, he'd be back in Los Angeles where he had three days to work in the recording studio and meet with the executives of the record label.

It was relentless, this schedule. During the peak of the concert season, he would perform four to five nights a week, usually on a Tuesday night and then over the weekend. Depending on the location, he would perform Thursday through Sunday, often traveling at night to the next city. This upcoming break in Los Angeles would be a welcome respite.

"We scheduled you for the Teen Choice Music Awards event," Mike mentioned. "Don't forget about that."

"When is it again?"

"Before Thanksgiving."

That was another busy week. With concerts in New York, appearances on morning news shows, interviews with talk show hosts, and a ride on a Thanksgiving Day float where he was to perform his new hit song, "Love Over Fame," the week would be downright exhausting.

When the SUV pulled into the airport, Alejandro let security guide him through the practically empty building. He went through the routine security check, then hurried down the corridor toward the airport gate. Two flight attendants smiled as he approached them, one brazenly asking for a photo. With a tired smile, Alejandro obliged before he was down a narrow set of stairs, through a doorway, and across the tarmac toward the private jet, a Gulfstream G650, that was waiting for him and his small entourage.

The pilot greeted him as he boarded the plane. Alejandro managed to spare another smile and shook the pilot's hand before hurrying to the closest seat. The leather seat shifted under his weight as he sank down, sighing heavily as he did.

A thin blonde approached him, a drink already in her hand, which she set down on the table before him. He smiled his appreciation and reached for it as Mike slid into the seat across from him, "I'll have one, too," said the manager, barely looking at the woman. "We need to go over the recording schedule for LA, Alex," he said as he dug into his briefcase.

Three more men entered the plane: two were security guards and the other was Carlos, Alejandro's personal aide. As Carlos walked past Alejandro, he slid a bag under the table by his feet. Exhaling, Alejandro reached down and, after digging into the bag, pulled out his laptop. He set it on the table and flipped the top open. "Jason booked the studio, *sí*?"

"First thing on Monday," Mike replied. There was a brief delay as the men were settled before two more people joined them on the plane. Alejandro looked up and nodded his head at the newcomers, a man and a woman, who nodded back but continued to tap away at their phones.

"What's the plan for tomorrow, Mike?" Alejandro asked as the door to the plane was shut and the engines began to rev up as part of the preflight check. The plane shuddered, just a bit, and the lights blinked off for a split second.

"Let's see," Mike mumbled, glancing through another stack of papers. "Chicago's schedule . . . Morning radio at seven thirty, a magazine reporter at eleven, another at two o'clock, and sound check at five."

He groaned. It was going to be another long day, preceded by a sleepless night. "What time do we land, anyway? One? Two?"

"And you're scheduled for a radio interview on Saturday in the morning when we get into St. Paul," Mike added, ignoring Alejandro's question about their arrival time in Chicago.

"On a Saturday?"

"Hey! They're doing us a favor, Alex," Mike retorted, an edge to his voice. "Recording it for their Monday show. Be grateful."

Rolling his eyes, Alejandro ignored his manager, despite thinking how easy it was for Mike to remind him to be grateful. After all, Mike wasn't the one who pulled eighteen-hour days of nonstop performances, whether for interviewers or crowds. It was a ruthless schedule, one that he had come to thrive on in the past, but now, without Amanda by his side, he felt something hollow growing inside him.

He reached inside his pocket for his cell phone. With a single swipe of his finger, he checked to see if there were any messages from her. None. It was after midnight. The flight wouldn't land until after one in the morning. By the time they were settled in the hotel, he imagined it would be close to two. He'd have no more than four hours of sleep, at best, followed by a full day with very little downtime.

He caught sight of Carlos and stretched so that he could see him. "You sent those flowers to Amanda, *sí*?"

Carlos gave him a thumbs-up. "*Sí*, Viper! Confirmed; they arrived at three."

He wondered why she hadn't texted him, to let him know that she had received them. He quickly sent her a message, knowing that, by the time she read it, he'd be on his way to the radio station in the morning, his eyes tired from the lack of sleep and a cup of hot coffee in his hand to perk him up.

"Alejandro," Mike said, in a concerted effort at remaining patient. "Can we talk business here? I won't get to see you tomorrow."

"*¡Ay, mi madre!*" He turned back in his seat and scowled at his manager. "What is it with you, Mike?" His blue eyes burned with anger and the muscles in his cheek tensed. "What exactly do we have to talk about? We talk every day, all day! I just wanted to check that my wife received the flowers! *¡Dios mío!*"

Holding up his hands as if in self-defense, Mike returned the harsh look. "Easy there, Alex! Just trying to keep you focused."

"Keep yourself focused," he snapped back, returning his attention to his laptop.

A silence fell over the sitting area of the plane; the other people busied themselves with their smartphones or perused through magazines. They kept their eyes down and avoided Alejandro at all costs. He didn't need to look over his shoulder to know what they were doing. They had worked with him long enough to know that, when pushed near the edge, Alejandro fought back. And when he fought back, he fought back hard with the usual result that heads rolled.

Chapter Three

```
Danke for finding Harvey.
He's such a good worker.
How was the concert last night?
Waiting to hear from you.
<3
A.
```

As she walked outside, Amanda pulled the black shawl that was slung across her shoulders tighter over the front of her dress. It was cold outside, and the sky was gray. The sun had not risen yet, despite the early-morning hour. She missed the blue skies of Miami and the smell of fresh sea air that permeated the penthouse where she lived with Alejandro, even though the sounds of the farm and smell of the cows comforted her. Whenever a horse-drawn buggy rolled down the road, she paused and lifted her head, listening to the musical humming of the wheels against the macadam. Yes, she had missed that, too.

"Gut mariye," she said as she greeted Harvey. He was already in the barn, tending to the morning milking. A soft-spoken man but reliable,

that was how Amanda would have described Harvey, had anyone asked. But she had no one to speak to. Not even Alejandro.

It had been two days since they had spoken on the telephone. With his concerts ending so late at night and then having to travel to other locations, he certainly slept until early afternoon. Amanda knew too well how taxing the concerts and the constant travel were on him, both physically and emotionally. When she was going to bed at night, he was just starting his work. Their schedules were too diverse, and she doubted that she would hear from him yet again today.

That realization saddened her.

Each morning, she'd glance at the calendar and try to figure out what Alejandro was doing that day. She knew he had finished recording in Los Angeles and thought he was now in Boston for two nights before heading to Providence for a Sunday night concert. After that, he would be in New York for almost a week. That had been the plan. But she never knew for certain since his itinerary could change at a moment's notice.

Soon it would be Thanksgiving, and he was scheduled to perform in the Macy's Thanksgiving Day Parade, whatever that was. And then, two more concerts in New York City: one on Friday and another Saturday. There would be more concerts after that: Houston, Milwaukee, Kansas City, and then back to Los Angeles for the Jingle Ball concert. There were a couple of weeks for a break before he was scheduled to return to New York City to ring in the new year at Times Square.

It was a grueling schedule, but when she had looked at the travel dates for the next year, she found herself in shock over where he would perform: countries in almost every continent. Some countries would include performances in multiple cities, Brazil in particular. When she had looked over the list, she had commented on the European leg of his tour.

"How is this possible?" she had asked, trying to understand the logistics behind all those dates and places listed on the schedule.

"*¿Qué?*" He had been flipping through some papers, numbers from recent concerts, when she had asked the question. "What are you looking at, Princesa?"

She had pointed to the paper. "This schedule. It's . . . it's . . ."

He had glanced at it and laughed. "Grueling, no?"

"*Ja!*" With a shake of her head, she had started reading it out loud. "Russia, Norway, Germany, and Sweden. All in one week?" He had continued laughing. "The next week, Finland, Poland, Croatia, and England." She had tossed the paper onto the table. "My word! I've never even heard of some of these places! Croatia?"

Now, just thinking about his schedule exhausted her. When she had traveled with him, she hadn't noticed how hectic the travel was. She just went along, not really paying attention to where they were going next. It was easier being on the inside looking out than on the outside looking in. Indeed, the more she thought about it, the more she realized she would barely be able to keep up with his innumerable flights, cities, and commitments. It was too hard to remember where he was staying and when he was leaving. She only wished that she could be with him.

In silence, Amanda began to move down the line of cows, trying to focus on the task at hand rather than the pain in her heart. She leaned her cheek against the warmth of the cow as she started milking her, breathing in the musky scent of the cow's hide as the machine worked the udder.

"Think she's done," a voice said from behind her.

Amanda looked up, her thoughts interrupted. "Hmm?" She was surprised that Harvey had spoken to her. He was usually so quiet that she often forgot he was even there.

He gestured toward the cow. "No more milk there," he said.

Quickly, Amanda looked down and, realizing that she had been daydreaming, laughed at her own mistake. The machine was drawing air at this point, and the cow was stomping her back hoof impatiently.

"I reckon you're right," she said lightly, and quickly moved on to the next cow.

The sun was just beginning to peek over the horizon when she heard the sound of an approaching buggy driving down the lane toward the house. She stood up and tried to peer out the open door, but the driver had stopped the buggy just on the other side. She looked over at Harvey. "Need to see who that is, I reckon."

"I can finish up," was his simple reply.

The bishop and the deacon were standing together by the buggy when she emerged from the dairy barn. It hadn't really surprised her that they would visit, just that it had taken so long.

"*Gut mariye,*" she called out, trying to sound friendly. She knew that the visit was not going to be pleasant, but she had been bracing for this moment since her return to the farm.

The bishop leveled his gaze at her, a stern look on his face. She had never realized how austere he looked prior to that moment, an awareness that took her by surprise, especially when she realized that she was not intimidated. With his long white beard and dark clothing, there was a suggestion of authority to the man. Yet, she had always been taught that God was the true authority for all humankind. The sudden and unexpected awareness of how his image conflicted with what she had been taught all of her life shocked her. Only time and distance could have shown her the truth behind the impression that he presented.

Whatever happened to *And whosoever will be chief among you, let him be your servant?* she found herself wondering, too aware of the sarcasm within her thought process.

"Amanda," the bishop said as acknowledgment, his eyes cold and piercing. "I trust your mother is inside?"

"*Ja,*" Amanda replied, trying not to sound too unaffected by his presence. Humility, she told herself. Even if forced, it was better to be perceived as humble with the bishop standing before her and inquiring about her *mamm*. "She'll be leaving for the hospital to visit with Daed later. They say he's to come home soon."

The fact that he did not frighten her, at least not for her sake, would not bode well for her parents. She remembered only too well how it was not that long ago that the bishop had insisted that she leave the community. He had wanted her to relocate the problem of the paparazzi to Ohio, far too willing to let another community deal with the stress of sudden fame for one of their members, a fame that had neither been sought nor wanted.

Now that she had returned, what would the bishop demand this time? She couldn't help but wonder why he had come to visit. She had been home almost two weeks now without any hint of support from the *g'may*. While *that* had surprised her, she had come to realize that the safety and protection of the community as a whole outweighed the needs of any individual.

As she gestured toward the house, indicating that they should follow her there in order to speak with her *mamm*, the two men nodded but did not speak. They shared no words expressing relief that Elias was going to be all right or that he was well enough to return to the farm. No hints of gratitude that Amanda had returned to help her family or that her husband had hired a local man to work the dairy. Instead, the cold looks on their faces told Amanda all that she needed to know: once again, this was not a social visit.

Inside the house, Lizzie was bustling about the kitchen, cleaning the morning dishes before her hired driver would arrive as scheduled each morning to pick her up for the twenty-minute drive to Lancaster General Hospital. With such a distance between the hospital and the farm, she wouldn't be returning until later that evening and wanted to finish her morning chores before leaving.

Amanda knew, however, that her *mamm* was really just trying to keep busy while she waited for the driver. Most of the chores would fall on Amanda's shoulders while her *mamm* stayed by her husband's side, holding his hand or reading from the *Budget*, while they waited for doctors to complete tests or share information. Amanda would do the house cleaning and laundry by herself before retreating outside to help the hired man with some of the barn chores.

At night, she was exhausted, but she enjoyed the work. How different, she had thought just the previous evening, from my life in Miami. In Miami, she had little work to do since Señora Perez ran the household. The days had passed by at a leisurely pace, often with Amanda waiting for Alejandro to awaken after long nights or return from business in Miami proper. After their marriage, she had lounged in his arms, despite being wide-awake as the sun cast an orange blush through the window curtains. Neither wanting to awaken him nor to leave his embrace, she had often lain there for hours until he stirred.

Now, as she was back at her parents' farm working, she found that hard work—physical labor—helped pass the time. Her body ached at night, but her mind felt at peace. She much preferred the hard work to sitting in the hospital at her *daed*'s bedside, now that she knew he would be all right.

When her *mamm* heard the door open, she called out, "Done already then, Amanda? Mayhaps you'll ride along with me to the hospital?"

"Mamm," Amanda said softly, glancing over her shoulder at the two men who were close on her heels. "Bishop's here."

The visitors entered the room and removed their hats, standing awkwardly in the middle of the kitchen. The bishop's stern eyes stared at Amanda with her dark plaid dress that was gathered at the waist. Her head was uncovered, exposing her hair, which was pulled back into a neat but braided bun at the nape of her neck. Over her shoulders, she wore a simple knit sweater and tall boots under the skirt of the dress.

His stare sent a chill through Amanda. The judgment that she could already feel from the bishop caused her to tilt her chin defiantly. Had it only been six months ago that whatever the bishop said was immediately taken as gospel by Amanda? Now, as she faced him for the second time in the same time period, she saw him in a new light. A very different one.

No longer did she fear the bishop and what he could do to her. Since she had chosen to not take the kneeling vow, the bishop did not make decisions for her. She was also steadfast in her acceptance that he would not frighten her away from her familial responsibilities. Her actions would not change, and this despite the bishop's hints that her presence would injure her parents, from both a social and a religious perspective. No, Amanda told herself, she had come home to help, and home was where she was going to stay, for the moment.

"We were surprised to hear that you had returned," the bishop started, his expression stern, but something in his eyes told her that he had become aware that Amanda was no longer intimidated by him. It was clear that her confidence unnerved him. It was not something that he was used to, not when facing his people. "And with you, those Englische men with their cars clogging the road and their cameras stealing our photos!"

"My father is in the hospital," Amanda said matter-of-factly, as a way of explanation.

Lizzie began to fuss, rubbing her hands together nervously. "Amanda was kind enough to return home to help with the farm while her *daed* is unwell," she offered.

The bishop turned to look at her, his eyes cool and emotionless. "So I have heard." He cleared his throat as he shifted his eyes to Amanda. "I have also heard that there is a hired man helping here as well."

"My husband arranged for that," Amanda stated, feeling a sense of pride that her own husband had stepped forward to offer extra help when the rest of the community had not. Had they expected her *mamm* to milk, feed, and muck the cows? Had they expected her to abandon her duties to her husband when he needed her the most? Or, she wondered, were they punishing her *mamm* for her daughter leaving the community?

"Is he plain?"

Amanda fought the urge to roll her eyes. What difference does it make? she wanted to ask. "He is Mennonite. From Ephrata." The bishop raised an eyebrow, and Amanda felt the need to explain. "He was a farmer but lost his farm. Now he hires himself out to others, and Alejandro is paying for him to help while Daed is unwell."

"Then you will be leaving soon, *ja*? And taking with you those people?"

Amanda wished that Alejandro had been next to her in order to confront the abrupt manner with which she was being addressed. However, she knew it was most likely best that he was not here, for she could only imagine what his response would have been. Always the gentleman, he would have found a way to defend her while letting the bishop know that his manner of speech was totally unacceptable.

But he wasn't there to speak on her behalf. Since the question had been directed to her, Amanda knew that the bishop was waiting for her response. While disappointed in his abrupt manner of addressing her, she knew that she had made the choice to leave the Amish community while her parents had not. She needed to respond and to choose her words wisely. The last thing she wanted to do was to say something confrontational that would jeopardize her parents' standing in the church.

With a deep breath, Amanda nodded and swallowed. "I am married now," she said. "I am not here to stay." Her eyes flickered at her mother, who seemed to cringe at the announcement. "My sister is to be married next week, and then she will travel here with her husband. We will decide how to best care for Daed as a family then."

The bishop nodded his head, approving of the plan. Apparently, family decision making was tolerable under his guidance for the *g'may*.

"That is *gut*," he admitted. Then, for the first time, he turned to look at Lizzie. "I have heard that he will recover, *ja?*"

"That is yet to be seen," Lizzie stated. "To what degree, anyway."

"We will pray for him at church," the bishop said.

"*Danke.*"

He looked at Amanda again but said nothing, his eyes disapproving. She wondered what he had thought when he had noticed her uncovered head, no prayer *kapp* pinned to the elastic headband to keep it in place. With her simple dress, one that was plain but clearly not Amish, she knew that she stood out as a non-Amish woman. Yet her mannerisms still reinforced the fact that she once had been one.

From the disappointed and fierce look on his face, she knew exactly what he thought of her: a lost sheep from the flock, one that had willingly drifted away from the shepherd and found peace in the company of wolves.

She felt the muscles in her jaw ache as she clenched her teeth, angry that the bishop's main concern had been her return to the farm, rather than her father's well-being. Still, she knew better than to say anything. She was no longer part of the community and, as such, had no voice or right to complain. Her heart felt heavy as she realized that she had changed more than she had thought. Never would the old Amanda have wanted to lash out at the bishop. Once again, she was stunned by how little she fit into the place once considered her home.

Chapter Four

Tried to call earlier. No answer.
Meeting with Mike in thirty minutes.
Tonight is the Teen Choice Music
Awards.
Wish you could go with me, Princesa.
V.

Alejandro stood against the window, one hand pushing back the sheer curtains as he peered outside, his blue eyes searching the crowded streets below. Despite it being November, the sky was blue and the sun shone. From the look of the people walking by the apartment building, he could tell that it was warm outside. After all, Los Angeles had near-perfect year-round weather.

Behind him, Mike leaned back in his chair at the table and tapped his finger against the stack of newspapers that were strewn across the glass tabletop. He watched Alejandro carefully, too aware of the tenseness in the man's shoulders and the way the muscle in his jaw contracted.

"You can't go alone," Mike said for the third time. "It's the Teen Choice Music Awards, for crying out loud, and you are being presented with the Latino Award!"

Alejandro sighed and shook his head. Was it only ten years ago that he was still struggling to make ends meet? Performing in raunchy bars for food and then fighting with others because they made fun of his singing songs onstage? Prior to that, he had mostly been considered a street thug, singing by the corner store in street sing-offs with other gangster-wannabe kids. It was lucky that he hadn't been killed. Several of his friends had been.

To have survived that lifestyle was nothing short of a miracle. Indeed, the fact that he had come so far in such a short period of time continued to amaze him. It was something that he vowed to always remember and respect. "Teen music? How did that happen?"

They both knew what he meant. His music was not necessarily teenager-friendly. Most of his labels were marked "Explicit" and "Parental Advisory." In order to get airtime, they always had to create softer versions that were appropriate for all audiences. To have been nominated for such an award was quite surprising.

Mike rolled his eyes. "That's not important. What is important is that you simply cannot go alone to the after-parties!"

"I'm not going with anyone but Amanda," he replied. "How would that look if I showed up with another woman?"

For the past four days, Alejandro had been in Los Angeles, recording new songs. Tonight, he'd attend this event and by the next day, he'd be in Boston for the weekend concerts. It was a busy schedule but that was the time of year: holidays meant appearances around the country, and that, in turn, translated into extra sales of songs and larger audiences at upcoming concerts.

"How will it look if you arrive alone?"

Alejandro laughed at the exasperated look on his manager's face. "Like a married man who is going out without his wife!" He stood up and smoothed at the creases of his black suit pants. He turned to look at the mirror on the wall and straightened his red tie. With the dark suit, the tie looked extra bright and sensual, Alejandro thought. "Teen Choice Music Awards, *sí*?" He glanced at his manager's reflection in the mirror. "That's quite surprising, no?"

His manager shrugged. "How many Latino stars are out there, Alejandro? Not many. How many have risen to the level that you have after coming from so little? None that have reached your level. Your lyrics might be questionable at times, but you are an inspiration." Impatiently, Mike glanced at his watch. "Speaking of inspiration, the car is picking you up in ten minutes for the radio interview. Remember? Justin Bell is joining you, too."

A sigh escaped from Alejandro. Evening rush hour on the radio: a joint interview with Justin Bell, the current teenage heartthrob of the music industry and the object of complete adoration from teen and tween girls around the world! Certainly there would be a mob scene at the radio station, just as much for Justin as for Viper. The eyes of every teenager in the United States would be on the show tonight, but the ears of every teenager in Los Angeles would be listening to KAMP-FM 97.1 that afternoon.

It had already been over a week and a very long one at that. The last information he had from Amanda was that her *daed*'s release from the hospital was scheduled for the following day and, so, her sister would be returning to the family farm shortly. With his travel itinerary, the days and nights flew by quickly. He was always busy and always on. That also meant that he was increasingly exhausted and irritable.

It was getting harder and harder to maintain the smiles and good mood knowing that the only person he wanted to see was thousands of miles across the country and working the family farm. To make matters worse, when he had to go out at night, he found himself increasingly distant from the women. In the past, he would have enjoyed his evenings at the restaurants, clubs, and parties. Having women throw themselves at him did have its benefits. But that was then; now he found that the women were playing a new game. The goal wasn't just to catch his attention but to drive a wedge between him and Amanda.

And that was simply becoming annoying to Alejandro.

"Any word on that nurse for Elias?"

Mike shut his eyes, lifting his hands to his brow and rubbing his temples. "Alex," he began calmly. "You have to snap out of this. It's been what? Ten days? Eleven? We have business to focus on, my friend."

Alejandro cast a quick glare over his shoulder at his manager. His blue eyes narrowed, and he took a second to catch his breath before responding. "I asked a question," he managed to say. "The nurse?"

Taking a deep breath, Mike nodded his head once. "Taken care of."

"When?"

"Next week." He glanced down at a folder, his eyes shifting over a piece of paper. "A week from Monday."

Alejandro nodded, although that information didn't necessarily please him. That was still ten days away. *"Bien, gracias."*

Mike shuffled some of the papers on the table and changed the subject. "Now, can we talk some business? Did you get a chance to see the video? They want to release it before Thanksgiving."

"Sí, sí," he replied dismissively, returning his gaze to the window. "I went to the production studio yesterday, although I already had watched it." He glanced over his shoulder. "You know that." He released the curtain and turned around, both of his hands behind his back as he stared at his manager. "I trust that you will arrange transportation for Amanda, *sí?"*

Mike glanced at his watch again and started to stand up, collecting his papers. "You need to get going. We'll catch up in Boston this weekend."

"Mike?"

Stopping what he was doing, Mike looked up and met Alejandro's steady gaze. "Yes?"

"Transportation for Amanda," he repeated, this time not as a question but a statement. "Get that nurse situated and then I want Amanda here . . . back with me."

"Of course, Alex," Mike said, rolling his eyes and clearly frustrated. "Whatever you request."

Alejandro reached into his pocket for his phone, clicked on the screen, and checked the time. With a deep breath, he reached for his suit jacket that hung over the back of a chair; then, without another word, he sauntered out of the room, leaving Mike standing there, alone. Just as he was about to walk through the front door, he heard Mike swear, loud enough so that Alejandro could hear before the door shut behind him. Alejandro stood in the hallway long enough to collect himself before he slid his arms into the jacket and strode over to the elevator, pressing the "Down" button. He didn't care if Mike was frustrated. It was time for his manager to step up and earn his salary, and if that meant he had to help manage Amanda as well, so be it.

Later that night, as he stood on the red carpet, his back to the Teen Choice Music Awards backdrop, he posed and smiled at the photographers, ignoring the questions about why Amanda was not with him. Despite the throngs of reporters with special access passes to the celebrities, Alejandro waved them away as he hurried along the carpet toward the entrance into the building.

He went through the motions of the evening, greeting his peers and different players in the music industry. Several times he posed with various singers whom he had featured in his songs and sometimes performed with onstage. The night was about sound bites and being photographed with the right people. It was a game that Viper played well.

Still, his mind continued to return to Pennsylvania. He found himself constantly glancing at his phone, checking the time and calculating what time it would be in Lititz. He wondered what Amanda was doing, what she was thinking, what she was feeling. He wondered if she was missing him as much as he was missing her.

"Excuse me," he said to the three people who were standing next to him, engaged in a conversation of superficial music-industry gossip. "I am expecting a call. *Permiso.*" He didn't wait for their response before he hurried through the crowd and found a quiet corner to use the phone. With shaking hands, he called Amanda. He needed to speak to her, needed to hear her voice, or else he simply couldn't get through the night.

"Hello?"

The sound of her voice, so sweet and innocent, with a hint of the Amish accent on that single word, caused his heart to beat faster. Oh, how he missed her! "Ah, Princesa!" He turned his back to the crowd and covered his one ear with his hand so that he could hear her better. "How are you this fine evening?"

"Alejandro!"

He laughed at the enthusiasm in her voice. "Who else would be calling you, eh? Were you expecting someone else?"

He thought he heard her gasp. "Oh, *nee, nee!*" There was a hint of panic in her tone. "I . . . I just never thought you'd call so late! I thought you had an awards thing tonight."

A smile crossed his lips. "I think the producers for the event would be disappointed to hear you call it an awards 'thing,' no?" He laughed again. He could only imagine the indignation on the faces of the producers if they had overheard Amanda's comment. In Los Angeles, ego was everything; a deflated ego was career suicide. "You know that you could probably watch it from your phone, Amanda."

There was a slight pause, and without being there, he knew that she had lifted the phone from her ear to stare at it. "Oh, I wouldn't know anything about doing that!"

"Oh, Amanda," he sighed. "We'll have to teach you how to use that device, no?" Quickly, he changed the subject. "I wanted to say good night before attending the 'awards thing,'" he gently teased. "And to let you know how much I miss you, Princesa."

"I miss you, too," she said softly. "Daed should be home soon, and then Anna will arrive."

"Everything else working out fine, Princesa?"

Another hesitation. It was as if she was collecting her thoughts before she responded. Immediately, he knew that something had happened. "*Vell*, not really," she admitted. If there was one thing Alejandro knew that he could count on from his wife, it was that she would always tell the truth. "The bishop was here."

He took a deep breath, waiting for his wife to continue. While he had never truly met the bishop beyond that one church service he had attended, back in the summer, he knew enough about the way the Amish worked; a visit from the bishop was most likely not one of a social nature.

"He's rather anxious for me to leave," Amanda said drily.

"As am I," Alejandro added, trying to lighten her mood.

She didn't respond.

"Amanda," he started. "There is nothing that he can do to you now. And your father is in the hospital. It makes perfect sense that you are there to help out until he is well or other arrangements can be made, no?" Someone tapped him on the shoulder and Alejandro peered around, smiling when he saw Justin Bell. "One minute, man," he said to his friend, holding up a finger so that Justin would wait for him to end his call. "Don't worry, Princesa. Before you know it, your father will be fine and we will be together again. Now, I must go. We will talk *mañana, sí?*"

"*Ja,*" she whispered.

"*¡Bueno! Adiós y te amo,* Princesa.*"

"*Te amo,*" she replied before he hung up the phone.

He gave Justin a quick embrace, slapping him on the shoulder in a gesture of friendship. The younger man had a small crowd of people behind him, people who Alejandro didn't know. In the distance, Alejandro thought he caught sight of Justin's girlfriend, Celinda, but she was talking to her own group of acquaintances. "What's up, man?"

"Heard you're going to be in New York for Thanksgiving, Viper," Justin said, running his fingers through his blond hair, his bright blue eyes searching the room as if looking for someone or something. "Having some people at my hotel on the Wednesday before. You should bring Amanda."

"Sounds good." He hadn't given much thought to that Thanksgiving week in New York City. All that he knew was that he was busy with back-to-back events on Wednesday and two concerts over the weekend before he returned to Los Angeles for another awards event. He also knew that he wanted Amanda to join him. "Hey, good luck tonight," Alejandro said before lifting his hand in the air to give Justin a high five.

For the next fifteen minutes, he mingled with the crowd. He was constantly surrounded by a group of people. There was an electric energy in the room as everyone lingered before slowly making their way into the main auditorium. It was as if no one wanted to be the first to sit down. To do so might mean missing something or someone important in the reception area.

Alejandro was relieved when the bell rang and ushers began to gently guide people through the doors and into the auditorium toward the front, which was reserved for those who had been nominated for awards as well as the big-name players in the industry.

The problem with the awards shows was that Alejandro had to remain on during the entire event. One of the first things he had learned was that the camera could always be pointed in his direction, even if not filming a close-up of him per se. There were too many stories of celebrities caught whispering to someone else, their lips easy to read, or putting on lipstick, or even worse, nodding off to sleep. For three hours, Alejandro had to be on high alert, to look his best from every angle, despite wishing he were anywhere else but here.

Once the show began and the majority of lights were on the stage, he let his mind wander back to the summer on the Beiler farm. He could almost feel the sun on his face and hear the rustling of the corn in the fields. Even the smell of freshly cut hay pervaded his memory. That one week had felt like a month to him, a month of peace and tranquility. And it had ended far too soon.

On the day he had left, he hated leaving Amanda behind. While he hadn't realized that he loved her, he had known that she was special, the type of woman that he would have wanted to get serious with if their lives were a little less extreme in their differences. He had never imagined that she would leave the Amish, never imagined that he would return to fetch her. Yet, when he had seen her on the television, those eyes pleading into the camera, he knew that she was reaching out to him, and he had dropped everything to rescue her.

Even then he hadn't realized that he was falling for her. His intentions had been honorable: take her away, let the furor die down, then bring her back to Lancaster to continue her future among the Amish. Life, however, had a funny way of stepping in and derailing the good intention train. Before he had known it, he had fallen for the dark-haired, dark-eyed Amish girl with her innocent outlook on life . . . his life in particular. The thought of not having her beside him, a man who had vowed to never get married, drove him mad at night as he slept alone.

He had never expected to fall in love, and certainly not with someone like Amanda. But then again, he had never met anyone like her. God had brought them together through the accident in order to ensure that two soul mates from the most unlikely backgrounds found each other.

Someone nudged him from behind his seat. Alejandro jumped, just a little, and turned around to see Celinda Ruiz sitting there. She smiled at him and gestured with her head toward the stage.

"It is with great honor tonight that, for the first time at the Teen Choice Music Awards, we have four nominations for our brand-new Latino Artist of the Year Award. It's an award that was long in coming, and with such an impressive pool of talent, the nominations were certainly hard to narrow down," the announcer said into the microphone. "Tonight, the nominations for Latino Artist of the Year are . . ."

Alejandro sat straight in his seat, knowing that the camera would pan to him when his name was called. He listened to the first three names, recognizing the irony that he had recorded songs with two of them. In a cutthroat industry, Alejandro had strived to avoid the typical backstabbing among the artists. That didn't mean, however, that others played by the same rule.

"And the fourth nomination is . . . Viper!"

The audience applauded and a few cheered from the back rows and balcony. Alejandro smiled, nodding his head toward the camera and lifting his hand in acknowledgment.

The announcer waited for the applause to die down before he shuffled the envelope in his hand to begin opening it. "And the award for the Latino Artist of the Year goes to . . ." There was a long pause, drawn out for more impact than was necessary. Alejandro sat there, staring straight ahead, dreading the moment whether he won or not. Either way, he would be judged on his reaction by the millions of television viewers who were tuned into the show.

"Viper!"

Alejandro paused for a moment, replaying the winner's name in his head to make certain he had heard correctly. When the people seated in front of him turned to smile in his direction, he knew that he had. He shook the hands of the people immediately surrounding his seat as he stood and made his way toward the stage to collect his award.

He had won previous awards during his career, but this was a special one. As a new award, it not only recognized the importance of contributions from the Latino community to the music industry but also proved that Viper was crossing into heretofore uncharted populations: not just Americans but also younger Americans!

He felt the heat from the lights on his face as he accepted the trophy, a large multicolored surfboard, and stepped toward the microphone. He smiled into the cameras and waited for the applause to die down. *"¡Dios mío!"* he said jokingly as he held onto the surfboard. "This is heavier than I thought!" The audience laughed. "But I am honored to be able to accept it tonight, not just for my work but for the work of all the Latino artists in the entertainment industry!" More applause and a few whistles came from the audience. "Not bad for a *chico* from Cuba, eh?" He paused again, waiting for the audience to quiet down. "I want to thank so many people: the record label and my producers in Los Angeles, my manager, Mike, for his continued support of my career, my buddies in Miami, who inspire me when I'm writing songs, my mother, who taught me to fight for what I want." He paused and looked directly into the camera. *"Te amo, Mami."* Polite applause. "And, of course, the young woman who honored me just a month ago by becoming my wife. Her love and faith inspire me!" He took a step back from the microphone and lifted the award over his head. *"¡Gracias a Dios!"*

The audience erupted into wild applause as Alejandro was led backstage so that the next award could be announced.

By now, he knew the drill. He had won other awards before this one. He would walk the gauntlet of entertainment reporters who were waiting to interview him, hoping for some exclusive sound bite that they could use on their programs. Then, there would be the endless photographs against another Teen Choice Music Award backdrop.

At some point, he would return to his seat, although Alejandro was tempted to slip away. Unfortunately, he knew that his absense would be noticed and certainly commented on by the tabloids.

It was almost an hour later when the ceremony ended. Despite being hounded by well-meaning partygoers who wanted him to attend the after-hours gatherings, Alejandro gave noncommittal answers and fought his way through the crowds to get into his awaiting car. He was tired. It had been a long day, and despite the fact that Mike would be furious, Alejandro leaned forward and instructed the driver to take him back to his condo. He had more long days ahead of him, and the last thing he wanted to do was spend the rest of the night partying.

No, he thought. Those days were over. Without Amanda, he told himself, he had no interest in drinking and dancing until the early hours of the morning. Instead, he'd relax at the hotel room and get a good night's sleep. *For once.*

Chapter Five

```
Wunderbar news about the award.
Danke for letting me know.
What is this about a nurse?
Another surprise?
<3
A.
```

Harvey slowed down the car before turning into the parking lot behind the natural food store. He glanced at Amanda before he put the car in "Park" and turned off the engine. "You alright, then?" he asked, concern in his eyes as she faced out the window, her hand covering her mouth and the color drained from her face. "You know you could never have gone in a buggy, Amanda. Driving was the only way."

She nodded and lowered her hand. Several other cars pulled in behind them. She already knew that those cars were driven by the more brazen of the photographers who had followed them. She had no choice but to face them, head held high and eyes straight ahead. "*Ja*, I know," she replied softly. "*Danke* for bringing me."

She hadn't counted on the paparazzi following them. But as soon as Harvey had pulled out of the driveway with Amanda in the passenger seat, three of the cars immediately followed. She hated the thought that they were taking her photograph with another man. She knew enough about the gossip magazines to suspect what the headline would read. There would be suspicions about who the man was driving the car and more speculation that her rushed marriage to Alejandro was already failing.

Oh, he had told her about those headlines when they had talked on the phone just two nights ago. He was in Los Angeles, working on several endorsements. He had told her about the concerts in Chicago and Detroit and St. Paul. And then he had told her about the tabloids.

Despite his casual manner about the stories, she had found herself in despair. The thought that people might actually believe those horrid stories upset her. Indeed, his news had broken her heart and she had felt increased pressure to rejoin him on the road. But he had reassured her that it was just part of the game.

Now, as she faced the intruding cameras once again, this time with Harvey Alderfer by her side, she did not need much imagination to visualize the headlines on the social media and tabloid papers that would grace the grocery store aisles within days.

Harvey glanced over his shoulder at the men who emerged from their respective cars, cameras in hand, busy snapping away, the lenses pointed in their direction. As usual, he remained calm and collected; nothing seemed to bother him. "Shall I walk in with you, then?"

Amanda hesitated. She hadn't dealt with the paparazzi one-on-one. Not really. At the farm, the police had kept them off the property. Now she was in the parking lot and her parents needed her to pick up a list of items. She could have asked Harvey to go without her, but she had felt the need to leave the farm, to escape the sorrow that had fallen over the house since her *daed*'s accident and her return. When Harvey had proposed that he drive her in his car, she had happily accepted, insisting that she pay him for the gas. She hadn't considered the possibility of the photographers following them.

"Or we can go back to the farm," he suggested.

The cowardly way, she thought bitterly. It was bad enough that she was apart from Alejandro, especially since they had barely been married a month, but she was not about to hide from these people. She didn't want him to worry any more than she knew he already did. She would do what Alejandro had taught her to do: face them and then move on.

"*Nee*, Harvey, but I appreciate your patience. I can handle this," she said, with more confidence than she actually felt.

Her hand shook as she opened the door of the car, dipping her head down as the men rushed toward her. To their credit, they kept a respectful distance while they photographed her as she walked into the store. She did her best to keep her head high then, staring straight ahead and not responding to them. She knew better than to encourage them. Alejandro had taught her that. Only respond when it's an event.

As she approached the door of the store, she saw it open. She was about to enter when she saw an elderly couple emerge, a box of goods in the man's arms. Amanda stepped aside, surprised to see the woman nod at her. It was a woman from her church district. But as soon as the woman saw the photographers, she shielded her face and hurried away from Amanda.

To her surprise, the photographers stayed outside of the store. She wasn't certain that they would respect the store enough to not enter; however, they remained poised with their cameras to take photos once she left. Amanda walked through the door and, with just a quick glance over her shoulder, shut the door behind her.

The store was well lit, despite the lack of electricity. Special skylights with tubing brought natural sunlight into the store, making it as bright as if fluorescent lights lined the ceiling. Amanda glanced around, trying to get her bearings. It had been a while since she had been here. She realized that it had been more than six months, just before she had gone to Ohio with her sister. Yet she immediately remembered where everything was located in the aisles and she felt a comforting sense of familiarity, one that she hadn't felt in a long time.

The only shopping she had done since leaving Lancaster in the summer had been with Alejandro, and it certainly had not been for groceries or supplies. No, it had been for dresses and jewelry, shoes and accessories. She had also shopped with Lucinda and Celinda, but it wasn't the same. The stores were new and exciting with racks of shoes and rows of clothing. Amanda had never seen anything like it; *obscene* had been the word that had come to mind. It was understandable why Englische people, women in particular, fussed over their appearance, for there were simply too many options to choose from.

But at the natural food store, Amanda felt at home. Everything seemed familiar, from the bulk foods that were packaged in simple clear plastic bags with white labels on the front, to the cold room with the fresh vegetables that were lined up so neatly in the produce cases.

She pushed the small cart down the broad aisles, pausing to pick up more flour, sugar, and dried beans before turning to the fresh produce section. She smiled at an Amish woman standing nearby, and to her surprise, the woman frowned and turned away without greeting her. Always, in the past, the Amish greeted one another, stranger or not. Amanda was puzzled by this woman's behavior, wondering why she had been snubbed. Was it because she was Amanda Diaz or simply because she was not in Amish garb?

In the pasta aisle, she noticed a familiar face: her friend Hannah. She hadn't seen much of Hannah since Aaron had died. For a while, Hannah had been one of her closest friends. They had shared almost as many secrets as Amanda shared with Anna. But their friendship had faded since Hannah had accepted that buggy ride home from Joshua Esh after the youth singing on a Sunday so long ago. Most of Hannah's free time had been spent with Joshua, for they were openly courting.

Indeed, after Aaron's death, things had changed on the Beiler farm. Neither Anna nor Amanda had wanted much to do with social activities. Anna had fallen into a depression, and her relationship with Menno Zook had ended. The family had taken a long time to grieve Aaron's death, as if something like that could ever be forgotten. As a result, they had withdrawn into themselves and friendships had been forgotten.

But life had continued for the rest of the *g'may.*

Amanda pushed her cart next to her friend and reached out to touch the woman's arm.

"Hannah!" She smiled. "It's right *gut* to see you!"

The woman turned from the bags of pasta that she had been surveying and eyed Amanda. It took her a minute to recognize the woman who stood before her. Despite her simple dress, Amanda was not wearing Amish clothing, nor was she wearing a prayer *kapp.* "Amanda? Amanda Beiler?"

"It's Amanda Diaz now," she replied, feeling the warmth of a blush covering her cheeks. Certainly, Hannah was aware that she had left the community and married the Englischer. The Amish grapevine was too strong to have ignored that tidbit of gossip, of that Amanda was sure and certain. "How are you?" She didn't really need to ask that, for Hannah's expanding waistline told Amanda all that she needed to know about her friend: married and expecting a baby.

"Just fine. Reckon I should ask you the same, ain't so?" Her friend smiled, a warm and welcoming smile. "Had heard that you were back in town. Awful sorry to hear about your *daed.* Hope he's doing well."

Amanda nodded. "He's soon to recover," she said. "Doing as well as can be expected. Not walking right now, but the doctors have hope that he will."

The door to the store opened and two men walked in, speaking in Pennsylvania Dutch to each other. Amanda heard the word *photographer* in the midst of their conversation and lifted her head to look at them.

The men walked past the aisle, one of them noticing her standing there. He paused, narrowing his eyes, and mumbled, *"Troovel,"* under his breath: trouble.

Hannah averted her eyes, embarrassed for her friend.

The word hit Amanda like a slap and she cringed.

"I . . . I best get going," Amanda said softly and, without waiting for a response, hurried down the rest of the aisle, pushing the cart before her as if it were a shield. She finished her shopping, her head down and refusing to look at anyone as she hurried through the store. She caught sight of the two men standing near an elderly couple, their tongues wagging and one of them gesturing toward her. Ignoring them, Amanda pushed the cart to the counter. She felt tears stinging at her eyes but refused to let them fall.

"How's your *daed*?" the woman at the cash register asked as she began to ring up Amanda's order.

It took her a minute to realize that the woman was speaking to her. "Excuse me?"

"Your *daed*. Is he doing better now?"

"Oh," Amanda started. "*Ja, ja*, much better. Should be coming home next week, I reckon."

The worker continued ringing up the order. "And your sister? I hear her wedding was announced just before your *daed*'s accident?"

"*Ja*, just before his stroke."

"They'll be returning here, then?"

Amanda nodded. "To visit. Around Thanksgiving week, I reckon."

The woman glanced over her shoulder toward the door. "Reckon you'll leave then, *ja*?" She looked back at Amanda, leveling a steady eye at the young woman. "And taking your friends with you?"

It took a moment for Amanda to realize exactly what the cashier meant. Slowly, it dawned on her that she was talking about the photographers. Amanda took a breath and squared her shoulders, refusing to let the woman see the pain she had felt from the hurtful insinuation of the woman's words. It was clear that the woman was telling Amanda that she was not wanted at the store, not if she brought with her the attention and cameras of the Englische.

The way she had been treated by the other customers and now by the cashier shocked Amanda. Hadn't it been just a few months ago that she, too, had been Amish? Hadn't she been treated with the respect and courtesy that the community practiced among their friends, family, and neighbors? However, today she had seen a different side to the people she used to consider her own. It was as if they had decided to unofficially shun her, and that feeling ripped through her in a way she had not expected.

Amanda had no response and, in typical Amish fashion, merely remained silent, her eyes staring straight ahead. *Best to let angry words remain unspoken,* her *mamm* had always told her.

Indeed, she told herself, I have nothing to say that would soothe either my raw nerves or hers.

Quietly, she paid her bill and pushed the cart with the food toward the door. She struggled to open it, finally pushing it with her hip and jerking the cart over the slightly raised metal bar that covered the threshold. When she approached the second door, she managed to maneuver the cart better and felt the cold air on her face as she stepped outside.

The photographers were waiting, eager to snap her photo as well as some shots of what was inside the cart. Amanda tried to look straight ahead, but a few of the men walked backward in front of her. She looked away, but there was no escaping their invasion of her personal space.

"That's enough," a deep voice said. Immediately, an arm seemed to come out of nowhere, pushing the photographers away and blocking Amanda from view. "Give the lady some space. You boys don't have much else to do, eh?"

Amanda blinked twice, stunned to see Harvey guiding her through the paparazzi and toward the car. He leaned over and whispered into her ear, "Get in. I'll take care of the food." Without a second's hesitation, Amanda did as he commanded, hurrying into the car, shutting the door and locking it. She covered her face with her hands, knowing that they were still taking photographs. After all this time, she wondered why they were still so interested in her.

After Harvey loaded the groceries and got into the car, he turned to look at her. "You all right, then?"

The concerned expression on his face touched her. It was all that she could do to simply nod her head, not trusting her voice to speak.

"I think I'll get a list from you or your *mamm* next time," Harvey said, putting the car into drive and pulling away from the photographers. "No need for you to go through that type of scene again."

It had been so different with Alejandro. Wherever they went, there had been crowds of people, true. But it had been controlled, and Alejandro knew how to handle them. Now, in her own hometown, along the small back roads of Lititz in Lancaster County, she couldn't even go to a grocery store.

She remained silent on the short drive back to her parents' farm. Staring out the window, she saw things in a different light. The large, open pastures and well-kept farmhouses, normally so serene and beautiful, now seemed barren and devoid of joy. Indeed, she realized as they approached the line of cars parked along the side of the road outside of her parents' lane, there is no joy left in Lancaster for me at all.

"Let me help carry in these groceries," Harvey said when he parked the car in front of the house. He didn't wait for an answer as he opened the door and grabbed the two large boxes of food.

Silently, Amanda followed him into the house, her mind reeling from what had just happened at the store. From meeting her friend to the unkind words uttered by an aging Amish man to the rebuff from the cashier at the register, Amanda was still in shock. How is this possible, she wondered, that people can be so cruel and insensitive?

"You alright, then, Amanda?"

"Hmm?" She looked up, unaware that Harvey had been watching her. The two boxes were on the kitchen table, and he stood behind them, one hand on the tabletop as he stared at her. "Oh, *ja*," she said dismissively, knowing that she wasn't telling the full truth. "I got this, *danke.*"

As she approached the table to begin unloading the goods from the boxes, she noticed that Harvey made no move toward the door. His presence did not disturb her, however. There was something comforting about him.

"It can't be easy," he finally said, breaking the silence. "For you or for them."

"Them?" His words surprised her, and she didn't know to whom he was referring. "The paparazzi?"

He chuckled and shook his head. "The Amish in your community."

"Ah," she replied wistfully, not certain that she wanted to agree with him, although knowing that he spoke the truth.

"They cannot understand your choice, I reckon," he continued. "And you probably cannot understand their harsh determination in dealing with it."

Harsh determination? She wanted to laugh at his choice of words. Harsh, indeed! She felt unwanted and betrayed by the very people among whom she had been raised. She had not realized that she could be treated in such a manner, especially since she had never taken her baptism. They were unofficially shunning her without officially admitting it. Yet Amanda knew that she couldn't abandon her family, not after all they had been through.

Oh, she knew that there was no home for her among the Amish. Not anymore. Her love for Alejandro transcended her desire to remain plain. And she knew better than to pressure him to consider such a move. She had made the decision to leave her family and her community for Alejandro. And now that they were married, she hadn't once regretted that decision. Still, the rejection she had felt during that shopping excursion stung at her soul. How could her own people be so cold?

"I reckon I can pray about it," Amanda finally admitted. "Mayhaps then I can gain some understanding." Forcing a smile, she took the empty box and set it on the floor before tackling the second one. "What does the book of Proverbs say? *All the ways of a man are clean in his own eyes; but the Lord weigheth the spirits.*"

Harvey reached down for the empty box. "The self-righteous heart can justify just about anything, ain't so?"

She wondered if he was directing that comment to her or toward the people of her *g'may* but decided not to ask. Either way, he spoke the truth. She had never considered herself self-righteous and could only presume that he meant the *g'may*. "I am not above correction or conscience," she said softly.

"I did not mean you," he confirmed, reaching his hand out for the second box. "Your actions speak of a contrite and honest heart, Amanda. Of the others, however, I am not so sure."

Amanda stared after him as he carried both of the empty boxes toward the door. He paused, just briefly, before he disappeared outside. She stared after him, his words haunting her.

Indeed, he had been speaking of the Amish, the people of her *g'may*. How could she have been so blind to the prejudices of her own community for all of those years? Despite the peace and tranquility of her youth, she was seeing things differently now. Where she used to see colors, so bright and vibrant, she was now seeing things in black and white. Her mind seemed flooded with conflicting information; it pulled her even further away from her upbringing.

Could it be true? Could the prejudices of the bishop and the lack of compassion of the people show a communally lofty heart? One that countered all of the teaching and preaching in school, church, and home? The idea was shocking to her, and she stood there, stunned, as the thoughts raced through her head.

She appreciated Harvey's insight. As a Mennonite, he was close enough to the Amish community to be knowledgeable about their ways, yet he provided an outside perspective that she had never bothered to seek. Was that what the Englische thought about the Amish? That they abandoned those who left the fold? That their hearts did not reflect the truth behind the spoken word?

"No!"

The sound of her own voice startled her. Perhaps from the outside looking in, the ways of the Amish seemed strange, even to someone like Harvey, who had lived among them for so long. Still, she felt inclined to protect the community, even the harsh bishop with his lack of emotion and compassion.

Among the Amish, the people were expected to live simple lives. The bishops of each *g'may* set the rules by which the people lived, the emphasis always focused on communal order and discipline. When those rules were broken, the consequences were accepted and followed. For some infractions, it meant a private confession. For others, it might be a public one. For the most serious transgressions, the perpetrator might fall under the *bann*, a shunning among the people until sins were properly confessed and repentance proved under way.

From the outside looking in, such a process might seem fierce and harsh. Yet everyone willingly agreed to live by those rules. There was no evangelism among the Amish, no pressure to join beyond that of parents pushing their children. However, no one fought the rules of the church. Indeed, had Amanda not met Alejandro, she would still follow those rules, despite not having taken her baptism. Now, because she had followed her heart, she had challenged the rules and, subsequently, the order of the *g'may*.

Oh, she understood it rather well now. The resistance that she had experienced on that very day from people who used to be considered friends as well as kin was a clear recourse spawned by her own actions and decisions. With the paparazzi stationed outside of her parents' farm and wandering through Lititz, there was a conflict between the rule and order that the people wanted to follow and the intrusion of the outside world, the very world that they wanted so much to avoid.

Sighing, she sank down onto the bench at the table. With her eyes closed, she lifted her heart to God and prayed, begging for the strength to continue her journey. She prayed for *Gelassenheit*, complete submission to the will of God. *Direct me, oh heavenly Father,* she asked. *Direct me so that I do the right thing for everyone: my* schwester, *my parents, my husband, and my community. I yield myself completely to your will, oh Lord.*

Chapter Six

```
Please stay on the farm.
I don't want you harassed.
It will only be for a few more weeks,
yes?
How is your father doing?
When is Anna to arrive?
V.
```

It was Carlos who had reluctantly handed Alejandro the stack of magazines and tabloid papers at the condo while his boss was having breakfast. The sun was already high in the sky, a sky clear as can be, totally devoid of clouds. A perfect autumn day in California, he thought. The only thing missing was Amanda.

However, when he picked up the first tabloid, she was right there on its cover, staring back at him, as disoriented as a fawn in the headlights.

He set down his coffee mug and began to scan the article, the words repulsing him to his very core. The first paper had a photo of Amanda with the hired man by her side; the gossip columnist, Harris Perez, speculated that she had returned home for more than just helping her family. The next paper had the same photo on one side of the page and another photo of Alejandro arriving alone at the Teen Choice Music Awards the other evening. The headline infuriated him: "Viper's Bite Too Much for Amish Belle."

"*Ay, Dios,*" he mumbled.

He didn't need this. Not today.

"What time is the car picking me up?" he asked Carlos.

"It's here already."

Scooping up the papers, he shoved them into a black leather portfolio. "Make certain this gets into the car," he demanded, thrusting the bag at Carlos. Without waiting for a reply, he disappeared through the sliding glass doors and hurried to his room to change.

The paparazzi thrived on speculation and controversy. That was a given. They took photos and published them out of context and with complete disregard for the truth. More celebrities would fight the practice but for two things: the enormous expense of the legal battle and the fact that, once a person achieved celebrity status, they became quasi-public property and different laws applied to them. Still, it didn't make the practice any more palatable.

Of course, Alejandro thought as he buttoned up his black shirt and stared into the bathroom mirror, the paparazzi had also helped jumpstart his career. During his early years, he had been a constant name in the Miami newspapers, both English and Spanish, just as much for his rapid rise to stardom as for the bar and street fights he had been involved in, some greatly exaggerated by the media. The stories had increased his fan base as young Latinos wanted to see what he would do next.

Still, he didn't want them bothering Amanda.

Thirty minutes later, he was sitting in Mike's office, a white mug of coffee in his hand while he waited for his manager to end a phone call. Setting the mug on the glass table by the sofa where he sat, Alejandro pulled the papers from the portfolio and glanced through them one more time.

He tossed them aside, frustrated at the photos that graced the entertainment section of a third tabloid that he hadn't seen earlier: Amanda at the farm, Alejandro onstage, not together; speculation that their marriage was on the rocks. But it was the actual story of the fourth paper that bothered him: the story about the hired man at the farm.

Indeed, the latest photo, the one of the hired man helping Amanda through the small crowd of photographers at the market, infuriated him. The article gleefully reported that social media had gone viral, circulating the photos with comments about Amanda returning to her plain roots and finding a new love interest. There was a split: half of the fans were thrilled, preferring a single Viper to a married Alejandro, while the other half seemed completely smitten with Amanda. However, what was more disturbing to Alejandro was how the former group was turning against Amanda while the latter turned against him.

Irritated by what he was reading, Alejandro brushed aside the magazine, stood up, and started to pace the floor in Mike's office, his hands clutched behind his back. His mind reeled, wondering what she was doing that morning. Already, he had tried to call her twice to no avail. It went directly to voice mail, so he knew she must have forgotten to charge the phone, something he had been very specific about instructing her to do each night.

"Dios *mío,*" he mumbled and rubbed at his forehead. He stared at Mike, who, having hung up the phone, had moved over to sit on the sofa. "I want this stopped, Mike." He gestured toward the papers. "Do something."

Mike took a moment and glanced through the small stack of papers. Alejandro noticed that he barely looked at the photos and articles, just scanning the headlines. It occurred to him that Mike might have already read the tabloids. Yet he had said nothing to his client. A wave of anger caused Alejandro to narrow his eyes and glare at Mike while he fingered through the papers. Finally, his manager looked up and shrugged his shoulders, a gesture of defeat as well as noncompliance. "And what exactly would you have me do, Alex?"

Alejandro ran his fingers through his hair and cursed in Spanish under his breath. "I don't know, but something," he muttered and turned to stare at Mike. Then, raising his voice: "Anything. Just divert the attention away from her while she's at her parents'. That's what I pay you for!"

If Alejandro had expected Mike to react to the unspoken threat, he was sorely disappointed. Instead of looking concerned, Mike merely leaned back into the sofa and put his hands behind his head, staring at Alejandro with no emotion in his eyes. "I can arrange interviews on the talk shows for you," Mike offered, his voice expressing the same lack of concern as in his facial expression. "I can arrange photographers at restaurants and hotels. But I can't do much for her while she's staying on a farm in Pennsylvania and you're traveling around the country."

"*¡Ay, Dios!*"

Mike shook his head as he cleared his throat. "Look, you just got married and now you are apart. People are going to talk. Speculation is part of the game. What does it matter? It's getting your name in front of people's eyes, and we both know what that does: sells your music and your image."

Alejandro knew that it was true. Without Amanda by his side, the rumors wouldn't stop. With more rumors would come more interest and more invasion of their privacy. But the bottom line was that the constant gossip and speculation did make money.

"Why are they so interested? Why does it matter so much to them?" he said, more to himself than to Mike. He didn't expect an answer.

"She's different," Mike responded. "That's the draw. If you were with any number of women, famous or not, they probably wouldn't care so much. But she's . . . Amish." As always, the way that Mike said the word, with a hint of disdain and disgust in his tone, infuriated Alejandro.

"She's not just any woman. She's my wife," Alejandro interrupted. "And she's not Amish. Not anymore."

Mike shrugged. "Whatever."

"There's a difference and we need to make it clear that she's no longer Amish!"

"Would it matter?" Mike asked before sighing and rubbing his face with his hands. "Look, maybe it will die down in a while. How long can they just camp out at her parents' farm taking photos of empty fields and cows?"

Alejandro narrowed his eyes and glared at his manager. "It's the intrusion on the entire community, not just the photos, that bothers me."

But he knew that what he had just said wasn't entirely true. It bothered him that people were speculating about Amanda and the hired man. Such rumors would also be noted among the community. What little he had experienced of the Amish during his brief stays on the farm gave him no false hope that such gossip in the entertainment world would escape the watchful eyes of the bishop and his ministers.

"She's there, Alex. I can't stop the photographers from intruding," Mike pointed out. "Need I remind you that those people, the ones who keep your name in the tabloids and on the lips of your fans, are protected by laws, laws that don't necessarily protect her anymore? Not now that she's crossed over to celebrity status."

"Then get her here!" Alejandro snapped back. At least if she were with him, he could shield her better. "Send a car. Send a plane. I'll arrange for more help for her parents for a few days; just get her to New York when I'm there next week!" He sank back into his chair, glancing at his phone. It was two in the afternoon. No calls. No texts. Where was she? Certainly she was home by now.

"What time is that talk show today?"

"You need to be there by three," Mike answered after consulting his calendar on his phone. "You best get ready. Car service will be here in thirty minutes. They want to do a dry run before the taping starts at four."

He didn't even have time to call her. "Well, do whatever it takes but get her to New York for next week. She can ride in the parade with me. That will quell the media," he snapped, annoyed that he had to tell his manager what to do. But, then again, everything was annoying him this past week. He had hated answering the questions, hated seeing that the paparazzi were back at the farm, and, most important, hated being separated from his wife.

Chapter Seven

Daed's resting at home.
Hope you can call before the show.
Glad we talked yesterday.
Avoid those photographers!
<3
A.

When Elias arrived home, Amanda was stunned and saddened to realize that her father was still limited to movement via a wheelchair. She hadn't been to the hospital for a few days and had thought that, upon his release, her *daed* would at least be able to walk. In addition, it further alarmed her that his speech remained so slurred and difficult to understand at times, especially when he was the slightest bit tired.

"I'll make a ramp," Harvey had said while they were milking the cows.

Amanda had looked up from where she sat, surprised that the usually quiet Harvey had spoken at all. "A ramp?"

"For the porch steps," he replied, his voice somber and serious. "So he can go in and out with ease. Fresh air will do him good, I reckon."

She wasn't certain how to reply. She had grown accustomed to few interactions and no kindness from the people in the community. During the past two weeks, she had felt isolated and alone, limited to her daily communications with Alejandro during which she attempted to mask her true feelings of sadness at being apart from him, a sadness which had been greatly heightened by the mistreatment from neighbors and other members of the church district. It would do no good to complain and add to his stress, she reasoned to herself.

"I . . . I don't know what to say," she finally said. "That's quite kind of you, Harvey."

He nodded his head but, as was typical for Harvey, said nothing in return.

It was two days later when Harvey brought in the mail that had just been delivered by the postal worker. In the past, Amanda would have walked out to retrieve the mail, usually in the evening. However, with the reporters camped at the mouth of their driveway, the police had decided to let the postal worker onto the property to hand-deliver the mail to whomever was in the barnyard. As chance had it that day, it was Harvey.

"Letter for you, Lizzie," he said as he set the mail on the counter. Without another word, he turned and walked back outside to continue with the barn chores.

Lizzie glanced at Amanda, who had been sitting next to Elias, reading aloud from a three-ring binder with handwritten letters in it. She had taken to reading to him at night, a way to entertain him. "I wonder from whom that letter could be."

Amanda shrugged. "Won't know until you look."

Just the day before, two of the young schoolchildren had stopped by the house with a brown paper bag in their hands. They had smiled shyly when Amanda opened the door. In the barnyard a buggy was standing, with a hitched horse stomping its hooves, eager to continue on its way home for the evening feeding.

"For Elias," the older of the two children had whispered. She had glanced at the younger one, clearly her sister. "From the schoolchildren, to help him recover."

Amanda had taken the brown paper bag and thanked the children, watching as they scampered back to the buggy. When it had finally disappeared around the barn in the direction of the road, Amanda had shut the door and walked back to the kitchen where she handed the package to her *daed*.

"Open it," he slurred.

It was a three-ring binder with sheets of paper inside, each one with a child's drawing and a Bible verse. It had been organized by age, Amanda had quickly realized. The younger students had their pages at the beginning of the book, easy to identify with the lack of detail in the drawings and the large, crooked writing. Toward the middle of the book, the drawings became more sophisticated and the verses written in much improved handwriting. Finally, the last several pages were clearly written by the older students, with detailed drawings and more involved Bible verses. Interspaced between the encouraging Bible verses were letters from the children that wished him a speedy recovery.

It had been, indeed, a very lovely gift.

Now, Amanda closed the binder and set it carefully on the edge of the sofa as she watched her *mamm* open the envelope. Lizzie slit the edge of the envelope with her pretty mother-of-pearl letter opener, a birthday gift from one of her sisters when she was a young woman. Patiently, Lizzie placed the opener on the table before she extracted the letter and unfolded it, her eyes skimming the contents quickly.

"Looks like it's from Anna," Lizzie said, moving toward the sitting area in order to pull up a chair and sit next to Elias so that he could better hear the contents of the letter. "See?" She pointed to the neat handwriting on the envelope and the two pieces of paper that had been folded and slipped inside.

"Read it," he said, his words a bit clearer and a sparkle in his eyes.

Lizzie scanned the letter first, a quick preread before she read it out loud.

"Dear family," Lizzie began reading after clearing her throat.

I hope this letter finds you in the best of health under the ever-watchful eye of the good Lord. May his blessings shine down on you, especially during this most trying time in all of our lives.

By the time you are holding this letter, I will have been married. While I am saddened by the thought of my family not being here to share in the joy of my union, I know that you will be here in spirit.

It is our intention to come to Lititz to visit for a few weeks and help Mamm care for Daed and the farm. We should be arriving the week of Thanksgiving, most likely on Tuesday by the dinner hour.

I am sure that Amanda is anxious to spend time with her husband, especially after having been so good as to help out while Daed was in the hospital. I can only imagine how torn she must have felt, but knowing how kindhearted our Amanda is, the decision must have been easy. Helping others is what she does best.

Jonas and his family have been right gut *about us visiting for so long, although I know his* daed *will miss the extra pair of hands on the farm. At least it isn't farming season.*

I will continue to pray for all of you, praying for your physical and spiritual well-being. We both look forward to seeing you in two weeks.

With blessings and love,
Anna Wheeler

Lizzie set the letter down on her lap and stared at the wall for a moment. Amanda studied her reaction to the letter and knew that her *mamm* had mixed feelings. Of course she was pleased that Anna had married, a good indication that she was healing after the loss of their brother, Aaron. Yet Mamm certainly felt sorrow at the fact that she had been unable to attend Anna's wedding.

With a sigh, Lizzie turned to look at her husband. *"Vell,"* she began, a strange tone to her voice. "Both our *dochders* have married, Elias. Seems time's upon us to make some hard decisions."

Elias tried to wave his hand, but the motion was choppy, lacking the strength of his pre-stroke physical condition. *"Nee!"* he managed to say loudly. "I will not sell this farm."

Amanda bit her lower lip, holding back her opinion, as she knew that this was a decision that only her parents could make. Keeping the farm was not practical; Amanda knew that, for sure and certain. Alejandro was of the world and would never farm. Jonas had family in Ohio and had no reason to move. With no one to work the farm, it was not logical to keep it. Yet Amanda knew that selling the farm was a sign of defeat to her father. After all, farming was all he knew how to do. Without farming, old age would surely set in. Without farming, what purpose did he have?

"Elias," Lizzie began gently. "Amanda must return to Alejandro."

To Amanda's surprise, her father slammed his hand down on the arm of the chair. "I will get better!" He paused to catch his breath from the effort of speaking. "I will farm again!"

Amanda knew there was no point arguing with her father. He was stubborn when shoved into a corner. She turned her head away, not wanting to see the strained look on her *daed*'s face. Her heart ached. She knew how difficult it would be for him to sell the farm, for it had been in the family for over four generations. To leave it would be very hard, but the reality was that her *daed* truly had no options.

The sun was beginning to set in the sky when Amanda pushed her *daed*'s wheelchair down the ramp that Harvey had built for him. She had wanted him to get some fresh air, and when she had offered, he had been quick to agree. After having been indoors for almost three weeks, Elias would certainly benefit from overseeing the afternoon chores.

Harvey was already working on the early evening feeding. The cows had been milked and the stalls were clean. The scent of fresh hay greeted Elias and Amanda as they entered the barn through the large double doors.

"You need help there?" Harvey didn't wait for an answer to his question as he hurried over to the chair. It was hard to roll it on the concrete flooring of the dairy, so Amanda let him take over the task of pushing it.

Elias stared at the cows, a look of longing in his eyes. It broke Amanda's heart to know that her *daed* could only watch, but not help with, the completion of the evening chores. She didn't need to read his mind to know what he was thinking as he watched Harvey: if only . . .

But there was no *if only*. Harvey Alderfer was a right *gut* man, with a strong work ethic and kind heart. But even if she had met him before her New York City encounter with Alejandro, Amanda would not have been interested in a relationship with Harvey. God had other plans for her, and those plans were centered on Alejandro. Still, seeing her *daed* watch Harvey, and imagining what he thought might have been, bothered her.

"Sister Anna's coming home to visit," Amanda told Harvey, breaking the silence. She hoped the news about Anna would awaken her *daed* to the fact that he had two *dochders*, both of whom had married, a fact of which he needed to be reminded. "She was married just the week last."

Harvey leaned against the pitchfork and smiled. "A happy time in a couple's life, no?"

Amanda frowned. It should be a happy time, she thought, fighting a sense of bitterness. She missed Alejandro and wished that she could be with him. Yet she knew that her duty was to help her parents until things could be properly sorted out. She owed that much to her parents as well as to Anna.

She could tell that Harvey sensed the shift in her mood, and he quickly changed the subject. "Planning on spreading manure tomorrow, Elias," he said. "'Less you object."

"Nee," her *daed* responded, pleased that he had been consulted.

"Right *gut* idea," she added. "November spreading will bring healthy crops in spring."

The mention of spring caused Amanda to ponder. Who would plant those crops? Would her *daed* still be living there on the farm in the spring? Or would they have moved to a smaller house, one that was more manageable for a man who was recovering from a stroke? Surely, Harvey could not work on their farm forever.

Chapter Eight

```
Went out last night.
Don't listen to the news.
Nothing happened.
V.
```

The weather was cold in Boston, and Alejandro dreaded the weight of a heavier jacket on his shoulders. Born in Cuba and having lived most of his life in Florida, heat was in his bones. When winter came and he toured in the North, he hated the long coats, leather gloves, and boots that his stylist insisted he wear. Today was no different. Already, he missed Los Angeles. He missed Miami, too. But most of all, he missed Amanda.

He spent a few hours at a gym, his personal trainer eager to get Alejandro back into his training program. Despite his notoriety, the other patrons merely stared and whispered; no one approached him, for which he was grateful. He needed the time alone to work with Marco. It had been too long since he had really worked out on a regular basis, and it felt good to push his body to its limit.

He hadn't wanted to go to the after-party the previous night, but his entourage and Mike had pressured him. "You need to get out," Mike had said. "For the media, if not for your own good."

The concert had been energizing, and Alejandro finally relented, knowing that his only other option was to go back to the hotel alone and sleep. With his blood pumping from the show, spending a few hours at a club with his friends began to sound like a good idea. Besides, he knew how important it was to be seen in public while on tour, especially in major cities.

Unfortunately, he hadn't counted on the crush of paparazzi that followed them, eager for a photo of Viper out on the town in Boston with his posse. When one photographer came too close, Alejandro had held up his hand to the lens of the camera as he slipped through the throngs of people waiting to enter the club. He headed toward the VIP level to escape the probing eyes and overeager fans.

Just as unfortunate was the fact that the photo of him pushing away the photographer was now the talk of social media. He hadn't been in the mood for dealing with an in-his-face photographer, and when the man had invaded his personal space, Alejandro had reacted without thinking. Someone else had caught the grimace on his face as he shoved the photographer, and as was to be expected, the photo was plastered on Facebook, Twitter, Instagram, and websites around the world.

Carlos had notified him in the morning, a stressed look on his face as he did so.

"What do you mean?" Alejandro had demanded, his temper beginning to flare. "They said what?"

Instead of replying, Carlos had handed him a piece of white paper. Screenshots of different social media outlets were on the paper. As Alejandro scanned the images, he clenched his jaw and shut his eyes.

"Another ten pounds?" Marco asked, interrupting Alejandro's thoughts.

Dropping the weights to the ground, he looked up and stared at Marco, a shorter version of himself, who was well built, with brown hair and a fast smile. The one main difference was that his accent was not Cuban but pure American. They had met as teenagers in Miami and had often worked out together before the Viper years. He was a good man and often accompanied Alejandro on tours in the States as both his personal trainer and a bodyguard.

"I'm done, man. That's enough for one day," Alejandro said and took the clean white towel that Marco handed him. He wiped at his neck and stood up. *"Gracias."*

"Just dancing won't keep you in shape, V," Marco said as he took back the damp towel. "Been too long."

Ignoring his friend, Alejandro slipped away and headed toward the private room that the facility provided to him in order to shower and change. He let the hot water pour over his head, one hand against the tiled wall, as he tried to make sense of what the media was saying.

Cheating on Amanda? Dancing with other women? Threatening the paparazzi? Each accusation was stated as a fact, despite being a complete falsehood. Yet there was nothing that he could do about it. Not without taking severe and costly legal action, and ultimately, for what purpose? Either Amanda would believe him or not.

A car was waiting for him outside the front door. Both Alejandro and Marco slipped inside before anyone recognized him. In silence, they rode in the back of the car as the driver headed toward Marco's hotel before taking Alejandro to his first official appointment of the day: a photo shoot for a magazine. Immediately after, his publicist had arranged for an interview with a Latino reporter. Finally, he would head back to the hotel for a short nap before returning to the arena for his second concert in Boston.

He took out his phone and fiddled with it. He wanted to call Amanda but didn't want to have that dialogue in front of Marco. He'd have to wait until later that afternoon when he was back at the hotel.

Still, he glanced down at his thirty text messages, hoping to see one from his wife.

Nothing.

"*Ay, Dios,*" he mumbled.

"What's up?" Marco asked.

Alejandro shook his head and, out of habit, began to scroll through his messages. Most of them were from Mike, two were from his publicist confirming times and locations, and the rest were from random friends who had his number. Nothing of any major importance. No, he corrected himself. Nothing from Amanda.

When they arrived at Alejandro's next stop, an old historical building in downtown Boston, a crew was waiting for him. He had barely been escorted into the building before he saw Mike standing in the back of the main room, talking with two women and a man. Dismissing the other people who were crowded around him, one with a clipboard, trying to go over the schedule for the shooting, Alejandro headed toward his manager.

"You're here!" Mike smiled and greeted Alejandro with a quick handshake and shoulder-to-shoulder hug. "Early, too! That's great. Busy day today, Alex." It often caused him a moment of pause when Mike called him Alex around other people. Most people in his traveling circuit called him Viper or V.

Glancing around the room, Alejandro saw the large white backdrop in one area, bright lights on stands surrounding it. There was also a section of another room through two double doors where people were scurrying around, setting up for more photos.

"What's the plan?" he asked, turning his attention back to Mike.

One of the women responded instead. "We have the building for another hour or so. Photos in the library, back there," she said, gesturing to the double doors. "Then a few stand-alone shots against the backdrop."

He looked at the woman, surprised that she sounded so authoritative. With her blond hair pulled back into a ponytail, he had mistaken her for a lowly assistant, not someone who was in charge. Indeed, her attire did not bespeak power or authority. She wore a simple white shirt and skinny jeans, not the wardrobe of a person in charge of a photo shoot for a megastar.

She must have seen him appraising her for she shifted the papers in her hand and stuck it out to shake his. "Marybeth Cook," she said and smiled. "Producer."

He nodded and shook her hand, taking in her bright blue eyes and chiseled cheekbones. A pretty woman, he admitted to himself. But young for such a job. He was used to working with older men . . . Latino men . . . for most of the photo shoots. *"Mucho gusto,"* he replied with a slight bow. "Point me in the direction of the stylist, and I'll get ready," he added, knowing that time was of the essence.

Without answering, Mike put his arm around Alejandro's shoulder and started guiding him toward a back room. "Alex, I want you to keep an open mind about this shoot, all right?"

Open mind. Alejandro frowned and looked at his manager. "What's going on?"

"Just promise me that, OK?"

"Mike?" There was an undertone of warning in his voice. "What are you up to?"

They stopped in front of the doorway as Mike gestured inside. "They'll get you prepped in here, and I'll see you in the library," he said, his cell phone ringing in his breast pocket and his attention immediately distracted.

It didn't take long to get changed into the black suit for the shoot and to sit through the application of makeup. After thanking the stylist team, Alejandro hurried toward the double doors, his curiosity piqued, despite the feeling of dread in his chest. There was music playing from speakers in the background and a crowd of people blocking the doorway. As he made his approach, someone noticed him and began to nudge others to clear the way. He nodded as he walked past them and into the room.

That was when he saw them.

Four women. Only these women were not the typical ones he worked with during photo or video shoots. No long, flowing hair. No skintight dresses with sequins and sparkles. No four-inch heels and fancy jewelry.

Instead, these were four women . . . beautiful women . . . dressed in Amish attire. Each one wore a different-colored dress with a simple white heart-shaped prayer *kapp* tied to the back of her head. Only Alejandro immediately saw that the heart part of the prayer *kapp* was too pronounced and the dresses were not real Amish dresses but poorly copied knockoffs. None of the women wore shoes, and he noticed that all of them had brightly colored nail polish on their toenails.

"What is this?" he exclaimed. He looked around the room until his eyes fell on Mike and Marybeth. The room filled with instant silence. "Mike? I asked a question."

"Alex," Mike said, trying to sound good-natured as he walked toward Alejandro. "I asked you to keep an open mind!"

As Mike reached out to place a hand on his shoulder, Alejandro shoved it away. "An open mind?" he repeated in disbelief. "What is there to keep an open mind about when you are completely mocking my wife?"

"It's not a mockery!" Mike laughed. "It's marketing!"

"I won't do it," Alejandro stated, raising one eyebrow as if daring Mike to argue with him. His voice was flat and emotionless. There was no questioning the conviction of his words.

It was the blonde, Marybeth, who cleared her throat and joined the two men. "Actually," she said slowly. "You will."

Her candor surprised him, so he turned his head to stare at her. "Excuse me?"

She flipped through a manila folder and produced a document. "If this is your signature, then you are obligated to do the photo shoot," she said, handing the papers to him. "You can keep that. It's a copy."

Quickly, Alejandro scanned the document. Indeed, it had his signature at the end of it.

"Page four has the section you might want to reread," Marybeth said casually.

Grimacing, Alejandro turned to that page and his eyes focused on a highlighted section. He felt his blood boil and clamped his teeth together as he read the paragraph about the agreement to possibly use Amish artifacts, including but not limited to farm equipment, clothing, housewares, and furniture, in the photo shoot.

He glared first at the woman and then at Mike. "You knew about this?"

"Just keep an open mind," Mike repeated for the third time. "There is no disrespect meant."

With a laugh, Alejandro threw the papers at Mike. "There is *only* disrespect meant!"

Without another word, he stormed toward the four women. They were beautiful, that could not be argued. But they were clearly anything but Amish. Still, he knew it wasn't their fault. Models took their jobs when and where they could get them. He tried to calm his temper as he nodded at them, too upset to trust any words on his lips.

Standing in between them, he turned around. "You want this done?" he snapped, his blue eyes narrowed and still fiercely glaring at Mike and Marybeth. "Then let's get going!"

For the next forty minutes, photographers directed the women to move around Alejandro: placing their hands on his shoulders, surrounding him, acting chaste behind him with folded hands, reaching out for him. Alejandro stood there, stoic and emotionless, dark sunglasses hiding his eyes. Occasionally, he would turn as directed, but he gave nothing more than the bare minimum.

As the photographers moved around him, Alejandro disappeared into his own thoughts. How would he explain this to Amanda? What would be her reaction? Knowing Amanda, she would not show her disappointment or disgust at the use of staged and very inauthentic Amish imagery to sell Viper. But there was no doubt that she would feel it.

His inability to prevent this angered him. He should have seen it coming. Mike had clearly crossed a line, and now Alejandro was faced with a bigger challenge. He had no choice but to replace his longtime manager. Yet to do so would create upheaval and turmoil that Alejandro was not willing to face. Not yet. Of course, there was the issue of Mike's contract. Alejandro made a mental note to contact his lawyer as soon as he could to find out what his options were.

"Fabulous!" the photographer shouted. "That's a wrap for this set."

Without a word, Alejandro stormed away, his arm brushing others as he moved toward the room with the white backdrop. Once again, he planted his feet in the middle of it, his hands clutched behind his back as he waited for the "Amish" models to join him and the photographer to continue taking pictures.

"Come on, Alejandro!" Mike stood on the sidelines, his arms crossed as he shook his head. "Work it a bit, eh?"

A raised eyebrow was the only response that he received.

Frustrated, Mike cursed under his breath and turned away, mumbling something to Marybeth, who never left his side. She didn't seem as frustrated as Mike with Alejandro's lack of enthusiasm for the photo shoot scene. That, alone, intrigued Alejandro.

When the shoot was over, Alejandro gave each of the models a hug and kiss on the cheek. His anger was not toward them, but he did refuse to stand with each one individually for a private photo. He knew that would disappoint the models; however, he didn't want to risk those photos circulating in the media. He could already envision the headlines, and not one of them was something he wanted Amanda to see.

"Could you have looked any more miserable?" Mike snapped as they walked toward the room set up for Alejandro to change. "I mean come on, Alex! It's marketing!"

Abruptly, Alejandro stopped and spun around, a finger pushed into Mike's face. "It's disgusting. Capitalizing on my wife's religion? You've crossed the line, Mike, and I'm done warning you. That part of my life is off-limits." As if to make his final point, he jabbed at Mike's shoulder. "Off-limits!" he repeated before turning around and storming away.

He could feel his blood coursing through his veins. It had been a mockery, and he had been trapped by legal documents that he hadn't read thoroughly. His anger was just as much directed at himself as at Mike. How could he have been so careless? he berated himself as he changed. It would be the last time that Mike did something so openly hostile toward Amanda, he told himself. And possibly one of the last things that Mike did for him, period.

He hadn't counted on Mike to wait for him.

"What's gotten into you, Alex?" Mike walked beside him, keeping up with Alejandro's brisk pace. "You have to learn to separate it, man. Separate your personal from your professional life or you are going to lose it!"

"I'm not losing anything, Mike," Alejandro snapped back. "But you are! You're losing your sense of decency, and I won't have Amanda be a casualty in whatever game you think you are playing."

"Hey!" Mike reached out and grabbed Alejandro's arm. The gesture startled Alejandro. He stopped walking and spun around. To his surprise, Mike's face was contorted in anger, a fierce expression in his eyes. "This isn't a game, Alex. This is real. And you brought her into it. You can't have selective fame, my friend."

"Selective fame?" He almost laughed at the expression.

Mike released his arm. "You know what I mean. You can't have some pieces of your life for the public and keep the rest private. It doesn't work that way. Not if you want to continue with this conquest of world dominance in the music industry, Viper."

The way he said *Viper* sent a chill down Alejandro's spine. "World dominance does not have to include the destruction of my soul," Alejandro countered. "Using Amanda to sell the image is not part of the plan."

Mike laughed. "Not part of the plan? I don't think you have a say in that matter. The public demands her. It's a bundled set at this point, Alex. You made sure of that when you married her."

"That's not fair!"

"Hey, you made the rules. I warned you about getting involved with her. It was to counter your image. Now, the softer side of Viper has emerged, and as always, you were right. The public loves it and is eating it up. Deny them the girl, and watch your fans fade, Alex. I've seen it before, and I do not want to see it again."

Alejandro shook his head at Mike. "You're wrong."

"Try me," Mike retorted. "But don't blame me when it backfires."

Disgusted, Alejandro walked away, his steps heavy and his fists clenched as he moved past the doors and hurried toward the waiting car outside of the building entrance. Alone in the car, Alejandro removed his dark sunglasses and rubbed at his eyes. When had it become so complicated? he wondered.

Chapter Nine

Are you in Boston yet?
Or Providence?
I can't keep up.
Missing you.
A.

It was Sunday and they had just returned from church. It had been a disastrous day from the moment she had awoken, and she was missing Alejandro more than ever. Had he been with her, she thought, he would have known what to do.

Earlier that morning, her *daed* had insisted on going to church, and Amanda knew what that meant: her *mamm* couldn't handle him alone, so she would have to go along. She had arisen early to milk the cows, knowing that it would take extra time without any help from Harvey. Mamm had come out to help her, but Amanda had quickly shooed her back inside, telling her to get Daed ready, when in reality, she was mostly concerned that it was too cold for her *mamm* to work.

By the time Amanda had finished the milking and harnessed the horse to the buggy, she barely had time to wash up and change, never mind have a quick bite to eat. She hadn't known what to wear, fluctuating between her regular plain clothing or a simple skirt and blouse.

"I'm not plain, Mamm," she said when her *mamm* had walked by the door and paused, checking to see what Amanda was doing. "What do I wear?"

"They know you aren't plain," Lizzie had responded. "Dress accordingly, then."

There were only two cars waiting outside of the driveway, something that had surprised Amanda. She hadn't left the property since the incident at the natural food store. With Mamm driving the horse and Daed seated next to her, Amanda had no choice but to crouch in the backseat of the buggy. She had hoped that the photographers would not follow them, but one glance out of the back window had quickly dashed that hope.

Once they pulled into the driveway of the farm where the service was being held, Amanda had breathed a sigh of relief: the two cars had not followed them onto the private property. For a moment, she dared to imagine that the rest of the day would go well.

She was soon proved wrong.

The men had come to help with Elias, expressing their surprise that he had arrived at all. Luckily, the worship service was being held at the farmhouse, which meant no steps and plenty of space for his wheelchair. To Amanda's relief, the men had promptly taken over Elias's care, which freed up Lizzie to go inside with the other women, a social outlet that Amanda had suspected her *mamm* desperately needed.

Unfortunately, once they had entered the farmhouse, the women who had been assembled in the empty kitchen next to the gathering room had stopped talking and stared at the two newcomers. Lizzie had ignored the silence and made her way through the line of women, first shaking their outstretched hands before bestowing the kiss of fellowship on the women's lips. Uncertain what to do, Amanda had walked behind her *mamm* but noticed that the women turned their heads while shaking her hand: the first rebuff of the day.

The second came only moments later. Rather than sit with the women she had always sat next to, her peers and friends, she was forced to sit up front with the elderly, a place of honor for guests as well as a separation from the younger women. Her cheeks had flushed red, this time from embarrassment, as she sat there beside her *mamm*, something she had not done since she was a child.

While the first hymn was being sung, the congregation had waited for the bishop and ministers to return. It was during this time that the leaders of the church usually left the room to decide, among one another, who was to preach the sermons. When they returned to the room, taking their seats in the front row of the men's side, that was the signal to stop singing the hymn at the next stanza.

It hadn't surprised Amanda to see the bishop stand and, for a few brief moments, pace the floor before his congregation. What did surprise her was his sermon.

"What does it take to be a disciple of Jesus?" he started in a loud, booming voice. "Is it praising his name? Is it turning the other cheek? It is speaking no evil? Or is it living a life that mirrors the words of the Bible? *'Whoever wants to be my disciple,'* the Ausbund says, *'he must forsake the world, in his heart also become pure and hate his own life.'*" The bishop stopped pacing and stood straight before the congregation. "We are a people who forsake worldliness because we want to be disciples of Jesus and follow his teachings. We choose being God's children over earthly treasures!"

Inwardly, Amanda had groaned, knowing full well that the sermon was directed, in part, toward her. After all, not only had she chosen to join the world, rather than forsake it, her very presence back in the community had brought the intrusion of the world with her. She tried to tune out the rest of his sermon, knowing that her cheeks were blazing red, the humiliation of his words too much for her to bear.

And then had come the fellowship hour.

The men had immediately converted the large worship room into a dining hall, creating long rows of tables by using trestles to slide onto the legs of the church benches. The younger boys had collected the Ausbund hymnals and neatly stacked them in wooden crates. Meanwhile, the women were dishing out the food, all of it having been prepared prior to the service so that the only true work was serving it to the church members. Still, plates and utensils had to be set out, cups had to be filled with water, and the platters of food needed to be placed on the tabletops.

When she had tried to help the women, they had simply responded by ignoring her. After all, Amanda rationalized, guests did not help serve food or clean up. Their silence and lack of accepting her help was a clear indication that they no longer considered her part of the community. She had chosen to not take the kneeling vow and had opted to marry outside of the faith. In return, they chose to keep her at arm's length in order to remain pure by forsaking the outside world, a world that Amanda was clearly a part of as a result of her own free will.

As if that was not bad enough, during the first seating Amanda had been forced to sit and eat with the older women and very young mothers who needed to feed small children. During the meal, no one had spoken to her, blatantly ignoring Amanda, although she had been somewhat pleased to see that her *mamm* had engaged in plenty of conversation.

The time to leave had not come fast enough for Amanda. She hadn't even cared that the photographers had snapped photos of her, using their intrusive telescopic lenses, when she had climbed into the buggy.

Driving down the lane toward her parents' farm had never felt so good before in all her life.

It had been not even fifteen minutes after they had returned when the cell phone rang. Having just come inside from unharnessing the horse, Amanda was at the kitchen sink, washing her hands, while her *mamm* sat in the rocking chair next to Daed. The room was silent except for the gentle ticking of the clock that hung on the wall. But the ringing of the cell phone caught the attention of everyone.

She had left it on the table and hurried over to get it, pausing for just a moment to wipe her hands on a dry hand towel. Only one person ever called her on the phone, and she felt embarrassed that she had to answer the call in front of her parents. Still, since she hadn't heard from Alejandro in a few days, she quickly grabbed the phone and answered it, moving away from the table and heading toward the door.

She placed the small device to her ear and turned her back toward the kitchen. "Alejandro!" she said happily as she answered the phone.

There was a brief pause. "Amanda, it's Carlos."

It took her a minute to realize that the voice on the other end was not her husband's. "Is everything all right?" she asked in a moment of panic.

"*Sí, sí,*" he reassured her. "Alejandro asked me to contact you."

"Oh." She couldn't hide the disappointment in her voice. It was almost two in the afternoon. She imagined that he was already engaged in interviews before the concert that evening. Certainly he was busy; he always was before a concert in a new city . . . even on Sundays.

Carlos cleared his throat on the other end of the phone. "He asked me to call you as he needs you to come to New York for the week."

New York? Amanda glanced over her shoulder at her parents, both of whom were watching her with apprehension and great interest. She shook her head, indicating that nothing was wrong, before she turned around again and lowered her voice. "I . . . I can't," she started. "My *daed* just came home. My *mamm* will need my help. And my sister isn't to arrive until Tuesday for dinner."

"He has hired a nurse to help. He needs you in New York," Carlos said, his voice matter-of-fact. "I have arranged for a car to arrive Tuesday at eight in the morning."

"I . . ." She didn't know what to say. If she was to leave on Tuesday morning, her sister would be there later to help her parents. Although Anna and her husband were not to arrive until dinnertime, surely her *mamm* could handle Daed for a day alone. And Harvey would be there in case of an emergency.

Her heart fluttered inside her chest. Part of her worried about the family's reaction to her leaving just before Anna arrived, but the other part longed to see him. "For how long?" she heard herself ask.

"A week," Carlos responded. "For the holiday."

After she ended the call, she took a minute to collect her thoughts. Was it possible that Alejandro missed her half as much as she missed him? Her thoughts turned back to the way she had been treated at church, more a stranger than a former member of their *g'may*. After so many weeks apart, she felt relief at the realization that in less than forty-eight hours, she would be reunited with her husband.

"*Wie gehts?*" her *mamm* asked.

"Hmm?" Amanda turned around and tried to smile. "Oh, that was Alejandro's assistant."

Lizzie made a face but did not speak her thoughts. She didn't have to. Amanda could read her expression loud and clear.

"He's busy, Mamm," Amanda said defensively.

"I see," was Lizzie's only reply.

She walked into the room and sat down on the sofa, her eyes drifting out the window. The fields were empty, the sky gray. With bare trees and a light breeze blowing dried leaves across the grass, it looked barren and unfriendly out there. Her mind returned to New York City, the bright lights and constant noise. She imagined that, even in winter, it was still an amazing place.

"He wants me to join him for the holiday," she finally admitted. Shifting her weight, she tore her eyes from the window and looked at her parents. "Tuesday."

Lizzie pursed her lips and glanced at Elias. He was tired, and when he was tired, it was harder for him to talk. Lizzie spoke for both of them. "Anna is due home on Tuesday night, Amanda," she said slowly. "Do you think that it is the right thing to do, then?"

"It's only for a week," Amanda offered. "She's home for two weeks, *ja*?"

Lizzie didn't respond, obviously disappointed with Amanda's answer.

"I miss him, Mamm," she continued. "It's been weeks."

"I understand that," Lizzie said, her eyes betraying her true feelings. "But Anna—"

"*Nee*, Mamm," Amanda interrupted her. "I came home in order to help Anna as well as to be here for you and Daed. But he is my husband, and I want to be with him. And it's clear from how I've been treated that I don't belong here anymore."

Her *mamm*'s eyes widened at the tone in Amanda's voice. "Amanda!"

"*Ach*, Mamm," Amanda said, a frown on her face. "I was all but shunned today at worship service."

Taking a deep breath, Lizzie pressed her lips together and averted her eyes. Clearly, she wanted to speak more but, in true Amish fashion, kept her words to herself. "We'll be sorry to see you miss the holiday, then," was all her *mamm* could muster.

"As am I," Amanda admitted truthfully. She had never spent a holiday apart from her family. Missing them was only natural. Still, she longed to be with Alejandro again, even if only for a week.

It was the following afternoon when she was sitting on the sofa and crocheting a blanket when her *mamm* approached her, a folded paper in her hands. The weather outside was frigid, and Amanda was already dreading having to venture outside for the evening chores. The cold air just seemed to whip across those empty fields, chilling her to the bone.

Lizzie stood before Amanda for a few seconds, hesitating as though something was on her mind that she didn't want to share. When

Amanda realized that this was certainly the case, she set the afghan on her lap and looked up.

"What is it, Mamm?"

There was no verbal response. Instead, Lizzie handed over the papers that she was holding to Amanda. There was a concerned look on her face as she did so.

Frowning, Amanda slid her crochet needle into the ball of yarn that was next to her on the sofa before she reached out and took the papers from her *mamm*. As she looked at them, a quick moment of panic washed over her: tabloids. She could only imagine what horrible things they said.

There were at least four of them, each with a different date. One headline screamed "Viper Sends Amish Girl Back to Farm." Her eyes quickly scanned the story, a story that speculated about a recent Viper sighting in Los Angeles without his new bride at his side. The article claimed that it was because of marital problems already, that Viper had sent his Amish wife away so that he could continue his lifestyle of clubbing hard and womanizing.

The other articles were similar, some even posting photos of Alejandro dancing with other women. That caught her by surprise, but upon closer inspection, Amanda realized that it was an old photo of Viper at a club in Miami. He hadn't been to Miami since they had left together and flown to Philadelphia.

Wondering where her *mamm* would have gotten such trashy newspapers, Amanda quickly handed them back to her, rolling her eyes and shaking her head. "Ridiculous," she mumbled, as her *mamm* put the tabloids onto the table.

"That's all you have to say about this?" Her mother sounded genuinely surprised.

Amanda looked at her mother and shrugged her shoulders. "It's predictable, I suppose. He's out there without me. They are going to gossip." She paused. Gossip was, apparently, not unknown to the

Amish, too, she thought wryly, for certainly her *mamm* didn't purchase these newspapers. And wasn't the Amish grapevine as potent as any tabloid? "They live for gossip," she added, not entirely certain to whom she was actually referring.

Clearly, Lizzie was stunned by Amanda's nonchalance. Taking back the papers, she folded them neatly. It was obvious that they were not going to make it into the garbage bin, the place where they belonged. "And you have joined the Englische world without reservation? A world of gossip and speculation about your private life?"

The irony of the situation was not lost on Amanda, but she remained respectful to her *mamm*. "Oh, there's always plenty of reservation about their world," Amanda admitted. "But not about Alejandro."

Her mother raised an eyebrow. "Perhaps not about Alejandro, but what about Viper?"

The question stung Amanda, the words as well as the tone of voice from her mother. In all of her years growing up, Amanda could not remember her mother ever speaking in such a manner. Rather than respond, Amanda lifted her chin and walked out of the kitchen.

The truth was that Amanda was worried about Alejandro. But for different reasons. They hadn't been able to connect via the telephone for several days. Oh, he sent her a text whenever he could, but he was busy and moving from city to city. She knew that his time in Los Angeles had been spent in meetings with advertisers, endorsers, and the recording studio. While he managed to send her texts, the phone calls had become less frequent.

A small piece of her constantly worried that he had forgotten about her, perhaps even slipped back into his old lifestyle. So the call from Carlos had come at the exact moment when, after a terrible day with grave disappointment in the people she used to consider part of her extended family, she desperately needed to hear from her husband.

Despite not having talked directly to him, she could tell that he missed her. She could tell that he longed for her to join him on the road. And tomorrow couldn't come soon enough to satisfy her intense longing to be with him once again.

Chapter Ten

```
I am waiting for you.
The minutes seem like hours.
Text me when the car passes through the
tunnel.
V.
```

He stood at the window, staring down at the street below. Cars were backed up, waiting for the morning traffic to dissipate. November in New York City marked the beginning of maddening rush-hour traffic from commuters and tourists alike. With Thanksgiving around the corner, people were flocking to the Big Apple to window-shop, skate at Rockefeller Center, and gaze at the huge holiday tree with its thousands of lights.

But Alejandro wasn't concerned with any of that. He had cleared his schedule until later in the afternoon because today was the day that Amanda was arriving. It had been over three weeks. Three long, painful weeks for him. He had traveled to so many cities that he had lost count. Performances, interviews, appearances at clubs. He had even managed to start recording a new song, one that he wrote just for Amanda. But none of it meant much anymore. The luster and the glory had disappeared. Without Amanda by his side, his enthusiasm was simply not there.

Oh, he had seen the tabloids. He hated those photos of Amanda with the hired man. But he had learned to compartmentalize his emotions, for he knew that his Amanda would never be anything but true to him. If the tabloids wanted to sell their papers by telling lie after lie, so be it. The truth was that Amanda was on her way into the city, a car and bodyguard having left at three in the morning to pick her up so that she would be with him before lunchtime.

He glanced around the suite. White roses were everywhere. His assistant had done wonders in following his instructions to have bouquets of gorgeous flowers, all white, in every room of the suite. There was a bottle of champagne chilling in the silver ice bucket by the cream-colored sofa. Despite it being daytime, the lights of the eighteen-armed chandelier cast a soft glow that sent mini-sparkles through the French-cut Swarovski crystals that hung from each of its curved arms.

With his hands behind his back, he turned his attention to the window again. He wore freshly pressed black slacks and a silk black shirt. He was waiting and would not move until he saw the black SUV pull down the street and stop in front of the hotel.

The week was going to be busy, no two ways about it. But facing the constant demands on his time would be so much easier with Amanda by his side. He had already instructed Carlos to work with Lucinda on outfits for Amanda to be coordinated with his based on the next week's schedule. With satisfaction, Alejandro had noticed just last evening that the closet was filled with outfits, each one with a note tag on it, instructing Amanda when to wear it and with which accessories.

But now he was staring out the window, his heart pounding inside his chest. At the realization that he felt like a schoolboy anxiously waiting for his date to arrive, he chuckled to himself and shook his head. Never in his life had he felt so overwhelmed by a woman. She was all-consuming to him, and he regretted having left her behind on the farm. Yet he was also aware of the fact that, had he not left her there, he would not be so cognizant of how dependent he had become on Amanda's presence in every aspect of his life.

It was an odd feeling, Alejandro realized. He had never depended on anyone except himself. From the days that he struggled for survival on the streets of Miami to fighting in the clubs just to sing a song onstage, it had only been himself in charge of his success. He wasn't proud of everything that he had done in order to survive, but he was proud that he made it out alive and with enough decency to try to help others escape the world of gangs, drugs, and crime to which he had nearly succumbed. Unfortunately, Alejandro had learned the importance of self-preservation in a world where people, including himself, often focused more on what they could get rather than on what they could give. His success only exacerbated that problem.

And then came Amanda.

He shut his eyes and, for a moment, leaned his head against the cool glass of the window.

She had been so different, so pure and good in thoughts and deeds. She had wanted nothing from him and that had taken him by surprise. For the first time in many years, he had let his guard down only to find out that the danger in that was love. But he regretted nothing. She was, after all, his true soul mate.

"Alejandro?"

He paused, collecting himself before he glanced over his shoulder at Carlos. "¿Sí?"

"She's here."

That surprised Alejandro. With such bad traffic, the driver must have taken back roads and side streets. "Is she coming up?"

Carlos nodded.

"Send her to freshen up, then bring her to me," he commanded, dreading even the smallest delay but savoring the anticipation. It was a quality that he had taught himself long ago. The best things in life were always worth working for as well as waiting for. He returned his gaze to the window, his arms behind his back, as he continued to watch the cars moving ever so slightly beneath him on the street.

It was almost twenty minutes later when he heard the door between the rooms of the suite open. It was quiet, the only noise being the sound of the door swooshing open, the bottom of it scraping across the top of the plush white carpet. He refused to turn around, savoring each moment, as his heart pounded inside his chest. He could hear her as she took a few steps into the room, her feet padding across the carpet. But then she stopped and he waited. It seemed like an eternity.

"Alejandro?"

Her voice was soft but full of questions, perhaps even a bit of concern, as to why he kept his back to her. With a deep breath, he shut his eyes and quickly counted to ten in Spanish. Then, he turned around, his eyes taking in the sight of his beautiful wife, who stood fewer than ten feet away from him.

A chill ran up his spine as he felt emotion well up in his throat. He had to calm himself as his blue eyes stared at her, drinking in the vision of Amanda, dressed in a simple navy dress with a belt around her waist. Her hair was pulled back into a bun at the nape of her neck. His eyes moved over her body, pausing just for a moment at the sparkling ring on her finger.

And then he could take no more.

He crossed the room with long, easy strides and stood before her. He met her eyes and stared as deeply into her soul as he could. Her eyes were dark and beautiful, full of curiosity at his reaction to her presence. But as he reached out for her hand and lifted it to his lips, kissing her skin ever so sweetly, he noticed that her eyes changed. They softened with emotion and a blush crossed her cheeks.

"Princesa," he murmured as he gently pulled her toward him. Wrapping his arms around her, he held her close, leaving his head resting on her head as he shut his eyes and breathed in deeply. She smelled like lavender, a flashback to the farm. "Oh, what you do to me," he said, his lips against her hair. He held her tight, feeling her heart beat against his chest. She was so small, so petite. He had forgotten how neatly she fit against his body.

"Alejandro," she whispered, and he realized that she was trembling.

He pulled back, just enough so that he could look down into her face. With one hand, he tilted her chin so that she was staring up and into his face. His eyes sought hers before he lowered his mouth onto hers, kissing her with all of the built-up passion that he had kept bottled up since the day he had left her at her parents' farm.

He moved his hand to the back of her neck, gently holding it as he kissed her. Without stopping, he slowly moved away from the sitting room of the suite and pulled her with him toward the bedroom. He felt her trepidation and that added to his desire to reclaim the only person who mattered in his life: his wife.

And as he stepped back to undress her, his eyes never leaving hers, he realized that he had stopped living the moment his car had driven away from the Beiler farm. For three weeks, he had merely gone through the motions, for his life had been on hold until this minute, this very second, as Amanda stood before him, a blush on her cheeks.

He reached up and unpinned her hair. He loved the feeling of the bobby pins sliding out from the bun. Collecting them in his hand, he waited for the cascade of brown hair to fall down her back before he leaned over and placed the pins on the nightstand by the bed. Then he returned his attention to Amanda, lifting his hands to run his fingers through her silky hair that hung down to her waist. He pulled it forward, and with his eyes shut, he inhaled the lavender scent.

Once again, she whispered his name. "Alejandro?"

He caught his breath and opened his eyes. Staring at her, he choked back the emotion that was building in his throat. He lifted a finger and pressed it to her lips. "Shh," he replied, his voice low and an all-too-familiar look in his eyes. "I need you, Princesa," he murmured, reaching up to unbutton his shirt. "I need to remember you in every way, to know that you are mine once again."

She lowered her eyes, but he caught the hint of a shy smile on her lips. It maddened him, and he tossed his shirt aside, letting it fall over the back of a chair.

"I saw that," he teased gently, taking her hand once again.

She lifted her eyes and silently questioned him with a simple look.

"*Ay,* Dios *mío,*" he groaned and pulled her toward him, crushing her against his body as he embraced her, his lips on her neck and one hand entwined in her hair. "No more words for you, Princesa. Only this," he whispered into her ear as he lowered her to the bed and reclaimed his wife in complete silence.

It was close to three in the afternoon when they sat in the sitting room of the suite, Amanda wearing a soft white robe, her legs bare. She sat next to Alejandro on the sofa, leaning against him as though afraid to be apart from him. With her legs tucked under her, she let her head fall onto his shoulder as she savored the memory of his love.

The room was silent, save for the muffled noise of the street traffic. It was a comfortable silence, as though words were not necessary. He kept one arm around her, holding her tight as he scrolled through the messages on his phone. She didn't mind. As long as she was next to him, touching him, smelling him, she didn't care what he was doing.

He reached over and placed his hand on her leg, leaning his head back onto the sofa and sighing.

"What is it, Alejandro?" she asked, her voice soft with a hint of shyness.

Despite the intimate and passionate greeting from just a few hours ago, she felt estranged from this man. He consumed her thoughts and her heart, but she realized that the three weeks apart had created a feeling of insecurity in her. She had to remind herself, over and over again, that he was her husband and not a figment of her imagination.

He looked at her, his blue eyes gazing at her face. With his free hand, he reached over and brushed her long brown hair away from her cheek. A smile on his lips countered the sadness in his eyes.

"I have missed you, Princesa," he said.

"And I, you."

He shut his eyes for a minute, as though digesting her words. Then, he nodded. "*Sí*, I believe that, Amanda. But you will be returning, no?" He didn't wait for her response. "I don't want you to return. I need you here . . . with me." He lifted his head and turned to face her, putting both hands on her hips and holding her tight in his grasp. "I can't let you go back."

She laughed at him. "I just arrived!"

"*¡Ay!*" He pulled her closer so that she was almost sitting on his lap. "But the thought of you leaving is tearing me apart. Do you understand?"

She didn't.

"I have arranged for a nurse to stay with your father after your sister leaves," he confessed, caressing her hand as he held it in his. "You must not return. I can't do this without you."

"You have, Alejandro. For years before me," she pointed out.

"No!" Releasing her abruptly, he stood up and paced the room, running his fingers through his hair. "You don't get it, Amanda!" *Aman-tha*. The way he said her name caused a shiver to run down her spine. "You have changed me, and it's too clear to everyone. If you leave . . . if you return to Lancaster . . . I can't do this." He spun around to face her. "Without you, I am nothing anymore. My heart is not in this if I cannot have you by my side."

While she was touched by the passion in his voice, she was equally concerned by the desperation in it. How could he have changed so much in such a short period of time? Standing up, she straightened her robe before crossing the floor to face him. She reached for his hands, hands that had been caressing her and touching her just an hour before. She shivered at the memory and pressed one of them to her heart.

"Feel this?" she whispered. "It beats for you." She stared up into his face, amazed at the intensity with which he looked back at her. "I am always with you, Alejandro. Don't you know that?"

She saw him take a deep breath as he held her hand tightly. *"Te amo,* Princesa,*"* he said, his voice low and sultry. *"Siempre."*

"And I love you, too," she whispered. "For always."

The look in his eyes told her what he wanted to do, to take her back into his arms and love her again. But a soft knock on the door interrupted the moment. He groaned, a soft noise that escaped his throat, and he leaned down to place his forehead against hers. She could smell the musky scent of his cologne and shut her eyes, inhaling it so that she would never forget it.

"We must get going," he sighed, the regret in his voice touching her heart. "I'll give you a few minutes to . . ." His eyes roved down her body and took in her hair, hanging over her shoulders in long, loose waves. He reached out and tugged at her hair, twirling it around his fingers. "Freshen up, although I prefer you just as you are."

She lowered her eyes, blushing at the compliment. She didn't think she'd ever get used to his amorous affection. She had never been raised with displays of emotion. No hugs, no kisses, except on Church Sunday. She had missed his sparkling eyes and playful words; she felt her pulse quicken when she realized just how much.

Reluctantly, she moved away from him, heading back to the bedroom to change her clothes and twist her hair into a large bun at the nape of her neck. Pausing at the open double doors, she looked back at him, not surprised to find that he was still watching her. "Where are we going?"

"Two television interviews and then a meeting about the parade."

She raised an eyebrow. "Parade?"

"*Sí, sí,*" he said, his attention turned to his phone, which had just vibrated. The screen glowed from his hand. "We're to ride in the Macy's Thanksgiving Day Parade."

Amanda frowned, wanting to ask exactly what that was. But she saw that his attention had shifted from her back to work. Respecting that, she padded across the carpet to the bathroom in order to fix her hair and apply a light bit of makeup, just the way Lucinda had shown her. She was just finishing when Alejandro poked his head around the corner.

"Lucinda sent clothes, Amanda. She has them marked for when to wear," he said. "I laid out the dress for today's interviews. It's on the bed." He glanced over his shoulder as he said it. When she followed his gaze, she saw that he had remade the bed and, indeed, left her outfit neatly on the white comforter. "I need to make a few quick calls. I shall wait for you in the outer room, *sí?*" He didn't wait for an answer as he turned and walked away.

It was a black dress, simple and conservative. Amanda was impressed with Lucinda's selection. Usually, the fashion consultant had tried to pick more seductive outfits for Amanda. This dress, however, was much more suited to Amanda's taste.

She stood before the mirror and took a long moment to stare at the reflection. She could hardly recognize herself. Gone was the plain girl who just the day before wore a dirty work dress with a scarf on her head and mud on her shoes. In her place was a woman, a woman who was no longer plain, and to her dismay, felt as though she fit nowhere. The farm and community of her youth no longer wanted her. That much was clear. Yet in Alejandro's life, more time was spent moving from hotel to hotel, traveling by bus, plane, or private car. There was no place that she truly felt comfortable calling home.

He rapped on the door before opening it. He wore the same outfit as before: crisp black slacks, a black silk shirt, and a black jacket. His eyes were hidden behind his sunglasses already so that she couldn't read his reaction; but she was more than certain of her own as she stared at the man who stood before her.

"¿*Listo,* Princesa?"

She could barely speak. He was breathtaking, a true gentleman with sophistication and class that she could only dream of ever understanding. Emotion welled in her throat, and it was all that she could do to nod her head.

His lips lifted just slightly at the corners into a smile, and he reached up to take off his glasses. It looked as if he could read her thoughts. Reaching out a hand, he waited for her to cross the floor to take hers in his own. "I understand," he murmured, leaning over to gently brush a kiss against her cheeks. "I'd like nothing more than to remain here, wrap my arms around you, and stay that way for the rest of the day," he whispered, his breath caressing her neck. "But I have obligations, Princesa. And as long as you are beside me, I can bear to suffer through them until we can return here tonight and spend an eternity in each other's arms to make up for lost time."

"Oh," she gasped, leaning against him. How could someone know her so well? How could this man, this gloriously wonderful man, see through her as if she were a simple glass window with all of her emotion right there in plain view for him to look at?

He leaned back and brushed his finger against the tip of her nose. "Besides," he teased. "I have a very special surprise for you tonight. Something that will leave you as breathless as you were earlier . . ."

"Alejandro!" She felt the heat rise to her cheeks as she pressed her face against his chest, hiding her reaction to his words, which only made him laugh. She had forgotten how much he loved to tease her, but forgave him immediately, for his love was so overwhelming that she could not help but melt in his presence.

Downstairs in the lobby, Amanda followed a step behind Alejandro, adjusting to the stares from the people who watched the star and his small entourage make their way from the elevator to the front door. She was mildly surprised that there was not a mob of people outside, although plenty of heads turned when they exited the door and made their way to the waiting SUV with the darkly tinted windows.

Alejandro held her hand and helped her inside, knowing that a few passing pedestrians were snapping their photos with their cell phones. He lifted a hand to wave before disappearing inside the car and sat next to his wife.

His phone buzzed, so he pulled it from his pocket, giving Amanda an apologetic look as he answered the call in Spanish. Since she couldn't understand him, she looked out the window and stared at the tall buildings and crowds of people on the streets. It looked so different to her, different from how she remembered it from the first time she had been here.

She glanced at Alejandro. How much her life had changed since that first day . . . a day with a bad decision to cross the street, but a day that had brought Alejandro into her life. She had been in awe of the city and the buildings. She had been awkward and a little intimidated by Alejandro, a stranger to her, who had seemed to know so well how to break through her exterior shell of reserve.

Now she was here, riding along with him in the SUV, her leg brushing against his, as he spoke on the phone to some business associate in a language she would most likely never learn. Tilting her head, she watched him, her eyes falling on the gold band on his finger. A shiver went up her spine, and she bit her lip, feeling a moment of overwhelming bliss. She shut her eyes and lifted her heart to God, thanking him for the gifts that he had given her and praying that she was worthy of the love he had shown to her.

"Princesa?"

Her thoughts interrupted, she opened her eyes.

"You are alright?"

She smiled at his concern and reached a hand out to stroke the back of his neck. "Alejandro," she said softly. "I was praying."

He lifted an eyebrow as he leaned into her hand. "Praying? About . . . ?"

"The gifts that he has bestowed upon me."

She could tell from his expression that he was intrigued. "And might I be so brazen as to ask about these gifts?"

"Oh, Alejandro," she laughed softly. "As if you have to ask. God led me to you, and I find myself amazed that he did so. I pray that I am deserving . . . for you are such a man." She paused, reaching out to place her palm on his cheek. "Such a good, kind, and wonderful man."

His chest rose as he took a deep breath. He was touched by her words. That much she could tell. But he had no response. It was as if the words escaped him. He slipped on his sunglasses and cleared his throat, which made her wonder if there was a hint of emotion that he preferred to hide from her. "Look, Princesa," he said, clearly changing the subject as he pointed out the window. "We are here."

There were no crowds as the vehicle pulled up to the building, although people began to stop and stare as soon as they recognized the couple that emerged from the black SUV with tinted windows. Alejandro reached his hand for Amanda to help her as she stepped onto the curb. She lifted her eyes and smiled at him, no words necessary to show her appreciation for his chivalrous action. As they walked toward the building, he kept his hand on the small of her back, gently guiding her toward the entrance.

It was an afternoon talk show and, unbeknownst to Amanda, she was to join Alejandro on the stage after he performed. If she wanted to argue or beg off the show schedule, one look at his face told her otherwise. He was glowing and vibrant, anticipating the chance to be seen on national television with his wife by his side. She knew that he wanted to prove the tabloids were wrong, that he had not discarded his wife, despite the blatant lies of their headlines.

Swallowing her fears, she said nothing about her apprehension for being interviewed in front of a live audience. She told herself to simply not think about it. Television meant nothing to her, and if Alejandro wanted her to sit in a chair beside him during the interview, so be it.

The dressing rooms were nicer than the ones at the different studios on the West Coast. Amanda didn't say a word as an assistant to the interviewer talked with Alejandro about how the show operated and the procedures for when they would join the host onstage. Meanwhile, makeup artists began to work on them. During their first interview in California, he had explained that television lights drained the color from their faces, and makeup was the only way to ensure that they didn't look pale and sick. However, she still found it amusing to watch as Alejandro was fussed over by two makeup artists, while only one worked on her face.

"Ready for the sound check, Viper?"

He nodded his head and stood up from the chair, turning to Amanda. "They'll bring you out when it's time, Princesa," he said, pausing to rest his hand on her arm. "You'll be fine. Don't be nervous."

She merely nodded, wishing that she didn't have to walk onto the stage without him. He'd already be there, seated with the host and waiting for her. At least that thought gave her some comfort. Besides, she told herself, for Alejandro she would find the courage to do anything.

Fifteen minutes later, she could hear the music as he began performing. The assistant who stood beside Amanda had explained that Alejandro would perform his song before joining the interviewer, Mallory O'Grady. It would be a one-on-one interview until after the next commercial break, and that was when Amanda would be escorted to join them onstage.

There was a small television hanging from the ceiling, and Amanda turned to watch Alejandro performing. As always, he looked so natural out there, not a worry in the world, as he sang to the audience. For

Alejandro, this was second nature, as comfortable to him as breathing air was to most people. And, as always, the audience was clearly enjoying themselves as they danced along with his music.

Once the music ended and Alejandro moved over to join Mallory O'Grady, Amanda felt the familiar butterflies in her stomach. She could watch him on the small television but couldn't hear what was being said. From the way that he sat, laughing and looking into the camera, she knew that it was a good interview for him. Still, she found herself wishing that he hadn't insisted that she be a part of it.

"Two minutes, Amanda," the assistant said. "I'll take you up to the stage area now."

By the time they arrived at the curtain that separated the stage from the waiting area, Amanda could see that the commercials were just ending and the cameras were in position to go live once again. While they waited, a man came over to her and clipped a small black microphone to her, hooking a small black box to the back of her belt at her waistline.

Swallowing her fears, Amanda smoothed down the front of the black skirt she was wearing and took a deep breath. I can do this, she told herself.

"Now," the assistant whispered and gently nudged Amanda toward the opening in the curtain. Two men, dressed in dark clothing, held it aside for her, and as if her feet had a mind of their own, she found herself walking toward the opening.

The lights from the ceiling were bright and warm. The noise from the audience was loud. For a brief moment, she hesitated, her eyes scanning the rows of seated people who were applauding her. They smiled at her, a few cheering, and she felt her nervousness return.

And then he was at her arm.

"Come, Princesa," he said, gently guiding her toward the two chairs next to the interviewer.

Once seated, Amanda felt more comfortable. She angled her body toward Mallory so that she didn't have to look at the audience. With her attention focused on the woman, Amanda found it easier to breathe.

"I must say," Mallory began, "I think I speak for everyone here that we are very pleased to have you on the show!"

"*Danke,*" Amanda said softly, casting a quick glance in the direction of the audience.

"Now, I understand that you just arrived in New York this morning," Mallory said. "I'm sure that's a big difference from having been at your parents' farm."

"*Ja*, that it is," she admitted.

"The first time you were here, in the Big Apple," Mallory continued. "That's when you met Viper, isn't it?"

Had that only been last summer? It seemed like a lifetime ago. Amanda looked over her shoulder at Alejandro. "It was indeed, wasn't it?" She turned back to Mallory. "I'm certainly more careful crossing streets now."

The audience laughed at her reference to how she had met Alejandro.

"I would certainly recommend that," Mallory replied, laughing, too. "Your life certainly has changed in the past year because of that accident. Lots of new cities to explore with Viper that you probably never even imagined visiting. What is your favorite place that you have traveled to so far?"

"Oh that's easy!" she replied, happy that she had a ready answer to the question. "Miami, for sure and certain! It's so beautiful there, and the ocean is magnificent. We haven't been to the beach yet, but Alejandro did take me on his boat. And we visited the islands after our wedding. I love being near the water. It's so . . ." She paused, trying to think of the word to explain what she was feeling. "Humbling, I reckon. I'd like to walk into the ocean from the beach and feel the sun on my face, to lose myself in the noise of the waves on the shoreline."

"I'm sure that can be arranged," Mallory teased. "You better get on it, Viper."

He laughed and reached for Amanda's hand. "I'm on it," he quipped playfully.

"For the past few weeks, I understand that you were back in Pennsylvania while Viper continued with his tour. It must have been hard to be separated for so long," Mallory started, redirecting her attention back to Amanda. "You've only been married about six weeks, right?"

Six weeks? It felt so much longer to Amanda. In fact, she had a hard time remembering life without Alejandro being a part of it. "It's right nice to be back with him," she finally said, figuring that was the safest answer. "Even if we are far away from Miami."

"Is that home now?"

Home? For a moment, Amanda frowned. Where was home, anymore? She had spent the most time with Alejandro on the road. While she favored Miami, she didn't necessarily think of the condo as home. *"Nee,"* she said thoughtfully. "Miami isn't home. You see, home is wherever we are when we are together."

There was a collective murmur of approval from the audience, and she felt Alejandro lift her hand to his lips, kissing it gently. When she turned her head to look at him, he smiled his appreciation at what she had said. And in that moment, she realized how much she had meant those words. Without Alejandro, her world was devoid of color and meaning. Even if they had to travel the globe, as long as she was with him, nothing else really mattered.

After a busy afternoon of interviews, Amanda had been thankful to return to the hotel. Alejandro had brought her back while he prepared to attend his last meeting of the day. Even if only for two hours, she was glad for the quiet time to relax and gather her wits about her.

Had it only been that morning when she had awoken on the farm? The smell of cows and manure still lingered in her memory, despite having spent so much time in the car, traveling to New York City. She rested her head on the back of the sofa in the hotel room and shut her eyes, reminiscing about the time she had spent with Alejandro earlier, upon her arrival at the hotel.

A blush covered her cheeks at the memory.

His love for her was insatiable, although she had to admit that she didn't really mind. When he held her in his arms, his lips pressed against hers, she felt complete, as though she had previously been lost, floating through life without any true purpose. When she was with Alejandro, she was truly lost no more.

It had been with great reluctance that she had even suggested being dropped off at the hotel. She had no interest in attending this parade meeting and knew that he would probably finish the meeting faster if she wasn't there anyway. Besides, she had been simply exhausted.

When he walked her to the elevator, he had given her a gentle kiss before reminding her that he had a special surprise planned for the evening. She would have been just as happy to stay at the hotel, to escape in his arms once again. But she knew that she'd never deny him anything. If he wanted her to dress up and go out in New York City, she would do exactly that. The way that his eyes lit up when he was planning special surprises for her made her realize that the gift of giving brought him great joy.

Glancing at the clock, she saw that she had exactly two hours. She hadn't slept well the previous evening and longed for a short nap. Instead, she decided to take a long bubble bath, knowing that it would relax her just as much and there was no risk of oversleeping. The last thing she wanted to do was to be late for Alejandro's surprise. So, instead of napping, she padded to the bathroom and turned on the water, leaning over the edge to sprinkle some colorful and fragrant crystals into the fancy tub.

While the water ran, she unpinned her hair, letting it fall down her back and reach all the way to her waist. Running the brush through it, she shut her eyes and remembered Alejandro's fascination with her hair. He always liked to be the one who carefully plucked each pin from her bun, setting them aside on the dresser or nightstand before running his fingers through her hair. Even earlier that morning, he had insisted on letting her hair down before he had taken her into his arms in the privacy of the suite's bedroom.

For forty refreshing minutes, she soaked in the tub until the water turned cool and her fingers puckered like raisins. Then, reluctantly, she stepped out and slid into the robe, once again. Her muscles felt relaxed, and despite still being tired, she felt ready to face the evening. Knowing Alejandro, it would not be over early.

She was still in the plush white robe when he returned to the hotel room. Sitting on a white stool by the dressing area, Amanda was just finishing with the blow dryer, her long hair taking extra time to dry.

It was his image in the mirror that caught her attention. He merely slipped into the doorway, leaning against the doorframe with his arms crossed over his chest as he watched her. She wasn't startled when she saw him. In a way, she realized that she had half expected him to show up while she was still getting ready. Flipping off the blow dryer, she set it down on the counter and smiled at his reflection in the mirror.

"Come here," he commanded, his voice soft and husky.

A shiver ran up her spine, and she bit her lower lip, her eyes never leaving his as she continued staring at him. When he raised an eyebrow at her, as if wondering why she wasn't doing as he requested, she caught her breath. There was no doubt in her mind as to what he wanted.

"Alejandro . . ."

"Come, Amanda," he commanded once again. "I have missed you for the past three weeks and you are too beautiful right now." He held out his hand. "Do not deny me," he whispered.

Nee, she thought as she stood up and turned to face him. Denying him was not something she could do. Nor did she want to, she realized. She crossed the room toward him but did not take his hand. Instead, she stood before him, the robe falling from one shoulder and exposing her skin.

He reached for the belt and tugged at it, pulling her closer to him. "That's a good girl," he teased, his hand slipping inside the robe and pressing against her bare back. The touch of his hand against her body sent another shiver down her spine and her heart fluttered inside her chest. "A very good wife, indeed," he murmured into her ear as he bent his head down to nuzzle at her neck.

She smiled a soft smile as she shut her eyes, losing herself in his touch.

"Now," he said as he stepped backward, pulling her along with him as he edged toward the bed, his breath warm on her neck. "We have an hour before we need to leave. I'd say that gives me enough time to show you, Amanda, just how much I truly missed you." He pulled at the belt to the robe, loosening it just enough so that the robe opened and exposed her to him. He glanced down at her and sighed, placing one hand on her hip as he pushed the robe from her shoulders. "Oh yes, how I have missed you," he whispered as he pulled her into his arms once again and pressed his lips on hers, unleashing the passion that he felt for her for the second time that day.

The theater was full of people, mostly couples, each and every one of them looking more distinguished than the next. Alejandro wore a tuxedo; the black bow tie perfectly straight after Amanda had fussed with it before they exited the car. Despite the stress of having to dress rapidly after their late-afternoon amorous interlude, she was in unusually affectionate spirits. He had hidden his amusement at her insistence that he needed help with his cuff links and with fixing his bow tie, claiming that it was crooked. Even when she commented about it again, in the car, he hadn't stopped her from gently twisting the bow tie until she felt it rested perfectly straight against the high collar of his tuxedo shirt.

When they had entered the main lobby, several people had turned their heads to watch the couple that had just walked through the double glass doors of the Metropolitan Opera House. Yet it wasn't because they knew who the couple was; it was because of how beautiful the woman looked.

She wore a simple, off-the-shoulder Giorgio Armani gown, the black velvet of the material shimmering in the lights from the chandeliers overhead. The bottom of the gown flared out, just enough, to allow only the hint of a peek at her shoes, simple black heels with rhinestones down the back of the heel. With her hair pulled back and the least amount of makeup that she could wear in order to escape Alejandro's scrutiny, she looked like royalty as she held on to his arm and entered the building.

And, best of all, no one seemed to know who they were.

Most of the attendees to the opera that evening were older couples, people who certainly had never heard a song by "Viper" in their life. She sensed the difference in the atmosphere immediately and almost breathed a sigh of relief. Tonight, she realized, would be one that promised a degree of normalcy that she had not experienced with Alejandro since he had first stayed at the farm.

"You are gorgeous," he murmured into her ear as he paused to hand their tickets to a man at the door.

She lowered her head and blushed at his words.

They were personally escorted through the crowd and toward a sweeping staircase. He held her elbow as they followed the man, a few heads turning as they passed; people wondered not only who the couple might be but also why they were being personally escorted to their seats.

They sat in the parterre, their seats front and center, looking directly at the stage. Amanda glanced down at the seats beneath them and felt queasy at the open space. He reached for her hand, holding it in his as he lifted it to his lips and planted a soft kiss on her skin.

"Sit back and don't look down," he whispered as if reading her mind.

She did as he said, trying to relax in the red cushioned seats as she looked around at the opulence of the theater. The gold-lined ceiling resembled the buds of a flower that had yet to completely blossom around the crystal chandeliers that sparkled like small explosions of light in midair. A heavy curtain hung like a golden waterfall of velvety material from the ceiling to the stage, the orchestra pit just barely visible beneath its edge. And everywhere surrounding the stage were people slowly making their way to their seats, eager for the opera to begin.

"It's beautiful," she said softly, leaning over toward Alejandro. "I never knew places like this even existed!"

He smiled at her innocence as he responded, "There are many things, Amanda, which I'm sure you will soon see that you never even knew existed." He paused and reached out to brush his fingers along her cheekbone. "I will live for those moments," he added before gently kissing her lips.

Ten minutes passed before the chandeliers began to slowly ascend toward the ceiling. Amanda watched in awe as the lights dimmed during their short journey. Only when they were as high as they could go did the music begin. She shifted her eyes from the ceiling to the orchestra pit, fighting the urge to lean forward so that she could get a better view of the people and instruments seated there.

And then the curtain rose, slowly at first. As it lifted into the air, she was immediately transported, not just to a new world but also into the past. Amanda was mesmerized by the stage, absorbing everything from the costumes and the set to the music from the orchestra and the singing from the performers. She was mesmerized by everything, even if she did not understand the words being sung.

At one point, she turned to look at Alejandro, wanting to thank him for bringing her to such a magnificent place. What she saw stunned her. His eyes were moist, transfixed on the stage, and at one point, she thought she saw his lips moving, ever so slightly. Despite the opera being sung in Italian, he seemed to already know the words. Yet that was not what startled her.

For Amanda, the singing was truly majestic, a hint of God in the voices that sang each word. The beauty of the songs and the performers' ability to sing them had floored her from the moment the opera had begun. She had never heard anything so amazing in her life. Indeed, she had never even imagined that something so overwhelmingly touching even existed. This experience was a true gift from her husband.

It had never dawned on her that Alejandro would actually be enjoying himself. That he would seem so touched.

His music was so different, so modern and fast. Between singing and rapping, Alejandro sang in a manner that was the antithesis of something as classical and heartfelt as this opera. She had presumed that he had brought her to the opera to treat her to a night out on the town, to expose her to more of the Englische world than just concerts and clubs, paparazzi and screaming fans. But as she stared at him, she realized that he, too, was enthralled with the opera, and it was obviously not his first time attending such an event.

"*¿Qué,* Princesa?" he whispered when he realized that she was watching him.

She merely smiled and shook her head, treasuring this new, golden discovery about the man seated beside her whom she loved so much.

As she turned her attention back to the stage, she said a silent prayer of gratitude to God for everything that he had given to her, for bringing Alejandro into her life and for blessing her with a happiness that she had never known was even possible.

Chapter Eleven

```
Mike,
What's the schedule for Los Angeles on
Sunday?
Did you make those special arrangements
that I
requested? Both for NYC and Miami?
Looking for flight information.
Gracias, Papi!
V.
```

Early in the morning, Amanda found herself standing outside of Rockefeller Center, a white wool coat styled in a flattering princess cut keeping her warm and shielded from the cold air. There were three security guards standing beside her, keeping the crowd that was screaming for Alejandro at a safe distance from her. Despite the cold weather, Amanda guessed that there were close to ten thousand people crowded outside of the studio in the plaza, screaming as they waited for Alejandro to perform for them. She had never seen such a crowd, not outside of the concert stadiums anyway.

The *NBC Today* show was hosting a pre-Thanksgiving concert each morning. With so many tourists in the city during this festive time of year, it was the perfect opportunity to entertain them before the holiday. The street merchants and store owners played along, thankful for the chance to display their wares and get the added business. Viper had been given the top billing spot of performing on Wednesday, the most bustling of days, as out-of-town guests planning a midafternoon matinee at the theater would come early into the city and wait for hours, hoping to catch a glimpse of the famous superstar and, as rumor had it, his Amish wife. They were being dubbed the new royal family of the Americas.

She knew that he was inside right now, being interviewed by the morning news anchors. She could see through the windows and caught a glimpse of her husband as he sat on a tall stool, laughing and gesturing with his hands. At one point, he swiveled on his chair and pointed in her direction. The crowd roared, and it took all of Amanda's self-control to not cover her ears with her gloved hands to block out the noise.

One of the security guards touched her arm and gestured toward the door. She knew what that signal meant: Alejandro was arriving in a moment. He had requested that she'd wait for him outside the door for two reasons: He wanted the crowd to adore her, and he wanted to have her accompany him when he exited the studio to walk through the crowd and to the stage.

Nodding her head, Amanda let the security guards guide her into position. Although there was a metal fence that separated the crowd from the walkway, several young girls were pressed against it, reaching out toward her, calling her name. She glanced in their direction and they waved their arms, begging her to let them take a photograph with them. Pressing her lips together, Amanda lowered her eyes and took a step farther behind the security guards. She was too aware that telephones and cameras were snapping her photo while she stood there.

It made her feel uncomfortable, and without Alejandro beside her, she didn't want to encourage it.

When the studio door opened, the noise from the crowd was deafening. Alejandro appeared, surrounded by his own entourage of security detail. He stood for a moment, smiling and waving to the crowd; then his eyes fell on Amanda, and he stepped in her direction. Taking her gloved hand in his, he paused, just a moment, before he lifted it to his lips. She flushed and looked away, the demure reaction on her face causing the crowd to roar in appreciation of the gesture.

"*¿Listo*, Princesa?" he said into her ear, his breath sending a shiver up her spine. Without waiting for an answer, he walked behind the security guards, still holding her hand. She followed behind him, finding herself amazed at how he would wave to people, reach to hold their hands, and occasionally pause, pulling her to his side for a photo for the fans.

She tried to smile, tried to follow his example, but she had forgotten about the mob scenes. Was it was possible, she asked herself, that these crowds were even worse than before their separation? No, she corrected herself: they were worse than before their marriage!

There were five steps that led to the stage. At that point, he leaned down and kissed her cheek, leaving her in the care of the security detail before bounding up the stairs and waving, again, to the crowds that were crammed into the plaza and beyond. Many people were holding signs in the air, waving them frantically as they tried to catch Viper's attention. Several signs had lights on them, while a few were cut out in the form of an Amish buggy with Amanda's name in big letters.

For the next twenty minutes, Alejandro did a sound check and graced the waiting fans with two songs as he warmed up for the televised portion of the outdoor concert.

"Coffee?"

Amanda turned in the direction of the voice. A tall, thin man was standing before her, the badge around his neck indicating that he was part of the show's staff. He was holding a steaming mug of coffee and gestured that she could take it.

"Oh, *danke*," she whispered, and then realizing that the man hadn't heard her, she repeated it, this time louder.

"Good crowd here today," he said, gazing over the heads of the people. "Probably over fifteen thousand."

Amanda gasped. Fifteen thousand people? Standing for hours in the cold? "So many! Whatever for?"

The man laughed at her question. "Certain celebrities bring a huge crowd," he explained good-naturedly. "Viper is definitely one of them."

"Oh, I see," she replied, although she didn't. The reaction to Alejandro on the West Coast had been completely different from this. Outside of the arenas, there had been crowds. That had been expected. In Los Angeles and Las Vegas, fans had waited outside the radio stations and, occasionally, at the hotel. In Las Vegas, people had crowded around to see them at the casino. However, she had never seen anything like this. This was different . . . worse.

"And you," the man added. "It circulated on Twitter that you were in New York City with him. I think that's why the crowd grew."

Twitter? She had heard the name before but had never asked about it, figuring it was one of those strange social media concepts that Alejandro always mentioned and she had no interest in understanding. Virtual world? She was having enough trouble navigating the real one that was Alejandro's life, that was for sure and certain.

When the commercial break was over, the cameramen began to take action and the host of the show stepped onto the stage to join Viper. Amanda watched, her eyes drinking in the transformation of Alejandro, her husband, into Viper the superstar. His entire demeanor adjusted, his words spoken with more of an accent as he used street lingo that he never used with her. He would lower his sunglasses and wink into the camera or smile and wave at the fans as he spoke. He knew how to work the crowd, and the crowd responded by shouting out his name and screaming for his attention.

"I understand you have a special guest with you today," the host said. The crowd went wild, and Viper laughed, winking and then pausing a moment so that their eager roar could die down.

"If you mean my Princesa, then *sí*, she is here, with me, today!" He looked in her direction and gestured for her to join him.

Amanda felt the color drain from her face. Without her realizing that it was happening, one of the security guards took hold of her arm and led her through the gate, ignoring the fans lining the walkway, toward the steps leading onto the stage. Amanda had no choice but to join him. It was one thing to sit on a stage and be interviewed by a reporter. It was quite another to stand before so many adoring fans and know that it was being televised to millions of people.

Viper crossed the stage and reached out his hand, the gesture one of such chivalry that it caused a murmur among the crowd. She looked up at him, her dark eyes wide and frightened. But one look at his sparkling baby blues that peered at her over his sunglasses and she knew that he would let nothing bad happen to her.

On the stage, Viper presented his wife to the crowd, giving her a slight bow as he gestured toward her. The noise that emitted from the studio audience surprised Amanda, so she took a step backward, pressing her body behind his, which only made the crowd roar louder. He laughed and brought her forward once again.

"Don't be shy," he whispered, just loud enough for the microphone to catch. "Just wave and smile. Be yourself, Princesa."

Reluctantly, she did as he instructed.

"Amanda, you've joined Viper for the week after having been home taking care of your father. How is everything back at the farm?" The host thrust the microphone toward her face, and for just a moment, she blinked, unsure of how to respond. With no urging from Alejandro, she decided to answer as he had instructed: by being herself.

"Daed is much better, *danke*," she said. "And it is ever so *gut* to be back with Alejandro."

"Congratulations on your first Thanksgiving together," the host said, a genuine smile on his face. "There's no place like New York City during the holidays."

At that statement, she laughed. "There's no place like New York City, period!"

Her comment brought laughter from the crowd as well as the host and Alejandro.

"I imagine it's a far cry from having grown up on an Amish farm, isn't it?" the host said.

"That's quite an understatement" was her simple response.

The host turned his attention back to Alejandro. "And I hear that Viper has something special for us today. A new release, is it?"

Relieved that she was out of the line of fire from the morning show host and no longer of interest to the cameras, Amanda waited patiently while Alejandro answered a few more questions before it was time for him to perform. Then the host gestured to her that they should leave the stage; she eagerly followed him down the steps and back through the crowds.

"Your autograph! Amanda!"

"A photo! Please, Amanda!"

Young girls were jumping up and down, screaming for her as they leaned over the metal barricade. The host paused and turned toward Amanda, indicating with a nod of his head that she could sign a few autographs with the fans if she wanted to do so.

She felt put on the spot. Turning to the closest group of girls, she tried to smile. "An autograph? You mean just my signature?" She had never understood that. She had seen Alejandro do that on numerous occasions, stopping to sign pieces of paper, shirts, even arms. It seemed to make the fans happy, but Amanda had never quite understood why.

"Please! Here! Sign this!"

The girl thrust a photo at Amanda. To her surprise, it was a photo of her and Alejandro. Before she knew what was happening, other girls were shoving their own similar photos at her and waving their pens. Giving into the pressure, she took the pens and signed her name to the photos, doing her best to accommodate as many as she could. After a few minutes, the security guard began to wave away the young fans before he directed Amanda toward a different area to wait.

"Where did they get those photographs?" she asked the host.

"Hmm?" He glanced at her, then back at the girls. "Street vendors are probably selling them. They try to take advantage of the situation. They always do."

It caught her by surprise that the host was not as friendly off camera as he was on camera. Most of the reporters and interviewers to whom she had been exposed had been genuinely nice people, regardless of whether the cameras were rolling. What a sad commentary and how it speaks about his true character, she thought wistfully and returned her attention to her husband.

It wasn't until they were back in the car, headed across midtown to another recording studio where they were scheduled to appear on a midmorning talk show, that she mentioned the rude behavior of the host from the morning show.

Alejandro laughed and leaned his head back on the neck rest. "Ay, mi madre, Princesa," he said as he caught his breath. "Nothing surprises me anymore. Nothing except what surprises you!"

She tried to hide her smile at his unexpected display of mirth at her complaint. "I fail to see what is so humorous," she said, pretending to pout. "There's no excuse for a lack of manners, I reckon."

"No excuse," Alejandro replied. "Only plenty of opportunity, especially in this business."

She made a face at him, which only caused him to laugh again.

It only took ten minutes to travel to their next appointment. Traffic was not as busy and so they arrived early. Without a crowd waiting outside the building, Alejandro and Amanda slipped through the front door, greeted at the reception desk by a security guard who escorted them to the elevators and upstairs to the studio.

People were bustling around, most of them dressed in casual attire, in sharp contrast to Alejandro in his freshly laundered black shirt and crisp black slacks. He had changed into them after the first performance that morning, always concerned about his appearance for the fans and cameras.

Amanda watched the activity, curious as usual about the cameras, lights, and process. It reminded her of the organized chaos following an Amish worship service: everyone was moving about to set up the room without being directed, as they simply knew what to do, despite the outward appearance of disorganization.

"Viper!"

A man approached Alejandro from the shadows and greeted him with a handshake that spoke of familiarity. He smiled politely at Amanda but focused on Alejandro.

"You ready for the big day, eh?"

Alejandro gave a shrug of his shoulders. "Just another day, *sí*."

"Big day?" Amanda asked.

Alejandro leaned over. "Tomorrow," he whispered.

She didn't understand what he meant but didn't question him further. Whatever this "big day" was, she'd find out in due time.

"Let's get you both to makeup," the man said and led them down a corridor toward a series of rooms where people were waiting to get the couple ready for the interview.

For the next fifteen minutes, makeup artists crowded around her, applying foundation and blush to her cheeks before attempting to work on her eyes. Taking a deep breath, Amanda turned her head away. Too much, she wanted to say but hoped that her gesture was enough to make her point.

Seated beside her, Alejandro glanced over, noticing her discomfort. He reached out and touched the artist's hand. *"Ay,"* he said, his voice commanding but kind. "She's beautiful enough, no?"

The artist rolled his eyes and took a deep breath before moving away.

"Danke," Amanda whispered. "I don't know why they need to put all of that stuff on our faces."

Alejandro laughed as he stood up from the seat and reached for her hand. "The lights wash out the color on our faces," he explained again. "But you are more than beautiful enough to not need so much, I agree." He smiled at the young man, who gestured for them to follow him.

There were television monitors in the waiting area by the stage entrance. Amanda sat quietly, her eyes on the monitor as she watched the screen. It was the live version of the show, and right now, the host, an older woman with blond hair, was seated at a desk and talking to the audience. Oblivious, Alejandro was on his phone, talking in Spanish to someone when a man walked in and motioned toward him.

"You'll go on first, and then we'll bring Amanda," he said to Alejandro, his eyes barely glancing at her. "OK, Viper?"

Within seconds, Amanda was seated alone in the room. It was quiet except for the television monitor, and once again, she lifted her eyes to stare at it. The host had moved away from the desk and was seated in a chair next to a white sofa. She was looking into the camera and announcing her next guest: Viper. The crowd applauded, several people calling out, as he emerged from behind the back curtain, a smile on his face and his hand lifted in the air, waving to the audience.

Despite knowing that he was just a few dozen yards from her, it felt strange to realize that he had, only moments before, left her side. She watched as he sat down in the chair next to the host's desk on the stage, smoothing his black pants so that they would not wrinkle. The smile on his face was a genuine one, not the forced smile that she had come to recognize during interviews when he was on tour and tired. His blue eyes sparkled, and he lifted his hand one more time toward the audience.

When they had finally settled down, the host began to ask him questions, mostly about his current tour and where he would be traveling to over the holidays and into next year. Amanda listened with an attentive ear, hearing him list the countries and continents, the audience laughing when he rolled his eyes at the exhaustive list. Prior to his having read this list of the planned tour a few weeks back, she had never heard of half the countries he had mentioned. Now, listening to him recite them, she felt a flutter in her chest. Was she really ready to travel all over the world in the next four months?

"Five minutes," someone said from the doorway.

Amanda looked up, startled by the voice. She never saw who had said it, for the person was already gone.

Her eyes strayed back to the monitor. Alejandro looked so comfortable as he answered question after question, his responses natural and charming. Amanda couldn't help but wonder how he had learned to be so comfortable in front of so many people.

Oh, she had listened to his stories about struggling to make it, so many years ago. Back in Miami, he had told her those tales while they lay in each other's arms, a candle flickering in the bedroom after sharing moments of intimacy reserved only for husband and wife.

He had told her about performing at clubs, often fighting with people who mocked him for his songs. Back in those days, most of his performances had been geared toward the Hispanic population, all of his songs in Spanish. Men teased him, jealous over his increasing popularity as both a singer and a star.

Still, he had persevered. Nothing was going to ruin his dream, he had whispered to Amanda, his lips against her ear and his hand stroking her bare arm.

His dedication to his career was something that she both wondered about and admired. Growing up Amish, Amanda had never seen such determination among any member of her community. There was no need. Success was a good crop of corn or a well-made quilt. Success was not something that was seen as progressive and continual; it was individual acts of obedience to parents, community, and God. That was the way of the Amish.

Her mind traveled to a verse from the book of James: *Humble yourselves before the Lord, and he will exalt you.* Despite Alejandro's success, she knew that privately he was a humble man. Unlike several other artists, Alejandro's contemporaries in the music industry that she had met, Alejandro did not take his stardom for granted. He spent time with his adoring fans, reached out to them through social media, personalized his approach with his music. And before each performance, she had always noticed that he took a moment to pray to God, thanking him for the rewards that had followed his hard work.

"Ready, Amanda?"

Her thoughts interrupted, she turned and nodded at the man who gestured for her to follow him. With forced confidence, Amanda walked onto the set and hesitated, just for a moment, a shy smile on her face when the audience began to cheer and applaud her arrival. She glanced into the seated crowd, startled that so many were excited for her entrance. Then, turning her eyes toward Alejandro, she saw that he was standing and walking toward her, his hand outstretched for her to take.

His presence reassured her, and she hurried toward him, comforted when he grasped her hand and led her to the chairs. As always, he waited for her to sit first before he joined her.

"Amanda," the host said, a big grin on her expressive face. "It's quite an honor to have you here today."

"It is?" Amanda asked back, surprised at the use of such a word. *Honor* was not a word that the Amish used lightly. And it was certainly never used in conjunction with meeting someone. After all, God created people and only God was above them.

The audience, however, laughed.

Alejandro squeezed her hand and laughed, too.

The blond woman behind the desk leaned forward, staring at Amanda with that same smile on her face. She seemed to be studying her, and it made Amanda feel uncomfortable. "The whole world seems to be watching you, Amanda. You've taken them by storm."

Again, Amanda professed to not understand this. "I don't understand why," she replied. "I'm just a person like them."

The audience laughed once again but seemed pleased with her humble responses.

"What is it like, Amanda?" the host started to ask, changing the direction of the conversation. "You grew up amid the Amish, but now you are traveling the world with your husband, Viper, the international superstar who seems to turn everything he touches into gold."

Inwardly, Amanda sighed. The same questions. Everyone always wanted to know what it was like to travel with him. She wasn't certain how to respond, not in a way that people might find interesting. So she just told the truth. "Every day is the same yet every day is different, I reckon," she replied, her soft voice mirroring the expression on her face. "But the only thing that matters is that Alejandro is happy. If I can help make that happen, then I am happy."

There was a collective sigh of empathy from the audience.

"Well, Viper," the host said, a teasing tone in her voice. "It seems that you both are happy these days, especially after having been apart."

"*Sí, sí,*" he began, as he leaned forward in the seat. "It was hard to be separated so soon after our wedding, but being reunited makes it worthwhile."

"And, Amanda, I hear that you will be riding in the Macy's Thanksgiving Day Parade this year. How do you feel about that?"

Indeed, how did she feel? Amanda chewed on her lower lip and raised an eyebrow. "I . . . I'm not sure since I haven't ever seen a parade," she replied. "But I'm sure it will be fine. Alejandro explained that we ride on the back of a big truck, smile and wave to people, and then he sings a song at one stop. That seems pleasant enough, especially since the weather is supposed to be quite lovely, *ja*?"

"Never seen a parade?" The host stared at the audience in amazement and they laughed. "Why, your first parade will be riding in the Macy's parade? I don't think too many people can claim that!"

"Is it so special?" she asked innocently.

The crowd roared, laughing at her question.

Alejandro leaned over and said to her softly, but loud enough for the microphone to pick up his words, "It's a fairly large parade, Princesa. It's very special."

"Oh."

The host turned her attention back to Alejandro, asking him another question about his upcoming events in New York City. "I heard there was quite a crowd at the morning show today," she said. "I also know that you tend to make a few surprise visits at clubs while in town. Any guest appearances at some local hot spots that you'd like to share with us, Viper?"

He squirmed in the seat, in slight annoyance, an act that he had perfected when he wanted to look as if he was put under pressure by the interviewers. Amanda smiled to herself, amused by his reaction, as she knew it was only to make the interviewer feel as though she was about to get special information out of Viper that no one else had been able to extract.

"I would be quite remiss if I did mention any special clubs where I might make an appearance," he finally admitted.

"The crowds, eh?"

"*Sí*, the crowds."

"Amanda," she said, turning her attention away from Alejandro. "How do you deal with all of these fans and the crowds that follow you?"

Hesitating before answering, Amanda glanced at Alejandro first. When he nodded, she finally spoke. *"Ja vell,"* she began slowly. "It sure would be nice if they would leave my family in peace, especially with my *daed* trying to heal and all." She lowered her eyes, hoping that what she was saying was a suitable reply. "Sure makes it hard for me, too, to return there to help with the farm."

"Creates problems in the community?"

She nodded. "Oh *ja!* The bishop sure doesn't care for the photographers stealing photos and asking so many questions." She sighed, too aware that one of the cameras was focused on her face. "The things that people love about the Amish way of life seem to be the things that they are so intent on destroying in order to learn more about us."

"Us?"

She felt, rather than saw, Alejandro stiffen at the interviewer's single-word question. "The Amish, I mean."

"But you are no longer Amish," the woman stated.

"Nee, I'm not," Amanda admitted. "You can be raised Amish but never join the church. There are cultural Amish, and there are religious Amish. While I have decided to not remain religiously Amish, I'll always have more than a touch of the cultural upbringing inside me." She smiled. "Can't remove that, I reckon."

The woman began to wrap up the interview before announcing a short commercial break. Afterward, Amanda knew that Alejandro would perform for the audience and then they would quickly depart the studio for their next appointment. To her relief, she realized that her part in the live show was over, so she relaxed, taking a deep breath as she shifted her eyes from the interviewer to her husband.

"And where do you go from here, Viper?"

He reached for Amanda's hand once again, giving her a gentle squeeze. "After New York, we will be traveling around the country for holiday concerts," he said, glancing at Amanda just briefly. He paused to smile at her before turning his attention back to the camera. "But as long as we are together, wherever we are is home."

This time, it was Amanda who felt herself stiffen at his announcement. He knew that she had to return to her parents' farm, that Anna and her husband were only visiting for a few weeks. She had no choice but to leave him in order to help her *daed* and *mamm*. As far as the holiday concert tour, this was the first she had heard him mention it since her *daed*'s stroke.

During the commercial break, Viper briefly walked toward the audience, shaking hands and posing for photos with the people seated in the immediate front of the theater. Amanda made no movement to join him, standing by the side of the stage as she watched Alejandro. His face lit up as he smiled for the cameras, that picture-perfect expression of delight that he had mastered for his fans.

The stage was a bundle of activity, the stagehands quickly transforming it into a concert setting for Viper's performance. Amanda turned her attention to watch, amazed at the activity in the studio. Within minutes, everything seemed to change. Men dressed in jeans and black shirts removed the furniture and desk while others set up the sound system and speakers.

During all of this, Alejandro appeared completely relaxed, ignoring the activity as he interacted with his fans, moving among those seated closest to the stage so that they could take photos with him and shake his hand. At one point, he took a woman's phone and turned around, snapping a photograph of himself with the woman and the audience behind them. Everyone cheered, and he waved his hand in acknowledgment before returning to the set.

Amanda stood near the host as the commercial break ended and the red light atop the camera flicked on. They were live.

"We're back!" the host said with a big white smile plastered on her face. "And without any further ado, let's give it up for Viper!"

Once again, for the second time that morning, Amanda watched as an audience applauded, their cheers wild and loud. The music began to play, and Alejandro transformed into Viper before Amanda's very eyes. And once again, she found herself transfixed as she watched him dance and sing, pandering to both the cameras and the audience as he did. For a moment, she turned her gaze to the adoring faces of the women in the audience as they stood, mouthing the words to his lyrics and dancing to the music of the songs, their eyes glowing and bodies moving in time to the energizing beat.

He moved about the stage, singing and dancing, his movement so natural and fluid that she, too, found herself swaying in time to the music. When he glanced over in her direction, pausing just briefly to lower his dark sunglasses and wink at her, the crowd roared in delight and Amanda felt color flood her cheeks. He had such a way of turning every moment into one in which she felt as if she were living in a dream.

She was silent when the performance ended and the cameras stopped filming, watching him as he thanked the crew before they began to rapidly dismantle everything. Alejandro waved once again to the audience, then after giving the host a warm hug, he grabbed Amanda's hand and led her out of the studio, pausing a few times to allow some of the crew to take photos with him.

When they were situated in the backseat of the SUV and headed toward the hotel, Alejandro sighed and removed his glasses, leaning his head back and rubbing at his eyes. *"Ay, Dios,"* he sighed.

"Tired, then?" she asked, her voice soft and caring. "Do you have time to rest a spell?"

He opened his eyes and stared at her, his blue eyes watching her as he reached out and caressed her cheek. "You are so beautiful, Amanda," he responded, avoiding her question.

"That wasn't what I asked." But she smiled as she answered.

"*Sí, sí,*" he murmured, lifting her hand to his lips and brushing it with a soft kiss. "I would like to rest a spell, but only if I have company."

She blushed and averted her eyes.

"Is that a '*ja*,' Princesa?" he teased, leaning over so that his body was pressed against her shoulder. "I saw you watching me," he murmured into her ear. "You liked it, *sí?*"

"*Sí,*" she whispered back.

"I thought so." He touched the tip of her nose with his finger and smiled before leaning back into the seat. "I saw it in your eyes." Watching her reaction, he seemed pleased that he had, once again, pushed her outside of her comfort zone. "We have a busy night, Princesa. I think some time alone is in order, but I don't think rest is on the menu," he said, his voice low and the intention more than clear. "Too much lost time to make up, *sí?*"

She let him pull her into his arms, her cheek pressed against his shoulder as he held her. When he kissed the top of her head, she shut her eyes and took a long, deep breath, enjoying the moment and knowing that, as long as she was with Alejandro, her life was, indeed, a dream. If only, she thought, enjoying his attention as well as the anticipation of an afternoon spent alone with him, I could live this moment forever.

Chapter Twelve

Dear Anna,

I hope this letter finds you well. Please bestow my thoughts, prayers, and well wishes upon the entire family.

I trust that your journey from Ohio was easy and safe. I understand that you took a bus, rather than the train as we did last spring. I'm sure that was much faster and probably a lot more comfortable.

So much has happened since then. I often think back to last year and can hardly believe the changes in both of our lives. It will be ever so gut to see you next week and to meet your husband, Jonas. I'm sure that I remember him from church service at the Troyer farm. I seem to remember him staring over our way several times.

Alejandro is performing in a big parade in New York City tomorrow. I'm not certain how big it is, but everyone seems very excited about it.

Today he had another morning interview on a television program. I did not accompany him this time, although I did yesterday. He also was on the radio *and then worked on a new song. I spent my morning crocheting for a while, waiting for his interview to be aired. It was fun to watch him on the television.*

Tonight we are going to go out to dinner. I sure do miss Mamm's home-cooked meals. Traveling so much does not allow for home cooking, I reckon. I can't wait to return to the farm for some of Mamm's fried chicken and meatballs.

There is a party tonight, too. So many endless nights. I find it hard to adjust to retiring so late only to have to wake up early. Alejandro does not seem to even notice. He sleeps when he can and never complains.

I best get going if I want to have the hotel people mail this letter.

May the Lord bless you and the family, keeping his face shining upon you as he bestows his graciousness upon all of you.

Amanda

It was on Wednesday evening when Alejandro surprised her with a single white rose and a gift-wrapped box, all in white with a bow atop it. They were standing in the living room of their suite at the Peninsula Hotel; Amanda had just emerged from the bedroom, dressed for an evening on the town before the parade the following morning.

Alejandro stood by the glass table near the window, a drink in his hand as he watched her walk through the doorway. It had been a long day, with more interviews and appearances. In the afternoon, Alejandro had met with several men in the suite, sitting on the sofa and staring at his computer as they played a recent recording of one of his songs. Amanda had taken the time to retreat to their bedroom and, with the doors shut, fell into bed for a late-afternoon nap.

She wasn't used to the busy schedule and constant movement between appointments. The crowds were worse than anything she had ever experienced while she had been on the road. Twice, someone had grabbed her arm when they were walking through crowds, and security had to intervene. Alejandro hadn't noticed, and despite being unnerved by the physical aggressiveness of his fans, she had not told him about those two incidents.

The constant "on" was exhausting, and she had been thankful for the time alone in the room. It was quiet and peaceful, the curtains drawn and the bed inviting. For a few minutes, she had lain in the king-sized bed with plush pillows and soft sheets, her eyes closed as she tried to make sense of the recent days in New York City with her husband.

She missed the days in Miami; that was the first thing she realized. When they were in Miami, there had been some semblance of routine and life as a couple. Yes, he had gone out late at night. Yes, he had people stopping by at strange hours. But still, it had been just the two of them and limited crowds.

She did not care for New York City with the crowded streets and aggressive people. Even though it was beautiful at night with the skyscrapers lit against the dark sky, she only saw the roughness of the screaming crowds wherever they went. She found herself thinking about home. When she realized that the word *home* conjured images of her parents' farm, she chastised herself. Home was no longer at the Beiler farm but by Alejandro's side. She had married him knowing that *home* would be on the road as much—if not more—as it would be in Miami.

And that thought disturbed her as she fell into a fitful sleep.

Now, however, as she stood in the doorway and caught his gaze, she felt ashamed of herself for having been so careless with her thoughts earlier in the day. He wore black pants and a light blue shirt, unbuttoned at the neck. His black jacket was tossed over the back of a dining chair, and the wrapped package sat next to the rose on the tabletop.

"Qué linda," he purred, setting down his glass and reaching for the gift and rose. Crossing the room in three easy strides, he reached for her hand. He lifted it above his head and motioned for her to turn around beneath it. "You are lovely as ever, Amanda," he said approvingly.

She wore a simple dress, black and pale blue, the colors matching Alejandro's apparel. The princess cut of the dress accentuated her small waist. The long skirt hugged her hips and flared out, just slightly, above her shoes. If she felt uncomfortable in the high heels and fancy dress, she said nothing. The look in his eyes, so approving and delighted, made up for her discomfort.

"Still, I think you are missing something, Princesa," he said teasingly as he handed her the wrapped box.

Color rose to her cheeks, but she knew better than to argue with him. In her world, presents were for birthdays, and even then, they were practical and useful. She didn't need to open the box to know that this gift was neither.

She unwrapped the ribbon and slowly opened the box. He moved behind her, brushing the soft rosebud along the side of her neck. It tickled and she smiled, lifting her shoulder in response to his touch. Inside the box was a beautiful necklace, sparkling with diamonds in a drip fashion on a white-gold chain. She caught her breath and tried to glance over her shoulder at him, but he was leaning against her, his lips touching her neck as he reached over her shoulders for the box.

"¿Permiso?" he asked, but did not wait for a response before he took the necklace and gently placed it around her neck. His hands lingered on her bare skin, his thumb gently caressing the edge of the necklace, before he turned her around to study her. *"Perfecto,"* he purred.

"That's too much," she countered, not certain how to respond to such a luxurious gift.

He laughed, a soft sound, as he leaned down to brush his lips against hers, quieting her demure protest. "Nothing is too much for *mi* Princesa," he whispered, pulling her into his arms and pressing her against his body. "Nothing . . ."

With his arms wrapped around her, Amanda felt safe and secure. The musky scent of his cologne wafted to her nose, and she breathed in deeply, shutting her eyes as she enjoyed the brief moment of intimacy that he had bestowed upon her.

The knock on the door interrupted them and Alejandro sighed. "Time to go," he announced, a hint of regret in his voice. "I'd much prefer to savor you alone, Amanda." He pulled back and touched her chin, tilting her face toward his. "But that is not to be tonight, no?" Without waiting for an answer, he leaned down to kiss her, a soft and sweet kiss, before he moved away, walking back to the table to get his jacket.

There was no one standing outside of the hotel when security escorted them to the awaiting SUV that was to take them to the restaurant and, later, to a special pre-parade party at another hotel, being hosted by Justin Bell and Celinda Ruiz. If nothing else, Amanda was looking forward to seeing Celinda, one of the few people she had met from Alejandro's circles, whom she considered close to being a friend.

When the SUV pulled up to the front door of the restaurant, an impressive entrance with double oak doors and simple greenery next to the Greek-style pillars, a man in a long black coat with white gloves opened the door, welcoming them to Daniel. Amanda followed Alejandro into the restaurant, just one step behind him, as he slipped through the door and into the reception area.

It was a beautiful restaurant with soft music piping through the sound system and dim lighting that cast a soft glow around the dining room. The tables were filled with a variety of people, mostly older men dressed in tuxedos or suits with middle-aged women in designer dresses. A few people turned their heads to look at the younger couple that had just arrived, but few seemed to actually recognize them. There was no fanfare over their arrival, and for that, Amanda breathed a sigh of relief. For once, they could dine in peace without being stared at or whispered about.

For twenty minutes, they sat in the lounge, Alejandro enjoying a cocktail while Amanda sipped a seltzer water, her alternative choice to alcohol. Only two other couples were in the lounge, both glancing at the famous international star and his wife. Alejandro nodded in their direction and instructed the waiter to buy both couples a drink. Amanda raised an eyebrow at his generosity, but Alejandro appeared as if nothing unusual had just happened.

Instead, he took off his sunglasses and absentmindedly shut them before sliding them into his breast pocket. His cell phone vibrated, and without thinking, he quickly glanced at it. *"Permiso,"* he said, politely excusing himself to check his text message, but he didn't wait for her response as he turned his attention to the phone.

She took advantage of his distraction to glance around the lounge. The two couples were enjoying their drinks and talking quietly among themselves. When Amanda caught the eyes of the one couple, they raised their glasses to her and smiled. But that was it.

Looking around the lounge, she took in the glass shelves behind the bar, lined with colorful bottles of liquor, lit up by lighting from the architectural arches above them. The walls were textured but plain white, which, with the dim lighting, took on an orange glow. The décor was more modern than Amanda was used to, although the bland colors reminded her of their Miami condominium.

"You like?"

Unaware that he had finished with his text, she returned her attention to Alejandro. "It's different, *ja,*" she responded, a smile on her face. "Reminds me of home." When he raised an eyebrow at her, a silent question on his face, she quickly added, *"Our* home."

He smiled when she said that. "You miss Miami, Princesa?"

"A little, *ja*," she admitted.

"Just wait until you see Brazil and Colombia," he said, leaning back in his chair and swirling his glass so that the ice tinkled against the side. "It is so beautiful. So different. And it will be warm. None of this cold winter weather." From his expression, she could tell that he was looking forward to escaping to warmer weather during the harsher months of the year. "Of course, we have to get through the holiday concerts first. But I think some time in Brazil will make up for that, no?"

"I . . . I think we need to talk about that," she said hesitantly.

Setting the glass down on the table, Alejandro stared at her. "Talk about . . . ?"

She averted her eyes and chewed on her lower lip. She didn't know how to tell him what she had been thinking the day before when he was being interviewed. "You know that I have to return to my parents, Alejandro," she finally said, her voice barely audible.

He tapped his finger against the side of his glass. Once, twice. *"Sí, sí,"* he responded, but she could tell from his casual dismissal that he didn't really mean it. "We can talk about that later, Amanda. Not tonight." He lifted his glass to his lips, his eyes staring at her over the rim. "Tonight is for us, to celebrate the holiday and to celebrate us."

When they walked into the main dining room, a few heads turned to watch them. A general murmur rose through the room, but to Amanda's relief, there was no general interruption at their entrance. Alejandro walked behind the maître d', his hand pressed lightly on the small of Amanda's back as he guided her through the tables toward the back of the dining room to a private section between two large white columns.

With the soft lighting and the gentle music in the background, Amanda found herself relaxing. Without crowds, without photographers, and without adoring fans screaming for his attention, she felt as though they were a normal couple out for an evening together.

Normal, she thought with an inward laugh. How could any of this be considered "normal"? she wondered.

"Why are you laughing?" he asked, his blue eyes drinking in her amusement.

"Was I?"

He gestured toward the waiter. "Champagne, *sí*?" He didn't wait for a response as he turned back to Amanda. "*Sí*, you were laughing, Princesa. I wonder about what?" He looked at her, his eyes sparkling.

"Life, I reckon," she replied. How could she explain to him what she was truly feeling? Leaning forward, she lowered her voice. "Don't you ever look back on where you came from, Alejandro, and just shake your head in disbelief?"

"Ah," he replied and leaned back in the booth where they were seated. "I see."

"You do?"

"*Sí, sí,*" he said, nodding his head. "The streets of Miami were tough, Amanda. And I look back on where I came from, often in amazement." He glanced around the room. "My mother always said that whoever made me over had their hands full!" He laughed as he remembered. "I'm glad you never met me then, Amanda. You would not have liked me."

"No?" She tried not to think about it, worried that he might be correct. It was a shocking thought that Alejandro could ever have been anything less than the gentleman who sat before her, the man who doted on her and made her feel as though the world stopped when he walked through the door.

"How did I manage to escape from being a foulmouthed little hoodlum and become this? From my mother working two to three jobs just so we'd have food on the table to my being able to enjoy this?" He gestured at the room and looked back at her. "To have you?"

"I was thinking more about the life, Alejandro," she corrected him gently.

"The life? *Sí*, it is different today from how it was so many years ago," he confessed. "But it was hard work and a lot of mistakes that turned me into a man, no?"

For a brief moment, she wondered about those "mistakes." Was he including the women he had loved physically but not emotionally? Did he ever think about his daughter, who he never saw? She had never asked him about that, worried that it would bring up bad memories for him. Besides, she had told herself whenever she remembered that he had fathered a child with an unknown woman so many years ago, it was an act that was committed by a different man from the one who sat before her now.

It was just after ten o'clock when the SUV pulled up in front of the Langham Place, the hotel on Fifth Avenue where Justin Bell was having a small gathering prior to the following morning's Thanksgiving Day Parade. However, from the looks of the suite, the festivities were only just beginning.

Amanda hung behind Alejandro, not recognizing anyone who greeted them. Music was playing while the guests were drinking and laughing. It was almost too loud to hear what anyone was saying, but by listening carefully, Amanda could make out the introductions as Alejandro made them.

She had been there a short while before she saw Celinda emerge from a back room. Immediately, Amanda smiled and felt a sense of relief wash over her. She moved away from Alejandro and made her way over to the sole person she recognized.

"Amanda!"

Celinda greeted her with a warm hug and a kiss on both of her cheeks. "I heard you might be stopping in," she gushed. "I'm so glad to see you!"

"And I you," Amanda said, genuinely meaning her words.

"How is your father?" Celinda asked, a caring look in her dark eyes. The fact that she had even asked about her *daed* touched Amanda. Few other people had been so thoughtful. "I heard he was unwell."

"*Ja, ja,*" Amanda admitted, nodding her head. "I was home recently, and he had just returned from the hospital. My sister and her husband have come for the holiday to visit." She glanced over her shoulder at Alejandro, seeing that he was standing amid several men and women talking. "I was glad to be able to see Alejandro," she added. One of the women, darker-skinned with long black hair and wearing a short red dress that accentuated her long legs, placed her arm on Alejandro's, and he laughed at whatever was said.

Celinda followed Amanda's gaze and smiled. "Don't pay any attention to that," she said, lowering her voice. "That means nothing."

"Nothing?" Amanda frowned. "Doesn't look like nothing."

"She's a hanger-on," Celinda explained. "Part of the regular entourage for Justin in New York City."

Entourage? Hanger-on? Amanda wanted to ask what Celinda meant but didn't have the courage. She was afraid that she would appear too unknowledgeable, just one more reason to feel insecure in this world of Alejandro's. However, Celinda seemed to notice the confused look on Amanda's face.

"That woman is part of a group of people that likes to hang out with celebrities," Celinda explained patiently. "Sometimes the paparazzi will take photos of them with Justin or others, speculating that he's dating her."

Amanda gasped. "That's terrible!"

This time, Celinda laughed. "Not really. Some of them are paid to pander to the media, to drum up interest in the celebrities. In fact, our publicists want us to break up for the holidays."

"Break up?"

Celinda raised an eyebrow and shrugged. "Sells more records for him if he's single before Christmas. Of course, when it comes time to ring in the New Year, we'll be officially back together again."

"I don't understand," Amanda said, shaking her head. "That's lying, isn't it?"

"Not really," Celinda replied. "It's more like marketing. Gives the fans what they want . . . that dream." She placed her hand on Amanda's arm and smiled. "Don't be alarmed. Much of what you read in the media is made up. If it hasn't happened yet, it will one day. Don't trust what they say."

She wanted to ask more questions, but she was still in shock over what Celinda had confided in her. During her courtship with Alejandro, she had known that he often orchestrated opportunities for the media to take photos or learn of information in a manner in which he would maintain control over the situation. But she had never suspected that entire relationships could be orchestrated just to gain media attention and boost the image of stars.

She kept her eyes on Alejandro, watching him. Indeed, now that she looked closer, she could tell that he was acting. He wasn't being his true self, not even in this crowd of supposed friends. His smile was electric, as usual, but the sparkle was gone from his eyes. Only when he looked around for her and caught her gaze did she recognize the light that she had grown to love in his expression.

He was always on, she realized. There was very little downtime for Alejandro. His life was a continuous string of events in which he had to constantly remain in the spotlight. No wonder he had wanted to spend the afternoon together, alone in the hotel room with his arms wrapped around her. He had made love to her in the quiet of the room and then held her, his breath slow and shallow as he rested. She hadn't been certain if he had actually slept, but she knew that he was at peace and relaxed, as she pressed her bare back against his chest. Yes, he had been at peace and relaxed, if only just for the moment. After all, she was his safe zone, the one person who was there for him with no expectations or demands beyond the need for his love.

Excusing herself from Celinda's side, Amanda made her way through the crowd and stood beside him. She rested her hand on his arm and smiled when he looked at her. "Mayhaps it's soon time, no?" she said softly. "It's a long day tomorrow."

He hid his smile and pursed his lips, amused at her forwardness in requesting to leave. With a raised eyebrow, he nodded his head. "And I have a surprise for you," he admitted. "So, *sí*, we should be going, Princesa." He took a final drink from his glass before setting it on the tray of a passing waiter. *"Vamos, mi amor,"* he said, wrapping his arm around her shoulders and tenderly escorting her away from the crowds and toward the front door.

Chapter Thirteen

It was a cold morning in New York City. Alejandro made a fuss over Amanda, buttoning her coat and tightening the beige cashmere scarf around her neck. With a proud smile, he tilted the matching hat on her head and leaned down to kiss her cheek. Despite not having returned to the hotel until after midnight, Alejandro looked fresh and well rested, something that Amanda did not feel.

"¿*Listo*, Princesa?"

She lifted up the steaming cup of coffee that was in her hands, indicating that, indeed, she was ready. Even if she didn't feel ready, she wasn't about to admit that to him. It amazed her how he had that endless energy, rising early and ready to face the day, despite the fact that the nights could be equally as long. Of course, midnight was early for Alejandro. For her, however, it had been a late evening.

Even though they were not scheduled to depart the staging area until half past ten, Alejandro had insisted that they wake early to see the balloons dangling from cables as they waited for the start of the parade.

He hadn't told her this. Instead, she had felt his hand tracing an imaginary line along her shoulder and down her arm. When she felt his lips kiss her skin, she had smiled to herself and rolled over, nestling into his arms. He was warm and already showered, his skin smelling of that fresh scent of soap and cologne.

"What time is it?" she had asked sleepily.

"Time to arise, Princesa," he had murmured into her ear. "I have another surprise for you."

Within forty minutes, he had led her out of the hotel and to the awaiting car. A man stood ready with two cups of steaming coffee in travel mugs, which he handed to them once they were situated in the car.

"Drink up," Alejandro had coaxed. "You will need caffeine for today."

Obediently, and also because she was cold, she took a deep swallow from the mug, pausing briefly to wave her hand in front of her mouth. "Ooo, hot."

He laughed at her reaction, placing his hand on her knee as he leaned forward, saying something in Spanish to the driver. Within minutes, the car was navigating the morning traffic and closed streets, taking them as close to the staging area as possible. When the streets became impassible, Alejandro opened the door of the car and helped Amanda get out.

Quickly, he took her hand and began hurrying through the streets. She was surprised that there was no one else with them. It was one of the very few times she could remember when he did not have security people accompanying him. While people were already sitting on the sidewalks, wrapped in blankets, no one paid much attention to the couple as they approached one of the security check-in areas. Alejandro reached into his jacket pocket and pulled out an envelope, which he promptly handed to the security guard. Within seconds, they were permitted entrance to the closed section of Seventy-Ninth Street, where, just beyond it, the helium-filled balloons and floats awaited their turn to join the parade route.

Amanda stared in amazement, her mouth hanging open as she followed Alejandro. The balloons that floated overhead were larger than anything she would have ever imagined. Cats, dogs, clowns, colorful characters that she had never seen before lingered over her head and between the large buildings near the parade route. Each balloon had dozens of lines hanging from it, each being held by a handler. Farther down the way, several balloons were still being held under thick netting, waiting their turn to be unleashed and readied for the parade.

Several handlers recognized Alejandro and Amanda, calling out "Viper!" to which he grinned and waved.

"Happy Thanksgiving!" he shouted back to their cries and cheers.

Just beyond the balloons were marching bands, dozens of young adults standing with their instruments in the lineup area, some stomping their feet to stay warm while others chatted with one another.

"They've been practicing since three this morning," Alejandro said into her ear.

"So early?"

He nodded as he led her farther down the street, his hand clutching hers tightly as they maneuvered through the people lining up.

As the sun rose overhead, the early-morning chill disappeared, and Amanda forgot how cold she had felt earlier. Instead, she stared at the people and the floats, the handlers and the balloons. It was something she had never seen before and doubted she'd see ever again.

"All of this for Thanksgiving?" she asked Alejandro.

"Sí, Thanksgiving."

She frowned, gesturing toward the streets lined with balloons and floats and people. "But what has this to do with Thanksgiving?"

He laughed and wrapped his arm around her neck, pulling her close and kissing the side of her head. "Ay, Amanda," he breathed. "How refreshingly honest you are!"

She wanted to say that there was nothing honest about what she had asked. It was clear that being thankful for God's love had nothing to do with larger-than-life balloons or oversized floats or bands that played far too loud for her taste. But his joy was too overwhelming, and she was just happy to be with her husband. Having been apart for too many weeks, she was especially thankful to be beside him on this first holiday celebrated together in their marriage.

"Viper!"

They both turned around at the calling of his name. A trio, all dressed in black with microphones and clipboards in their hands, was approaching. As they began to address him in Spanish, pointing farther down the road at a large float, Amanda looked away, taking in the excitement and energy that packed the street.

She had truly never seen anything like it before in her life. So many people and so much activity! Despite the perception of chaos and the noise that issued from the instruments warming up and the people cheering along the street, there was something familiar about it. An organization that could only come from years of practice. It reminded her of the organized chaos that often ensued after the worship services back at home.

"We have to go to the staging area," Alejandro said, motioning toward a white golf cart that had just pulled up behind them. He gestured for her to step into the backseat, and once she was settled, he sat beside her.

A very different Thanksgiving indeed, she thought as she turned her attention to watching the floats and bands that they passed as the driver sped through the crowd to take them to the staging area. When the golf cart stopped, Alejandro was quick to help her off, then thanked the driver with a quick handshake.

"Viper," someone else called out. Within seconds, the man was leading them through the throngs of people lining up as they waited to join the parade that started on Seventy-Seventh Street. They stopped walking near Central Park West and stood before a monstrous float that resembled something Amanda had seen only once as a child in a fairy-tale book, at a doctor's office.

The man was saying something to Alejandro that she couldn't hear, but she saw him point out a section of the float: a platform that was at least fifteen feet higher than the rest of the decorated vehicle and looked like a giant gray castle. There was flooring around the castle on all sides for people to dance and wave to the crowd.

"¿Listo, Princesa?" he asked as he turned to her. "They want us to climb up now as this unit will start moving out shortly."

Without waiting for her response, he reached for her hand and helped her climb the small ladder to the first platform. He quickly followed behind her, then led her through the castle doorway. Inside, it was dark and she could barely see. Alejandro waited for someone to flip on a flashlight and direct their attention toward a narrow metal staircase that led to the top of the castle.

After eight or so steps up, Amanda emerged atop the castle tower, amazed that she was staring down at the street below her. Around the top of the castle, there was a wooden railing with gold fabric hanging from it. She walked to it and leaned over, amazed at how high up they truly were.

"Is this safe?" she whispered to Alejandro.

He laughed at her. "You're fine," he teased. "No fretting. I want you to enjoy this day. It's not everyone who gets to ride in the Macy's Thanksgiving Day Parade." He leaned over and kissed the top of her head. "In fact, I would wager that you are the first Amish woman who ever did!"

She frowned, not wanting to point out that she wasn't truly Amish anymore. It would do no good to bring *that* up, she figured.

It was almost twenty minutes later when the line of parade floats, balloons, and bands began to move. At first it was slow and Alejandro leaned against the railing, his arms crossed over his chest as he watched Amanda. His eyes seemed to sparkle, and when she realized that she was the object of his attention, she turned toward him and, through lowered eyes, met his gaze.

"What is it, Alejandro?" she asked softly.

"You are so beautiful, Amanda," he answered, reaching out for her hand. "And I am so honored to have you standing beside me."

She felt his arms wrap around her as he embraced her. For a moment, the buildings and the noise disappeared and it was as if the two of them were standing alone, on top of the fake castle that slowly moved down the street. She was oblivious to everything except the power of the man who held her, the warmth from his body keeping away the chill in the air.

And she was happy.

Where was I last year? she asked herself, knowing full well what the answer was: with her parents and her sister, trying to cope with yet another year without Aaron. It had been just one more holiday of sorrow and disappointment. It had been hard for the family to praise God for their blessings when each of them still felt the loss of a life that had been taken far too suddenly for any of them to comprehend.

Faith only goes so far, Amanda had often told herself during those difficult times. She had never voiced those words out loud. Her parents would have scolded her for thinking such a thought.

It was almost twenty minutes after nine when their float turned down the side street that joined with the main avenue. Immediately, Amanda caught her breath. Alejandro stood beside her, his arm wrapped around her waist as he watched her reaction. Indeed, she was stunned.

For as far as her eyes could see, the streets were lined with people. Thousands upon thousands of them. They stood as thick as could be, along the sidewalks and behind the barricades, screaming and yelling as they waved their hands to the float as it passed. Police were everywhere, their backs to the floats as their eyes scanned the crowds, looking to identify any potential mischief.

Up ahead of them, she could see balloons in the air being held along the parade route with marching bands leading the way. The noise from the crowd was almost loud enough to wash out the music that was being played from a speaker on their float.

"You like?" Alejandro asked, brushing his finger across her cheek.

She could barely contain her excitement as she looked up at him. "It's like nothing I've ever seen before!" she gasped.

He leaned down and gently pressed his lips against hers, ignoring the cheers from the crowds that had just witnessed this public display of affection. Amanda, however, flushed and pulled away, lowering her eyes. Her reaction only caused him more delight and he laughed, pulling her close as he raised his arm and started waving to the people lined up along the streets and the reporters in the starting line broadcast booth.

For the next fifty minutes, they smiled and waved to the crowds. There was a palpable energy along the parade route, and despite the chill in the air and having awoken so early, Amanda felt herself pulsating with it. The faces of the people lit up when they recognized Viper and his wife, some people screaming and yelling for his attention. Several people even called her by name, which made her flush with embarrassment.

And then the float stopped. They had approached the staging area just before the television zone. People hurried around the float, and a man approached Alejandro to give him a microphone. Amanda stepped aside, trying to stay out of the way and wishing that Alejandro would let her disappear inside the castle so that she wouldn't have to be in front of all those people.

He caught her attention and, as if reading her mind, raised an eyebrow. "And you would disappoint fifty million people?" he teased, as he took off his coat and handed it to the man.

"That doesn't help," she said, frowning at him.

He laughed at her nervousness but turned his attention back to the man who was giving him instructions. Alejandro appeared to be only half listening, being far too familiar with performing and having already reviewed the procedures earlier in the week. Still, he remained respectful and nodded his head as the man talked, only pausing once to wink in her direction.

When the float finally moved forward into the television zone, Amanda felt a moment of panic. Television cameras were focused on them and the people in the official viewing area. When the float finally stopped again, the music began to play, and before her eyes, Alejandro transformed into Viper.

She had never been on the stage with him, not like this. For a moment, she was transfixed as he began to sing one of his songs. And then she realized that he was singing it to her. It was a new song, one that she had not heard before, but as soon as he reached for her hand, she knew exactly what was happening. It was upbeat and lively with words that seemed to flow from his heart.

She found herself swaying to the music and clapping along with him. When he nodded his head at her, she knew that was exactly what he had wanted. He gestured toward his heart as he looked at her, his words flowing into the microphone and being broadcast to the millions of people listening.

On the street beside the float were dancers dressed in blue and white, their outfits sparkling as they moved in perfect coordination with the music. Amanda managed to look into the crowd and noticed that people were watching not the dancers, but Alejandro and her. She pushed aside her nervousness and smiled, knowing that was what Alejandro would want her to do.

When the song ended, the crowd roared with applause and he waved to them, lifting his arm into the air and, with his other hand, blowing a kiss toward the sea of people. The float began to move again, and within minutes, they were nearing the end of the parade route.

Alejandro posed with several people for photographs, occasionally pulling Amanda into the picture. The people were full of smiles, their eyes glowing. Amanda watched with enormous curiosity, realizing that this moment was very special to her husband's fans. But time was limited and security was quick to approach him, eager to escort him to his waiting vehicle in order to clear the area as swiftly as possible.

As they headed back to the hotel, Alejandro entwined his fingers with hers and leaned over, kissing the side of her head. "I have a surprise for you," he said. "I hope you will like it."

She smiled, her eyes sparkling. "Another surprise?" She wasn't certain that she would ever get used to his gestures of affection. "What is it?"

Touching the tip of her nose with his finger, he winked at her, his blue eyes flashing at her. "You will have to wait, *sí*? That is what makes it a surprise!"

It didn't take long for her to realize that the surprise was not back at the hotel but at the airport. A small private plane waited for them on the runway.

"What is this?" she asked.

"Our ride to Thanksgiving dinner," he answered, leading her onto the plane. "Thanksgiving is for family, and we have not been home for a while, no?"

She stopped moving toward the plane and blinked her eyes. "Home? Lancaster?"

He frowned and rolled his eyes. "No, Amanda. Miami!"

Immediately, she flushed and quietly apologized.

"But you have a concert here tomorrow night!" she exclaimed, changing the subject.

He laughed, that look of delight in his eyes. "Today is today. We have thirty hours to ourselves, and we are going to enjoy them, Princesa."

Chapter Fourteen

It was four o'clock when they finally arrived at their condominium in Miami. Everything felt out of place and surreal to Amanda. The weather was warm and the sun shone overhead. Unlike New York with its cold weather and gray landscape, Miami was in sharp contrast. Reaching into her small handbag, she pulled out a pair of sunglasses and slipped them on, shielding her eyes from the bright sun that felt oh-so-good on her face.

Amanda found it hard to believe that just four hours ago they had been in New York City. As the car maneuvered through the traffic, she peered out the window at the tall palm trees that lined the streets, breathing in the smell of sea air.

"I think I missed Miami," she said as she shut her eyes and breathed in deeply.

She felt his hand on her knee, a soft reassurance that he had heard her. Glancing over at him, she saw that he was scrolling through the messages on his phone with his other hand. She smiled to herself, wondering how it was possible that he could always work and still remain so attentive. With a soft sigh, she returned her attention to the window.

The car pulled up at the building, and the doorman was quick to assist them out of the vehicle. Amanda thanked him and wished him a happy Thanksgiving, all the while wondering when, indeed, he would have a Thanksgiving. In the past, she had never thought much about Thanksgiving or any holiday among the Englische. She had just presumed that they all spent it together: families enjoying food, relatives having fun. However, as the doorman nodded at her well wishes, she realized that the world of the Englische was different, and in that world, some people did not get to celebrate with their families.

When the door to their condominium opened, Amanda paused. While it felt like home with the open doors and high ceilings, something was different. The air smelled of home-cooked food, and there was noise coming from the rooftop patio.

"Is someone here?" she asked as she set her bag down on the chair by the front table.

Alejandro gave her a mischievous look. "It is Thanksgiving, no?" He said, reaching for her hand and, after pausing to kiss the back of it, leading her through the foyer and toward the kitchen. The noise increased and she began to realize that Alejandro had planned something much more than a brief twenty-four-hour trip to Miami for Thanksgiving.

It was when they walked through the French doors that led outside to the patio that she saw the people. His family was gathered there: his mother, aunts, uncles, cousins. People she had not seen since their wedding. She felt the color rise to her cheeks, feeling shy at this unexpected Thanksgiving dinner at their home.

"¡Hola!" he shouted happily as they stood in the doorway, lifting his arm in greeting to the people gathered around the pool. A collective cheer filled the air, and people began to crowd around them, embracing both Alejandro and Amanda.

When Alecia approached, the group of people quieted down and moved aside, watching as the matriarch stood before her son and his wife. For a long moment, her eyes searched Alejandro's face, her expression devoid of any emotion. But when she turned to Amanda, something changed.

To everyone's surprise, she reached for Amanda first, pulling her into her arms to greet her with a warm embrace and kissing her on both cheeks. When she pulled away, she placed her hands on Amanda's cheeks and stared into her eyes.

"My daughter brought my son home for the holiday," she said, her tone full of pleasure and admiration. "I see that your words were spoken in truth. My son is a changed man, and I see that it is you who have changed him."

Not knowing how to respond, Amanda looked down at the ground and felt the heat rise to her cheeks. Her humble response caused Alecia to laugh softly.

Then she turned her attention to Alejandro. For a long moment, she studied his face. Amanda tried to read her expression, but as usual, she remained stoic and inscrutable. "My son comes home and arranges a holiday gathering for the family," she began. "The first holiday in years that we have seen you."

No one spoke, waiting to see in what direction Alecia was headed with her statement. There seemed to be a cloud of suspense lingering over the family members seated at the table. Amanda noticed that Alejandro stood there, his hands clasped behind his back and his chin jutting forward without so much as a twitch of a muscle in his cheeks. He, too, was as unreadable as his mother.

And then she smiled. "I am most pleased with you, Alejandro."

There seemed to be a collective sigh among the gathering, as if the family had been holding their breath to see in which way the day would turn. With Alecia's stamp of approval, the direction would surely be one of festivity and joy, a day to truly give thanks for the goodness that God had bestowed upon their family.

After greeting everyone and reintroducing Amanda to those family members she had only briefly met at the wedding, Alejandro excused himself to go change into more comfortable clothing for the afternoon. He reached for Amanda's hand and took her with him, climbing the stairs two at a time.

Alone in their bedroom, Amanda stared at Alejandro, her mouth hanging open and her eyes sparkling. When he saw her, he laughed and pulled her into his arms, nuzzling his lips against her neck as he held her tight. Their bodies were pressed tight together, and he gently pushed her backward toward the bed. While she protested weakly, he ignored her and forced her onto the mattress.

He covered her mouth and kissed her, his one hand entwined in her hair. Putting her arms around him, she responded with an equal passion, feeling her heart burst with love for this wonderful man.

When he pulled away, leaning over her and staring into her face, he smiled. "You like your surprise, Princesa?"

"You are truly an amazing man," she whispered. "And just when I think it is not possible to love you any more than I do, I find that there is no limit to the depth of love in my heart for you."

He rolled over beside her, his hand resting on her waist as he pressed his forehead against her neck. "Ah, Princesa," he murmured. "You have a way of making me feel six feet tall and as though I could walk on water."

She laughed. "You are almost six feet tall, but only Jesus could walk on water."

He pulled her closer to him, her hip tucked neatly against his stomach. "Seven feet tall, then," he teased.

Placing her hand atop his, she caressed his skin. "It does feel good to be here, doesn't it now?"

Leaning on his elbow, he stared into her face. "Does it feel like home?"

She had to think about that. When she heard that word, *home*, blurry visions came to her mind: the farm, the hotel rooms, the condo in Los Angeles, the condo in Miami. In the past, home was her parents' farm. Today, she wasn't certain where home truly was. But one thing was for sure and certain. When she thought of home, Alejandro was always standing next to her.

"You are here," she replied softly. "That makes it feel like home."

He shut his eyes for a bit, and she saw the muscles along his jawline twitch. His breathing seemed to quicken, and before she knew it, he abruptly pulled away. Sitting on the edge of the bed, his back turned toward her, he ran his fingers through his hair.

"What's wrong, Alejandro?" she asked, sitting up and placing a hand on his shoulder. "Did I say something wrong?"

He stood up, and her hand dropped onto her lap. "We best get changed, no? We have guests for our first Thanksgiving."

The abrupt change in his mood startled her. What could she possibly have said to upset him? "Alejandro?"

He turned around, a forced smile on his face as he looked at her. "Nothing is wrong, Princesa," he said, his tone tense and guttural. "But I cannot stay one more second in this room with you, or we will never get back downstairs. I will hoard you to myself and make love to you all night. So please go get changed before I can no longer control myself."

The heat rose to her cheeks, and she bit her lower lip, partially in embarrassment at his words but also because she found herself inwardly pleased with the passion that this wonderful man felt toward her. She had never known passion before . . . hadn't even known that it existed and the form it took. And then, she had met Alejandro.

Obediently, she stood up and disappeared from the room to the adjoining bedroom, where she used to sleep before they were married and which she currently used as her dressing room. Her heart pounded, and her stomach felt as though she had butterflies as she shuffled through the many hanging clothes on the cedar rod, looking for a dress to wear that was modest enough for her taste but suitable for a Thanksgiving dinner with her husband's family.

After having selected a short-sleeved floral print dress and gold sandals that matched, she stood in front of the mirror, brushing out her hair before twisting it into a bun. She pinched her cheeks, hating how pale they looked compared to the freshly tanned skin of her in-laws.

"Ah," she heard him say from the open door between the two rooms. "Is that vanity I see?" He wore that half smile, the one that made his eyes sparkle as he looked at her.

She tried not to smile, despite her embarrassment at having been caught studying her reflection in the mirror. "A little pinkness is not vanity!" she retorted playfully, although she wasn't certain that was true. How many times had she watched her sister, Anna, do the same thing before they had gone to church and then later that same evening before singings? "Just makes me look . . ." She hesitated as she tried to find the right word. "Healthier."

"And prettier," he added. "If that is possible."

He crossed the room and pulled her into his arms once again. Only this time, he pushed her against the wall, one hand over her head and the other on her waist. His blue eyes stared down at her as he pressed his body against hers.

"I thought you wanted to enjoy your family," she teased, a soft and demure tone to her question.

"I do," he admitted. "But only for you. I want our first Thanksgiving together to be special." He dropped his hand from the wall and cupped her chin in his hand, tilting her face so that she was forced to look up at him. "But later, Amanda, I will have you to myself, and that is when I will show you what I am thankful for."

He didn't wait for her response before he lowered his lips onto hers, kissing her once again with a passion that she could only reciprocate, her heart pounding.

Downstairs, the family was back outside, the younger cousins swimming in the pool while the adults sat around the tables and lounged on the poolside beds with thick white cushions and multicolored pillows. Music played from the stereo system by the cabana, and a few of the younger women hung out in the shade with frozen drinks in their hands.

The woman seated next to Alecia stood up and indicated that Amanda should sit there. To her dismay, Alejandro wandered over to join a group of young men on the other side of the pool. She felt shy as she sat next to her mother-in-law, wondering what in the world they could possibly discuss, for the only thing that they had in common was their love of Alejandro.

"Your father," Alecia began. "He is well?"

That was a good a start, Amanda thought as she nodded her head. "Oh *ja*, much better. His speech is a bit hard to understand when he is tired, and he still cannot farm." She turned and looked at Alejandro. There was a glow of love in her eyes as she did so. "But Alejandro has arranged for a nurse and physical therapist to come to the farm to help him."

"He did now, did he?"

The tone of Alecia's voice did not go unnoticed by Amanda. "*Ja*, he did," she replied respectfully. "Amish Aid would not pay for that, you see."

No one else around the table spoke, but they watched with great curiosity the two women who did. It dawned on Amanda that, once again, she was the outsider. No different from in Lancaster, they were staring at her and wondering about her lifestyle and upbringing, as well as how she had fallen for a man like Alejandro.

"And you, too, have been helping him, no?"

Her eyes flickered around the table, feeling uncomfortable under the scrutiny of Alejandro's family. "*Ja*, I have," she admitted. "My *schwester* . . ." She paused, realizing that they would not know that word. "My sister, I mean, has just returned for a visit with her new husband. But they will soon return to live in Ohio, so I will be helping with the farmwork until we can figure out what to do with it."

"Do with it?"

Amanda sighed. This wasn't a conversation that made her happy. "Without my brother, no one is left to take over the farm. They will have to sell it, I reckon. There are a lot of decisions to be made, now that my *daed*'s not well."

To her surprise, Alecia reached over and patted Amanda's hand. "You are a wise woman, Amanda Diaz," she said. "You will make the right decision, I am sure."

"God willing," Amanda added softly, not certain if anyone heard her, for Alecia had turned her attention to her sister, who was seated on her other side.

For the next thirty minutes, Amanda sat silently, watching the interactions between the different family members. She counted upwards of twenty-two people there, not including Alejandro and herself. Surprisingly, there were few young children. It was a lot different from family gatherings in Lititz where over a hundred people might gather for one holiday celebration, with the children accounting for more than half of them. Still, she enjoyed the overwhelming sense of love that she felt among the Diaz family.

As she continued to observe everyone, her eyes continually returned to where Alejandro stood with his cousins, a glass in his hand and a smile on his face. He was relaxing as he leaned against the bar near the cabana, his dark sunglasses shielding his eyes. With his white shorts and turquoise button-down collared shirt, a color she had never seen him wear before, he looked as if he had never left Miami. Unlike her, his skin had not paled and seemed to drink in the sun. She realized that her husband was breathtakingly handsome.

A young woman who Amanda had never seen before approached Alejandro and leaned over, whispering something in his ear. From the way she was dressed, Amanda realized that she had been hired to help Señora Perez with the meal. She was grateful that he had thought to have others helping Señora Perez and was momentarily ashamed of herself for not having offered assistance in the kitchen.

Alejandro walked toward the table where Amanda sat with his mother and aunts. "Señora Perez says that it is time to go inside," he said, placing a hand on Amanda's shoulder. "The dinner is *listo*."

After holding out the chairs, first for his mother to his left and then for Amanda to his right, he took ahold of his wife's hand and entwined his fingers with hers. The gesture caused the heat to rise to her cheeks. Public affection was not something that she was used to, and she wasn't certain if she would ever feel comfortable with such gestures. Still, his touch sent a shiver through her as she remembered his passionate kisses earlier that evening in their bedroom.

The dining room was set up with extra extensions in the already long table. Señora Perez had arranged for an elegant white tablecloth to cover the length of the table, and it was laden with multiple silver candelabras with orange candles burning, the flames flickering as people moved around the table to find their assigned seats. As was to be expected, Alejandro sat at the head of the table with Amanda beside him.

In all of her life, at church fellowship, weddings, and even barn raisings, Amanda had never seen such a feast of food on one table. Multiple platters of already sliced turkey, cranberry sauce, different varieties of salads, bowls of rice and beans, fresh vegetables, various dips and salsas, and even platters of roast pork graced the table. The smells that rose to her nose were different from what she was used to at home: orange, garlic, and onions.

Alejandro waited until everyone was seated before he cleared his throat and stood up, a wineglass in his hand. A silence fell over the room, all eyes on him. With a smile, he lifted his glass and began to speak.

"American Thanksgiving is traditionally held to honor the survival of the Pilgrims who started their settlement after leaving oppression in Europe. For most of us gathered around the table, we, too, celebrate our survival from escaping the oppression from our homeland, Cuba." He paused for a moment, but it was clear that he was not finished. "But just like other Americans, we celebrate the love of God as he has provided us with the ability to survive in this country as well as to sit together today with our family. It is not always easy to get together, and I thank you from the bottom of my heart for celebrating this joyous day with me and my wife, Amanda."

Everyone raised their glasses and gestured toward Alejandro first and then Amanda. Uncertain of what to do, she reached for her own glass of wine and lifted it, glancing at Alejandro to make certain that she was doing the correct thing. He winked at her, then lifted the glass to his lips and took a small sip.

Sitting back down, Alejandro glanced around the table, pausing at the far end where his mother, the matriarch of the family, sat. Her younger sister was seated on one side, and her brother on the other. To Amanda, she looked like a grand dame holding court. She was not an unattractive woman, although her face was round with wrinkles at the corner of her eyes and mouth. But there was definitely something intimidating about her.

"Mami," Alejandro asked. "Would you say the blessing?"

Amanda glanced at him. In all of the time that she had been with him, both before and after their marriage, she had never seen him pray before a meal. While she knew that he prayed with his band and dancers before the concerts, she had quickly learned that many entertainers did that. For some, it was rumored to bring bad luck to not do so.

Alecia lifted her head, her chin jutting forward for just a moment. *"Claro,"* she said, acknowledging his request. She reached out her hands, taking her sister's in one and her brother's in the other. Quickly, the rest of the table followed her example until everyone was holding hands, in a never-ending circle. With their heads bent down, they waited for Alecia's prayer.

"*Gracias a* Dios,*"* she began, her eyes shut and her words spoken with authority and strength. "*Por todo lo que nos han dado y gracias por dejarme estar con mi familia. Te doy gracias por toda la comida y por todo lo que tu me has dado en mi vida. En el nombre de Jesus, amen.*" (Thank you, God, for everything that you have given us and thank you for having me here with my family. I thank you for all this food and for everything that you have given me in my life. In the name of Jesus, amen.)

If Amanda had felt uncomfortable celebrating Thanksgiving with so many people who she didn't truly know, that feeling quickly passed. Unlike the holiday dinners with her own family, there was a lot of catching up and sharing, joking and teasing. While Thanksgiving was not necessarily solemn back in Pennsylvania, it was certainly not as jovial and festive as what she was experiencing with the Diaz family down here in Florida.

As the evening wore on, she found herself listening to the stories and laughing with Alejandro's family. The male cousins liked to tell stories about when they first moved to America and how Alejandro took them under his tutelage to learn how to survive on the streets of Miami. One story, in particular, ended with Alejandro causing his younger cousin, Victor, to get into a fight with another Cuban-American boy.

"*¡Ay, chico!*" Alejandro laughed, shaking his head. "Let's not go there, eh? I'm sure you don't want to know why he called you out, no?"

Victor laughed, taking a long sip from his wineglass before he responded. "And I'm sure you don't want Amanda to know what role you played in getting me called out, *chico!*"

The younger people seated around the table laughed, and despite being horrified to hear about Victor having fought someone, Amanda found herself smiling at the teasing banter between the two men.

Alejandro's mother and aunts merely shook their heads while the uncles joined in the laughter. It was clear that there was a gender divide over the appreciation of the antics of youth.

What she quickly recognized was that Alejandro was just . . . Alejandro with these people, his family. They saw him as he had always been and not as Viper, the international superstar. Unlike the crowds of other people who hung around Alejandro, his family wanted nothing more from him than to enjoy his company.

Of course, Alejandro helped his family. She learned about how he had helped his aunt Maria with mortgage payments when her husband left her, cousin Adolfo with some legal fees, and cousin Marisol with her college bills. Family was important to Alejandro, and while he wasn't about to give away all of his money, he certainly wasn't going to let any of them suffer for lack of having it.

"Aman . . .tha," Tía Maria asked, her accent so thick that Amanda almost didn't realize that she was being addressed. "Alecia told us that your father has been unwell, sí?"

Nodding her head, Amanda glanced around the table, hating the fact that everyone had fallen silent and was now staring at her. Their curiosity about her and her family was more than apparent. "Sí," she responded, ignoring the snickers from the younger adults at her use of Spanish. "But he is home now. Just not well enough to tend to the farm chores."

Alecia shifted her gaze toward Alejandro. "I heard that you have hired nursing help, no?"

"Sí, Mami," Alejandro said, tensing ever so slightly but just enough that Amanda noticed he was uncomfortable.

Reaching out to cover his hand with hers, Amanda smiled at his mother. "Oh ja, Alejandro has been wonderful! And ever so understanding of my need to help my daed and mamm. He also arranged for a man to come help with the dairy and the fields. In fact—" She turned her head and stared at her husband. "My family could not have survived through this without his help."

"Amanda . . . ," he said in a low voice. "Don't."

"But it's true," she replied emphatically, unaware that everyone was watching the exchange.

It was Alecia's turn to interject. "You still have much faith in my son, Amanda."

Amanda was surprised by his mother's words. She looked at Alecia, confusion in her eyes. "Why wouldn't I have faith in him? He is my husband, and he is my friend." She glanced back at Alejandro. "My best friend. I have all the faith of the world in him."

With a raised eyebrow, Alecia then rolled her eyes at Alejandro. The expression on her face was one of amusement; it was not lost on Amanda. She felt a tightening in her chest, wondering what the underlying, unspoken message was that lingered in the room.

Alecia lifted her wineglass and gestured toward her son. "To Alejandro," she said, but Amanda could not understand why there was such a scornful tone in her voice. "For proving that people can change, no?"

"Mami," he mumbled, shaking his head and refusing to acknowledge her toast. "Why do you have to be like that?"

Sensing the sudden tension that was filling the room, Amanda quickly stood up, forcing a smile on her face. "Perhaps I should go see about clearing the table and dessert, *ja*? Alejandro? Mayhaps I could use your help in the kitchen speaking with Señora Perez." She gently touched his arm, and to her relief, he set his linen napkin on the table by his plate and slid back his chair.

"*Con permisso*," he said. Then, with his own forced smile, he gestured toward the wine. "Have some while I ask Rodriego to bring more." He didn't wait for a response before he turned and followed Amanda out of the room and into the kitchen.

She didn't ask any questions about what had just happened. Instead, she pretended that everything was normal. Her upbringing was one that permitted personal privacy and discouraged interference unless the subject was brought up. So rather than talk about the obviously uncomfortable exchange that had just happened, she tried to shift his attention to something else.

"The food was wonderful, Alejandro," she started. "Please let Señora Perez know that."

There were two other young women, dressed in all black, working in the kitchen, helping the *señora* with the cleanup of the dishes. Amanda approached Señora Perez and touched her shoulder gently, gesturing toward the two women and then the dining room. "Perhaps they might clear the table for dessert?"

Alejandro leaned against the counter, his arms crossed over his chest. When Amanda started to move toward the butler's pantry to retrieve the pies and cakes that were stored there, he reached out and gently grabbed her arm.

She looked up at him, but, as was her way, said nothing.

"You don't want to know?"

With a simple shake of her head, Amanda smiled at him. She placed the palm of her hand against his cheek and stared into his eyes. "I don't *need* to know, Alejandro," she said softly. She felt him press against her touch. "There is nothing that has happened in your past that could possibly change the way my heart leaps with joy every time I am near you, when I think about you, when I dwell on the gift God has given to me."

"*Ay*, Dios," he mumbled and put his hands on her waist, pulling her close to him. With her cheek now pressed against his chest, she could feel the rapid beating of his heart. Whatever had just happened had truly bothered him; however, she got the distinct feeling that it was more about what she would have thought as opposed to what his mother had actually said. *"¡Gracias a Dios para ti!"* He kissed the top of her head, still holding her tightly.

She let him hold her, just long enough to feel the tension begin to ease from his body. Then, pulling back, she looked up and into his face. "Now, let's enjoy the rest of this evening," she said. "You were having such a joyous time with your cousins. Perhaps dessert is best served outside." A quick glance over her shoulder and out the window told her what she needed to know. "It looks like it is gorgeous weather, and I, for one, would much prefer the fresh air of your Miami since I know that we will soon have to return to the frigid air of New York!"

It was almost an hour later when people began to leave. Amanda stayed by Alejandro's side, feeling as though her presence would ward off whatever issue had been broached by his mother. She would never be anything but respectful to Alecia, for she was Alejandro's mother. Still, she felt that her presence calmed him, soothing his raw nerves.

At the door, Amanda embraced Alecia and told her how nice it was to have been able to spend the evening with her. Deep down, she meant it. After all, family was important to her. Whatever this rift was between mother and son, Amanda hoped that one day it would heal.

"You keep that faith, Amanda," Alecia said, the hint of haughtiness in her voice. "It's what makes you so special."

"Mami!"

Amanda reached for his hand and gave it a soft squeeze. "It would be nice to see more of you," she managed to say. "Perhaps when we return, we could spend more time together. I would enjoy making lunch for you and visiting a spell."

The invitation seemed to soften Alecia, and she reached out to pat her daughter-in-law's cheek in a gentle, maternal way. "Special indeed, Amanda." It was clear that Amanda's offer had surprised her, and, at the same time, pleased her greatly.

With hesitation, Alecia permitted Alejandro to hug her and kiss her cheeks before she thanked him for arranging the family gathering.

Yet the tension remained, and she departed from the condominium without any further words.

He shut the door and leaned against it, his hand above the lock and his shoulder slouched forward. She gave him a few seconds to collect his thoughts before she walked toward him and gently rubbed her hand across his back. At first he didn't respond, but she could feel him begin to relax again.

"She is so unforgiving," he finally said, exasperated with his mother. "But I do not want that to ruin our evening." Turning around, he clasped her hand and raised it to his lips. "You, Princesa, are an amazing hostess, even among people you barely know and especially in a situation you did not even know you were hosting!"

"How long were you planning this?" she asked, lowering her eyelids just enough so that she had to tilt her head to stare at him. "It was a *wunderbar* surprise, Alejandro."

Still holding her hand, he led her toward the living room and gave her a playful twirl as he guided her to the sofa. "Since I knew that you were coming to me for the week." He smiled at her as she sat down. "I wanted our first holiday to be spent together, at home and with family."

"We must properly thank Señora Perez, *ja*? She must've worked very hard."

Alejandro nodded as he hurried to the back of the room and fiddled with a piece of equipment that immediately filled the space with soft music. "I agree," he said. "I'll give her a week vacation to go visit her family." He paused as he walked to the sideboard where crystal decanters of liquor were sitting. "No, two weeks." He poured himself another drink and took a deep swallow.

A slow song came on, and Alejandro made a noise deep inside his throat. With a smile, he set down his glass and reached for her hand. "Dance with me, Señora Diaz." He pulled her to her feet and wrapped one arm around her waist while the other sought her hand. "I love this song," he murmured.

"I find that surprising," she replied, looking up and into his face as he held her. He looked relaxed and happy, even more so than before when he was enjoying the company of his cousins. "Your own music is so fast-paced and . . ."

Lifting an eyebrow, he glanced at her as they swayed to the music. "And what?"

Flushing, she wasn't certain how to respond without offending him. But he pressured her to answer and finally she blurted out, "*Ja vell* . . . your music is rather . . . explicit."

If she thought he would be offended, she was wrong. Instead, he laughed and swung her around, raising his arm so that she could dip her head under it, before pulling her back into his embrace. "*Ay, Princesa,*" he laughed. "The music I write and sing sells. It's not that I do not like it." He wrapped his arms around her waist, holding her even tighter. "I do like that type of music. It's like poetry, no? But I can still like other types of music, too."

"I see," she said in a soft voice.

"When I was younger," he began. "*Mi tío* would take me to the local bar in our neighborhood. He would have me recite poetry in exchange for money, which we'd split. I kept my half to give to my mother while Tío Miguel kept his for booze."

"Poetry?"

"*Sí*, poetry."

She tilted her head as she looked at him. "Can you still recite it, then?"

He paused for a moment, thinking before he smiled. "I won't recite the whole poem. It's rather long. But these were always my favorite few verses." He cleared his throat before he began to recite the poem's verses, a serious look on his face as he spoke:

I have seen across the skies
A wounded eagle still flying;

I know the hole where lies
The snake of its venom dying.

I know that the world is weak
And must soon fall to the ground,
Then the gentle brook will speak
Above the quiet profound.

While trembling with joy and dread,
I have touched with hand so bold
A once-bright star that fell dead
From heaven at my threshold.

On my brave heart is engraved
The sorrow hidden from all eyes:
The son of a land enslaved,
Lives for it, suffers, and dies.

All is beautiful and right,
All is as music and reason;
And all, like diamonds, is light
That was coal before its season.

I know when fools are laid to rest
Honor and tears will abound,
And that of all fruits, the best
Is left to rot in holy ground.

Amanda watched him with curiosity. The fact that he could remember so many words, written by a man from so long ago, impressed her more than anything else. Yet, as he recited the words, there was such feeling in his voice, emotions that showed how he felt about what he was actually reciting.

"That was beautiful," she whispered.

"That was the beginning of my career," he replied. "Poetry, especially Cuban poetry that celebrated the needs of the people, taught me much about songwriting. Before I knew it, I was using that skill to remember long passages and to understand the meter of the poems, which I imitated to create unique rhythms of songs."

"That's quite impressive, Alejandro," she said, and meant it.

He reached out his hand, wiggling his fingers for her to take it. "Come, dance with me again. It's just us, Amanda, in our home. I want to enjoy this moment for as long as I can."

They danced to the music, swaying slowly as their bodies were pressed together, moving in time to the song's beat. At one point, she looked up and saw that they were dancing under the chandelier in the foyer. He clutched her hand to his chest and kept his eyes staring into hers. And then, his feet stopped moving and he lowered his mouth onto hers, his lips pressing against hers, kissing her with a gentle passion that sent shivers up her spine.

"Come," he said, his voice hoarse. "Enough of this dancing. I want to spend time with my wife, to love her all night long so that when you return to Lancaster, you can do nothing but think of us and this moment. To remember that passion of our first holiday together, spent at our home and full of love."

He didn't wait for her response as he headed for the staircase, slowly ascending to the second floor, Amanda obediently following behind him.

Chapter Fifteen

The following morning, Amanda woke up to the smell of freshly brewed coffee. Opening her eyes, she rolled over and saw Alejandro sitting on the mattress beside her, staring at the wall in a daze. She reached out and touched his leg, smiling when he jumped. "Good morning," she said softly.

"*Sí*, Princesa. *Buenos días, mi amor,*" he replied, leaning down to kiss her shoulder.

"What were you thinking?" she asked.

He took a deep breath and gave a short shrug of his shoulders.

"Tell me," she urged, sitting up and leaning against the headboard. Something was bothering him. She had never before seen him so pensive.

"It was nice to wake up here," he admitted, looking down at her. "It's been a long time on the road and there's more to come."

She brushed her hair back from her cheek and chewed on her lower lip. This wasn't like Alejandro, to complain about the travel. "You love what you do," she said pointedly.

"*Sí, claro.* I do." He took a sip of coffee and handed the mug to her. "But I'm getting tired. The holidays are especially tough, and this year is even harder."

"Why?"

"Because of you."

"Me?" she asked, surprised that he had said that. The last thing she ever wanted to do was burden him. She tried hard to be positive and supportive. The thought that she contributed to any hardship in his life upset her. "Why because of me?"

He leaned back, stretching out on the bed, and rested his cheek on his hand. The sheets rustled beneath him. "I'd rather be here with you, Amanda, than on the road."

His words were matter-of-fact and emotionless. It alarmed her, and she felt her heart begin to race. What was he saying? "Alejandro," she whispered. "You love traveling."

He shut his eyes and rolled onto his back, his arm tossed casually over his forehead. "I do, *sí*," he said reluctantly. "But I need some downtime, Amanda. It's too much."

"You have months of shows ahead of you." She knew she wasn't telling him anything that he didn't know. Still, she had to state the obvious.

"*Sí, sí,*" he mumbled, an edge to his voice. "I know this. But I want some time. Time to cruise the islands or relax on a deserted beach. I want time for us, Princesa. And we have other things to think about . . . the future."

Future? She raised an eyebrow. "What do you mean?"

"What happens when we start a family? I want to be with you, not living apart."

She felt the color rise to her cheeks at the mention of a family. They had never discussed it. They didn't have to. Despite the fact that he had no siblings, she had seen how important family was to him. As for herself, she just presumed that they would have *kinner*. Among the

Amish, children were never planned or discussed. They were just born and cherished, gifts from God.

"Oh, Alejandro," she sighed, trying to collect her thoughts. "You can't think about that right now. You have commitments, and your fans count on you. Disappointing them would be bad."

"I want you on the road with me," he said. He opened his eyes and looked at her. "It's the only way I can do it."

Ah, she thought. So that's what this is about. "We've talked about this," she said softly. She didn't want to disappoint him, and she was unhappy about having to make a choice. Her heart belonged with Alejandro, but she knew that she had a responsibility to her family. A filial obligation to fulfill.

"We have, *sí*," he said evenly. Sitting up once again, he studied her expression. For a moment, she thought he was going to repeat his argument about the hired man and the nurse that he had arranged to help her parents. Instead, he gave her a soft smile. "Let's not discuss this now. We have the morning to ourselves. Let's enjoy it, no?"

They spent the morning hours by the pool, Alejandro drinking in the sun and swimming laps while Amanda lounged on a recliner with her e-reader. From time to time, she would look up and watch him, his even strokes breaking through the water as he swam. She couldn't help but think about his words, wondering what was truly troubling him.

For years, he had been building up his career for this very moment of fame. He was at the peak of success, and she wondered if he might be burning out. Was it truly too much? Or had she become a distraction to him? That thought worried her the most. What would happen when she did return to the farm? They both knew that it would be temporary; she had to return to him, and she wanted to do just that. However, she knew that her father still needed her. She couldn't just walk away from them, not after everything they had been through. Not after Aaron . . .

He splashed some water at her, the cool drops breaking her train of thought. Startled, she looked at him, surprised to realize that he had been watching her from the edge of the pool. "You almost ready?" he asked.

She shook her head. "It's so nice here," she said, smiling. "So warm! I had forgotten how much I like Miami."

"Dade County, baby," he teased, lighting up at her words. "Might not have cows, but we sure do have sun!"

She laughed. His improved mood felt like a weight was lifting from her shoulders.

His cell phone rang from the table next to her lounge chair. He made a face but quickly pulled himself out of the pool, water dripping from his shoulders, chest, and swimsuit. He shook his head as he walked toward the phone, purposely getting Amanda wet, teasing her.

"*¿Hola?*" he said into the phone, reaching out to take the towel Amanda handed him. He rubbed it over his neck and chest before sitting down on the empty lounge chair. "*Sí, sí,*" he said, rolling his eyes and leaning back into the warm cushion.

She listened to him speaking in Spanish, wishing not for the first time that she could understand his native tongue. It was a pretty language, musical in nature, especially when he spoke it. Occasionally, he would laugh, a short devious laugh. She always smiled when he laughed like that for she knew that, whatever he was saying or doing, he was being naughty in a way that only Viper could be.

"*Ay,*" he said as he set the phone down after the call ended. "It's going to be a long weekend, *sí?*"

"Who was that, if I may ask?"

"Carlos. About the awards dinner on Sunday."

She looked away. When she had come to New York, they had agreed that she would return to Lancaster on Sunday when he left for Los Angeles. His disappointment that she would not be attending the dinner with him was apparent, and she still felt bad about that. However, she knew that Anna would need to return to Ohio and she had wanted to see her sister and meet her new husband before they left.

While he had been supportive of that arrangement, they had several discussions about when she would rejoin him on the road.

Noticing her averted eyes, he leaned over and touched her arm. "Amanda," he said gently. "It's not a problem."

She nodded but still couldn't meet his gaze.

"Alejandro!"

They both looked up at the sound of his name. Rodriego was standing in the open doorway. "The car will be here in thirty minutes," he called to them.

With a big sigh, Alejandro lifted his hand in acknowledgment. He squeezed her knee before standing up. "*¿Listo,* Princesa?" Reaching down, he helped her to her feet and paused, just for a minute, before he brushed his fingers over her warm skin. "Soon we'll be back, Amanda. Between the weekend concerts in the Southwest."

She shut her eyes, enjoying the last few minutes of sun and her husband's attention. Once they left for the airport, she knew that it would be back to business as usual: the city lights, the endless nights. But for now, for just this one minute, she had him to herself. The twenty-four-hour escape to Miami had been a tease, a mini-vacation, but it had relaxed both of them. Unfortunately, she could already see the stress beginning to return to his face. When he pulled her into his arms, her cheek pressed against his shoulder, she could hear his heart beating and knew that, despite his embrace, his mind was already on the concert tonight.

The flight to New York seemed quicker than the prior day. Amanda had read her book while Alejandro sat next to her, humming to himself as he scribbled words on pieces of paper. Several times, she glanced over, smiling at the serious look on his face. At the halfway mark of the trip, he pulled out his laptop from his carry-on. She wondered what he was working on but didn't dare break his concentration to ask.

At five o'clock, they arrived at the airport. After being escorted through the crowds that quickly materialized out of nowhere, security helped them into the waiting car, which took Alejandro to Madison Square Garden. He needed to meet with his staff, conduct a sound check with his band, and talk with different reporters who had requested a quick preconcert meeting with him. He gave her a quick kiss before leaving the car, pausing only to instruct the driver to take Amanda to the hotel and make certain she was escorted inside, in case of fans mobbing her.

Returning to the suite felt a little like coming home to her. They hadn't packed any bags when they had left for their whirlwind holiday getaway. Everything was neat and tidy, exactly as they had left it. She wandered to the small kitchenette and pulled out a bottle of sparkling Voss water. The tall glass bottle made a hissing sound when she twisted off the large gray cap. Alejandro had introduced her to the sparkling water, and she found it very refreshing. As a result, he had made certain that his staff kept it stocked in their hotel rooms whenever they traveled together.

Her cell phone rang and she looked up, startled at the noise. No one ever called it. She hadn't even charged it while she was with Alejandro. There was no need. The only person she communicated with on the device was him. He had charged it overnight and made certain that she knew it was working.

Retrieving it from her handbag, she was not surprised to see that it was from him. "Miss me already, then?" she asked teasingly when she answered it.

"Uh . . ." A female voice hesitated on the other end of the phone. "Amanda?"

Amanda sank down into a chair, shutting her eyes in embarrassment. "*Ja*, it's me," she managed to say, despite wishing that a hole would open in the floor and swallow her.

"Alejandro asked me to call you," the woman said. "A car will come for you in two hours. He wanted you to meet with some people here before the show."

"Oh?" Amanda couldn't help but wonder why this woman had called her. Why hadn't he? And why had she used Alejandro's phone and not her own?

"Someone will come to your room and escort you downstairs to the car," the woman explained politely.

After thanking the woman, Amanda set the cell phone down on the table. *Two hours?* She couldn't imagine what she would do for two hours. It was too early to start getting ready. She sighed and leaned her head against the back of the chair.

She missed the farm. That was the bottom-line truth. She liked working the land; she liked the routine of each day. Having returned to the farm so recently had been refreshing. She admitted it. Yet she knew that her place was with her husband.

Without a doubt, she loved being with him. He made her heart soar, that was for sure and certain. A simple look or a simple gesture from Alejandro was all that she needed to make her realize that she was the luckiest woman in the world. Prior to meeting Alejandro, she had never even imagined such emotions. Love had seemed like a fuzzy concept, one that was steeped in the spiritual, certainly not in the emotional or physical. Indeed, her upbringing had not focused on anything but the spiritual for all aspects of life, from a community perspective.

But after she had fallen in love with Alejandro, all of that had changed.

Now, despite the grueling schedule of his international tour, she was looking forward to seeing some of these countries. In her entire life, she had never imagined that she would have such opportunities. It was never something that was even considered. Now, however, Alejandro's enthusiasm for showing her different parts of the world, exposing her to different cultures, was rubbing off on her.

Still, in the back of her mind, Amanda knew that she needed to temper her immersion into the Englische culture by returning to her roots, even if only occasionally and for short periods of time. Over the past few months, she had seen enough to know exactly why the Amish church leaders were so opposed to their youth and community being exposed to worldliness: it could be, indeed, corrupting, to say the least.

It was almost seven thirty when Amanda was escorted through a secured back entrance into Madison Square Garden and through a long and narrow corridor to the artists' lounge where people would soon gather to meet Viper during the VIP Meet and Greet. For now however, there was just a lone woman seated on a sofa, a laptop next to her and a pile of papers on her lap.

Confused, Amanda looked around for Alejandro, and when she didn't see him, she thought that security had perhaps brought her to the wrong room. She was just about to exit when the young woman looked up and saw Amanda standing there.

"Oh!" The dark-haired woman did not seem as surprised as Amanda was. Quickly, the woman placed the papers she had been reviewing on top of her laptop and stood up, smoothing down her navy-blue skirt and approaching Amanda, her hand outstretched and a smile on her face. "You must be Amanda!"

"I was looking for Alejandro," she said as she reluctantly shook the woman's hand. The woman was pretty with large dark eyes and olive-toned skin. Her hair was almost jet-black and cut in a bob that curled around her ears.

"He'll be here in a moment, I'm sure," the woman said with a confidence that made Amanda suddenly wonder who, exactly, this woman was and why she knew Alejandro's schedule. Despite the questions that floated through Amanda's mind, she did recognize that the woman seemed pleasant enough, especially when she asked, "Would you like anything? Coffee? Water? Wine?"

"Nee," Amanda said, glancing over her shoulder toward the open doorway. People were walking by, some glancing inside, but no one stopping. "Do you know where he is, then?"

Before the woman had a chance to answer, Amanda heard his voice in the corridor. He was speaking in Spanish to someone, and whatever he said, the response was laughter. Amanda turned and took a step toward the door just as he walked through it.

"*¡Ah,* Princesa!" He greeted her with a warm embrace and kissed her lips before he turned to the other woman in the room. "You have met Dali, *sí?*"

"Dali?"

The young woman suddenly seemed a little nervous as she glanced from Amanda to Alejandro. "We hadn't quite gotten that far yet, Viper."

There was a familiarity between the two that did not go unnoticed by Amanda. Yet it was clearly a professional relationship. It piqued her curiosity since it was more than apparent this meeting was arranged for Amanda's benefit.

"I see." Alejandro turned to Amanda and rubbed his hand down her arm in a loving yet possessive gesture. His expression was not his usual one of adoration or love, but the look she often saw when he was in work mode. His next words explained why. "I have hired Dali to work for you. As your assistant."

"Work for me?" She was stunned. What on earth did she need an assistant for? "I . . . I don't know what to say."

He gestured toward the sitting area for the three of them to be seated. A young man walked through the doorway, carrying a tray of beverages. He handed a glass to Alejandro and two bottles of water to the women. When he exited the room, he shut the door behind him.

"Dali will help you with scheduling and media relations, Princesa. She will monitor social media and the tabloids. She will also schedule interviews and social appearances." He lifted his glass to his lips and took a long sip. "She will be a big help to you, Amanda."

Amanda barely heard the last part of what he had said. She was stuck on the previous sentence. "Social appearances? Interviews?

Whatever for?" She almost laughed, but, knowing that he was serious, thought twice about doing so.

Clearing her throat, Dali leaned forward and answered for Alejandro. "There is a lot of demand from the public for getting to know you better, Amanda. Whether you know it or not, you have become an overnight sensation."

"I don't want to be an overnight sensation," she responded in a matter-of-fact tone, staring at the woman seated beside her. Dali stared back but gave no indication of any emotion nor made any attempt to conjure a response. Frustrated, Amanda looked at Alejandro. "I just want to be with you," she whispered, too aware that this Dali woman was right there and listening. "I don't want to do interviews or those other things."

He reached out and touched her knee. His blue eyes met hers, and she could see that he was pleased with her response. Still, without him saying another word, she knew that she was fighting a losing battle. "Remember I told you once to trust me, *sí*? Do you?"

Amanda took a deep breath, biting her lip to hold back the tears that she sensed were close to the surface. She did remember that. It was after he had come to the farm to rescue her from the paparazzi who had found her parents' farm and from the bishop who was insisting that she leave the community until the fervor died down. "*Ja*, this I do," she said softly.

"Then I am asking you to trust me once again, Amanda," he said, never once breaking eye contact with her. "Dali will help arrange your schedule and the logistics surrounding your appointments. There will be no inconvenience for you beyond just showing up at these events. But the public is enamored of you, Amanda, and to deny them some access, even if it is very sheltered access, will create more problems in the long run. You have to give them a little of what they want, but with Dali's help, it will be structured and organized in a way that will limit the intrusions on your privacy."

Knowing that she had no choice, Amanda swallowed and nodded her head, not trusting her voice to say anything.

"*¡Bueno!*" He clapped his hands, looking pleased. "Now, Dali will have access to your cell phone. Since you have met, she will call you using her own phone and help you program her number into yours. That way you will know when she is calling and that it's a safe phone call to answer."

Amanda nodded again, finally understanding why a strange woman had called her using Alejandro's phone. Long ago, he had instructed her to never answer her phone if it wasn't from him or her family, should she choose to give them the phone number.

"There are two reporters coming in just a few minutes," he continued as he stood up. "I want Dali with you when you speak to them as I must go get ready for the Meet and Greet. I'll talk with them later. Dali will take good care of you, Princesa." Leaning down, he placed a gentle kiss on her lips and gave her hand a reassuring squeeze. "I know you will do wonderful, Amanda. And after the show, we can go out for a late-night cocktail at the Top of the Strand, *sí?*"

"Top of the Strand?"

He headed toward the door. "You'll like it, Princesa. It's quiet." Then, with a quick wink, he opened the door and disappeared, leaving Amanda alone with this new personal assistant, Dali.

Immediately, Amanda realized that Dali was a "take charge" type of person. "Let's sit for a moment, shall we?" she asked, and without waiting for Amanda to respond, she sat back down on the sofa and moved the papers off her laptop. "I have a few things scheduled already for tomorrow," she said as she tapped at the keyboard and her eyes searched the computer screen. "Easy things to start; I think that is best."

Sighing, Amanda sat down in the seat that Alejandro had just vacated. "What exactly are these 'things' that you are scheduling, then?"

Dali glanced up and smiled. "More reporters who want to interview you. New York is a bustling town, Amanda. Several companies have contacted us for endorsements, but Alejandro thought that was a bit too much."

"Endorsements?" It was a word she didn't understand in the context in which Dali used it.

"Advertisements, in a way," Dali patiently explained. "Photos of you holding the product, videos of you recommending the product, stuff like that."

That thought horrified Amanda. "Oh no!" she exclaimed, alarmed that something of that nature would even be considered. "I could never do that!"

To her surprise, Dali laughed. "That's what Viper said." She turned her attention back to the laptop and tapped a few more keys, the noise a clicking sound that seemed oddly out of place in the lounge room. "Now, he had asked me to look into charities for you. He felt you might like that . . . perhaps a bit more comfortable with such a role for the public."

Charities? Amanda frowned. "I don't understand."

Again, Dali looked up and patiently explained. "Most celebrities have a cause, a charity that they support. Viper does not. He felt that it might be something of interest to you."

"What do other people do?" Amanda asked, curious about this idea.

"Literacy, hunger, poverty, animal rescue, things of that nature," was the simple response from Dali. Her answer didn't really help narrow down what "charity" might interest Amanda.

"Religion?"

Dali shook her head. "Too controversial."

"Religion is controversial?"

Again, Dali laughed. It was a gentle sound, not one that hinted at any sort of mockery. "You have no idea."

Amanda frowned. *Ja vell,* she replied. "I have no idea, indeed." Her frustration was rising. Alejandro had never mentioned this to her. When she married him, she thought she was to be his wife. Now she was getting the sense that there was much more involved in being married to Viper than what was required to be married to Alejandro, and that was not something she had considered beforehand.

"He made one suggestion," Dali offered. "Helping disadvantaged children get educated."

"Aren't they already?"

"Not always," Dali admitted. "Down in Miami, there is a lot of poverty. Many of those children have a hard time in school, and the schools are not equipped to deal with them. As a result, they drop out and work the streets. There are a lot of children with good potential who are overlooked and lost as a result."

"That's horrible," Amanda gasped.

Dali scribbled something on a piece of paper and glanced at her cell phone. "It's almost time for the first reporter. You think about that other idea and talk it over with Viper. There's no need to decide today, Amanda." She handed Amanda a piece of paper, then collected the rest of her things and put them into a leather bag that was beside the sofa. "Here's your agenda for tonight."

"Agenda?" She wasn't even certain she knew what that was.

"Schedule," Dali explained. "*Women Daily* is interviewing you at seven thirty and *People en Español* is scheduled at seven forty-five. They are both going to stay and take some photos of you and Viper during the Meet and Greet at eight. At eight forty-five, you will go to your stylist in the dressing room adjoining Viper's. At nine thirty, you should be ready for an escort to your seat. Two guards will remain with you in case of any problems. But you should expect the crowd to react and be ready for requests for photos."

It amazed Amanda that Dali was reciting the schedule from memory. Everything that she said was listed exactly the same on the paper in her hand. "Oh help," she muttered. "I'll never remember all of this."

Standing up, Dali smiled at Amanda. "You don't have to. That's what I'm for!"

As if on cue, another woman was escorted into the room and Dali was quick to greet her. The first reporter had arrived, promptly at seven thirty. To Amanda's relief, Dali took charge of the interview, first introducing the reporter to Amanda, then remaining nearby while the reporter asked her questions. The questions were no different from those asked by previous reporters: how had they met, what was life on the road like, did she miss her Amish community. When ten minutes had passed, Dali kindly indicated that the reporter had to wrap up her questions because an escort had been arranged for the reporter to stand backstage and watch the behind-the-scenes action before the Meet and Greet.

By the time the second interview was finished, Alejandro joined her in the room, pausing to greet the reporter from the *Latina Ahora* magazine. Then, at both Dali and Carlos's urging, Alejandro led his wife toward a door at the back of the room to greet the fans who had been waiting for a chance to meet Viper and Amanda.

Unlike some of the other Meet and Greets, this one was more structured, with the people waiting in a queue for their turn to stand next to Viper and have their photos taken. He would spend a few seconds talking to them, but there was a noticeable lack of time spent with each guest. When she mentioned this observation to Dali, she was told that there were too many people to grant more time.

A few times, Alejandro waved Amanda into the photo. Dali had explained that there were a few extra-special people in the group: investors, producers, and other important people from the entertainment industry, and Alejandro had wanted to introduce them to Amanda and include her in the photos.

Before Amanda knew it, Dali was walking with her to the dressing room. An attendant handed an outfit to her, then pointed her toward a screen behind which to change into it. A stylist came in to brush out her hair and then, at Amanda's insistence, restyle it in a bun. Only this time, the stylist added some flare to it, with tendrils hanging down Amanda's neck and the bun twisted in a unique way so that it looked fuller. With her hair finished, a makeup artist came in and spent ten minutes putting foundation, blush, eye shadow, and lipstick on Amanda's face.

"Is this really necessary?" she whispered to Dali.

Dali leaned forward and whispered back, "Yes."

Amanda let out a big sigh, realizing that she was not going to get any empathy or support from this Dali woman, at least not on the makeup issue. While the man worked on her face, Amanda shut her eyes and wondered what her family was doing at that moment. Surely Daed was sleeping already. Mamm would be sitting in her chair under the kerosene lantern, the heat thrown from the light keeping her warm while she worked on a quilt. Knowing Anna, she was most likely crocheting an afghan. As for Jonas, he would probably be reading the *Budget* or the Bible, depending on whether he had yet to catch up on the weekly news.

If they could only see her now, she thought with a twinge of apprehension. While their day was winding down, hers was still in full swing. The concert would energize her. There was no doubt about that. Seeing Alejandro transform into Viper onstage, listening to the women screaming for him, listening to the music that he sang . . . all of it would pulsate throughout her entire body and awaken all of her senses. And then afterward, he wanted to take her to that rooftop lounge. Time alone to enjoy the beauty of the New York skyline before calling it a day.

The stark contrast between the two worlds was almost too much for her to grasp. How on earth had this happened?

"It's time, Amanda," Dali said, placing a gentle hand under her elbow to help her step down from the raised makeup chair.

Together they walked through the corridor and to an open doorway that was draped in black. Amanda glanced through the opening and saw Alejandro standing with some men, reviewing the set list. The dancers were stretching their muscles, ignoring the rest of the commotion as the stage crew finished changing the set from the opening band.

"This way, Amanda," Dali urged, guiding her toward two large men dressed in black.

Obediently, Amanda followed her, watching the organized chaos that went on behind the scenes. Everyone seemed to know what they were doing, even though half of the stagehands were racing around as if in a panic.

"I wonder what they think . . ." she began to say.

"Who?"

"The people, before they go onstage to perform," Amanda responded. "I can't imagine doing something so . . . so public."

Dali almost smiled but tried to maintain her professionalism. "In due time, Amanda," she said. "For right now, he wants you in the audience. That is public enough, no?"

When the two bodyguards, dressed in suits as opposed to regular security guard uniforms, escorted Amanda to her seat in the pit, the section of the seating directly in front of the stage, a low roar erupted from the audience. Those who had front-row seats in the stands next to the pit leaned over railings and screamed for her attention. Security guards dressed in yellow shirts and black pants lined the way, positioning themselves between the fans and Amanda.

Dali had instructed her to look at the fans and smile, pausing several times to permit them to take her photo. Several of the fans on the floor in the pit crowded around her, and the guards with the yellow shirts stepped forward and tried to clear a path. Amanda glanced at the bodyguard beside her, but he merely stared straight ahead as if surveilling the sea of people before them.

It took almost five minutes for the men to escort Amanda to her seat, located in the fifth row and directly in front of the stage. They sat on either side of her, their heads constantly in motion as they watched the crowd around Amanda to ensure that no trouble was brewing from any direction.

When the lights went down and the music began, the attention shifted from Amanda to the stage. For that, she was grateful. It didn't matter how many times she saw him perform, she was always amazed at his transformation before his tens of thousands of adoring fans. Even more important, he always looked as though he was enjoying himself, as if the performance was just as special to him as it was to the audience. Between vocals, he would dance, laugh, and even lean down to shake hands with those who stood closest to the stage. There was no doubt that Viper was a performer, born to do what he was doing: entertain others.

It wasn't until just after his first encore that one of the bodyguards touched her arm as the second man nodded his head, pointing in the direction of the nearest exit. It was time to leave, before the mad rush of fans realized that she was about to do so. Otherwise, once the concert ended, they would have created a mob around her, no longer concerned about being thrown out of the stadium.

Discreetly, they made their way to the backstage area, easily passing through security. Patiently, she waited near the steps down from the stage so that she could be there to congratulate him on yet another amazing concert. When the music finally ended and he emerged, a crowd of people surrounded him, but he merely smiled, pausing for a few quick photographs, before hurrying in the direction where Amanda stood.

"Come," he commanded. "I want to get showered and changed so that we can enjoy New York City tonight . . . just the two of us, *sí*?"

His words were music to her ears. Following his concerts, she was usually subjected to after-concert gatherings or crowds of people. Those late nights in clubs or at parties were not her thing, but she would never think to complain to Alejandro. So the fact that he had planned a special late night without hordes of people was extra special to her, especially since she knew that their time together was coming to another pause. In just one more day, she would return to Pennsylvania to see Anna and meet her new brother-in-law while Alejandro would fly to Los Angeles again.

As usual, he didn't waste any time getting showered and changed. She waited patiently in the dressing room, seated on one of the plush chairs and leafing through a magazine that someone had left on the coffee table. There were bottles of Voss water in an ice bucket on a buffet table along with pieces of sushi that she had picked at while waiting earlier. When he emerged from the bathroom, his hair still damp but his clothes changed and the scent of his musky cologne teasing her senses, she set down the magazine.

"It's cold out, Alejandro," she said. "You shouldn't go out with a wet head."

To her surprise, he laughed at her.

She frowned back at him. "You'll get sick. I see nothing funny about that."

He reached down for her hand and pulled her to her feet. "I wouldn't dream of upsetting you, Princesa. Give me another moment, *sí*?" Planting a soft kiss on her lips, he quickly turned to the dressing table and picked up the hair dryer, turning it on and shaking it around his head.

Wandering back over to the buffet table, she put a few pieces of sushi on a plate and carried them over to him, wordlessly setting it on the dressing table. She knew that he tended to not eat well when he was on the road, either skipping meals or eating too late. It worried her, especially if she was not around to keep an eye on him.

"Voilà!" He set the hair dryer down and picked up the plate of sushi. "You take great care of me, *sí?* What will I do without you on the road with me, Amanda?"

From the other side of the room, she turned around and faced him. "Need I remind you that you *do* have a large staff. Perhaps you need to have them pay better attention to *your* needs."

He raised an eyebrow at her and gave her that half-crooked smile. "I much prefer you to pay attention to my . . . needs, Princesa," he said before popping a piece of sushi into his mouth. Then, setting the plate down on the counter, he wiped his hands on a napkin and headed toward the door. "Let's go, my amazing wife, for I have something wonderful to show you this evening." He held out his hand for her before leading her out of the door to the dressing room.

It didn't take more than twenty minutes for the driver to navigate the streets of Midtown Manhattan and arrive at the Strand Hotel. Amanda gave Alejandro a curious look but asked no questions. When the doorman opened the car door, Alejandro hastened to jump out and assist her to the curb. Quickly, in order to avoid anyone noticing them, Alejandro hurried her inside the small lobby and navigated to the elevator, pausing just briefly to greet the security guard at the entrance.

She wasn't prepared for the elevator doors to open at the rooftop lounge. Despite it being cold outside, there were tall propane gas heaters positioned around the lounge, especially near the far wall. She looked up as Alejandro led her toward the back of the lounge. The glass roof was open, affording the most magnificent view of the skyline, especially the Empire State Building, which towered over them. It was beautiful, unlike anything she had ever seen before, and she caught her breath as they walked past the bar and toward a small table facing the view.

"Alejandro!" she breathed. "It's . . . it's simply amazing."

He gestured toward a server and said something rapidly in Spanish before turning his attention back to Amanda. "I thought you would enjoy this. I know how much you loved your first visit to New York City, no?" They both laughed at the inside joke, knowing full well that her first stay in New York City, while bringing them together, was spent in a hospital bed, rather than sightseeing.

When the server approached their table, she set two drinks down before them and paused, just for a moment, as she recognized the famous couple seated before them. Alejandro ignored her as he lifted his drink and raised it to toast his wife.

"Here is to our wonderful week spent together, *sí*?"

Reluctantly, she raised her own glass, wondering what he had ordered for her to drink. Champagne. She sipped at it, then set the glass on the tabletop. "It has been a magical week," she sighed. "I dread thinking about tomorrow."

Tapping his finger against the edge of his glass, he stared at her as if considering her words. That was when she knew that he had an alternative agenda for the evening. It didn't take long to learn what it was.

"*Aman-tha,*" he began slowly. "I have made arrangements for you to come with me to Los Angeles."

She greeted his news with silence.

"I want you with me at the award ceremony," he continued, his gaze unwavering as he watched her, waiting for her reaction. There was none. "We will fly out tomorrow after the concert and have all day Sunday and Monday."

From the corner of her eye, she noticed a few people stealing photos of them. She ignored them as she considered Alejandro's request. Or was it a request? she wondered. He hadn't asked her. Nee, she thought. Instead of asking her, he had *told* her that the arrangements had already been made. Still, he was her husband and, as such, he was the head of their small household. Arguing with him was not something she would consider doing. It simply was not in her character.

"When would I return to Lititz?" she finally responded.

"Tuesday morning, there is a flight. You would get back by supper." He paused. "Unless you wish to travel with me to Phoenix that day?"

She ignored the last question, knowing that she simply could not travel with him to his next concert stop in Arizona. However, leaving Tuesday morning provided enough time to visit with Anna, she told herself. "I see," was all that she could think to say. She'd have to find a way to get a message to her parents so that they would not worry. And, she rationalized, it was only an extra two days.

"That's it?" he asked. "Just 'I see'?"

Not wanting to ruin his good mood, Amanda lifted her champagne flute and gestured toward him. "It will be nice to see Los Angeles again, I reckon."

A look of relief washed over his face, and it immediately warmed her heart. Despite his having made the arrangement, he had clearly been apprehensive about her reaction. Seeing him happy and so obviously pleased made the sacrifice all the more worthwhile.

Chapter Sixteen

Dear Mamm and Daed,
Mayhaps I will be home by the time that you receive this
letter. Please apologize again to Anna that I delayed my
return to the farm. I shall be there soon enough, however.
Alejandro has been nominated for an award, you see. It
is only proper that I should be by his side at the event.

Amanda

It felt strange waking up in the condominium in Los Angeles. It was the first time that she had slept there as his wife. To wake up and not be surrounded by support staff or hotel security felt odd at first. Slipping her feet out from underneath the bedcovers, she glanced at Alejandro as he slept. He wore a sleeveless white undershirt that accentuated his chest. His tattoos peeked out from beneath the fabric, and she resisted the urge to trace one of them with her finger.

The sun was barely rising from behind the long vertical blinds that hung over the large windows. Golden rays seemed to sparkle against the backdrop of a budding blue sky. It promised to be a beautiful day, and he had mentioned to her it would be a day of relaxation and no appointments. Just the two of them, he had said, after a chaotic week of concerts, events, and travel.

Their last day in New York City had been spent in leisure, until it was time for Alejandro to return to the arena in preparation for the final show before flying out to Los Angeles, immediately afterward. On Saturday, they had slept late and enjoyed a lovely brunch, specially prepared for them by the chef and served in the privacy of their suite. In the early afternoon, Alejandro had insisted on taking her shopping on Fifth Avenue, two bodyguards in tow in case there were any issues with people recognizing them. Fortunately, there were none.

Later, they had enjoyed a quick meal together at Tao, a fancy Asian restaurant. It had felt odd to Amanda to be able to maneuver the streets with Alejandro and not have crowds of people surrounding them. While a few recognized them, most people were too involved in their own lives to even notice the famous couple. Still, as a precaution, the two bodyguards accompanied them everywhere.

After the concert, they had been driven to LaGuardia Airport where the private plane awaited them. Amanda was secretly glad that his manager, Mike, hadn't joined them. He had left for Los Angeles on Friday before the show, his presence required to make arrangements for the awards ceremony on Sunday evening. A few of Alejandro's usual entourage accompanied them on the flight, but they remained toward the back of the plane, leaving the couple alone.

It had been early in the morning, California time, when the Gulfstream landed. She had tried to sleep most of the journey, with little success, curled up with her head on Alejandro's shoulder. By the time they made it to the condominium, she merely crawled into bed and sank into a deep sleep. She didn't even know whether Alejandro followed her to bed or spent another hour catching up on his e-mails.

They had spent most of Sunday in the condominium, relaxing until it was time for the awards ceremony. It had been nice to do nothing for once. He watched some television, in between phone calls to Mike, Carlos, and several other people who were part of his publicity team. Due to the time difference between the East and West Coasts, the awards ceremony had started earlier in the late afternoon. Afterward, they hadn't returned to the condominium until well into the wee hours of the morning. Reluctantly, Amanda had accompanied Alejandro to the after-parties. He had clutched her hand, introducing her to endless faces and countless names that she knew she'd never remember. Wherever they had gone, the flashes of photographers greeted them, and eager reporters, hoping to get that thirty-second interview that would get picked up by some entertainment station, shoved microphones toward their faces.

Barefoot, she padded into the kitchen and began to search for coffee. She knew that he'd sleep for a while longer, but her eyes were itchy from her own lack of sleep and she wanted to sit on the veranda with a warm mug of coffee in her hand and watch the morning sun rise over the tops of the buildings. It took her a moment to orient herself to the kitchen and figure out where the small pods were for the fancy coffeepot. Unlike at home, on her parents' farm, this coffee machine made one cup at a time. There was no boiling water to pour over the instant coffee that her parents often used.

By the time she slid open the sliding glass doors in the living room—a room that was dressed all in white from the carpet and walls to the curtains, adornments, and furniture—the sun had already changed the colors in the sky to pale yellow and orange. She sank into one of the chairs and curled her legs beneath her as she held the coffee mug.

In hindsight, she was glad that she had changed her mind and accompanied Alejandro to Los Angeles and the awards dinner. He had been so pleased with her decision and proud of her presence that she had immediately recognized that she had done the right thing. He had not won the award but had stood up when the announcement was made for his colleague, applauding the entertainer who had won. His public display of genuine happiness for the winner warmed Amanda's heart and made her proud. The goodness that continually poured out of her husband was something that she had never expected to see in an Englischer.

"You are up?"

She glanced over her shoulder as she felt his hand on the top of her head. As expected, he leaned down and kissed her neck, pausing to whisper, "I love you" in her ear.

Shutting her eyes, she leaned back so that her head was pressed against his stomach. His hand moved from her head to her shoulder, and he massaged it for a moment before reaching down to steal her mug of coffee. "Did you sleep well, Alejandro?"

"*Sí, sí.*" He took a long sip from the mug. "I sleep as well here as I do in Miami," he said. "Or perhaps it is because you are beside me."

She smiled.

"And you, Princesa?"

How to tell him what she was feeling? She felt as though she were living a dream, sitting on the patio outside of his Los Angeles condo, his hand on her shoulder and her back pressed against him. Like a true princess, she thought, living in a castle with her knight in shining armor. "I slept quite well, *danke*," was all that she could muster, too embarrassed to tell him what she wanted to say.

He knelt down behind her, his arm wrapping around her throat as he nuzzled her once again. "I think you were too tired, no?" He kissed her skin. "From more than just the award ceremony . . ."

She blushed. He had the habit of teasing her in the mornings, reminding her of the intimacy they shared behind closed doors. "Alejandro," she whispered. "Don't tease."

Laughing, he planted a final kiss on her cheek before he stood up and headed back inside. "Let me refresh your coffee, Princesa. And then we have a busy day today."

She turned around and watched him, her dark eyes wide and sparkling. The tone of Alejandro's voice told her that their "busy day" did not entail interviews, meetings, or anything else related to Viper. Instead, she suspected that his "busy day" indicated a day of fun, just the two of them . . . a rare treat before she headed back to Pennsylvania. "We do?" she asked breathlessly, anticipating what he had in store for her.

"*¡Sí! ¡Vamos a la playa!*" he called out as he disappeared around the corner.

Inwardly, she hid her smile, knowing that he was using Spanish on purpose, to stretch out the suspense. "You know I don't know what that means!" she called out after him.

"Then you must wait, Princesa!" he called back. "I read in a book somewhere that patience is a virtue, no?"

A few minutes passed before he emerged, two mugs of coffee in his hands, one of which he handed to her. "The beach," he translated. "We are going to the beach."

"Oh help!"

He laughed at her again. "Why 'oh help'? You have been to the beach before, *sí*?" Sinking into the chair next to her, he crossed his legs and shut his eyes. She watched as he lifted his face toward the sun. "You will love the California ocean, Amanda. The beautiful water and warm sun . . . it will lift your heart and soul to stand on the edge of the water and look out, seeing nothing but the ocean before you."

"What will I wear?"

"A bathing suit, of course!" He raised his eyebrows and grinned. "And a small one at that, *por favor*!"

"Alejandro!" But even she couldn't help laughing at his expression, so playful and relaxed. "I don't know if I'd be comfortable wearing one of those bathing suits in public. It will make me feel as if I am wearing just my underwear! Will other people be there then?"

"*¡Claro!* It's the beach!"

"Then I definitely won't wear a bathing suit!" she insisted.

With a sigh, he gave up. "It's probably not warm enough anyway," he admitted. "Perhaps it will get up to the seventies. Not swimming weather. But I still want to go walk along the beach with you. Will you do that, Amanda? Will you go with me?"

She tilted her head and looked at him over the rim of her coffee mug. His blue eyes stared back at her, full of intensity and passion. He seemed to be waiting, breathlessly, for her answer. And that surprised her. For a moment, she didn't know how to respond. Was he truly asking her? Did he have any doubt she would come? "Oh, Alejandro," she whispered. "Don't you know that I would go anywhere with you?"

At first, he didn't respond. He turned his head away from her, gazing over the side of the balcony, his eyes scanning the sky. Then, slowly, he set down his coffee mug and stood up, pausing to take her hand and pull her to her feet. He set her coffee mug on the table next to his before he wrapped his arm around her waist and held her close, his hand pressed against the small of her back.

"Anywhere?" he repeated.

Her only response was a simple nod of her head.

"Hmm," he whispered, taking a step toward the sliding door and pulling her along with him. "I can think of only one place where I would like to take you right now." He glanced over his shoulder, making certain to carefully guide her inside. "And I think you know where that is, Princesa," he murmured, as he walked backward, his arms still tight around her waist, and led her back to the bedroom.

.   .   .

It was two hours later when they stood on the beach, the white sand warm and soft under their bare feet. She held her sandals in one hand and the crook of his arm in her other. For a long time, they stood there, staring at the enormous mass of water that ebbed and flowed onto the coastline.

The waves broke onto the shore, uphill over the darker wet sand, toward them on the edge of the incline. With each break, the waterline crept closer to them, but never quite reached their toes. Some of the waves brought frothy white foam, while others pushed seashells in their direction.

Farther out, the waves looked gentle and peaceful, a constant motion that kept the horizon alive. In the distance was a ship. It was too far away to know whether it was a commercial or pleasure vessel. But that didn't matter to Amanda. She was amazed by the sight of the ocean, in love with the sound of the waves and immune to the casual stares of people walking past them just over the ridge.

"I want to feel it," she whispered.

"¿Qué, Princesa?" He hadn't heard her and bent down so that she could repeat her request.

She managed to tear her gaze from the ocean to look at him, suddenly noticing that his eyes were almost the same blue color as the water before them. "I want to feel it!" she said, her eyes ablaze with excitement. "May I do that?"

He tilted his head and smiled at her, that half-crooked smile that spoke of his amusement with her innocence. *"Claro,* Princesa," he said. "Let's go down to the water's edge together, *sí?"*

To his surprise, she shook her head. *"Nee."*

He lifted an eyebrow, that half smile still on his face. His only response was a simple nod of his head. He understood. It was a magical moment, one that she wanted to feel alone . . . to reflect on the magnificence of the wonder of God's creation. Reaching down for her sandals, he gestured toward the water's edge as he took a step backward. "Don't go in too far," he said playfully. "I would prefer to not have to rescue you again today."

She made a face at him before turning back to the ocean. With great reverence, she slowly walked toward it, reaching for her skirt as she approached the edge. Her fingers entwined with the soft material as she crumpled it in her hands and lifted it so that the hemline would not get wet.

And then she felt it: the coolness of the water on her bare feet.

At first, she jumped back. He must have been watching her, amused at her reaction for she heard him laugh from behind her. Ignoring him, she ventured forward again. With her eyes cast down, she watched the water recede away from her feet, back into the great ocean. The sand beneath her feet felt cold and hard. As she walked, little puddles formed beneath her footprints. She almost knelt down to touch them when she saw another wave racing up the incline toward her. She was closer to the ocean this time, and the water wrapped around her ankles.

Lifting her skirt higher, she forced herself to walk even deeper into the water. When it reached her knees, she knew that her skirt would be drenched, but she decided she didn't care. With each breaking wave, drops of water splashed onto her arms and hands. She released the material and let it get soaked as she lifted her arms into the air; then, swirling around like a little girl, she tossed her head back to feel the warm sun on her face, in contrast to the cold sensation of the rhythmical influx of the waves splashing her legs.

The realization that she was experiencing this for the first time—standing in the sand and staring across the Pacific Ocean. Witnessing the power and beauty of the water—something fashioned by the hand of the Creator—triggered an overwhelming feeling of awe and reverence within her. She wanted to shout "God made this!" Instead, she said a silent prayer, thanking him for guiding her to this moment, a moment that she could feel inside her very core. Only someone as powerful and almighty as the Lord could create something so majestic and poignant as this sight, she thought, and immediately wished she could share it with her *schwester* and her *mamm* and *daed*.

Oh, she knew of Amish people in her community who went on cruises. Some of them even brought back photographs or picture postcards of the ocean. But that was nothing compared to actually standing on the shore and looking out, as far as the eye could see, along the water-filled horizon. It was even different to simply stand at the water's edge, feeling it against her feet, than when they had visited the islands on his yacht.

She jumped when she felt his arms around her.

"Alejandro!" she gasped, half laughing and half from fright. "You scared me!"

"I did, *sí*?" He pulled her close to him, the water rushing around them as they stood in the surf. "You have nothing to be scared about, Princesa," he whispered as he pressed his chin against her shoulder. Softly, he began to hum into her ear, a gentle version of one of his songs.

Amanda shut her eyes and leaned against him, loving the powerful feeling of both the water and his embrace. Safe and protected from harm, she relaxed against the gentle pulling of the tide and listened to his humming.

After a few minutes, he released her and turned her around so that she was facing him. She caught her breath when she realized that he was soaking wet, up to his waist. "Oh help!"

He laughed. "It's only water, no?"

"You're drenched!"

"So are you!"

Smiling, she looked back at the horizon. "It's worth it," she said. "*Danke,* Alejandro."

"For . . . ?"

"For everything."

Not caring that people were gathered on the shoreline, watching the interaction of the couple standing in the water, she let him bend down and brush his lips against hers. The touch of his kiss sent a shiver down her spine and she clung to him, not caring that she was beginning to shiver from the cold water. As long as she was with him, she was warm, both inside and out.

"Stay with me, Amanda," he breathed into her ear. "Don't go back."

His words tugged at her heart. How she hated the thought of leaving him, but she knew that she had to get back to Lancaster. It wasn't fair to put so much pressure on Anna when she was about to return to Ohio with her husband. Besides, Amanda had promised to come home to visit with her and she had already broken that promise once. To do it again would not sit well with her family and with her own conscience.

"You know that I can't," she said, the regret more than evident in her voice. "It's not fair that you ask me that, Alejandro."

"Fair?" He didn't seem to appreciate the use of that word. The way that his facial expression changed made that obvious to her. "You are my wife, no?"

"Alejandro . . ." She didn't want to end their time together on a sour note. Everything had been so wonderful over the past week. And it wasn't as though she wanted to leave him; it was that she *had* to do so. "Please don't make this harder for me than it has to be."

The water was getting cold; silently, they walked back to the shoreline. The warm air did little to help take the chill from their bones, so Alejandro bent down to pick up their shoes and gestured toward the car.

It wasn't until they had returned to the condominium that he brought up the subject one last time. She was changing her clothes into something dry and warm, too aware that he was not. Instead, he leaned against the doorframe, watching her with his arms crossed over his chest.

"When will we see each other again?" he finally asked, breaking the silence.

His question didn't surprise her for she had been wondering the same thing. Unfortunately, she realized that neither had an answer. "I need to help my parents . . ."

He held up his hand. "I keep hearing you say that, Amanda," he said, with a sharpness in his tone that caught her off guard. "I have hired a man to help with the farmwork and a nurse to help with your father. What else do you need to do?"

She took a deep breath. How could she explain this to him? The last thing that she wanted was to upset him, and she could see that he was unhappy with her. Feeling torn in two directions, she didn't know how to respond. She sat down on the edge of the bed, fighting the urge to cry, but the tears were forcing their way to the surface. "Please, Alejandro," she whispered. "Don't do this."

He didn't seem moved by her emotions. "Do what, Amanda? Miss you? Want you with me?"

"You are forcing me to make a choice," she managed to say. "I don't want to have to do that."

"What is this 'choice'?" he asked, a stunned expression on his face. "Is it choosing between your Amish roots or your husband? I hate to remind you, but you already made that choice, *mi amor.*"

She wiped at her eye just in time to catch the first tear. "You will be traveling to all of those cities. You will have all of those interviews and meetings and people. Let me return to Lancaster and visit my sister. Let me have some time to figure out what is best for my *mamm* and *daed.* Please," she implored.

Her tears finally touched him and he sighed, giving into her by walking to the bed and kneeling before her. "Hey, Amanda," he said softly. "No crying."

"I don't want you angry with me," she whispered, embarrassed for not having been able to control her sorrow at his reaction.

He reached up and wiped away a tear. "I'm not angry," he explained quietly. "I'm just missing you so much already that my heart breaks to think that we will be apart." He tried to smile. "And we don't know for how long. That makes it worse, no?"

She nodded her head and pressed her cheek against his hand. She wanted to tell him that it was hard for her to leave him, too. But expressing her emotions and feelings was not something she was used to doing.

Chapter Seventeen

Just landed at airport.
So cold here.
Smells like snow.
Missing you already.
<3
A.

When the car service returned her to her parents' farm on Tuesday evening, Amanda sighed, hesitating long enough to collect her thoughts, before she opened the door to get out. It had been a long flight and the first one that she had taken alone. It didn't matter that Alejandro had arranged for her to fly first-class or that security had escorted her both to and from the plane. People had recognized her, small mobs had formed, and security had to intervene.

Arriving at the Philadelphia airport, her presence was immediately known and the speculation that she was returning to her parents' farm in Lancaster created a virtual whirlwind of movement in cyberspace. By the time that she had arrived at the farm, there were already photographers positioned at the end of the driveway, eager for a picture of Amanda leaving Alejandro and returning to her Amish roots.

On the plane, she had picked up a few of the magazines that Dali had packed for her in her carry-on bag. Many of the magazines were written in Spanish, so Amanda merely flipped through the pages, looking at the photos. Whenever she had found a photo of Alejandro, she found herself catching her breath and pausing. It continued to amaze her how much the media followed him.

But it had been the two English magazines that had caught most of her attention. Dali had made certain to leave a pink sticky note inside both of those magazines so that Amanda had not needed to search for the articles. Instead, she had been able to open right up to the section to see what Dali, or Alejandro, she imagined, wanted her to read.

Photos of Alejandro alone. Photos of Alejandro with Amanda. Photos of Alejandro performing. *Study the photos,* Dali had told her. *Learn what works and what doesn't work. Take the time to practice at home, in front of the mirror.* Dali's words had echoed in her mind and she had tried to do just that: practice facing a mirror.

It had felt strange to lock herself in the bathroom and spend time staring in the mirror. Her reflection was something she tried to avoid. Her entire life had been spent without looking in mirrors, without studying her expressions or how she looked. Still, if Alejandro had hired Dali to help Amanda with her image and presence to the media as well as with her scheduling, she knew that she would listen.

Now, when she emerged from the car and realized that photographers were taking her picture, she held her head high and ignored them. Still, she remembered to keep her sunglasses on, a trick that Alejandro had taught her so that people could not see her eyes. *Seeing the eyes,* he had explained, *means they can read your thoughts and your emotions. When in doubt, hide them.*

The door to the house opened and a figure dressed in a green dress with a black shawl tossed over her shoulders rushed outside and toward her: Anna. Not caring about how she looked to the photographers, Amanda squealed and ran toward her sister. It had been months since they had seen each other. Now, they were greeting each other as married women, each with new lives that were unfolding before them.

Embracing Anna, Amanda couldn't help but enjoy the feeling of her sister in her arms. They had grown up together, shared many secrets, and weathered many storms. Until the moment that Anna had rushed out the door to greet her, Amanda had not realized how much she had missed her sister.

"Oh, Anna!" Amanda gushed, pulling back to stare at her. She looked the same with her rosy cheeks and bright smile. The only major difference was the style of her prayer *kapp*, which, unlike the heart-shaped *kapps* from Lancaster, was far more stern looking in the way that it clung to her head. "How *gut* it is to see you!"

Her sister's eyes sparkled. "And you, too, *schwester*! It's been far too long now, *ja*? Six months?"

Clearing his throat, the driver interrupted the reunion. "Shall I take your bags to the porch, ma'am?"

Amanda glanced over her shoulder and nodded. "*Ja*, please," she affirmed, too aware that her voice had easily picked up the Pennsylvania Dutch way of speaking in a singsongy manner. As she looked at him, she noticed the photographers snapping pictures once again. Returning her attention to her sister, she motioned toward the house. "Best get inside, *ja*?"

Her sister's eyes flickered over Amanda's shoulders, and she caught her breath. "Oh help," Anna muttered, a dark cloud passing over her eyes. "I heard about those people."

They hurried into the house, Amanda pausing to politely thank the driver, who merely nodded his head and retreated to his car, eager to return to Philadelphia.

The past week seemed to have flown by, but nothing had changed at the Beiler farm. Daed sat in his wheelchair, a blanket tucked around his lap and his head tilted, just ever so slightly, toward one side. The left side of his face seemed to droop, but his eyes lit up when Amanda walked into the kitchen. Lizzie was setting the table and greeted Amanda with a pleasant "hullo" and not much more.

And then there was Jonas. He stood up from the sofa where he had been reading the *Budget* and crossed the room to greet his new sister-in-law with a firm handshake. He was tall and thin with straight hair cut in the traditional Amish style. He wore glasses that rested on the tip of his nose, but his eyes seemed to peer over the top as he studied his *fraa*'s younger sister.

"So, Amanda," he said, the lilt and accent of his voice different from that of the Lancaster Amish. "Heard a lot about you."

Feeling shy in front of this stranger that was now a part of her family, Amanda merely nodded and glanced at Anna. She didn't know how to respond. He was Amish, through and through. Plain and simple with a friendly face and a kind voice. It dawned on her that, one day, Jonas and Anna would meet Alejandro. How very different they were, just in appearance, never mind lifestyle.

"It's right *gut* to meet you," she managed to finally say.

She moved over to greet her *mamm* before turning to her *daed*. She tried to force a smile and knelt by his side. "How you feeling there, Daed?"

He mumbled an answer, the words slurred and barely recognizable. She thought she heard him say something about being glad that she was back. She glanced up at her *mamm*, questioning her with her eyes. His speech had not improved since she had left but had, in fact, gotten worse. She wondered why but knew better than to ask such a question in front of her *daed*.

"I was in California, Daed," she said slowly, staring up into his face. "Alejandro has a condominium out there." For a moment, she almost corrected herself, for indeed, it was *their* condominium now. She felt too prideful to say that out loud. "It's beautiful. Warm all year round with palm trees and bright blue skies." She glanced over her shoulder to look at her sister and Jonas. "As blue as in Holmes County, Anna."

Anna smiled. When they had first arrived in Holmes County, Ohio, earlier that year, both of them had commented on the rich blue color of the sky. While Lancaster was beautiful in its own right, there was something different about Holmes County: rolling hills, more compact farms, and majestic blue skies.

"And so much traffic! If you think Route 340 is bad in the late afternoon or summer weekends . . ." She let the sentence trail off but laughed. "His condo is just a few miles from the ocean!"

Anna caught her breath. "The ocean, then?"

Amanda nodded, standing up and resting her hand on the back of her *daed*'s wheelchair. "Oh, Anna!" she said. "It's just the most amazing thing you could ever see! Water everywhere. And it's a strange, changing color . . . blue and green. But when the waves break on the sand, they rise up out of the water and curl over into frothing white foam. I even saw people using planks to ride those waves!"

"Ride the waves!" Anna repeated, glancing at Jonas, a look of wonder in her eyes. "Well! If I ever . . ."

Jonas scratched at his head. "Can't say I ever saw the ocean," he interrupted. "Sounds mighty nice."

"It's more than nice," Amanda said lightly. "It's simply . . . majestic. You can actually feel the power of God as you stand there, your toes in the warm sand, and realize that he made it all. He planned every drop of water that's in that great enormous ocean! And as I stood there," she continued, her mind racing back to that day, "I looked off to the horizon and realized that if I could walk, simply walk across that water, I'd reach China! What an amazing feeling of how small and insignificant we are as individuals. A truly humbling experience."

The room was silent.

She took a deep breath and sighed. Without being told, she knew what they were not saying . . . what they were thinking. They didn't need an ocean to experience those feelings. It might be a strong reminder for the Englische, but the Amish knew those feelings and lived them every day. Their silence spoke of how much she had changed in the past few months.

Taking a deep breath, she placed her hand on her *daed's* shoulders and turned her attention back to him. "Things are going *vell* here, then, *ja?*"

Another mumble. She thought she heard the word *fine* but wasn't certain.

"He's doing much better," Lizzie translated for her husband. "That nurse that your Alejandro sent has been helping him with his arm movements and speech." Lizzie raised her eyebrows and tilted her head a bit. "She said that his speech will improve again shortly. Just a small setback from so much activity. And he's starting physical therapy for his legs next week."

This was news, indeed! If Amanda wanted to ask about the prognosis, she didn't. She'd inquire about that later, after her *daed* was in bed, with no risk of him overhearing the answers.

"So he will walk again, *ja?*"

Lizzie glanced at Anna, then back at Amanda, a look on her face that answered the question without words. Immediately, Amanda was sorry that she had spoken aloud, knowing that the answer was probably one that no one wanted to hear.

After taking her suitcase to the *grossdaadihaus*, Amanda changed out of her clothing into something more plain and suitable for helping with the evening chores. She paused to place her cell phone on the desk by the window, her hand lingering on it as if willing Alejandro to call her at that very moment. By now, he was in Phoenix and most likely busy with his preconcert interviews and sound checks. He would have no time to contact her that day, of that she was most certain.

It felt strange to return to the family kitchen, full of light and good smells, to see Anna and Lizzie working together to wash the dishes from the evening meal. She felt like an outsider, watching something play out before her: something so familiar to her and yet something that she was no longer a part of, despite having been an insider for over twenty years.

After the kitchen was almost cleaned, Lizzie excused herself, taking Elias into the first-floor master bedroom to prepare him for bed. Anna was putting away the final dishes before she placed a kettle of water on the gas stove to make some tea. Feeling useless, Amanda sat on the sofa, leafing through a daily devotional book that was resting there but not really reading it.

Jonas rose from the table where he had remained, the newspaper open before him. He leaned down and neatly folded it before shoving his hands into his pockets. He seemed to shuffle his feet as he looked first at his wife and then at the clock on the wall. "*Ja vell*, I reckon I'll leave you two to catch up for a spell," he said. "Best go on out and help Harvey."

"Is he still working here, then?" Amanda asked, surprised, for she had assumed that Harvey would no longer be needed once Jonas and Anna had arrived.

"Oh *ja*," Jonas replied as he headed toward the door. "No finer a fellow and a right hard worker, too. Helped me get the lay of the farm and all real quick."

"Let's go sit at the table, then," Anna said. "I made pumpkin pie yesterday. We can visit a spell, *ja?*"

While they sat at the table, listening to the movement of their *mamm* preparing Daed for bed in the other room, they both picked at the pumpkin pie, neither really eating it. So much had happened, and for Amanda, it felt as though her *daed* had regressed rather than progressed. The thought worried her, and Anna must have read her mind.

"He seems to be trying," Anna said, her brown eyes staring at the closed bedroom door. "I just hate seeing him like this, Amanda." Tears welled in the corners of Anna's eyes, and she wiped at them with her finger.

"I know what you mean," Amanda admitted, using her fork to poke at the pie. "He was ever so much better before."

"You mean the speech, then?" Anna nodded her head, not waiting for Amanda to answer. "He does get tired early in the evening. The nurse said that is because he is trying so hard and tiring so easily."

"How will he ever farm again?" Amanda wondered out loud.

"Listen, *schwester*," Anna continued, taking a deep breath and turning to meet Amanda's eyes. She reached out to cover Amanda's hand with her own, a change in her expression. "I have some big news for you. We all agreed that I should be the one to tell you."

"News?"

Anna nodded her head and smiled. "Jonas and I have decided that our place is here, with Mamm and Daed. We're going to move here in time for the holidays. Need to pack up our things back in Ohio and say our good-byes to folks."

An answer to my prayers, Amanda thought. "Oh, Anna, that's just *wunderbar gut* news!" she exclaimed, immediately wishing that she could contact Alejandro and tell him the amazing news. With Anna moving to the farm, her problems were solved. Once they were established in Pennsylvania, she could rejoin Alejandro with a clear conscience. "And Jonas is willing? What a blessing!"

A bigger smile lit up Anna's face as she nodded. "He is that, indeed. Such a *gut* man. So kind and focused on God and family. It was his idea," Anna confessed. "To move here, that is."

Amanda raised an eyebrow, surprised to hear this news. "Really now?"

"*Ja, ja!*"

That spoke worlds about the character of Jonas Wheeler. Of course, land was expensive everywhere. Even in Holmes County, land would be hard to purchase. It made sense for Jonas and Anna to return to

Lancaster County and take over the Beiler farm in Lititz. But for Jonas to have made the offer without being asked? To volunteer to leave his family and church district? It would be hard on him, that was for sure and certain. He'd have to start over, but with Anna's help, he'd adapt in a short time.

"Oh, Anna! That will be such a relief," Amanda admitted. "I was so worried about what would happen to Mamm and Daed . . . what would happen to the farm."

"It makes the most sense," Anna replied. "And we would not be forced to rent a *grossdaadihaus* back in Holmes County. No land to farm on our own, just helping one of Jonas's *bruders*," she added.

And then Amanda saw it. Within a year or two, Anna would be living in the main house with her husband and a baby. Her parents would eventually fulfill their dream of moving into the *grossdaadihaus* that was connected, the very section of the house where Alejandro had stayed when he first came to the farm and where Amanda was staying now. Eventually, the bedrooms upstairs would be filled with children, who would help with the chores, worship on Sundays, and bring laughter back to the lives of everyone on the farm.

It was more than Amanda could possibly do for her parents, not even with all of Alejandro's money.

"We'll help in any way that we can," she offered, knowing that it was a weak offer.

"I think the nurse is a great help, Amanda," Anna admitted. "And that electricity in the *grossdaadihaus*, why, that will be right *gut* for Daed. Surely the bishop will approve the use of some store-bought fans in the hotter weather."

A fan? Amanda wanted to comment that the solar power could be used for so much more. But she checked her tongue. That was not an Amish comment; it reflected more of the changes that she had recently made in her own life. Recognizing that caused her to catch her breath. Had she truly changed so much in such a short period of time?

Anna hesitated and glanced around, making certain that no one was listening. When she apparently felt comfortable that no one would barge in on their conversation, she leaned forward and whispered, "Tell me about him."

"You mean Alejandro?"

Anna nodded her head. "It was all the talk in Ohio, you know."

"It was?"

"Oh *ja!*" There was a gleam in Anna's eyes. "Apparently, there was talk of sending *you* to Ohio. The younger Amish were hoping it would happen, eager to see what it was like to be surrounded by Hollywood."

That comment caused Amanda to laugh. "It's not like that, Anna."

"Then tell me," she whispered, reaching out to grab Amanda's hand. "What *is* it like?"

How could she start to explain? Amanda wondered.

"I can't answer that question, I reckon. It's too hard to describe," Amanda finally said. "It's just so . . . different. But even though I don't like all of the crowds and the women and the noise and the constant travel, it doesn't really matter."

"Women?" Anna's eyes grew larger as she questioned her younger sister. "What do you mean by that?"

"It's hard to understand. I didn't at first," she confessed. "But women like Alejandro." Not true, she told herself. "No, they like Viper, the image that he portrays to the media and to his fans. They scream and yell for him. They throw things like flowers and little gifts at him. They cry when they see him. I've never seen such a fuss before, and I have to admit, it was most strange and intimidating in the beginning."

Anna gasped. "I can't believe you!"

"It's true. He had warned me about it when he was here at the farm," she continued. "Warned me that women would try to . . ." She let the sentence fade, not willing to share that part of Alejandro's past with her sister. "Well, they just aren't always nice women, *ja?*"

"I reckon not!"

"None of that matters," Amanda hastened to say. "That's not who he is. You see, his fans don't really know him at all." That thought saddened Amanda. She paused, mulling it over in her mind, her eyes glazing over as she looked away. "It's the man behind the image, the man who took care of me in New York, the man who saved me from the paparazzi here at the farm, the man who loves me . . . that is the man that I love and married."

"Enough to have left all of this?" Anna said, gesturing with a wide wave of her hand. "Our upbringing? Our land? Our religion?"

Amanda pursed her lips as she contemplated how to answer. She had known that it was coming: the million-dollar question that everyone wanted to ask, but few dared. But she was surprised that the question came from her own sister, and after such a short time reconnecting. There was just no way to explain to Anna how she felt . . . how Alejandro made her feel.

"Do you remember that time before Aaron was born?" she began. "When Mamm took us to that Englische doctor she was seeing. We had to wait in the sitting room and there was that book, the colorful one with the mice that talked and the mean stepsisters?"

A frown creased Anna's forehead. "*Ja*, I do remember that," she whispered.

"Do you remember how we sat there, looking at the book, but we didn't really understand the story?"

Anna smiled. "Oh *ja*, it was all in English and we had barely learned how to read yet."

"But there was that one part, the part at the end, where the pretty woman was dancing with the handsome man."

"He was a prince!" Anna smiled as the memory came flooding back to her.

"*Ja*, a prince."

Anna laughed once again. "Oh, we thought we were going to get in an awful lot of trouble if Mamm came out and caught us looking at that fancy book. But we were so young, and the dress and the woman and the man . . . they were so beautiful, weren't they? A prince with his princess. Things that we knew very little about, ain't so? But that book sure made it look right nice."

Lifting up her hand, Amanda pointed her finger into the air, too aware that her wedding ring sparkled on her hand as she did so. "That is how I feel with Alejandro," she said slowly. "I feel like a princess in his arms."

The joy left Anna's face, and she stared at her sister. Amanda waited for her reaction, the silence that fell between them long and awkward.

Finally, the silence was broken.

"But you are forgetting something, Amanda," Anna whispered. "There was no God in that story. Where's God in that story? Where's God in *your* story?"

The sorrow in her sister's eyes caught her off guard. How could her sister question her faith in God? How could she not see that God was behind every aspect of her relationship with Alejandro? From the accident to the hospital to the time spent on the farm, it had been his hand guiding the man and the woman together.

"But you see, God is at the core of it, Anna," Amanda replied evenly. *"For where two or three are gathered together in my name, there am I in the midst of them,"* she quoted from the Bible. "Alejandro is certainly not plain, and he's definitely not Amish, but that does not mean that God is not at the core and center of his life. He thanks God every day, every minute of the day, for having blessed him with so many opportunities. And he is fixated on giving back to help others achieve their own dreams."

A soft sigh escaped Anna's lips as she shook her head. *"Nee, schwester,"* she said. "I meant where is God in *your* life?"

The shift in the question caused Amanda to remain silent. It sounded more like a statement than a question. And indeed, it was not a question that she had considered in the past. Not really. Yes, she prayed to God, she read the Bible, she did all that she could to honor her upbringing while being immersed in Alejandro's very Englische lifestyle. Still, her focus had shifted to supporting Alejandro rather than obeying God's will.

At that moment, the door opened and Jonas walked through it, a gust of cold air following him. He glanced at his wife, his eyes lighting up from behind his glasses. Quickly, he removed his coat and hung it on the peg by the door. "Getting cold out there," he said. "Think it might flurry tonight."

Anna continued to watch Amanda as though waiting for a response. When neither spoke, Jonas shuffled his feet, realizing that he had interrupted a sisters-only discussion and one that appeared to be quite serious. He quickly excused himself and began to head toward the staircase.

Amanda stopped him as she stood up abruptly and glanced at the clock. "Getting late. Reckon I'll go retire for the night," Amanda mumbled, aware that she had avoided answering Anna's question. With an attempt at a light smile, she retreated to the *grossdaadihaus*.

Chapter Eighteen

```
Missing you, A.
Concert was good last night.
VIP people missed seeing you too.
Crowd loves the new music video.
We played it on the screen while
performing.
Love you, Princesa.
V.
```

Texas was definitely not his favorite state. He was glad that he was playing a different city each night. A busy schedule meant that each day flew by much faster. By the time he was finished with a show, he'd be escorted to his bus and driven to the next city. Mornings always brought radio interviews, and afternoons were spent with reporters. He managed to sneak in a few visits to the local gym while on the road and found that working out kept his mind focused.

Despite the constant motion of his life, he worried about Amanda. The snowstorm sounded serious with over six inches in early December. The community had been caught off guard by road conditions that had been poor for two days. The only good news was that the paparazzi had seemed to dwindle away. Whether it was the lack of activity or the increasingly cold weather, Amanda had reported that she hadn't seen anyone camped out at the end of her parents' driveway for three days already.

Small blessings, he told himself.

He had tried to call her earlier, but her phone just rang and rang. He suspected that she had forgotten to carry her phone with her, for he doubted that she had left the farm. He had warned her about taking the buggy anywhere, especially after his publicist had forwarded him two news clippings about horse-and-buggy accidents, one in Indiana and one in Pennsylvania, from trucks trying to pass them on the road. Knowing the aggressive way that the paparazzi pursued their targets, he didn't want her taking any chances. Even if they were no longer lingering nearby, it did not mean that they had abandoned their interest in her.

When he had left Amanda at the airport, he had felt a tugging at his heart. She looked so despondent as she was escorted down the corridor to board the plane. For a long while, he had stood at the window, watching until the plane was finally pushed backward in order to taxi to the runway. He ignored the pleas of the men beside him, members of Mike's team who often traveled with Alejandro when Mike was back in Los Angeles. He didn't care if he would be late to catch his flight to Phoenix. It was a private charter and it could just wait, he thought as he continued to watch the plane taxi out of sight.

After Phoenix, he had traveled to Houston on Wednesday, thankful that Mike had scheduled multiple appointments and interviews for that day, as he had nothing else to do since the concert was on Thursday evening. And then began his five-city tour of Texas over a two-week period of time, broken up by a quick jaunt back to Los Angeles for three days to work on a new music video that was due for release before Christmas.

In all of that time, Amanda was never far from his mind. He would text her several times a day, often before meeting with people. His free time was limited, but he wanted her to know that he was thinking about her.

However, it was her phone call after she had arrived home that had stuck with him. The news that her sister, Anna, had told Amanda that she would be moving home with her husband to take over the farm had made his day. Their separation would be almost over, he had told himself, mentally counting down the days until he could be with her once again. They had agreed that she would fly to Miami, just before Christmas, just three weeks from now. And then, he had vowed, there would be no more days and weeks apart. With her sister and brother-in-law at the farm and the hired help that Alejandro was committed to continuing, there was no further reason that Amanda could not be with him.

Of course, he had to get to that point in time.

"Viper?"

He looked up at the man who approached him. *"¿Sí?"*

"Sound check?"

Alejandro sighed and stood up. It was always something, he thought, wondering when his life had become so overscheduled. After his Dallas concert on Saturday night, he had four days until he needed to return to Texas and then start heading north to Kansas and then Wisconsin. He had contemplated scheduling a trip to Pennsylvania until he had learned that Mike had booked time in the recording studio in Los Angeles.

"Los Angeles? Again?" Alejandro had mumbled when Mike had told him the news. He had always hated Los Angeles, with its traffic, smog, and crowds of people. Concrete City, he called it in private.

"What did you say? 'Again?' Perhaps you'd like to explain what that's supposed to mean!" Mike had snapped back. "Last time I checked, you were a businessman, Alex, a leading artist in the entertainment industry. You don't stay that way by avoiding LA, of all places! And you certainly won't stay that way by running off to hide on Amish farms in Pennsylvania!"

While he hadn't appreciated Mike's crude approach, he knew that he was right. After all, he needed to record new songs and tape another music video. Without new material, fans would lose interest, and once lost, it was hard to regain.

Disappointed, Alejandro had rationalized that it was better this way. Without Amanda to distract him, he could probably get both things done and crossed off his list before the holiday. Afterward, he'd have plenty of time to spend with his wife since he didn't have much scheduled in January beyond meeting up with the band to practice his new songs and with the choreographer to practice new dance routines with his backup dancers.

He had a lot planned for January, starting with some time alone with Amanda, cruising the islands on the yacht. He'd have some of his friends flown down to meet with them when the yacht reached St. Maarten, a great island for partying, snorkeling, and fishing. Carlos had managed to arrange for her passport to be expedited, and Alejandro was eager to show her the world. From what little he had shown her of the United States, he knew that she would continue to find everything that he showed her to be completely fascinating and awe inspiring.

It was Andres, his security guard, who found him in the corridor heading from the backstage lounge toward the stage.

"They want you to see the video," Andres said. "Issue with the big screens projecting it."

"¡Ay, Dios!" There was always something. Tonight was the big debut of his new music video during the concert. Didn't he pay people to take care of these things? Technical glitches and incompetence were two things that he had absolutely no patience for, especially when he paid so well to avoid both.

He hurried to the front of the stage and joined a group of men dressed in jeans and T-shirts. One of them was his technical director, Johnny, and Alejandro spoke directly to him. "How bad?" he asked, getting straight to the point.

"Projector ain't working," Johnny answered. "We can't show it."

Alejandro stared at the man before him. *Can't* wasn't a word in his vocabulary. "I suggest you fix the problem, Johnny," he said, speaking slowly, careful to enunciate each word, a trick that he had learned long ago, which helped mask his anger. "You have a backup system, no?"

"Yes, but it's not nearly as good as the one we've been using," the man admitted, avoiding eye contact with his boss.

"That's not what I want to hear." He glanced around at the other men. "I want it fixed, and I want to see the video within the next thirty minutes, *entiendes*?" While he spoke to the group of men, he was staring directly at Johnny. "I suggest you jump on it, *chico*." Without another word, the men hurried away, their heads bent together as they regrouped in order to meet his demand.

"Sorry, Viper," Andres said. "Just thought you'd want to know."

Alejandro shook his head, indicating that he wasn't upset with Andres for alerting him. He turned to the director for audio who was waiting patiently nearby for the sound check. "Let's do this," he said as he gestured to one of the audio assistants to pin him with the microphone before handing him his earpiece so that he could test the sound and practice a quick song with his band.

Nothing ever seemed to go smoothly on the road lately, he thought as he tried to shake the feeling of complete irritation. He had too much to focus on to deal with such problems. That's why he had a team of people working for him. His production manager, Eddie, needed to handle these issues, not him. It was Thomas's job to deal with the local staff and make certain that things went smoothly. Just as it was Bobby's responsibility, as hospitality manager, to oversee the VIP Meet and Greets as well as taking care of the band and any special guests who were often invited to his shows; and Rudy, as the road manager, was supposed to manage the logistics of getting from point A to point B in the most efficient and comfortable way. Everyone had a job to do in order to make the show run. Panic was just not an option on a concert day.

"Viper!"

He cringed as he heard Bobby running up to him. He had been headed back to the lounge, wanting a few minutes to try to call Amanda and grab a bite to eat.

"Wanted to alert you that I just learned Enrique Lopez will be here tonight," Bobby said, trying to catch his breath.

Alejandro smiled at the news, good for a change. Enrique was an old friend and one whom Alejandro had performed with many times over the years. "To perform or watch?"

"Both," Bobby said. "If you want, that is, his manager said."

"¡Sí, sí!" He reached out and placed his hand on Bobby's shoulder. "Tell Eddie to update the set list and notify the band." He wondered if Mike had arranged this chance meeting. It wasn't unusual for other artists to show up and perform with him at concerts, but it was a bit unusual to receive such late notice. It was usually organized in advance. But Alejandro didn't mind. It would be good to see his old friend.

When he finally escaped to the semi-quiet of the lounge, he reached into his pocket for his cell phone, taking a moment to shut out the noise that surrounded him as he dialed Amanda's number. The phone rang five times before he was interrupted.

"Video's ready," Andres called out to him from the doorway.

"Un momento," Alejandro said, lifting his hand up to wave away Andres.

A sixth and then seventh ring. No answer. He glanced at the clock and realized that it was after four in Pennsylvania. Amanda was most likely outside, helping Harvey with the evening chores. He shut off the phone, disappointed that he wouldn't have a chance to talk with her before the show. By the time she was finished with the chores, he would be in full swing with the final concert preparation. He'd have to wait until the following day to try to speak with her again.

Quickly, he typed in a short text message, apologizing for having missed a chance to speak with her. Then, after he hit the "Send" button, he slipped the phone into his pocket and turned around, not surprised to see Andres waiting for him at the doorway.

"It's fixed?"

Andres shrugged his shoulders, a silent indication that the final verdict would be up to Alejandro, not him.

With a sigh, Alejandro reached for a sandwich and napkin before heading to the door. He looked up at Andres and took a deep breath. "Let's go, then," he said, knowing full well that his afternoon would be spent fixing more problems like this one. After all, no matter what, the show always had to go on.

Chapter Nineteen

```
I have a surprise for you.
Curious?
You'll know soon.
<3
A.
```

Dali had greeted her at the airport, escorting her through the throngs of people, a few recognizing Amanda, without much of an incident. However, a bodyguard had trailed behind them, prepared to intervene in case there were any issues with a sudden mob. The car was waiting out front and they hurried into the backseat so that the driver could get them to the stadium in time.

"Does he know I'm here?"

Dali had given a slight shake of her head. "I don't think he knows that you are coming."

In response, Amanda frowned, glancing at her phone that she clutched in her hand. "I texted him before the plane left Philadelphia. But I didn't tell him. I wanted to surprise him, so *danke* for not letting him know." He hadn't texted back to her.

As always, Dali traveled with her leather bag that contained her papers and her laptop. She reached overhead and flipped on the light before rummaging through her bag for a manila folder. "Here is your schedule for the weekend," she said and handed the paper to Amanda.

"Schedule?"

"*Sí.*" Dali slipped on a pair of reading glasses and began to read from her own sheet of paper. "He goes onstage at nine o'clock. The plan is to sneak you onto the stage when he is singing with the video playing."

"Oh help," Amanda muttered, her eyes looking down at the paper. "I really hadn't planned on that, Dali."

With a flicker of her eyes, Dali merely glanced at Amanda from over the top of her reading glasses. "You wanted to surprise him, no?"

Amanda sighed.

"After the concert tonight, he is scheduled to fly to Milwaukee. It's a private jet, so there is no problem with you accompanying him. There is one radio interview in Milwaukee, and I believe he is scheduled to meet with some Hispanic leaders about a child care facility and then visit the children's cancer center."

"The what?" Despite having heard Dali correctly, Amanda was taken aback by what she had just been told. "The children's cancer center?"

"At the children's hospital, *sí*," Dali replied as if it were the most natural thing in the world for Alejandro to do.

"I'm afraid I don't understand," Amanda said. "Why would he do that?"

Dali took a deep breath and removed her glasses, staring at Amanda for a second before she responded. "A young Hispanic boy in the center wanted to meet Viper. The letter was vetted and everything checked out. Viper's going to the hospital to meet him." She slipped her glasses back on and returned her attention to the papers on her lap. "Besides, it's a nice thing to do."

Stunned, Amanda sat back in the leather seat and stared at the piece of paper.

"And I delayed his LA flight after the Milwaukee concert until Monday at two. Your flight leaves just before his." She put her paper back into the leather bag. "Gives you a little time alone without appointments and rushing all over the place."

Amanda nodded, only half listening to Dali. Instead, she was focused on surprising Alejandro. "I can't thank you enough!" she gushed at Dali. "I'm so excited to see his reaction."

Lifting her head from her bag, Dali reached up and removed her reading glasses. She raised a perfectly manicured eyebrow and stared at Amanda. "*Sí,*" she said. "I think he will be excited." But there was an edge to Dali's voice, something left unspoken.

"What is it?"

Dali shook her head. "*Nada,* Amanda."

Nothing? It was nothing? Amanda frowned, realizing that Dali's idea of "*nada*" was most likely "something" in her own world. But she asked no more questions. Instead, she looked out the window at the passing signs on the highway as they headed toward the arena. It had taken quite a few phone calls back and forth with Dali to make all of the arrangements. Everything was orchestrated to keep her appearance secret, from the public as well as from her husband.

The parking lot was jam-packed with cars, and the arena lit up with brilliant lights. It was late, already past eight thirty, when the driver pulled the car up to security and rolled down his window. Amanda couldn't hear what he said or see the identification that he showed the security guards, but she could see the crowd of people gathered around the barricade. It surprised her that there were people still waiting outside during the concert, and Dali quickly explained that those were people who didn't have tickets but hoped to catch sight of Alejandro when he left the arena.

Inside the secure compound of the arena, Dali quickly escorted Amanda through the long corridors to a private dressing room. She checked with one of the men hurrying down the hallway to find out if Alejandro was already backstage or still at the VIP Meet and Greet with Bobby's assistant.

"He's backstage," Dali said as she shut the door and leaned against it, her arms crossed over her chest as she watched two women begin to fuss over Amanda. An outfit was set aside for her to change into, and the stylists were helping her with her hair and makeup. "The plan is to have you wait until the video starts, Amanda. You'll emerge from the shadows atop the large staircase so that when he turns around, he'll see you there."

Amanda tried to hide a nervous smile. She had been backstage at a few of his concerts, although he seemed to prefer having her escorted into the pit. He had told her that he liked knowing that she was right in front of the stage to watch him perform. While she was slowly getting used to the fans at the concerts, for they often went crazy when she was escorted to her seat, she had never stood on the stage in front of so many of them. Still, she could visualize the look on his face when he would see her. That image motivated her to shelve her fears and agree to surprise him onstage.

Someone rapped on the door as the hairstylist finished with Amanda's hair: an updo, something different from her usual style. Curly tendrils hung down her neck and over her ears. For a few moments, Amanda stared in the mirror, barely recognizing herself.

"Five minutes," the voice called out from the other side of the door.

Turning to look at Dali, Amanda blinked her eyes and swallowed, her nerves feeling as though they resided in her throat. "And he truly has no idea?"

Dali glanced at her phone, checking the time, then looked back at Amanda. "No, he does not," she said, her eyes scanning approvingly over Amanda's outfit. "And you look lovely, by the way." She smiled. "You should wear your hair like that more often."

"It's so fancy," Amanda complained, glancing back into the mirror. With the tight black dress of sequins and the soft leather high-heeled boots, Amanda felt like a different person and wondered if she even recognized herself. It was too much of a contrast with the image still in her mind, just earlier that day, when she said good-bye to her *mamm* and *daed*. Mamm had been dressed in her plain dark-green dress with her white prayer *kapp* pinned to her head. If her *mamm* could see her now, Amanda thought, what on earth would she think of her?

"I don't know if he'll recognize me!" she said, chewing on her lower lip as she stared at her reflection.

"*¿Listo*, Amanda?"

Was she ready? Amanda shifted her eyes in the reflection of the mirror toward Dali, who was watching her, an emotionless look on her face. Amanda swallowed, wondering what had ever possessed her to consider doing such a thing. How many thousands of people were in the arena? All of them would see her before Alejandro did. It was the perfect plan. Her palms were sweating, and she suddenly felt her stomach in complete turmoil. "I don't know if I can do this," she whispered.

Dali took a deep breath and reached into her pocket. "You can and you will," she said matter-of-factly. "Now, take these and let's go." She extracted a pair of dark sunglasses and handed them to Amanda. "Just don't fall down those stairs in those high boots, for crying out loud, even though that would be a grand entrance no one would forget!"

The serious look on Dali's face caused Amanda to burst out laughing. A hint of relief swept through Dali's expression, and she tried to hide a smile, but Amanda could see it. "I'll try not to, then," she replied, standing up and walking toward the door, her hand outstretched for the glasses. "*Danke*, Dali," she said. "You are a right *gut* friend."

"Humph! We'll see about that when Viper gets a look at you."

Amanda frowned at Dali, just long enough to challenge her. "We'll see about that!" she shot back teasingly. Then, she opened the black sunglasses and put them on. *"¡Listo!"*

This time, it was Dali who laughed. "I suspect you are," she managed to say. "Let's go, then."

She could hear the music as they made their way to the stage. They walked down long corridors and passed groups of people dressed in black shirts and black jeans. No one seemed to pay any attention to Amanda as Dali led her toward the area directly behind the stage. Two men nodded at the women, one of them stepping forward to reach for Amanda's arm.

Without a word, he helped her walk up the back steps so that she was standing behind a curtain. He leaned over and shouted into her ear, "When the lights dim after this song, you step through. There will be fireworks and then a brilliant light on you. The band will start the music, and two men will help you walk down the stairs to Viper."

She nodded her head, her heart pounding. She could barely believe that she was doing this, but she knew that she was beyond any point of return. With a trembling hand, she reached out and grabbed the man's arm, steadying herself as she waited, her breath coming in short gulps.

Calm down, she told herself. Do this for Alejandro.

And then, everything went dark. The man helped guide her through the split in the curtain, and she was suddenly standing atop a platform, her eyes hidden behind dark sunglasses. She could barely see anything around her, but in the distance, she saw faint flickers of light coming from the audience. Her heart pounded so hard that, for just a moment, she felt faint and worried that she would collapse.

Two loud noises shook the stage, and seconds later, white lights flared into the air. Flashing lights almost blinded her, and she was thankful that Dali had forced the sunglasses on her. The music began and the lights remained on, a spotlight on Viper who was pandering to the crowd while a second spotlight focused on her.

The music began and Viper sang. The crowd began to notice her standing atop the platform, especially when two men in black suits stepped out from the shadows, each taking one of her arms and helping to slowly escort her down the stairs.

If the noise of the audience was loud and unruly before, when they realized that Amanda was descending the stairs and Viper was still singing, completely unaware, a loud roar almost drowned out his music.

He laughed at their enthusiasm and, in high spirits, turned to look at one of the band members. And that was when he saw her.

She was halfway down the stairs and paused, just long enough to make certain that he had, indeed, recognized her. The expression on his face caused her heart to soar. When he first glanced over his shoulder, he was smiling and laughing. But when he caught sight of her, his mouth fell open as he stopped in his tracks, staring at the apparition before him.

"Princesa?" he said, the microphone picking up his word and causing the audience to roar once again. He handed the microphone to one of the dancers and walked toward the staircase, a broad grin on his face as he reached a hand out to take hers as she approached the bottom and joined him onstage.

Not caring that tens of thousands of people were watching, he swept her into his arms and lifted her off her feet.

"What on earth . . . ?"

She could barely hear him but laughed at the look of complete joy on his face. "I told you that I had a surprise for you, *ja*?"

Holding her hand, he walked toward the front of the stage and retrieved his microphone, returning to singing with Amanda by his side. When he danced in time to the music, he danced toward her, laughing when she blushed and backed away. At one point, she let him grab her hand to dance with him. When they parted, she looked at him and lowered her sunglasses, playfully leveling a look at him that prompted another roar from the audience.

He tossed his head back and lost the words to the song, laughing at her.

"*Ay, mi madre,*" he said into the microphone before turning to the audience and gesturing toward Amanda. "*¡Mi Princesa!*" he shouted and the crowd screamed back, flashes from cameras lighting up the arena like tiny fireflies in a field at night.

She lifted her arm up and waved at the audience before blowing a kiss in his direction and then retreating offstage. Dali was waiting for her in the wings and greeted her with a beaming smile.

"It's hot out there!" Amanda gushed as she took the bottle of chilled water from Dali.

"You were charming," Dali admitted. "And you were right. He seemed not only surprised but delighted."

Ninety minutes later, the concert was over and Alejandro burst into his dressing room. His face lit up when he saw her sitting there, ever so nonchalant on the leather sofa that was against the far wall. In three long strides, he was standing before her and pulling her to her feet, a smile on his face, his arms wrapped around her.

"You!"

She tried to act demure. "Me? What about me?"

"I forgot the words to my song because of you!"

A simple shrug of one shoulder and a lift of her eyebrows added to her gentle teasing. "I can't help it if you don't practice, I reckon," she said.

He laughed and hugged her. "What a fabulous surprise, Princesa!"

Someone knocked on the dressing room door. "Five minutes, Viper. We have to get going."

Pressing his hands on her cheeks, he knelt down and stared into her eyes. "What brought this on? What is the plan?"

She lifted her hands and covered his. "I missed you," she said softly. "And I'm going with you to Milwaukee. Dali arranged it so that I don't have to go back to Pennsylvania until Monday."

A frown crossed his brow, and he pursed his lips. "I'm to fly to LA on Sunday."

"Nee," Amanda said, shaking her head. "Dali arranged for you to fly out Monday after me."

"Really?" He seemed genuinely surprised and definitely pleased. He leaned over and kissed her. "Remind me to give that *chica* a raise, *sí?*"

Five minutes later, after what Amanda thought must have been the world's fastest shower, Alejandro had changed into fresh clothes and they were hurrying down the corridor to the car. It would take them to the airport where the private plane was waiting on the tarmac to fly them to Milwaukee.

On Sunday, Dali spent the afternoon with Amanda while Alejandro was busy, first at the gym working out, then meeting with several Hispanic leaders in the city before heading over to the arena. There was talk about opening a new center for the children to provide after-school care in the city, and Alejandro had agreed to help fund the charity.

Amanda hadn't wanted to accompany him, knowing that they still had a busy night ahead of them. He had, however, insisted that she come with him to visit the hospital and meet the little boy with cancer. "He wanted to meet you, too," Alejandro had explained.

"What type of cancer?" she had asked.

"The kind you don't get better from," was his vague reply.

While he was busy with his other appointments, she had spent some time with Dali, reviewing upcoming events and fund-raisers that had requested Amanda's presence.

"Will Alejandro attend these with me?"

Dali shook her head. "Doubtful," she responded. "He has his own schedule, plus his new recordings."

That didn't sit well with Amanda. "Why on earth would they want me, then?" she asked.

Exasperated, Dali removed her reading glasses and stared at Amanda. "I can't answer that," she said evenly. "But they do."

"*Ja vell*, that seems awfully silly," Amanda commented.

A sigh escaped from Dali's lips. "Amanda," she managed to say, remaining calm. "When are you going to realize that you are part of this package?"

"What package?"

"The Viper package!" Dali set her glasses down on the papers spread out on the table between them. "The public adores you, and you are becoming a celebrity in your own right."

"Oh bother," she mumbled. "I don't want to be a celebrity. I just want to be his wife."

"And with that, my dear, comes the spotlight," Dali retorted. "It will be no different in South America, trust me."

It was too complicated for Amanda to comprehend. She barely listened to Dali as the woman rattled off things she had scheduled for Amanda during the week they would be in Miami over Christmas and then back in New York City for New Year's Eve: a fund-raiser here, a charity auction there. It was too much for Amanda, so she simply shut down and realized that she would have no choice but to follow Dali's schedule in the near future. After all, she reasoned, that *was* why Alejandro had hired her.

Dali glanced at her watch. "We need to get going," she said. "The car service will be here in ten minutes to take you to the hospital. Viper's joining you there to meet the boy, and then we need to get you ready for the concert."

At the hospital, she noticed a small crowd gathered outside the main entrance. Security guards were waiting for her arrival, the public apparently having caught wind of the visit by Viper and his wife to the children's cancer center. Both Dali and Amanda emerged from the car and were immediately escorted inside the building by security.

A hospital administrator greeted her, introducing herself as Kathleen Papp, the liaison who would accompany them on their tour of the cancer center prior to meeting Sean, the little boy who had wanted to meet Viper so desperately. Since Alejandro had yet to arrive, Kathleen took advantage of the time to express her gratitude to Amanda.

"It's a wonderful thing that he's doing," Kathleen said, a big smile on her face. From the glow in her eyes, it was clear that Kathleen did not have many special guests who visited the patients at the hospital. "He's such an amazing young boy," she continued. "So brave. And all he ever talks about is football and Viper."

"That's an interesting combination, isn't it?" Amanda said, smiling at the pleasant woman.

"He wanted to be a rapper," Kathleen said, the use of the past tense too obvious. "Meeting Viper is the next best thing, I imagine. He idolizes your husband."

Amanda heard a cheer from the small crowd outside and knew that Alejandro had arrived. "I look forward to meeting Sean," she heard herself say before turning her attention toward the door and wondering where Alejandro was. She could see him with the fans. He had stopped and posed for several people to take photographs with him. His bodyguards waited patiently for him to finish with his fans, rather than rush him inside as they had done with Amanda.

"Princesa!" he cried out happily. "You have beat me here!" He kissed her on the cheek before turning to the woman standing next to her. "And you must be Kathleen Papp! *Gracias* for arranging this meeting!"

"No," she responded, her eyes glowing even more. "Thank you! We know how busy you must be."

"Never too busy to visit fans like Sean," he replied.

For the next fifteen minutes, Kathleen took them on a short tour of the children's cancer center. Amanda trailed behind Alejandro, her eyes taking in the playful decorations on the walls in the hallways and waiting rooms. One of the empty patient rooms, she noticed, was decorated with bright colors and framed paintings of animals. Unlike the bland gray hospital room where her *daed* had stayed, these cheerful rooms were geared specifically for children.

"Some of our young patients have spent more time here than at their own homes," Kathleen proceeded to tell Alejandro and Amanda. "We want them to feel comfortable, especially the ones like Sean who are terminally ill from the disease."

Terminally ill? Amanda caught her breath and bit her lip.

Kathleen stopped at a closed door and motioned to the hand sanitizer on the wall. "This is his room," she said. "Please wash your hands first, and then we can introduce you to Sean."

He was lying on the hospital bed, a blue cap on his head and tubes connected to his arm from bags hanging on a pole. When the door opened, the boy turned his head and tried to focus on the visitors. When he recognized who entered, his eyes widened and he attempted to sit up.

His mother was at his side and placed a hand on his shoulder. "Easy now," she said and pressed a button on the side of the bed that helped to raise it into a sitting position. Her attention was focused on her son, not on the two people who had just entered the room.

"Hey there, *chico!*" Alejandro said as he approached the side of the bed, a big smile on his face. "I heard you're doing some time in here, no?"

"Viper!" The boy grinned and turned to his mother. "Mom! It's him! It's him!"

"I see that!" she laughed.

"You have to take a picture! The guys will never believe this!" He turned back to Alejandro. "Can we take a picture so my friends know I'm not making this up?"

Alejandro laughed. *"¡Sí, sí!"*

He posed for a few photos with Sean, putting his arm around the boy's shoulders and smiling into his mother's camera. At one point, he gestured for Amanda to join them and the boy's face lit up as he exclaimed, "I'm the luckiest kid in here!"

Then, the photos out of the way, Alejandro asked permission to pull up a chair. For ten minutes, Alejandro sat beside Sean, talking with him as if they were old friends. They discussed football and which team Sean thought would make the playoffs that year.

"I bet you like the Dolphins!" Sean said.

"*Sí*, I do," Alejandro admitted.

"They'll never make it! I'd bet on the Green Bay Packers, though. They're looking good this year!"

Alejandro groaned and shook his head. "Double or nothing, my friend. The next game they play against each other, Green Bay wins and I'll fly you to the next concert I have in the US!"

"Really?" Sean's face glowed. "With my mom?"

"*¡Sí, sí!* Mom has to go to keep you in line, I bet!" he laughed, glancing at Sean's mother, who was smiling down at her son.

"What if the Dolphins win?"

Alejandro made a face as if he was deep in thought, then he snapped his fingers. "Dolphins win, you get better and don't come back to the hospital! How's that?"

Amanda watched the exchange, a sorrowful smile on her face and a bittersweet pull at her heart. She had never before witnessed such a touching moment. Alejandro acted as if he had been lifelong friends with this boy who looked to be no more than fourteen years old. According to Kathleen, the chances of him surviving to graduate high school were slim. Late-stage acute myeloid leukemia did not have a high rate of survival, especially not at his age.

And it was at that moment that Amanda knew what charity she wanted to choose as her focus: children's cancer. If Alejandro's visit could bring so much happiness into the life of a young boy like Sean, then Amanda knew that she wanted to devote herself to helping other children forget their disease, even if only for one moment, so that they, too, could feel as if they were the luckiest kids in the world.

After the previous evening's surprise appearance by Amanda at the Viper concert, there was not a seat left for sale at the Milwaukee concert. He had laughed over his morning coffee as he perused the social media, commenting that Amanda was a marketing genius. He had even tried to get her to make the same grand entrance, but she had refused, asking to sit in the audience as she usually did.

It amazed Amanda that, despite having seen so many Viper concerts, she never grew tired of watching him perform. His presence onstage was riveting and made her blood pulse. He was exciting to watch, but so was the response from the audience: they simply adored him and his music.

As she was walked to her seat, some fans reaching out to her and begging for a photograph, Amanda realized that the adoration now included her, as well. The thought struck her as odd for she had not done anything to warrant such attention: she couldn't sing, didn't dance, and rarely spoke in public. It dawned on her that simply being loved by Alejandro made her loved by his public.

While she didn't understand it, she decided to just accept it.

Once the concert started, she found herself lost in the music and in watching Viper perform. Early on, she had realized that each show was different in some way, and she loved to try to find those little changes that he added to the concert. Tonight, however, she knew in advance that the big difference was the display of the recently released music video on the big screen while he sang the song. They had played the video the night before in Kansas City, but she had not been able to see it as she had been onstage instead of in the audience.

It was almost halfway through the concert when the lights dimmed and she heard the introduction to the song. Her eyes shifted to the large screens, eager to see the video. She could remember, too well, having been in the studio for some of the recording.

And then the screen came to life.

It was only a four-minute video, but she felt as though it took three times as long. She was too aware that the people surrounding her were watching it and, at several points, turned to glance at her.

True to form, Amanda maintained no expression on her face, despite feeling the humiliation of seeing herself on the big screen. Someone had recorded her during the video shooting, capturing her discomfort at watching Alejandro holding another woman in his arms and trailing his finger along her lips before kissing her. The videographer had even captured the moment when a tear fell from Amanda's eye and she had reached up to wipe it away.

Despite her embarrassment and humiliation at such a public display of her private moment of emotion, the audience cheered at the end of the video and Viper's live performance. It was clear that they had loved the song as well as the video.

Dali's words came back to her: the Viper package. Amanda suddenly realized what that meant. She no longer had any privacy . . . not really. Her life was on display for the public to see and analyze. Obscure and anonymous nights like they had experienced in New York City when Alejandro had taken her to the opera were the exception, not the rule. In fact, Amanda was quickly realizing that there *were* no rules in her new life.

Withdrawing into herself, Amanda tried to get a handle on what she was feeling. At the top of the list was hurt and disappointment. How could Alejandro have thought that it was appropriate? How could he not have shown the video to her before now? How could he have left her so unprepared?

It wasn't until they were almost back to the hotel that he finally realized she was extra quiet and not her usual bubbly self. Immediately after the show, he had been surrounded by a crowd of fans that had special backstage access as part of the Hispanic center he was funding. He spent a few minutes posing for photos and signing autographs before being able to finally slip away to his dressing room. He had taken a quick shower before both he and Amanda were rushed to the waiting car in order to leave the arena for the hotel. Too many fans were blocking the exit, so a police escort was called to accommodate them.

"What shall we do tonight, Princesa?" he asked as he fiddled with his phone, quickly scanning his messages. "A movie in the suite, perhaps? Something low-key?"

She stared out the window, uncertain how to respond. She wanted to tell him what she was feeling, to describe how hurt she had been. Yet she didn't want to ruin their last evening together. The following day, she would return to Pennsylvania and he would return to Los Angeles.

"That sounds fine," she managed to say, hoping that her voice did not give away her true feelings.

There was a moment of silence in the car, and she realized that he was responding to some messages on his phone, not even aware that she was upset about the video. His obliviousness to her feelings upset her even more. How could he not sense that something was amiss?

They were in the elevator, a doorman reaching inside to use his key in order to select their floor, when he finally noticed how quiet she was. Slipping his phone into his pocket, he reached out for her hand. "It will go quickly, no?" he said.

It took her a few seconds to understand what he meant. They would be apart for two more weeks, and he obviously suspected that her silence was due to their impending separation. As gracefully as she could, she withdrew her hand from his and averted her eyes. She didn't want him to see the disappointment reflected in them.

"*Escúchame*, Amanda," he said, reaching out to cup her chin with his hand, forcing her to look at him just as the elevator doors opened on their floor. "You don't have to go," he said. "You could come with me to Los Angeles. Your sister will be back in another week or so, no?"

Taking a deep breath, she moistened her lips as she stared into his eyes. "That's not it, Alejandro," she said in a flat, emotionless voice before stepping out of the elevator.

He followed her down the hallway to the door of their room at the end. There were four private suites on the secured floor, so they were assured of having the most privacy possible. As she stood at the doorway, her arms crossed over her chest, she was glad that the floor was so isolated.

"Do you mind telling me what is bothering you, then?" he asked as he opened the door to their suite. "I should hate to have our last evening together spent in silence, *mi amor*. Without knowing what is wrong, I cannot fix it."

"Mayhaps this cannot be fixed," she snapped back, immediately ashamed of herself for sounding so angry.

"Hey, hey!" He took ahold of her arm as she tried to walk past him. "What is this about?"

"The video!"

He blinked twice, releasing his grasp on her but following her inside the suite. After shutting the door, he quietly unzipped his black leather jacket and tossed it over a chair in the main sitting room. His eyes never left her as she crossed the room, pausing to lean against a table to reach down and remove her high heels. Holding them in her hands, she walked barefoot toward the bedroom door in order to change.

"The video?" he finally said, breaking the silence as he leaned against the doorframe. "What video?"

"Alejandro!" She spun around, surprised at herself. She had never heard her parents quarrel before and immediately disliked the hot feeling that swelled inside her chest. "How could you not have shown that video to me?"

He seemed genuinely perplexed. "The music video?" he asked, the expression on his face showing his genuine confusion. "What was wrong with it, Amanda?"

"It was humiliating!"

To her surprise, rather than demonstrate any empathy for her feelings, he laughed. "You are angry about the video?"

Standing with her hands on her hips, she faced him, the color racing to her cheeks. How dare he laugh at me? she thought. "I find nothing humorous about it!" she snapped, her words harsh and her tone ugly, even to her own ears.

Quick as a flash, he crossed the room and pushed her up against the wall, one hand resting above her head and the other gently pressed against her waist. He stared down into her face, still smiling, despite the anger in her eyes.

"I have never seen *mi* Princesa angry before," he murmured, an all-too-familiar look in his eyes. "Such fire!"

Amanda tried to wiggle free from him, knowing perfectly well what he had on his mind. She tried to break away, but he was too strong. "Alejandro! I'm perfectly serious."

"As am I," he whispered, leaning down to kiss her neck. "I think I shall do more things to get you angry in the future!"

Frustrated, she gave up fighting him but resisted his affection. "That video was insulting," she said. "I cannot believe that you permitted them to use my image!"

"You are beautiful on the big screen," he breathed into her ear. "You are even beautiful when you are angry, too."

"You should have shown it to me first!" she demanded.

He shrugged. "*¿Por qué?* You would have said no, *sí?*"

"I would have said no, *ja!*"

He smiled. "And that is why I didn't show it to you."

His hand traveled from her waist to her back, and he pulled her so that she was pressed against him. Placing her hands against his shoulders, she tried to push him back, but it was a futile effort. And as his kisses trailed from her neck to her lips, she gave up entirely. There was no fighting Alejandro, she realized, although the fight had left her as well.

"Stay with me," he pleaded, taking her into his arms and maneuvering her toward the bed. "I don't want to be without you, Amanda."

Aman-tha.

She swallowed her previous anger at him as he held her tight. His arms, so muscular and strong, refused to loosen their grip, and soon the backs of her legs touched the side of the bed frame. With her anger quickly ebbing away, giving way to his passion, she responded to his plea by kissing him back, her free hand caressing the nape of his neck. How could she remain angry with him, this man whom she loved so much?

Chapter Twenty

```
Sure is cold here today.
Reckon it's warm in LA.
Know you are busy.
Please call when you can.
A.
```

Despite the chill in the air outside, the sun was shining and there was not one cloud in the sky. From the kitchen, Amanda gazed outside the window and scanned the blue sky behind the barn. A flock of birds, Canada geese, flew in a V formation toward the south. Their wings seemed to flap in unison, but she knew that it was just a visual trick.

Hurry and be safe, she thought, wishing them a speedy journey as she turned away from the window.

She had been home almost four days and had only spoken with Alejandro once. While she hadn't completely forgotten about being upset with the video and his nonchalant attitude toward it, his romantic attention to her their last evening spent together in the hotel had made the hurt disappear. However, a new hurt was rapidly arising that came from four days of limited communication with her husband.

Oh, Dali kept her well posted on what was going on. The ever-diligent Dali, Amanda had privately nicknamed her. Despite Amanda being in Lancaster County, Dali continued to work hard behind the scenes. Already Amanda had two telephone interviews with reporters, one based in England and one in Canada. And Dali had been quick to report that the music video, the one that Amanda found so distasteful, already had over four million views and there was talk of a possible music video award for it.

As for Alejandro, Dali had merely told Amanda that she knew he was in Los Angeles and suspected that most of his time was spent at the recording studio. Dali was quick to remind Amanda that her own job was not to manage the public relations for Alejandro but for her, his wife. However, she had reported that there had been no gossip in the social media about their separation. From the tone of Dali's voice, that lack of journalistic interest did not please her. For a publicist, media silence meant public relations failure. Amanda, however, had been overjoyed by the lack of stories and gossip in the media. While she would never admit it to anyone, she needed a break from the speculative and usually false stories that circulated about her and Alejandro.

"Going to market today, Amanda?"

She looked over at her *mamm*, ho had just walked in from outside. Lizzie's cheeks were flushed with the cold as she hung up her thick black jacket on a peg jutting from the wall by the door. "I can, Mamm," she answered. "Did you write a list?"

"Ja, ja." Lizzie rubbed her arms as she walked to the desk near the sofa. "Sure is cold out today," she muttered. "Be certain to bundle up, then."

"I will, Mamm," Amanda said, hiding a quick roll of her eyes. "If Harvey's taking me, his car does have a heater in it, ain't so?"

Lizzie glanced up. "No need to be sassy," her *mamm* scolded gently. "Besides, I want you to take the horse and buggy. That mare needs exercise anyway."

Inwardly, Amanda groaned. On a cold day, the buggy would never warm up during the ride to the market. She'd have to make certain to bring extra blankets to huddle under during the ride. At least the paparazzi had not been hanging around, the cold weather chasing them away as much as the boredom from not being able to take more than a few redundant photographs of Amanda walking to and from the barn.

When she had put on her coat and taken the list from her *mamm*, she ventured outside, shivering as the cold ran through her bones. She carried two afghan blankets over her arm as she hurried toward the buggy, puffing out small clouds of steam as she breathed.

Harvey had just finished harnessing the horse and was backing her up when Amanda approached the side of the buggy. He paused and eyed her, concern on his face. "You sure 'bout this, then?" he asked cautiously. "Not certain you should be going alone."

"*Danke* for caring," she replied, genuinely meaning it. Harvey had become a quasi-member of the family over the past few weeks, his help on the farm invaluable and his loyalty to the family irreplaceable. "I'll be just fine. Those photographers haven't been around since I returned now, have they? And besides," she said as she slid open the buggy door and tossed in the blankets, "I need to get off the farm for a while."

For the first mile, the horse seemed to prance along the road, tossing her head and trying hard to break into a canter. Amanda was glad that there were but very few cars on the road as her *mamm* had been correct: the horse needed the exercise. Inside the buggy, the rumbling of the wheels against the road and the jiggling sounds accompanying its motion drowned out her thoughts. As soon as the horse calmed down and began to amble at an even pace, Amanda started to lose herself in the hypnotic trance of the noise and motion.

Despite the blueness of the sky and warmth of the sun, she found herself looking around at the fields and farmhouses, seeing them with a fresh perspective. When she had been younger, taking these same roads with her little brother, Aaron, at her side, they had pointed out the different cows, crops, and birds that they encountered along the way. Now, however, she saw it differently.

She barely saw the color of the farms. Instead of the blue silos and red barns, everything looked black and white to her. Perhaps it was the bare trees or empty fields that made it look that way. More likely, she realized, it was her exposure to so many things in the Englische world. The bright lights of the cities. The energy of the concerts. The sounds of the opera. The smells of fancy restaurants. The hustling street vendors. In the past months, her world had changed so much that she could only compare the peaceful life that she had known for so long to the life she knew was now her future.

Yet being apart from Alejandro made her feel as though she was bridging a stream, unable to quite cross from one side to the other. She wanted to have both feet on the Englische side even though she wasn't certain if she was truly ready to say good-bye to the Amish side in its entirety.

There were few people at the market. Amanda tied the horse to the hitching post and hurried across the parking lot to the steps that led to the glass doors. She held the list in her hand as she grabbed a small shopping cart and began to push it through the aisles, quickly filling up the cart with the items on her *mamm's* list: flour, brewer's yeast, sea salt, aloe vera water, natural sugar, tea, vegetables, and bran.

She was walking through the vitamin aisle, looking for Graviola, the last item on the list, when she felt the heat of someone's stare on the back of her neck. Hesitating, she contemplated not turning around but curiosity got the better of her. She stopped walking, pausing just long enough to look over her shoulder to see the bishop standing beside his wife at the far end of the aisle.

For a moment, Amanda thought about ignoring him. He had been rude to her one too many times, she thought. But just as quickly, she realized that it would mean she was stooping to his level. Leaving her cart in the middle of the aisle, she approached the bishop and his wife, quick to smile as she greeted them.

"*Gut mariye,*" she said, holding out her hand to shake theirs. It did not surprise her that neither one hurried to respond in kind. "I hope you are staying warm today. It's right cold out, ain't so?"

Reluctantly, the bishop accepted her outstretched hand. "Reckon so," he mumbled.

His wife followed his example. She was a small woman with a wrinkled face and faded blue eyes that hid behind thick, round spectacles. Her hand was cold when Amanda shook it. It was a hand that had changed many diapers and made just as many pies over a lifetime. The only life that the bishop's wife had known was the one that she was living now. The realization that had she not met and married Alejandro, she would have been just like this woman struck Amanda, and for just a moment, she felt a wave of relief.

"Your *daed* is better, I hear," the bishop managed to say, a forced degree of civility in his voice.

"*Ja, danke* for asking," Amanda said. "There's a nurse visiting each afternoon. She works with him on his muscles. Sure does tire him out."

The bishop's wife nodded her head. "Long journey ahead of him, that's for sure and certain," she said.

"Reckon you heard that Anna and her husband are moving from Ohio to run Daed's farm," Amanda added, uncertain how to extract herself from the awkward conversation.

"As it should be," was all that the bishop said. And then silence.

As politely as possible, Amanda bade them good day and hurried back to her cart, her cheeks stinging from the coldness of a man who professed to be so close to God. Oh, she knew that it was the lot that had chosen him to lead their *g'may*. But after so many years doing so, he was looked upon as a most godly man. His lack of compassion continued to stun her, but she realized there was nothing she could do about it.

At the cash register, she was still thinking about the cold response from both the bishop and his wife when the cashier, a younger Amish woman who Amanda had known from the youth singings, cleared her throat. She glanced around the store before she leaned over and whispered, "Those men are outside, you know."

Frowning, Amanda wondered if she had heard properly. "What men, Mary?"

"The men with the cameras."

Quickly, Amanda turned her head and stared out the window, trying to see what men the woman was referencing. Sure enough, there were three cars positioned near her buggy, one almost blocking her exit. The photographers were unabashedly leaning against the cars, cameras in hand, waiting for her to exit the store.

"Oh fiddle-faddle," she muttered. How had *that* happened? There was no way around it; she would have to face them head-on. With two boxes to carry, she needed to make two trips. And then she'd have to make her way home, praying that they did not drive their cars too close to the horse and buggy.

Trying to hide her fear, Amanda took a deep breath as she placed the supplies into a box while Mary continued to ring up her total. Several men walked into the store, pausing when they recognized Amanda and glancing back toward the door. She knew what they were talking about, even if she could not hear them. Having seen the photographers in the parking lot, they had probably suspected that Amanda was inside. Seeing her had only confirmed their suspicions.

She paid Mary for the goods, trying to smile as she thanked her, then carried the boxes to the window, resting one on the ledge as she peered outside. One of the photographers was smoking a cigarette while the other two men held their cameras, talking to each other. They were waiting for her to exit the store and didn't look in a hurry to leave.

As she contemplated how she was going to manage the inevitable confrontation, she felt a hand on her shoulder. Surprised, she turned around and found herself face-to-face with the bishop. "Reckon you need some help with those boxes, *ja?*"

She didn't quite understand what he was asking. "I . . . I can manage."

His eyes flickered toward the window. "Might not hurt if I carry one box out first," he said. "And pull that buggy around to the back doors so you don't have to carry it down those stairs."

The realization that he was offering to help struck her, and she could barely do more than nod her head. She was suddenly moved by this gesture from the bishop, a man who had fought so hard to alienate her ever since Alejandro had returned her to the farm after her accident in New York City. When he took the first box and headed toward the door, she could hardly believe that he was confronting those men on her behalf.

She watched from the window as he descended the stairs and headed directly for the buggy. Instead of getting into his own buggy, he placed the box in the back of her *daed's*. The photographers moved, one of them taking a photograph of the bishop while the other two got out of his way. The bishop ignored them, a scowl on his face as he untied the horse and backed her up before getting inside the buggy. He slammed the door shut before the photographer could take another photo and slapped the reins on the horse's back to get her moving.

The buggy rolled out of the parking lot, but rather than head down the lane, it turned down the narrow road alongside the store. To Amanda's amazement, the photographers didn't pay any attention as they settled back into their former positions, waiting for Amanda to exit.

Lifting the second box into her arms, Amanda followed Mary to the back of the store and through a door that led into the storage room. At the rear was a doorway that led to the back of the building. When Mary opened the door, Amanda saw that the bishop was already waiting there, standing beside the horse and gesturing for Amanda to hurry.

She didn't need to be told twice. She pushed the box through the open buggy door and slid it over the seat so that she had room to climb in. The bishop held the horse's bridle as Amanda settled in. He kept glancing over his shoulder, as if expecting the photographers to come around the back of the building. But there was no sign of them.

"You take that dirt road to the Millers' farm," he instructed. "Then exit out of their driveway to the main road."

"*Danke*, Bishop," she said quietly, emotion welling up and into her throat. Of anyone to step up to come to her aid, she never would have suspected this man. She was ashamed of herself for having thought so little of his character, despite their differences in the past.

The bishop didn't respond as he stepped away from the horse and motioned for her to get moving before the photographers caught on to their ruse. But as she directed the horse down the dirt lane, she looked into the side mirror and saw that he turned to watch her leave. At one point, she thought she saw him lift his hand to wave to her, but she couldn't be sure of that.

As she maneuvered the buggy down the dirt lane toward the white farmhouse, she breathed a sigh of relief. No one was following her. In her mind, she could see the confusion of the photographers when the bishop reemerged from the front door, this time with his wife. She wondered if the men would even recognize that it was the same Amish man who had just driven away in a buggy. She doubted it. By the time they would finally realize what had happened, Amanda would most likely be home already, helping to unload the groceries in her *mamm*'s kitchen.

And all of that because the bishop had stepped forward to assist her, protecting her even though she was no longer a member of the *g'may*. It dawned on her that his gesture had taught her an even more important lesson: despite the choices that she had made, she didn't necessarily have to jump from one side of the stream to another. While she would never truly be accepted as an Amish woman, she would also never truly be an Englischer. Indeed, the bishop had just shown her that she would always have a connection with the Amish and, as such, would fall under the protected wing of the Amish community.

Chapter Twenty-One

```
Getting ready for the Jingle Ball
concert.
Will call later.
Remember to stay put.
No more excursions to the store, mi
amor.
V.
```

It was his fifth year performing at the Jingle Ball concert in the City of Angels, Alejandro realized. Each year, he had enjoyed himself as much during the concert as afterward, at the after-parties. The entertainers were always in a jovial mood, often drinking backstage both before and after their performances. Last year, a somewhat inebriated Lil Juan had barged in on Viper's set, the two of them immediately breaking into a joint song, a throwback to the old days, singing at clubs in Miami.

This year, the general mood backstage was no different.

With so many entertainers performing on one stage, the behind-the-scenes areas were filled with people: managers, girlfriends, stagehands, and well-wishers who belonged to various entourages. Like the others, Alejandro was never alone, his own entourage of friends having joined him in Los Angeles for the big event. And as they were talking with other people who they knew from previous concert tours, Alejandro found himself floating among the different groups, embracing old friends whom he hadn't seen in a long time and shaking hands with those whom he had never met before that evening. This was a night when ideas for future collaborations on songs and videos flowed as easily as the holiday cheer.

The only thing that could have made the night even better was if Amanda had agreed to join him.

He hadn't spoken to her since Friday morning. His week had been spent at the recording studio, creating new beats to go with the two new songs that he had written while on the road. Then he had spent the evenings helping two friends with their beats, drinking beers while they sat around the computer and adjusted the sounds until Alejandro was satisfied.

He had been upset with her when he had heard about the incident at the store.

"I thought I told you to not go anywhere, Amanda," he had said sharply. "You should have stayed put. It's not safe to be riding around alone and you know that."

She hadn't responded right away to his reprimand. Her silence had said it all. And he knew that he had upset her. He had learned that Amish trait of hers, shutting down when upset with a situation or a person. Only once had she ever vocalized her emotions when upset and that had been just recently over the video.

"What's up, man?"

Alejandro turned around, grinning when he recognized his friend Dricke Ray. The last time they had seen each other was at an awards event before he had married Amanda. They embraced, clapping each other on the back.

"Where's that pretty little woman of yours?" Dricke asked, looking around as if he expected Amanda to be hiding behind Alejandro.

"Not here tonight," Alejandro admitted.

"When the cat's away . . ." Dricke started to say, but Alejandro lifted an eyebrow, stopping him in midsentence. "Aw, you're an old married dude now. I keep forgetting 'bout that!" Dricke laughed and held up his hand in the air, waiting for Alejandro to slap it, a gesture of friendship and understanding. "But you can still be a mouse and play, Viper! I'll be seeing you at that party later, no?" He laughed as he walked away, a stagehand chasing after him as it was almost time for his set.

There were reporters everywhere, most of them in high spirits from having joined the entertainers in toasting the holiday season. Carrying his drink, he paused for the obligatory photo shoot by the sponsor's backdrop and spent a few minutes mingling with several reporters, all of whom had asked more questions about Amanda than about his songs or upcoming international tour. That hadn't bothered him. In fact, he much preferred talking about Amanda than about his tour. When he talked about her, he felt alive and closer to her, especially given their current separation. Being apart was increasingly difficult, and Mike was not making it any easier.

Afterward, he moved over to join a group of people who were seated in the back lounge area. He was laughing with them over a story about a crazy fan at a concert when she sat beside him in the empty seat. For a moment, Alejandro had to do a double take, and it was all that he could do to not make a scene.

Maria sank down into the seat next to him, her blond hair twisted into a sexy French knot with rhinestone pins pushed into the side. Alejandro knew exactly who was behind this trickery: Mike. Only Mike could have arranged for Maria to not only be in Los Angeles but also backstage at one of the hottest events of the season.

Instead of confronting her, for he had long ago learned to always behave in public as though a dozen cameras were trained on him, capturing both audio and video, he smiled and sat up, just enough to appear gentlemanly, as she smoothed the front of her dress so that it would not wrinkle.

"What a pleasant surprise," he managed to say, the smile still plastered on his face. Inside, he was seething. "I'll have to remember to thank Mike later, no?"

She returned the greeting by leaning over to kiss his cheek, her hand lingering on his knee as she did so. "It's wonderful to see you, Viper."

He responded with a short, low grunt, shifting his leg so that her hand fell away as he turned his attention back to the man sitting next to him. But it was already too late. He could sense the reporters taking his photo, seated next to the mysterious woman who seemed all too familiar and comfortable with Viper.

The after-party was packed with people. Alejandro accepted the congratulations of his peers, too aware that Maria was constantly a few feet behind him. As photographers snapped his pictures, she was by his side. Despite glancing often at his security companion, trying to get his attention to remove her without making a scene, nothing happened.

"Viper!" someone called out. "Over here!"

He lifted his hand in acknowledgment and excused himself from the photographers as he made his way over to Dricke Ray. Lifting his hand in the air, he smiled as Dricke did the same and they greeted each other by clasping their hands.

"Yo, man!" Dricke said. "Great performance!"

"*¡Gracias, chico!*" He laughed as Dricke grabbed two drinks from a nearby waiter and shoved one into his hands. "*¡Salud!*"

"You changed your mind about playing while the cat's away, I see!" Dricke glanced over Alejandro's shoulder. Maria stood nearby, talking with two other women, both clearly typical entourage hanger-ons. "Or are you breaking the hearts of all the lovely ladies tonight?"

"Nah, man," Alejandro said, lifting the glass to his lips. "Not my style."

Dricke made eye contact with one of the women and nodded his head. "It's my style," he retorted, a gleam in his eyes. "That life don't leave your blood too fast, my friend." Tapping his glass against Alejandro's, he winked and teasingly growled at him, imitating a cat. "Excuse me, man. I see a fine feline calling out to me over there!"

For a moment, Alejandro stood alone. It was rare that people weren't crowded around him, and he took the moment to catch his breath. He hadn't wanted to come to the after-party. However, with so many of the industry greats gathered in one place, he knew that it would be career suicide to miss it. Mike had been certain to point that out to him when he showed up backstage.

Alejandro scanned the crowd, looking for his manager. He thought he saw him by the bar, talking with Justin Bell's manager. A future collaboration in the making? Alejandro wasn't certain how that would fly with his fans. Justin Bell appealed to a younger age group, mostly teenage girls. However, he was a popular artist and a collaboration certainly couldn't hurt Viper's new "good boy" image.

When Mike finally noticed him, Alejandro dragged him away from the crowds and questioned him about Maria's presence. He feigned innocence, but the shifting of his eyes did not go unnoticed by Alejandro. He was lying.

"Why'd you have to do that?" Alejandro said, shaking his head.

"I have no idea what you're talking about," Mike professed, glancing over Alejandro's shoulder and nodding at someone who was passing by. "She knows a lot of people here, Alex. Anyone could have invited her. It's not like she hasn't been here before."

Alejandro didn't believe him. Mike had been insistent that Viper not show up alone to the after-party, wanting a young woman on either arm as he walked into the event. "It's all for show," he had pleaded with Alejandro. "Just tell your wife that, for crying out loud."

It had been the way that Mike said "your wife" that bothered Alejandro as much as the suggestion that Viper flaunt being apart from Amanda. There was always contempt in Mike's voice when he referenced Amanda. It had dawned on Alejandro that Mike resented no longer being number one in his life. Prior to Amanda's presence, Alejandro had relied on Mike, never letting anyone, especially a woman, come between them. Women had been temporary objects in his life, not lifelong partners.

Adjustments, Alejandro had thought as he shook his head at his manager. "No women, Mike. Not even for show."

Now, with Maria at the Jingle Ball concert, hanging with his entourage and floating among the others, Alejandro realized that Mike had arranged for her presence on purpose, a type of punishment for Alejandro not permitting the young women to escort him into the after-party.

"Hey, you!"

He heard the greeting before he felt the hand on his shoulder. Glancing over, he saw the impeccably manicured red nails and, immediately, knew that Maria had zoned in on him.

Sighing, Alejandro turned to face her. "Happy holidays to you," he managed to say. He had to remind himself that he wasn't upset with her, although he had noticed how cold she had been to Amanda on the few occasions they had been together in Miami. Without complaining or saying anything negative, Amanda had made it clear that Maria's presence bothered her. Out of respect, Alejandro had quietly severed his ties with his former friend and occasional lover. After all, he had reasoned, it was the right thing to do, especially now that he was married.

"I think you should buy me a drink," she purred. "A proper holiday toast, *sí*?"

People were watching, and Alejandro knew that he couldn't make a scene. As always, Maria played the part well: femme fatale to the end. If he denied her the drink, the reporters would catch wind of it and present Maria as the scorned ex-lover. Certainly they remembered her from the summer when she had pretended to be his girlfriend in order to draw attention away from Amanda. It hadn't worked then, but Alejandro suspected the tabloids would love to revive the story.

He gestured to a server, lifting up his glass of vodka on the rocks and pointing toward Maria's empty champagne flute.

"*Gracias*, Viper." She smiled when he turned his attention back to her. "It's been so long! How have you been?"

"Busy."

"As usual," she laughed. "You live to be busy."

He smiled. She knew him too well. Slowly, he tried to relax, continually reminding himself that it was not Maria who was at fault. For all Alejandro knew, Mike had arranged for someone to invite her on his behalf. "You've been well, *sí*?"

Nodding her head, she watched as the server returned and Alejandro handed her the glass of champagne. "*Salud,*" she said, raising the crystal flute to touch the rim to his glass in a gesture of friendship. "It's good to see you, Alejandro," she said, gazing at him as he took a sip of the drink. "Haven't seen much of you since your wedding."

He shrugged, not certain how to respond.

"I was hurt that you didn't invite me," she admitted. "Our paths go a long way back, *chico*. I would have liked to have celebrated with you."

He laughed. "Oh really?" The thought of Maria wanting to celebrate anything that did not center on her amused him. She had grown too used to being the only woman permitted in his life to know him. Being supplanted by Amanda was certainly not a cause for celebration in Maria's world.

"*¡Sí!*" she insisted, trying to sound sincere, but the gleam in her eyes told him otherwise.

"In that case," he said, raising his glass one more time. "*¡Gracias por la felicitación y feliz navidad, mi amiga!*"

The music was loud and the lights were flashing. The general ambiance of the gathering was one of celebration and happiness. It was a good after-party, and he was starting to feel more festive as he sipped at his drink.

Maria glanced over her shoulder at the dance floor. Looking back at him, she brushed a tendril away from her cheek and smiled, hesitating just a moment before she spoke what was on her mind. He knew what she was going to say before the words slipped through her lips. He could see it in her eyes, and he was prepared.

"Let's dance, Viper," she said. "I feel like getting on the floor a bit, no?"

Without hesitation, he reached for her champagne and set both of their glasses on a nearby table before grabbing her hand and leading her through the crowd. The people parted, a few smiling at the handsome couple as they made their way to the already crowded dance floor, no one seeming to notice or care that the woman accompanying Viper was not his wife.

Chapter Twenty-Two

```
I haven't heard from you all day.
How was the concert?
<3
A.
```

By two in the afternoon, Amanda was worried. He had not contacted her since the evening before, a short text during the limousine ride from the condominium to the Jingle Ball concert. He had promised to call her in the morning. But her phone never rang, despite it almost being afternoon.

"I don't understand," she mumbled, checking that it had properly charged overnight. To her dismay, the battery indicator was full. "Something must be wrong."

"Relax, Amanda," Lizzie said dismissively. "You tell us all the time how busy his schedule is. He'll call, *ja*?"

She knew her *mamm* was right. There was nothing to worry about. He would contact her when he had the time. Still, with the dark December skies that hid the sun and the bare trees resembling bony skeletons reaching up for the sky, she was already depressed enough and not having heard from him was adding to it.

It was almost an hour later when Amanda sat with her parents, her *mamm* working on the hem of a dress and her *daed* in his wheelchair by the window. Mamm looked up and glanced out the window. "Sure hope Anna and Jonas get back soon," she fretted. "Weather sure looks bad."

Just the previous afternoon, Anna and Jonas had arrived from Ohio. It had been a happy reunion in more ways than one. With the Christmas holidays only a week away, Amanda was looking forward to being reunited with Alejandro in time to celebrate their first Christmas together.

Her surprise visit to Kansas the previous weekend had been too short, leaving more longing than satisfaction in her heart. Plus, they had parted after she had spoken cross words with him about that video. It still bothered her that she had spoken so sharply to him and wondered if that had anything to do with his unusual lack of communication over the week.

Oh, he had texted her every day. But far and few between were the phone calls. She longed to hear his voice, to share a conversation and to know that he still missed her. One of their last conversations had been after her excursion to the market. His sharp words to her, reprimanding her for not having listened to him about not leaving the farm, had bothered her. Rather than say something that she would later regret, she had not commented on his tone or scolding. But it had stung her soul to know that she had disappointed him and that he had so harshly made her feel that way.

The day before, she had texted Alejandro about Anna and Jonas having arrived four days earlier than expected. While she knew that he was out in Los Angeles for that Jingle Ball concert, she had certainly expected that he would have contacted her before now. She had hoped that he would be as excited as she was about their early arrival from

Ohio. With her sister and Jonas back in Pennsylvania, Amanda was now able to leave the farm and rejoin him.

His last communication, however, hadn't inquired about her sister's arrival or mentioned Amanda joining him on the road.

"Who're they visiting today, Mamm?"

"Daed's cousins in Ephrata," Lizzie responded, her head bent over the dress as she sewed. "Thought they'd be back by now, with the weather looking so bad and the afternoon milking to be done."

Nodding her head, Amanda turned her attention back to the *Budget* newspaper in her hands. In the early afternoons before chores, she liked to read the paper out loud, sharing the stories of the different Amish communities from around the country with her *daed*.

"Daed, you know the Yoders from Walnut Creek, *ja*?" She looked up and waited for her *daed* to nod his head. "Says here that his *mamm* just celebrated her ninety-fifth birthday!"

"Can you imagine?" Mamm gasped, tsk-tsking with her tongue. "Ninety-five years!"

"Seems like they had a big birthday celebration, says here," Amanda continued. "Over a hundred and twenty-five people!" She set the paper down and looked at her *daed*. "Can you imagine the size of that cake?"

Elias tried to smile. "Big, *ja*?"

Lizzie set down her sewing and looked out the window. Amanda glanced at her, studying the serious expression on her mother's face. She had aged, Amanda realized, more than she should have over the past few years. Amanda imagined that a lot of that had to do with Aaron's death but certainly the other recent events could not have helped. For a moment, Amanda felt pity for her mother. How life could change so quickly, she pondered.

"I'm just not liking this weather," Lizzie muttered, turning to her husband and *dochder*. "Amanda, go on out and see if Harvey needs help," she ordered. "Looks like another snowstorm is brewing, and he best be heading home if that's the case."

Obediently, Amanda set down the paper, folding it neatly before she did so. With a smile, she reached out and touched her *daed*'s shoulder. "We'll read more later, *ja*?" She didn't wait for his response before she hurried toward the door, pausing for a moment to wrap a thick black shawl around her shoulders before she slipped outside.

It was good to be outside, she thought. The house was depressing to her. With her *daed* being immobile and her *mamm* fretting so much over everyone and everything, there was a thick sense of gloom permeating the room. She felt out of place and didn't like the feeling. What had been so familiar to her not that long ago now seemed foreign. She found herself missing not just Alejandro but the world of the Englische. Or, she corrected herself, *his* world of the Englische.

As she walked into the barn, she noticed that two kerosene-powered lanterns were already burning. The bright glow from the lanterns also threw off some heat, so once she entered the barn, she was pleased that the air was not bitter cold.

"Harvey," she called out cheerfully. "Mamm sent me to help you now."

"Over here," his voice called out from the back of the barn.

Amanda walked in the direction of the voice, ducking under a metal bar in between two cows so that she didn't have to walk all the way around in order to get to Harvey. It was early to be milking the cows that stood at the back of the barn. When she approached him, he looked up and nodded his appreciation for her assistance.

"Would be mighty happy if you helped me, Amanda," he said. "Radio in the car said we're due for a big storm tonight. I'd sure like to make it home before the snow starts."

"A big storm?" she repeated, clicking her tongue. "In early December. My oh my! Must be a strong winter ahead of us, then!"

He nodded his head as he placed his cheek against the flank of the cow he was milking. "So I heard," he commented but then concentrated on the task at hand.

Amanda knew better than to break his concentration. Harvey preferred to work in silence, his thoughts his only companions. She didn't know whether he was reflecting on things of a personal nature or strictly focusing on the milking.

The silence was fine by her, however. She put on a dirty apron to protect her clothing and hurried to the line of cows waiting to be milked. The heat of the cow's flank warmed her cheek, and she breathed in the musky scent of its hide. She knew that she'd be leaving soon, and while eager to return to her life with Alejandro, she also knew that she'd miss the farm.

With so much travel ahead of them, she wasn't certain when she would return. Surely they would have time to visit in the summer, she told herself. But just as soon as she thought that, she realized she didn't have any idea whether that was true. Alejandro had his South American tour, and then he had mentioned something about Europe. At some point, he would need to relax, and for that she was certain he would want to be in Miami. And, of course, he'd want to head out to Los Angeles, spending a few weeks in the summer at their apartment outside of Beverly Hills so that he could work on his new recordings.

Perhaps, Amanda thought sadly, there would be no joint return to the farm. If anything, she'd most likely return on her own for a short visit while Alejandro was on the road. With his busy schedule and constant travel, finding a few days to vacation together seemed nearly impossible.

It was a half hour later when the buggy pulled into the driveway and Jonas appeared in the dairy. He apologized to Harvey for his late arrival and quickly got to work. Amanda finished what she was doing and carried a full bucket of milk to the containment system in the back room. Glancing out the window, she noticed that Anna was unhitching the horse from the buggy.

Amanda set the empty bucket on the ground and wiped her hands on the front of her apron as she hurried toward the barn door. The sting of the cold air sent a chill up her spine, and she wrapped her arms around her chest. Snow indeed, she thought as she glanced up into the sky.

"Let me help," Amanda said as she approached her sister in the driveway. "Faster with two sets of hands, *ja*?"

Anna smiled her appreciation and the two of them quickly began to unharness the horse from the buggy. "How was your visit, then?" Amanda asked as she lifted one of the buggy's shafts to help move it inside the barn before the snow fell.

"Right *gut*," Anna replied. "So nice to see the family. Such a shame they couldn't come to Ohio for the wedding."

Amanda thought back to her own wedding and smiled. It would have been nicer if her family could have been there, but with that one exception, she wouldn't have changed anything else about that day. Besides, she realized, Alejandro's family and religion were so different from the Amish that she knew they would not have appreciated the ceremony in the same way that she had.

With the horse wiped down and the buggy safely stored away, Amanda and Anna hurried back into the house. After hanging up their coats, they stood by the heater and tried to warm up.

"So tell me about our cousins, Anna," Amanda began. "I haven't seen them in such a long time. I should have ridden along with you and Jonas, I reckon."

The chime on her cell phone rang, announcing a text message. Amanda stopped speaking in midsentence and hurried over to pick up the phone on the counter where she had left it. A smile was on her face as she slid her finger across the phone to unlock it and read her message. The thought crossed her mind that he had not called her but texted her instead. However, she figured he had been busy with interviews and recording, whatever Mike and his publicist had put on his schedule.

Only the message was not from Alejandro.

It was a photograph from an unknown number. And it was of Alejandro. But he was not alone and, from the looks of it, he was intoxicated. His glasses were atop his head, his eyes bloodshot, and his skin pale. The smile on his face was lopsided and not the typical expression of control that he wore.

That, however, was not what concerned her the most. It was the way his arm was wrapped around a woman's neck, pulling her close to him, her head almost resting on his shoulder. And it wasn't just any woman; it was Maria.

Maria wearing the very same white bathrobe with the pink embroidered A over a rose that Alejandro had gifted to Amanda on their first trip to LA. Maria with her blond hair in an updo, tendrils dripping down her neck. Maria with sparkling earrings and a necklace that brought attention to her bare chest peeking out from under the garment.

Maria in the arms of Amanda's husband.

"What's wrong, Amanda?"

She could barely tear her eyes away from the photograph on her phone. Briefly, she glanced at her *mamm* and *schwester* but merely shook her head. There were no words that could pass her lips. She knew that the color had drained from her face. She felt her hands trembling.

And then the chime rang again.

Another photo. This one was worse than the first. She shut her eyes and said a silent prayer. Please God, she prayed. Make this not be true. But when she opened her eyes, she saw that her prayer was not answered. The photograph was still there. The photograph of Maria and Alejandro walking into the lobby of a building together, his arm slung around her neck. There was no question what the insinuation meant. What was worse, she recognized the building: their condominium in Los Angeles.

Trying to maintain her composure, Amanda took a deep breath and shut off the phone. She set it down on the table, facedown, and lifted her eyes to meet the curious gazes of her mother and sister. "It's nothing," she said, forcing a smile that hurt her soul. The lie pained her, but she knew that she could never share those photos with her family. They'd never understand something that she, herself, could barely comprehend.

"Think I'll go outside for a spell," she mumbled.

She was partially down the walkway when she heard the screen door open and footsteps on the porch. "Amanda!" her sister called as she ran toward her. "Your shawl! You'll catch cold!" With great affection, Anna wrapped the wool shawl around Amanda's shoulders and tucked it tightly under her chin. She spared her a smile and said, "If you need to talk . . ."

Amanda nodded but could not speak. She was struggling to fight back the tears and the painful lump in her throat. She needed to be alone. Talking wasn't going to help, not this time. "I'm fine," she managed to say, knowing that her voice was not as convincing as the words she had spoken.

Turning her back toward the house, she let her feet take her down the road. She stared at nothing as she walked, breathing in the crisp air and listening to the crunching of the snow under her shoes. The noise created a filter in her mind; she could only use it as an escape from the thoughts that were causing darkness in her heart.

As she approached the end of the lane, she ignored the paparazzi that had, once again, set up a twenty-four-hour team, just in case something happened in the wee hours of the night that warranted reporting to the rest of the world. Their reemergence at the farm didn't surprise her, and she suspected that they, too, had been privy to those photos of Alejandro and Maria. They snapped her photograph, eager to report to the world how Viper's wife had responded to the news that he had spent the evening with another woman.

Only their presence didn't matter to her, not in her current state of mind.

Anyone could have sent her those photos, she realized. Even the paparazzi could have sent them, eagerly awaiting her reaction to such heartbreaking images of her husband seeking comfort in Maria's arms.

But Amanda didn't care. For the moment, her only thought was to concentrate on trying to calm down and control her emotions. It would do no one any good to fall apart, she told herself, knowing that falling apart was the one thing she wanted to do.

Her mind traveled back to the argument that they had had prior to her leaving. Her tears on account of that awful video had been mirrored by the tears she had cried on her flight back to Philadelphia. Since their separation, their communications had been stressed, that was undeniable. But to think that Alejandro would slip so carelessly into his Viper mindset and be seen in public with another woman, especially that Maria? To take her in his arms? To bring her to their home? To do something so unthinkable?

She could not even finish her train of thought! The images in her mind caused her stomach to twist and turn, an ache that spread throughout her body.

Her feet carried her down the road, unconcerned by the slow-moving car behind her. Let them take photos, she thought bitterly. All they will see is my back, and what interest would that be to the insatiable fans? Immediately, she recognized the bitterness in her own feelings. In her entire life, she had never felt this way, and the feeling completely drained her emotions while darkening her heart.

Please, God, from whom all blessings flow, guide me through this in the true manner of being your child.

She felt a wave of nausea and hurried to the side of the road. Tears streamed down her cheeks as she bent down and vomited. Her back convulsed from her predicament, and she didn't care that the photographers in the car following her were taking picture after picture at a frenzied pace, having finally found what they were out to get: a photo of the despondent Amanda, the most famous Amish woman in the world and now the most brokenhearted.

Chapter Twenty-Three

When he finally awoke, the room was dark and he had no idea what time it was. A thin trickle of light shone in through the crack in the curtains, which had been shut. By whom, he had no idea. His head ached and his eyes felt bleary. Groaning, he rolled over in the bed, tossing an arm over his forehead as he thought back to the previous evening. What had happened? How had he returned to the condo?

After a few minutes, he slid his legs over the side of the bed. He leaned his elbows on his knees as he rubbed his face. He remembered being angry with Maria at the after-party, how she continued to cling to his arm and linger nearby with those other women. But after hanging with Dricke Ray and Justin Bell, he had begun to loosen up a bit. And then they had convinced him to sing, something that he did not need much encouragement to do.

After that, too many people had sent over congratulatory drinks to him. As his head lightened, so did his mood. Dancing, laughing, photos with the different ladies. For a few hours, he had been Viper, living *la vida loca*, the crazy life that he had abandoned only a few short months earlier. Now, the morning after, as he tried to piece together the fuzzy missing sections of the previous night, he realized that the switch had been far too easy for him. He had forgotten what it was like to be young and wild and free. He had forgotten what it felt like to be among adoring fans and sexy women. And he had forgotten the fact that he was married and wildly in love with his wife.

Amanda!

He scrambled for his phone, and despite his still-unfocused eyes, he punched at the buttons so that it turned on, the clock clearly displaying 1:04 p.m. Had he truly slept that late? He searched his memory, trying to recall if he had any appointments today. Probably. When didn't he have appointments? he thought bitterly. Mike would have to deal with his no-show appearance.

"Hey, you're awake!"

The female voice from the doorway startled him. He jumped and quickly looked in the direction from where her voice came. Leaning against the doorframe in a sheer white dressing gown was Maria, her blond hair hanging over her shoulder in wild curls. As always, her makeup was impeccable and she was the vision of beauty. But it was the glow in her eyes that scared him.

She crossed the room and handed him a white mug with hot coffee. "Black, the way you like it, baby," she said, a knowing smile on her face.

He didn't speak as he took it from her, a sense of dread building within his chest.

She took his silence for an unspoken invitation and sat down on the bed next to him, too close for his comfort. "Wow!" she said, laughing lightly as she flipped her hair over her shoulder. The curl immediately swooped back across her cheek in that particularly unique Maria type of way. "That was some party last night, *sí*?"

He sipped at the coffee, knowing that she was going to tell him whatever he needed to know. She always did. He also knew that it would serve no purpose to admit that he barely remembered what had happened and was extremely curious as to why she was in his condo. In due time, he told himself, she will tell me, no doubt.

She reached out and ran her fingers through his hair. He stiffened at her touch, but she ignored it. "I can't *believe* what we did last night," she laughed, tilting her head back. Her hair brushed against his bare skin. "That was so much fun! I'll simply never forget it!"

"Maria . . ." He reached up with his free hand and brushed away her touch. "Stop."

Despite his protest, her hand lingered on his shoulder. "It's so good to have my Viper back," she whispered and leaned over to kiss at his neck. The gesture shocked him. It was too unexpected. Even more unexpected was the familiar way in which she had done it. As if he shouldn't have been surprised. As if he should have expected it. As if it was the most natural act in the world between the two of them.

Abruptly, he stood up. His heart was pounding. He needed time alone . . . time to think and collect himself. He searched his memory, fighting the cloud of mystery that hung over the throbbing in his temples. He tried to think why she would have kissed him, why she had entered his room, and, most important, why she was even there.

"You need to leave, Maria," he said, his tone low and even. Get in control, he told himself. Control the situation. "I'm not sure how you managed to get in here, but it's time to leave."

She laughed again and leaned back on the bed, one leg bent seductively. "You invited me," she purred, her eyes drooping just enough to indicate that she was flirting with him. "Multiple times, Viper."

He shut his eyes and clenched his fist. No, no, no, he screamed to himself. "Please get out," he said calmly.

She laughed, a noise that sounded more sinister than friendly. "Oh, Viper," she said softly. "I don't think you mean that."

What have I done? He wanted to scream at the top of his lungs, to wake up and find that this was just a bad nightmare. Yes, he had gone out with Dricke Ray and some of the usual entourage after the Jingle Ball. Clearly, he had consumed far too much alcohol. But to actually break his sacred marriage vow to Amanda? Impossible, he told himself.

"Maria," he said calmly. "I have asked you to leave. It's time." He stared at the wall, waiting to hear movement . . . the rustling of sheets, her footsteps on the padded carpet, the noise of a door opening. Instead, he heard nothing. When he looked over his shoulder and saw that she had made no move to exit, a mischievous smirk on her face, he hissed at her. *"¡Ahora!"*

She gasped and hurried off the bed. With narrowed eyes, she faced him and met his glare with her own. "It was only a matter of time, Alejandro!" she snarled, venom in her voice. "Marrying a quaint little farm girl and thinking you could change!" She laughed. "A tiger's stripes can fade, but they never go away; a tiger never stops being a tiger." Tilting her chin into the air, she smiled at him smugly. "Neither does a player!"

"Andres!" he shouted, calling for his security guard. It took a few minutes for the large man, dressed all in black, to appear in the open bedroom door. "Please escort this young . . ." He hesitated, trying to force himself to remain composed. ". . . Woman to the exit."

"I don't need an escort," she snapped as she hurried toward the bathroom to change into her clothes. It only took her a few minutes to emerge, a small bag in her hand and dressed in a plain body-hugging dress with tall black stilettos. For a moment, he frowned, wondering about her change of clothes.

He waited until he heard the door to the suite shut before he allowed himself to pick up his phone and walk to the large, plush white chair by the window. Sinking into it, he used one finger to pull back the curtain and winced, as if in pain, at the bright light.

The phone felt heavy in his hand. He had to call Amanda. Surely she was waiting for him. He hadn't called after the awards ceremony to tell her the good news. There hadn't been time. He had been whisked behind the stage where reporters and photographers were lined up to interview him. It was a gauntlet, moving from one station to the next, smiling into the cameras and repeating words of appreciation for having been recognized, especially given the strong competition of the other nominees.

Then he had been hurried to the dressing room where he had changed in order to perform in the final half hour. After his song, he had quickly showered and changed once again before leaving the venue and heading to the after-party.

And that's where the trouble had begun.

Drinks, toasts, congratulations, celebration. The music, the laughter, the pride of having won the award. It had been too much, and after weeks of not having partied with his entourage, it had gone to his head. Slipping back into the role of Viper had apparently been easier than he thought.

He stared at the phone, which seemed to stare right back at him, mocking him, for he knew that he needed to call Amanda, but he had no idea what he was going to say. He had never lied to her, never really lied to anyone, except during his bad days on the streets of Miami. If only he could remember everything . . .

"Viper?"

He looked up at Andres, who stood in the open doorway. *"¿Sí?"*

"Mike is here to see you."

Alejandro frowned and shook his head. There was no way that he could see Mike right now. His mind was swarming, his temples were throbbing, and he felt weak in the knees. He had to collect himself, had to sort his jumbled thoughts. "Tell him later."

There was no need to tell Mike anything, for he stormed through the bedroom doors. "What did you do last night, Alex? You missed your morning appointment and now you're late for your interview! My phone is ringing off the hook!"

"Not now," Alejandro responded, walking past his manager and heading toward the bathroom. He slammed the door shut and turned on the faucet. The cold water poured down the drain, and he quickly splashed it over his face. It felt good, calming him down for a moment as he stared into the mirror.

Glimpses came back to him. The music was loud. The lights were flashing. And Maria had been by his side the entire night. They had danced; he remembered that much quite clearly. She had tried to kiss him at the nightclub, but he had pushed her away. That image came to him, too. But how had she managed to wind up in his condo? Had he truly invited her to accompany him? Had he been so intoxicated that he had betrayed his marriage vows?

Knowing that Mike was going to wait until he reappeared, Alejandro took his time. He switched on the shower and waited until the steam began to cloud the mirror. Only then did he strip and step inside, the hot water pouring over his head and down his back. His muscles began to relax, and he leaned one hand on the wall, his head hanging down as he tried to reconcile himself to the fact that, indeed, he had no memory of what had actually happened.

He cursed out loud and punched at the wall.

In all of his years as a grown-up man, he had never been faithful to a woman. He did not feel the need for it, and neither did they. He hadn't expected anything different from those few women with whom he had relationships, either. Life was too short to be committed to one person, he had always explained. If nothing else, he had been honest about his infidelity. No one could ever claim that he was less than up front.

His entire reputation and image as Viper had been built upon that model. It was expected that he would leave clubs with different women each night and surround himself with any number of gorgeous hangers-on. His life was about living it, never about settling down. And the fans seemed to thrive on it, for he did it with style and class. When other celebrities fought the tabloids for reporting on their philandering ways, Viper had embraced them, and, as a result, his adoring public rewarded him with more loyalty than any other star.

But that had all changed when he met Amanda. He had evolved, and as unlikely as it had seemed at the time, the fans had changed along with him. His devotion to Amanda changed his image, and the public ate it up.

He remembered all too well that Mike had chastised him, telling him that a married Viper would never make it in the industry. The public would never accept it, Mike had claimed. Alejandro had proved him wrong. Viper was a different man, and the fans liked what they saw.

It had never crossed Alejandro's mind that once dedicated to Amanda, he might not be able to give up his ways. How would she react to infidelity? How would the public react? The realization that these two questions were something he needed to face struck him as if someone had punched him in the stomach. The truth was that he had been unfaithful. A night of debauchery and lust had stolen his senses, forced him to his knees, and possibly ruined his life.

He shut his eyes and wished that he would wake up again, wake up alone and with the taste of a bad nightmare in his mouth instead of stale liquor. He wished that everything he was currently feeling would simply disappear. But he knew that it wouldn't. He had to face the facts that he had awoken in his bed, the morning stained by the memory of another woman. He couldn't deny it. It was something he had to face. After all, Amanda was better than that. She *deserved* better than that.

How could I have done something like this? His mind fought hard to try to make sense of the situation. He loved Amanda, loved her with his entire soul and being. Yet the truth was that he had awoken with another woman in his apartment. Had nothing changed? He was left wondering if Maria had been right. A tiger's stripes never go away. They just may fade a little.

"¡Dios *mío!*" he muttered and abruptly turned off the water. He would have to confess to Amanda, to let her know that something had happened and he had no memory of it. There was no way that he could live with himself by pretending last night hadn't happened. She would forgive him. He took a deep breath at that thought. Yes, forgiveness was something that ran deep in the Amish culture and religion.

With a towel wrapped around his waist, he exited the bathroom and walked past Mike, unabashed as he headed for the closet. His head began to clear, and despite being unhappy with the choices he had made, he knew that there was a path to redemption.

"The social media has gone insane," Mike said. He was sitting in a chair by the window, the curtain now open so that bright light streamed through. Little bits of dust seemed to float in the sun rays. "They're saying Viper is back, and from the looks of it, they like it."

"Shut up, Mike," Alejandro growled. "It's not about marketing."

"Everything is about marketing!" He laughed when he said it, a laugh without any mirth. "Alex, you're an international star and you're a man, two strikes against you right there. The public will forgive your infidelity. Heck, they expect it from you!"

"It's not their forgiveness that I need!" he snapped as he slipped on a pair of freshly laundered black slacks. "You seem to be rather amused by this."

"I am," Mike admitted.

"That makes me sick."

"Come on, Alex," he said, standing up and crossing the room. "You're Viper, for God's sake. No matter how you look at it, no one can expect you to remain faithful to a little country gal who is insisting on staying in the middle of nowhere, Pennsylvania, while you're traveling the country. I mean, it's sex, right? Just sex. It doesn't mean anything."

Alejandro brushed off Mike's hand. "It means everything. And you can cancel any appointments. I'm going to Pennsylvania."

A look of panic crossed Mike's eyes. "Whoa, now slow down there, Alex. You're scheduled for Atlanta in a couple days. You can't just cancel it."

"Cancel it." The words surprised him almost as much as they surprised Mike. But as soon as the words slipped from his lips, Alejandro knew that he meant them. How could he possibly perform when he had to confess to Amanda? Too much was at risk, and he couldn't possibly afford losing the only thing that mattered to him: his wife.

Mike frowned. "You've got to be kidding me."

"Cancel them all." He slipped his arms into a white shirt and turned toward the mirror as he buttoned it. "I want the first flight out of here for Philadelphia."

There was a long moment of silence. Alejandro focused on the buttons, ignoring the piercing glare from his manager. He knew that Mike's earlier amusement at the matter of his infidelity angered him even more. The media attention was right up Mike's alley, the type of negative publicity and speculation that increased sales, despite ruining lives. In the end, the bottom line was always the money. At least for Mike.

"You cancel that concert and you're finished," Mike said slowly, his voice low. "I can't let that happen, Alex."

"If I don't go to her, then I am finished anyway." He straightened his arm and buttoned the cuff at his wrist. "Don't you get it?" He stared into the reflection of the mirror, meeting Mike's eyes. "I need to get to her before she hears about this from someone else."

"She's on a farm in the middle of Amish-land!" Mike snapped, the word "Amish-land" rolling off his tongue as if it were distasteful. "How would she hear? It's not like they have television or tabloids, for crying out loud!" He lifted his hand to his brow and rubbed at his temples. "Come on, Alex. Just two more days, and then you have a break. Just hang on. Do the Atlanta concert, and then you can go get her. Confess all that you want. But don't hang us out to dry here. You can't cancel the concert."

Frustrated, Alejandro groaned out loud and spun around, walking toward the window. He shoved the sheer curtain back and pressed his forehead against the cool glass. Atlanta, he said to himself. Just one more concert, and then he would be free to go. He had off for a week . . . Christmas week. He'd fly her down to Miami, and they could make up there, in the comfort and safety of their home.

"Fine!" he finally said. "But get her on a flight to Miami. I want her there on Tuesday when I arrive. I'm finished performing without her. I don't care what you have to do, but get her sister situated on the farm and bring her to me, Mike. I won't do this anymore if she's not with me."

Satisfied, Mike nodded. He reached for his phone and began tapping the keys as he talked. "Great! There's a flight on Tuesday at eight in the morning. I'll get her gal working on it. What's her name again? Dali?" Alejandro nodded, but Mike continued to prattle on. "And I've already rescheduled your missed appointments for later this afternoon. Let's get moving on those, Viper."

Mike headed toward the door, pausing to glance back as he slid his phone into his pocket. "Get back in the swing of things and forget about this little . . ." He gestured with his hand. "Little slipup. That's all it was, right?"

He was drained of emotion and didn't fight back. Instead, he acquiesced to Mike's demands, feeling a touch of relief that, for once, his manager was in charge of the situation and making the decisions.

Chapter Twenty-Four

She ended the call and stared out the window, the small cell phone still in her hand. For a moment, she held the phone, the warmth of the battery pressed against her palm. When it vibrated, she glanced down and noticed, yet again, another text from Alejandro. Had Dali already gotten in touch with him? Had she already relayed the message?

Angry, Amanda turned the power off, waiting for the screen to turn gray before completely shutting down. Setting the phone on the windowsill, she turned around and tried to block out the feelings of pain and hurt that flowed through her. She hadn't wanted to speak to Dali that way, not when Dali was caught playing the intermediary.

For the past two days, he had been trying to reach her. Amanda had refused his calls and ignored his texts. If she had known how to forward those horrible photos to his phone, she would have. However, from the content of his texts, he knew why she was not responding: the media had already jumped all over the story that Viper had spent the evening in his Los Angeles condominium with another woman. The tabloids were eager to fill in the missing pieces that Amanda had already visualized. Clearly, he suspected that she had heard the gossip.

Had he known that someone had leaked the photos via text to her phone, she imagined he would have been horrified.

And then Dali had called.

There had been no warm-and-fuzzy greeting. As usual, Dali jumped right to the point. "He wants you to fly to Miami," Dali had said. "I can have a car picking you up at five thirty in the morning tomorrow."

For some reason, Dali's directness had incensed Amanda. Whether it was her assumption that Amanda would just go along with the famous "schedule" without an argument or whether it was Alejandro's presumption that she would be so quick to forgive a transgression of such magnitude and come running to him, she had felt angry once again. It was a feeling she wasn't used to, at least not prior to the past few days. Now, anger had become part of her life, and that was something Amanda didn't like one bit.

"Cancel it, Dali," Amanda had heard herself say into the phone, turning to look out the window, her finger tracing circles in the frosted glass. "I'm not going."

On the other end of the phone, there had been a pause, just long enough for Dali to collect her thoughts, Amanda suspected. Standing up for her own rights was not something that anyone expected from Amanda.

"That's not what he wanted," her assistant replied.

Amanda could hear papers shuffling in the background. She imagined Dali was staring at the Miami schedule, quickly calculating all of the appointments that had been scheduled for Amanda. It gave her a hint of satisfaction to realize that Dali would be inconvenienced canceling them. She wasn't certain why she was so irritated at Dali, but she was.

"He was rather clear . . ."

"Dali!" Amanda had interrupted abruptly. "I'm not his possession!" The harshness of her words surprised even Amanda. She had never before spoken in anger to another person. That was not the Amish way. Trying to take a deep breath and calm down, Amanda tried again. "You'll just have to explain to him that I simply won't be flying to Miami tomorrow."

Another pause. For a moment, Amanda had thought that their connection had failed. But when she heard Dali clear her throat, she had known that the silence was from the shock at Amanda's defiance to Alejandro's request.

"He won't like this," Dali had mumbled.

"He knows why," was all that Amanda had replied before politely ending the call.

Anna looked up as Amanda walked into the kitchen. Jonas was outside with Harvey as they mucked the stalls and dairy. Daed had happily joined them, bundled in a heavy coat with a thick blanket across his legs. Mamm had pushed his wheelchair outside, eager for her own breath of fresh air. It had been only a few minutes after everyone left that Amanda's cell phone had rung and she had escaped to the privacy of the *grossdaadihaus* to speak to Dali.

"Was that Alejandro, then?" Anna asked, a warm smile on her face. Her hands were buried in fresh dough, flour covering the front of her apron. "I reckon he'll be happy to see you again. It's been a few weeks, *ja*?"

"A week," Amanda retorted, her voice flat and emotionless. "I flew out to Kansas last weekend, remember?"

"*Ach, ja!*" Anna turned her attention back to the dough. "Mamm told me about that. What was it like? Kansas?"

Sliding onto the bench, Amanda shrugged. She didn't feel like talking. "Who knows? You fly in at night, get whisked away, and then return before you have a chance to see anything. I hardly even remember the airport, never mind the state."

Clicking her tongue against the roof of her mouth, Anna shook her head. "Such a pity," she said as she kneaded the dough. "To travel such a distance only to turn around and return so fast. It's a shame he doesn't get to enjoy those places more."

Amanda wanted to tell her sister that she thought Alejandro had enjoyed Los Angeles far too much during this last stay. But she held her tongue. It would do no good to hang her dirty laundry on the clothesline for everyone to see.

Her heart felt heavy, and she disappeared inside her thoughts. She had to figure out her next step. At some point, she reasoned with herself, she had to confront Alejandro and hear his version of the story. She remembered the Bible verse in Luke about forgiving those who confess their sins. It had seemed so easy to do when she was reading the Bible. Now, however, when she was faced with having to actually do it, she realized how difficult Jesus's directive truly was. She had never heard of such a thing as adultery among the Amish. She had suspected that it existed, although it was very rare, but it was not something that would be made public or mentioned in the *Budget* at least. If it did happen, well, it would have to be strictly dealt with by the couple. Probably suppressed and forgiven, if not forgotten, because divorce was virtually unknown and considered unholy by the Amish. It was, simply, not in their way of life. But then again, she pondered, she had not taken her kneeling vows, so was she really, truly Amish?

Maria, she thought with a sour taste in her mouth and a hollow feeling inside her chest. How could he have allowed that woman into their apartment? How could he have tainted their marriage with such an awfully brazen and unchristian person? How could he have so little respect for the commitment they had made to each other?

Despite wanting to cry, Amanda had no more tears left. She had cried them all over the course of the previous few evenings in the solitude of the *grossdaadihaus*. Each morning, when she had awoken, her eyes had been puffy; she had splashed cold water on her face for a few minutes before resorting to a cool cloth to calm the swelling.

But her family had noticed.

That first morning, after she had received the images of her husband in another woman's arms, the tears had still been fresh in her eyes. Indeed, no sooner had she walked into the kitchen than she had noted the quizzical look on her *mamm*'s face and the worried frown on her sister's. Yet, in true Amish fashion, no questions were asked. Privacy was respected in all situations. They knew that if Amanda wanted to share what was troubling her, she would do it in her own time.

A buggy pulled into the driveway. Amanda didn't have to look to know that it was most likely the bishop. He was the only one who dared visit anymore, especially since the paparazzi had returned after the Jingle Ball concert. The fact that they were so eager for a photograph of her added to her irritation. Was heartache something that lifted up the souls of the fans?

When the bishop walked into the kitchen, he removed his hat and cleared his throat. Anna greeted him with a smile. He had been to the house before, spending time getting to know Jonas prior to welcoming him into the *g'may*. In anticipation of the interview, Jonas had arranged for a letter from the bishop of his former *g'may* in Ohio so that he could present it to the leaders of Anna's church district. No one had anticipated any problems as Jonas was clearly going to be a valuable addition to the community.

However, the silence that continued in the kitchen indicated to Amanda that the bishop was not there to visit with Jonas or Anna.

"A word, Amanda," the bishop had said uncomfortably.

Since the incident at the grocery store, Amanda had noticed a new attitude from the bishop toward her. While it wasn't warm and friendly like it had been before she had married Alejandro, there was a new hint of understanding in the way he addressed her. Distant understanding but an understanding, nevertheless.

"Something wrong, Bishop?" she asked, wondering what this was about. Most likely the paparazzi's return to the community in such numbers. "You may speak in front of my *schwester*."

He took a step toward Amanda and reached into his pocket. "This came to my attention just yesterday," he said, his aged fingers unfolding the piece of newspaper that he withdrew from his coat. Again, he cleared his throat as he handed it to her. She didn't need to look at it in order to know what it was.

The photo of Alejandro with Maria in the suggestive pose glared at her from the pages of the tabloid newspaper. She had expected to see it. However, there were two new photos on the page, a picture of Alejandro with several women dressed in Amish clothing standing behind him, their hands on his shoulders. The shock of such a photo left her speechless. Not only had he dishonored their marriage vows, but now he was mocking her religion as well? But the worst one was the larger picture in the middle, showing her, Amanda, bent at the waist and obviously vomiting on the side of the road, on the night that she had found out about his infidelity. There was a caption under it that said: "Will Viper's naïve and unsuspecting young Amish wife be able to . . . stomach the star's new antics?"

She blinked her eyes to force back the tears that were quickly threatening to fall.

Sensing her discomfort, the bishop glanced toward the window. "I see that the camera people have returned. I imagine this is why, *ja*?"

Amanda couldn't respond, the humiliation of the moment far too great for any words to form on her lips. She merely nodded her head, her eyes still on that horrible photo. It was just like an advertisement; she saw that right away. Swallowing hard, she tried to accept the fact that he had used her Amish upbringing as a promotional tool to help build his image. Her frustration turned to fury, and she crumpled the paper in her hand, not needing to read the article that accompanied the photographs.

The bishop cleared his throat once again. This was uncharted territory for him. Amanda regretted that his discomfort was caused by choices she had made in her life. "Amanda," he finally said, shuffling his hat in his hands. "If you need some counseling . . ." He did not finish the sentence.

"Counseling?" She looked up upon hearing the word.

"Spiritual, of course," the bishop added.

"I see," she replied. She was disappointed. She hadn't lost faith in God, only in Alejandro. She wasn't certain how spiritual guidance would help with that. "*Danke*, Bishop."

"I trust the camera people will lose interest and disappear soon, *ja*?"

Ah, she thought bitterly. *"Ja,"* Amanda said, knowing that it was what he wanted to hear. With Christmas just a week away, the last thing that the Amish community wanted was photographers interfering with such a holy celebration. "They will, I'm sure," she added.

"Gut," he said, satisfied with her answer. "Now, I should like to visit with Elias. Is he in the *haus*?"

Anna directed him toward the barn and watched as the bishop bade them both good-bye before leaving to walk through the chilled air to the dairy. For a few long moments, the kitchen remained silent, Amanda staring at the crumpled piece of paper in her hand while Anna stared at her.

"Schwester," Anna started, moving to the table where Amanda sat. "If you want to talk, I am here."

Forcing a smile that she didn't feel, Amanda reached out and touched her hand. *"Danke*, Anna," she said, genuinely touched by her *schwester's* concern. "But there is nothing to talk about." She stood up and walked to the wood-burning stove in the corner of the kitchen. Opening the front door to it, she tossed the paper inside and watched as it immediately caught fire. "Nothing at all," she whispered, staring at the blaze until the flames began to die out, the paper now nothing more than a pile of fluttering black ashes.

Chapter Twenty-Five

"How good of you to join us," Mike sneered, glancing at the clock on the wall as Alejandro walked through the door into the recording studio. He wore a simple pair of black slacks and a black short-sleeved polo. He flipped his sunglasses up so that they rested atop his head. There was a carefree manner about his gait, despite being greeted by a visibly angry manager. "You're two hours late, Alex! We've got people on the clock waiting for you!"

Alejandro glared at him. "They'll get paid!" He knew he sounded testy, and he didn't care. Ever since his return to Miami, when Amanda did not show up and continued to refuse his calls, Alejandro's temper was increasingly short with Mike. His manager's lack of empathy and compassion grated on his nerves.

"That's not the point," Mike snapped back.

"That *is* the point. It's always the point. The money is what matters, *sí?*"

"Aw, Jesus," Mike said, running his fingers through his hair and turning around. "What is this? I mean, come on, Alex! We have songs to record and people on payroll. All you can do is mope around and bark at people."

Alejandro ignored him, walking over to the mixing board, leaning down to speak to the producer, Joel, seated before it. "What have you got so far?"

"Backing tracks were recorded last week, but I may want to re-record the drums. Just need your vocals, and we can begin tweaking it," he replied. "Need to capture your levels when you're ready."

"Bueno." Alejandro strolled past Mike and opened the door that led to the iso booth, the soundproof room where vocals were recorded. Once inside, he reached for a bottle of water that was waiting for him on the stool near the microphone. "Play me the track so far," he called out.

Within seconds, music filled the iso booth and Alejandro listened intently, his head bobbing in time to the beat. He ignored Mike, who stood behind the glass window, his arms crossed over his chest and a scowl on his face. When the music ended, Alejandro nodded his head. "Not bad," he called out. "Now let's get the demo rolling. You can start recording whenever."

He set the bottle of water down on the stool and reached for his sunglasses, folding them up to hang on the front of his shirt before reaching for the earphones. Once he put them on, all noise was drowned out except for what was piped through them.

For the next hour, he sang into the large diaphragm microphone that was hidden behind the pop filter. Several times, Joel played it back for Alejandro, who would give it a thumbs-up or thumbs-down, depending on how he felt the vocals sounded. During the entire time, Mike continued to stand there, scowling. Not once did Alejandro acknowledge the man's presence, nor did he ask for any input from his manager, a fact that continued to visibly infuriate him.

They took a short break, and Alejandro reached into his pocket for his smartphone. He glanced down at the screen after typing in his passcode. It was blank. Clenching his jaw, he rolled his eyes to look up at the ceiling for a moment. He had texted Amanda earlier in the morning. Still no response. It had been days since Dali had given him the message that Amanda was refusing to leave Pennsylvania to meet him in Miami.

In the meantime, Mike had booked his days with appointment after appointment: meetings with producers, corporate executives, interviewers, radio shows. He had signed on to endorse an energy drink that was popular with the upper- and middle-class Caucasian teenage population. The marketing team wanted to break into the Latino market, and Viper would be the face for their product line.

And then there had been meetings with the choreographers, who had put together new dance routines for the dancers, some moves that would appeal more to the South American market when that leg of the tour began.

Through all of this, Alejandro barely listened in the meetings, relying on Mike to summarize everything afterward. Instead of paying attention to the talking heads in suits seated around conference tables, Alejandro was fighting the pain in his heart, knowing that Amanda had somehow seen the tabloids' fodder about Maria staying at their condo in Los Angeles after the Jingle Ball. Her abrupt shunning was all the evidence that he needed to know that she knew the truth.

"We need to talk," Mike said behind him.

Alejandro held up his hand. "Not now," he snapped.

"What is *wrong* with you?" Mike demanded, the frustration more than apparent in his voice.

Ignoring him, Alejandro pushed a few buttons on his phone and then held it to his ear. He waited a few seconds, the line ringing on the other end, until someone picked it up. "Dali? Have you heard from her?"

"I have not, Viper," she said apologetically.

"Keep trying."

When he ended the call, he turned around, surprised to see Mike still standing there. There was a look of contempt in his eyes as he stared at his manager. It was a look that was returned in kind. "Alex," Mike began. "Don't forget you are showcasing at the Liv Nightclub. You have to snap out of this mood."

"I'm not in a mood," he retorted.

"Really?" Mike snorted. "Then what would you call this?"

Alejandro shook his head, refusing to answer Mike's question. "Just send a car to get me after the shows. I'm not hanging out there afterward."

Mike grimaced, clearly annoyed with Alejandro's announcement. "Are you trying to kill your career?"

"What does it matter at this point?" He didn't wait for a response before he grabbed the bottle of water and left the iso booth. With the door open, he knew that Mike could hear him as he said, "Joel, I'm done for the day. See what you can use from that, and if you need it, we'll schedule another session." Slipping his sunglasses on, he turned and passed through the door, unfazed by the furious look on his manager's face as he watched his client walk away from the recording session.

Sitting under the cabana, he absentmindedly spun his smartphone on the table with two fingers as his mind wandered. Ever since Dali had delivered Amanda's message, he had barely been able to concentrate. His concert in Atlanta had been the first after the Jingle Ball, and he had done his best to appear nonchalant about the situation, despite the stares and whispers from the people who surrounded him.

"Señor Diaz?"

He looked up and saw Señora Perez walking toward him, a strained look on her face. Since his return from Atlanta, her avoidance of him had not gone unnoticed. Just one more disappointed person, he thought as he responded with a weary *"¿Sí?"*

"Tu madre está aquí," she said.

His mother was here? That was a surprise and, knowing his mother, not necessarily a pleasant one. While he wanted to tell Señora Perez to inform his mother that he was busy, he knew that he couldn't put off the inevitable. *"Bueno,"* he said with a sigh. *"Traiga mi madre aquí, por favor."* He took a deep breath, trying to brace himself for the storm known as Alecia Diaz. He was, however, curious as to why she had shown up at all. He wasn't even certain that she knew he was in Miami.

"Alejandro," she said by way of a greeting.

He stood up as she crossed the patio. She wore a simple floral dress and had her beige handbag hanging over her arm. "Mami," he said as he leaned forward and embraced her. "I'm surprised to see you here, *sí?*"

Alecia lifted an eyebrow but did not respond.

"Sit, please?" He pulled out a chair for his mother, but she made no move to take a seat.

"What is this that I hear about you and Amanda?" She exhaled sharply, her nostrils flaring. "Or, rather, I read about in the tabloids. God forbid I hear anything from you directly."

Inwardly, he groaned. He should have known better. Of course, he thought wryly. Not only was this about Amanda but also about how infrequently he contacted her. "Mami . . ." he started, shaking his head as he began to attempt to defend himself, but she held up her hand and stopped him before he could speak.

"I will not see this happen again," she said, her tone completely devoid of emotion. "It was bad enough with that girl and your daughter."

He felt his spine stiffen, and he clenched his teeth. It was the one topic, the *only* topic that seemed to always come between them. "Don't go there, Mami."

"That is my granddaughter, Alejandro, and your daughter! Need I remind you of that? You have nothing to do with her. You tossed her away!"

He raised his hand to his head and tried to keep his temper in check. How dare she bring this up! "It was a one-night stand, Mami! And you know that I send money to care for the child!"

"She has a name."

Alejandro shook his head. How many years ago had that happened? He had paid his dues many times over for that mistake. More important, he had made certain that it never happened again. While he didn't want the child to suffer or live in poverty, he had never felt compelled to be involved in her life. "What does that have to do with Amanda, anyway?"

She lifted her hand and pointed her finger at him. "You have a habit, Alejandro, of walking away instead of fighting."

"That's not true, Mami!" He was angered by her words. "I'm giving her space."

Alecia made a face and waved her hand at him in disgust. "Space? No. You are going about your business and not fighting for that woman!" She lifted her chin and leveled her eyes at him. "You make this right, Alejandro! Whatever you did with that other woman, you make this right with Amanda! She is special. She deserves better."

"She won't answer my texts or respond to my phone calls," he said, the excuse sounding lame as the words slipped past his lips.

Once again, Alecia raised an eyebrow as she stared at him. He had seen that look many times during his youth, especially during his days on the streets of Miami. She had never liked the crowd that he hung around with, and she certainly didn't care for the number of times the police had shown up on their doorstep. "You seem to be able to fly around the country for interviews and other appointments, no? Are you suggesting that those are more important than your marriage?"

He shut his eyes and exhaled loudly. How could he explain to his mother that Amanda simply didn't want to see him? "She doesn't want me there," he replied.

"Do you blame her?"

"*¡Ay, Dios, Mami!*" He shook his head, lifting his hand to his forehead.

Once again, Alecia leveled her gaze at him, narrowing her eyes as she studied his face. "You have done many things wrong in your life, *mi hijo*. Now, you do something right, Alejandro." She took a step backward, a clear indication that the conversation was over, staring at him with a steely coldness that felt all too familiar to him. "Do something right *for once*," she repeated.

And with that, she turned and walked back toward the sliding doors that led into the kitchen.

He watched her disappear, his heart pounding. Out of respect, he would never tell his mother what he wanted to say. Still, after she had disappeared, he sank back into the seat and seethed, knowing all too well that, in many ways, his mother was right.

Despite the fame and the money, he had done many things wrong in his life. The one bright spot had been falling in love with Amanda. He had thought that his wild days were over when he had found her. He had been only too happy to say good-bye to his years of sleeping with strange women and loving no one but himself and his career. Amanda changed all of that: the one person who wanted nothing from him. But she had expectations, one of which was certainly fidelity.

He held his head in his hands, too strong to cry but too weak to do anything more than feel sorry for himself. He had always known who he was: a young, wild, and strong man with his eyes on the prize. Nothing ever got in the way of success. He had contemplated that prior to deciding on marrying Amanda. She would support him as well as contribute to the goals that he had in mind for himself. He was strong enough to balance both his success and Amanda. At least that was what he had thought.

Now, after what had happened in Los Angeles, he didn't know who he was anymore. He had lost faith in himself and that broke his heart almost as much as losing Amanda. The heavy feeling in his chest seemed to grow with each passing day that she refused to take his phone calls, respond to his texts, or return to Miami to be with him for the holidays.

"Where've you been, man?"

Alejandro ignored the stage manager, who was walking behind him. He was dressed all in black and wore his sunglasses, even though the Liv Nightclub was dark enough, despite the colored lights that surrounded the main floor. From where he stood, Alejandro could see the people crammed into the pit, arms in the air, laughing and dancing to the music on the stage.

Viper's appearance had not been advertised. There were moments, whenever he had downtime in Miami, when he liked to perform at the Liv or other well-known clubs. The club owners welcomed his appearance as it always added to the popularity of the venue in the subsequent weeks.

"Paolo's set is almost done," said the scrawny man with the clipboard in his hands and wire hanging from his ear. "You're up next, Viper."

He remained silent as people crowded around him, their hands moving quickly as they hooked up his earpiece while an artist touched up his makeup. Alejandro didn't move or interact with them. He focused his gaze on the back wall, paying attention to nothing that was going on around him. Instead, he sank deeper into despair. His mother's words haunted him, and he knew that, once again, he had proved incapable of doing the right thing when it came to the women in his life. Only this time, he realized, it was about one special woman . . . it was about Amanda.

"Time, Viper!"

He took a deep breath and walked onto the stage, trying to put on his game face. He smiled at the audience and lifted his arm in the air, acknowledging their cheers. The music began, and Alejandro grabbed the microphone, moving his hips and feet in time to the beat. For a moment, he felt as if he might escape the feelings of self-pity that had been drowning him since he had left Los Angeles.

The crowd was responding to him, apparently not caring that he was torn apart on the inside. They only cared about the music and the partying. As always, they were standing and dancing as Viper performed for them, the mood in the club full of energy and life.

And then, in the middle of the song, he stopped singing.

The music continued to play, the band members looking at each other as they repeated the beat, waiting for Viper to continue singing.

But he didn't.

He stood there, the microphone in his hand as he stared into the audience. After a few long moments, the band stopped playing and the audience quieted. They watched as Viper stood there, almost in a trance.

"I can't do this," he said and placed the microphone back into the stand before walking off the stage.

For a long moment, the audience stopped dancing and a silence fell upon the club. Then, after the realization hit them that Viper was not returning to the stage, people began to boo and shout, angry that he had abandoned them.

Alejandro heard them but didn't care as he passed the stunned faces of the backstage crew at the club, heading toward the dressing room.

"What just happened out there?"

It didn't surprise Alejandro that Mike was on his heels, his face red with rage as he screamed at him. As his business manager, of course

Mike would be enraged by watching his client walk offstage in the middle of a set. But Alejandro didn't care. Not anymore.

"Are you out of your mind? Have you completely lost it?"

"Leave me alone," Alejandro snapped. He felt a hold on his arm as Mike grabbed him. The shock of the gesture caused Alejandro to spin around and face his manager. "I'm finished! Cancel everything."

"Is this still about Los Angeles? Are you still wallowing in such guilt?"

Jerking his arm free from Mike's grasp, Alejandro glared at him. "Don't you talk to me about Los Angeles! You're the one who brought Maria to the concert!"

To his surprise, Mike laughed, his eyes narrowing and a smirk on his face. "I don't believe this. I never thought you'd take it this far."

For some reason, Mike's words cut through Alejandro. Taking a step forward, Alejandro leaned in close and lowered his voice. "What is that supposed to mean?"

"Oh, come on!" Mike shook his head. "Don't tell me that you didn't know!"

"Know what?"

"The whole thing was a setup! A publicity stunt," Mike snarled. "And a chance to get the real Viper back, not this . . . this lovesick Alejandro."

"What are you saying, Mike?"

Mike glanced around, too aware that people were watching from a respectful distance. He reached up and rubbed his forehead, small beads of sweat starting to form over his brow. "Nothing happened with Maria that night," he finally admitted in a low voice. "You kept talking about Amanda. Maria slept on the sofa after we put you to bed."

"We?"

"Yes, we!" Mike shouted back. "I was there!"

A silence fell between the two men as Alejandro tried to digest what Mike had just told him. And then it dawned on him. Something

Mike had said that morning. "That's how you knew to reschedule my appointments," he whispered, more to himself than to Mike. "You planned the whole thing." He lifted his eyes and glared at the man standing before him. "You let me believe . . ."

"Now, Alejandro," Mike said, holding his hands up and taking a step backward. "Your numbers are off the charts. Your concerts are sold out. If anyone knows that the bad-boy image sells, it should be you."

"You let me believe that I was unfaithful to Amanda!"

"Alex . . ."

Alejandro didn't let him finish the sentence. Within a split second, Mike was on the floor, Alejandro towering over him. Not caring who was watching, for everyone was silent and staring at the two men, one flat on his back and the other enraged above him, Alejandro pointed a finger at Mike. "You, my friend, are fired!" He didn't wait for a response as he took a step back and lifted his chin, defiantly glancing around at the people who were staring at them. He knew that this story would break in the tabloids by morning and certainly spiral out of control on social media within the hour. He didn't care. Instead he felt elated, and vindicated.

Without a word, he turned and retreated down the corridor toward the dressing rooms. Once inside, he found his cell phone and quickly punched a few numbers in it and then lifted it to his ear. The phone rang only twice. "Carlos? Get me a flight to Philadelphia. I don't care how, but I want to get there first thing in the morning. And call Rodriego to get my things ready. *¡Pronto!*"

Chapter Twenty-Six

When she answered the door, Amanda wasn't surprised to see another deliveryman standing there with a large bouquet of flowers in his arms. The flowers came every three days, like clockwork. Some days they were roses. Other days they were a mixture. But they always had the same card: *Missing you. Please speak with me. V.*

"More flowers, then?" Mamm said, tsk-tsking with her tongue, clearly disapproving. "Such an expense."

"But they sure are beautiful and brighten the room, ain't so?"

Amanda looked up at her sister. Leave it to Anna to look at the positive side and try to cheer up a bad situation, she thought.

"Never saw such pretty flowers in winter!"

Without a word, Amanda carried the flowers to the kitchen sink and set them down. She moved in a robotic fashion, not speaking and showing no emotion. It had been over a week since she had last spoken to him. Almost ten days. She knew that he had performed in Atlanta over the previous weekend and that he continued to text her multiple times during the day. But she didn't respond. How could she? Those photos of Maria in his arms and entering their condominium in Los Angeles haunted her. And if that had not been enough, the tabloids had run wild with the story. Someone had been kind enough to forward *those* stories to her attention as well.

"You best be putting those in fresh water, Amanda," her *mamm* scolded. "No sense in wasting them!"

"I'm tired," she replied, ignoring the flowers as she turned to go to her section of the *haus*. She needed to lie down. Her energy level was gone . . . had been since she had learned about Alejandro's infidelity. Her heart was heavy with grief, and her stomach churned each time she thought about it. The only things that could make her feel even a touch better were to pray and sleep. Today, sleep sounded like the better of the two options.

Not fifteen minutes had passed when she heard a knock on the door. Amanda tried to ignore it, but whoever it was persisted. Sighing, she sat up on the bed and turned toward the door. *"Ja?"*

"May I come in, then?"

Anna. Of course it was Anna. The peacemaker. *"Ja, ja,"* Amanda said with a heavy sigh and sat farther back in the bed so that she leaned against the headboard.

Anna walked in slowly, carrying two mugs in her hands. "I thought a little hot cocoa might cheer you up on such a chilly December day," she said as she handed one mug to her sister. "I even put in those yucky little marshmallows you always liked."

"They aren't yucky," Amanda said, a halfhearted smile on her face. The steam from the cocoa caressed her chin as she lifted the mug toward her lips. *"Danke, Schwester."*

The bed shifted as Anna sat down beside her. For a few long seconds, neither spoke. Instead, they sipped their mugs of hot cocoa and stared out the window. The sky was gray and hinted at more snow. Amanda couldn't help wondering if this would be a tough winter with lots of snowstorms. She had been looking forward to spending Christmas week in Miami. Now, however, it did not seem that was likely.

"What's going on, Amanda?"

Ah, she thought. Time to talk. Amanda set down the mug on the nightstand next to her bed. "I really don't know what to say," she started.

"You need to talk to Alejandro about this," Anna stated, her eyes leveled at Amanda. "You can't hide here at Daed and Mamm's. You've made a choice, and you have an obligation to the man who you married before God."

She shut her eyes and leaned her head back so that it touched the headboard. *"Ja, ja,"* she mumbled. "I know that I made a choice. I took vows before God. But so did he, Anna."

"You haven't even spoken to him, Amanda," Anna said, a hint of reproach in her voice. "It's as if you have given up on him without understanding the situation."

"Understanding? The situation?" She practically croaked the words. How could she explain this to her *schwester*? How could she expose sweet Anna to the ways of the music industry? Amanda could remember when Alejandro had first talked to her about the dark side of his world. She had been sitting on the porch, her leg broken, as he crouched before her while they talked. He had told her about sleeping with women whom he didn't know and certainly didn't love. She had learned to overcome that, knowing that the past was just that: the past. But what he had done with Maria? She wasn't certain that she could ever forgive that, despite her upbringing within a tradition that held forgiveness as one of the highest virtues.

In truth, his actions had broken her heart and, with shattered faith, forgiveness was simply impossible.

"I know what those horrid tabloids are saying," Anna said softly. "I saw one at Smart Shopper."

Amanda's mouth fell open. She had never considered that possibility. The shame of what that meant flooded over her and she covered her face with her hands. If Anna knew, that meant that others in the community knew, including her parents. Before she knew it, the tears began to stream down her cheeks and she felt the weight of the emotions that she had been holding back lift from her shoulders as she began to sob.

Her *schwester* shifted her weight on the mattress so that she was sitting closer to Amanda. She rubbed her back, trying to soothe Amanda's tears. "Now, now," she said softly. "You need to calm down, now."

"I can't," Amanda cried. "I simply can't. The thought of Alejandro with that . . . that . . ." She thought many different words, but not one of them was suited to say aloud. "Woman!" Removing her hands from her tear-streaked face, Amanda looked at Anna. "My heart broke, Anna. It simply broke. I love him so much, and to think that he could do something like this? I don't know how I can go on!"

"Shh!" Anna pulled Amanda into her arms. "Don't say such things. We all felt that way after Aaron joined Jesus. Do you remember? And we got through that, as a family. We will get through this, too."

"I'm so ashamed," Amanda sobbed. "How can I ever face anyone again in the *g'may*?"

"You can and you will."

But it was so much more than that. Amanda struggled to find the words to express to her sister exactly what she was feeling. "It will never be the same, Anna," she said, extracting herself from Anna's arms. "Nothing seems right here. Not anymore. I look around, and where I used to see such vibrant life and colors . . . *vell*, it's all black, gray, and white to me now. I will spend my days dreaming about what could've been." She paused and wiped at the tears in the corners of her eyes. "What should've been."

"It could be again, Amanda," Anna offered.

"I'd have to get used to settling," Amanda replied. "To go from that life back to this?"

"What's wrong with this?" Anna asked, no hint of any contempt in her voice. "It worked fine for us for years, ain't so?"

"After having tasted that life, Anna, I don't know if I could be plain again." She laughed through her tears. "There was something magical about those endless nights and all of the city lights in New York, Los Angeles, and Miami! So much life and so many colors!" Her laughter turned back to sobs. "All of those memories . . . just crumbling to dust with that one photo!"

"Now, Amanda," Anna said, her voice a bit more stern. "You are the one who always said not to believe those horrible tabloids. You haven't even given him a chance to explain."

"I just can't face it," she whispered through her tears.

"You can't hide here forever, either," Anna pointed out. "He *is* your husband."

"He was unfaithful to me!" Saying the words out loud hurt twice as much as having thought them over and over again in her head. There were not enough tears in her body to cry away the pain that she felt.

There was a soft knock at the door. "Amanda?" Lizzie opened the door and peered inside. "You best be coming out here, Dochder." She paused, her eyes taking in the sight of Amanda's tearstained face. She lowered her voice as she added, "He's here."

Amanda wiped at her face, staring at her *mamm* as she tried to understand what she had just said. "Who's here, Mamm?"

"From the looks of the car that just pulled in, I reckon it must be your husband."

The color drained from Amanda's face as she looked to her sister. Anna forced a smile and patted Amanda's leg in reassurance. "You can do this, Amanda," Anna said. "You've always been the strong one among us. Listen to what he has to say, and let God guide you. You can never go wrong when you cast your worries into his capable hands."

Nervously, Amanda got out of bed. Her hands were shaking as she hurried to the small mirror and looked at her reflection. Her face was blotchy from crying. There was nothing she could do about that. Not caring that her *mamm* and *schwester* were watching her, she smoothed back her hair and quickly pinched her cheeks.

She was wearing a plain black skirt and a white shirt that was tucked in at the waist. The skirt was dirty from when she had worked outside in the morning. Luckily, her shirt had been shielded from dirt as she had worn a jacket to keep herself warm.

"Come now, Amanda," her *mamm* urged and pushed the door open so that Amanda had no choice but to hurry out of the room and follow her into the main *haus*.

He was standing in the doorway, the frame of his body taking up the entire opening. His legs were apart as he stood there, and his hands were behind his back. For a split second, she had the distinct feeling that she had lived this moment before. It was the day that he had first come back for her, to rescue her from the bishop demanding that she be sent away. He had worn the same expression on his face with the same air of confidence surrounding him.

This was not the look of a man coming to confess his sins to her.

"Amanda," he said, nodding his head in her direction.

She remained silent as she stared at him, ashamed of herself for feeling her heart race and her knees weaken. She willed herself to remain strong and not to break down in tears at the sight of this man, this man whom she loved with her entire being. The very same man who had broken their marriage vows.

"Excuse me," he said, turning to Lizzie and Anna. "It's good to see you again, Lizzie. And you must be Amanda's sister?" He crossed the room to shake Anna's hand. "I wish we were meeting under different circumstances."

Anna didn't reply and lowered her eyes.

"I saw your father in the barn," Alejandro said, directing his attention back to Amanda. "He looks well."

Amanda had to blink her eyes to fight back the tears.

"*¿Permiso?*" he said to Lizzie and Anna. "I should like to speak to my wife alone."

He didn't wait for their response as he walked toward Amanda and reached for her hand. When she didn't take it, he frowned. "Come," he demanded, his voice soft but firm. "Enough is enough, Amanda. We must talk, and that is best done in private, no?" He took her hand and led her through the door toward the *grossdaadihaus*, having witnessed her walk through that same door just minutes before, a clear indication that she was staying there.

In the privacy of the *grossdaadihaus*, Alejandro released her hand and turned to stare at her. His eyes roved over her, from head to foot, as if drinking in the sight of her. For a moment, she thought he was going to pull her into his arms, embrace her, and kiss her. She felt ashamed of herself for realizing that had he done such a thing, she most likely would have let him.

"You do not return my texts or my calls." There was no accusation or tone to his statement, just the clear facts. "You did not come to Miami. Why?"

She lifted her chin.

"Ah," he said, jabbing at the air with his finger as if he had just realized why, despite the fact that they both knew what the reason was. "The tabloids, no? The story about Maria at our place in Los Angeles made its way to Lititz, Pennsylvania." He narrowed his eyes as he looked at her. "And I bet that . . . what do you call it? The Amish grapevine was quick to share that with you, no? For a community that professes to be so plain and against worldliness, they certainly like to follow the gossip in the entertainment world, no?"

"That's not fair!"

"Nor is spreading gossip!" he retorted quickly, obviously pleased that she had finally broken her silence. "Since you are so eager to believe the gossip from those god-awful tabloids, Amanda, perhaps you would like to hear some more of it."

He turned his back on her and walked toward the window. She watched as he peered outside, seeming to take in the empty fields, some with slight patches of snow on the ground that hadn't thawed out from the previous snowstorm.

"This story," he began, "it is about a man who fell in love with a woman, *sí*? Before he met her, he was carefree and full of sin. But once he met her, everything changed. It was as if God had placed this beautiful angel in his path. The man's life changed, and that change had a ripple effect." He glanced over his shoulder, pausing long enough to make certain she was paying attention. "You see, there were other people who benefited from this man's success. They didn't want him to settle down with a woman, especially a woman as special and magnificent as this particular woman. So they did everything they could to break up the relationship. They mocked her in music videos, they poked fun at her upbringing in advertisements . . ." He turned around and took a step toward her. "They even made it appear that he had been unfaithful to this woman. They convinced him, too, that he had broken his marriage vows and let him believe that he had betrayed the one woman in his entire life whom he had sworn to love, honor, and protect."

She felt her heart beat faster as she listened to his words. Was this true? Was it possible?

"The woman wouldn't take his calls nor respond to his texts. She had lost faith in him. The man wallowed in self-pity and despair. He had lost faith in himself." By now, Alejandro was standing before her. There was a sorrow in his blue eyes, something she had never seen before. And at that moment, she knew that he had been suffering as much as she had. "But it was all a lie. A lie to tear apart the man and the woman."

A single tear fell from her eye. "A lie?"

"*Sí*, Princesa," he said, nodding his head as he placed his hands on her shoulders. "It was a lie, orchestrated by the man's former manager and played out in front of the media."

"But the photos that were sent to my phone . . ."

Alejandro raised an eyebrow. "Only four people know your number, Amanda, and Mike was one of them. He must have had someone send you those photos." He reached into his pocket and pulled out a folded piece of paper. He placed it in her hand. "Here's more proof of Mike's lies."

She glanced down at the paper in her hand and unfolded it. Another tabloid article. Only this time it included a photo of Mike, flat on his back with an angry Viper hovering over him. Quickly, her eyes scanned the article, an article that told the same story as the one Alejandro had just shared with her.

"Mike set me up, Amanda," he said. "And he arranged for you to learn about it. But nothing happened between Maria and me. Mike confessed and told me that everything was a publicity stunt. One giant lie." He raised an eyebrow. "And he was consequently terminated," he added tersely.

"A lie?" She repeated the two words as if in shock. Oh, how she wanted to believe him! How she wanted to know that what he had said was the truth. But the pain of accepting this as truth would mean that she, too, had sinned by having lost faith in him. "How can I be sure, Alejandro? My heart is . . . it was broken," she said, holding back a sob that wanted to escape her throat.

"My heart was broken, too, Amanda," he admitted. "I could not continue singing onstage. That was when Mike admitted everything."

None of this made sense to her. How could someone be so cruel? Even though she never cared for Mike, their first meeting in Los Angeles over lunch having been all but disastrous, she simply could not imagine that he would do something so cruel to Alejandro. It was coldhearted and evil. As much as Mike disliked her, she knew that he cared deeply for Alejandro.

"I . . . I don't know what to say," she whispered. "If this is true . . ."

"It is true," he interrupted. "Maria admitted it, too. He paid her for it." Gently, he pinched her chin and tilted her head so that she had no choice but to look into his eyes. "Look at me, look me in the eye, and you will know that it is true. I never should have doubted myself, Amanda. I should have known it was a lie. And you should have, too."

His words cut through her, and she knew that he spoke the truth. Yet there was no reproach to his words. That, too, was painful to realize. She tried to lower her eyes as she whispered, "If this is true, then I am ashamed of myself."

It was at that moment when he pulled her into his arms, pressing her head gently against his chest while she let the tears flow from her eyes, not caring that she was sobbing. The shame of having lost faith in him, of not permitting him the chance to explain, was more than she could bear. If the thought of Alejandro having let her down was devastating, the realization that it was she who had let him down was twice as painful.

"Oh, Alejandro," she sobbed, clinging to him, unleashing the pent-up emotions that she had been trying so hard to hide, for far too long. "I'm ever so sorry!"

"Shh," he soothed, holding her as tight as he could. "You didn't know any better, and I should have."

"I thought horrible things," she admitted through her tears. "I don't think I can ever forgive myself."

"*Ay, Princesa,*" he moaned. "None of that. We have punished ourselves enough, no? We have to move beyond this and get back on track." He kissed the top of her head. "I love you more than anything, Amanda Diaz. You have to know that, Princesa."

"I do," she whispered, shutting her eyes and feeling his arms around her, a feeling that she had feared she would never experience again. "Oh, I do know that!"

For a long while, they stayed hugging, clinging to each other as they let the emotions of the past week shift into a new direction. When he finally pulled back, just enough to peer down at her, he reached up and wiped away her tears. "No more tears except for tears of joy, Amanda," he said. "In just a few days, it is Christmas. This is a joyous holiday, *sí*? And I want to give you happiness from this day forward."

"You always give me happiness," she said softly. Then, as if something dawned on her, she looked up at him. "What will we do for Christmas?"

He frowned. "What do you mean?"

"Do you have to go back to Miami?"

"Ah," he said, realizing what she meant. "We will do whatever you wish, Amanda. We can fly to Miami or we can stay here with your family. The only thing that I care about is that we are together. There will be no more of this back and forth. Not for a while, *sí*?"

She laughed through her damp eyes. *"¡Sí!"*

"Are you teasing me?" he asked, bending down just a little so that they were eye to eye. "I like it when you tease me."

"Then I shall do more of it!" she proclaimed, life slowly returning to her eyes.

Leaning forward, he kissed her lips, soft at first, but when she placed her hands on his shoulders, his kiss became stronger and more passionate. With his hands on the small of her back, he pulled her until she was pressed against his chest, his arms holding her as tight as he could. He rested his chin on top of her head, sighing as he embraced her.

"I thought I had lost you," she whispered, the tears returning to her eyes. "And it was a feeling I never want to have again."

He soothed her by rubbing his hands along her back, still holding her as tight as he could. She let the tears fall again, sobbing against his shoulder as she realized how relieved she was to not only have learned the truth but also to have him before her, holding her and comforting her. For the first time in almost two weeks, she knew that everything was going to be all right and that they could survive whatever the future would throw at them. Together, she realized, they would overcome anything.

Epilogue

The noise from the crowd was deafening, a constant roar of voices and noisemakers, with the occasional blast from a police car somewhere in the distance. The lights from the buildings lit up the area, creating an even more festive mood. Everyone seemed to be facing one direction, looking into the sky toward the roof of One Times Square. In less than thirty minutes, the ball would drop and the crowd would begin counting backward, saying good-bye to the old year and welcoming the new one.

Alejandro stood beside Amanda, his arm protectively around her waist as they waited for the security detail to indicate that it was time to leave the comfort of the building. They would then proceed to the area facing the crowd, where Alejandro would perform his last song for the year to both the people jammed into Times Square and the millions of viewers who watched from the comfort of their television screens at home.

He leaned down and nuzzled her neck, his warm breath tickling her ear. *"Te amo,* Princesa, *"* he whispered.

She smiled but did not respond.

"Ready, Viper?"

She didn't have to look to know that Alejandro had nodded to the head of security. With a slight increase of pressure on her waist, he indicated that she should walk beside him as they followed the men outside and through the cordoned-off walkway toward the stage that was set up, facing the waiting crowd. Those who stood nearby cheered when Viper emerged with his wife by his side. Unbeknownst to Amanda, a camera was simulcasting their entrance and displaying it on the enormous screen that was on the side of the Times Square building.

Despite the unusually cold temperature, Amanda found that she was warm, wrapped in the black faux-fur jacket that Alejandro had given to her just that morning. Like Alejandro, she wore dark sunglasses, which helped to shield her eyes from the bright lights shining down on them as they made their way to the stage.

He had insisted that she join him up onstage. She hadn't wanted to, proclaiming that it would be awkward for her and distract his fans. But Alejandro said he didn't care.

"I want the world to see you," he had said as they dressed in the hotel before leaving earlier that evening. "They will always see you by my side and never again will anyone have reason to question the depths of my love for you."

Now, as they climbed the stairs to the stage, Amanda took a deep breath and fought the pounding of her heart. She tried to remember where she had been the previous year at this time. Home, she thought. Home in bed, for sure and certain. The Amish certainly didn't stay up to ring in the new year, at least not the farmers who had to arise at four in the morning. After all, their daily chores didn't care whether it was the old year or the new year . . . not on a farm.

She stood toward the back of the stage, trying to stay in the shadows of some of the equipment. His transformation into Viper had begun the moment they had walked through the black curtain, strolling through the crowd toward the stage. She watched from behind as he grabbed the microphone and greeted his fans. They responded with a roar of cheers and screams.

It was hard to see into the crowd, what with the lights from the stage shining down on them. Those who were closest to the stage were easier to see, while the rest of the people morphed into a never-ending sea. The young women who were up front screamed and waved their hands in the air. Viper leaned down and touched several of their hands before he stood up and turned back to the band, nodding his head for them to get started.

The music began, and Viper started dancing, the microphone clutched in his gloved hand. He wore a broad smile on his face, laughing as he moved across the stage, interacting with the five scantily clad dancers through their choreographed moves. The energy from the crowd was contagious, and Amanda found herself swaying ever so slightly in rhythm with the music. The deep bass seemed to pulsate throughout her body. She found herself getting lost in the excitement and actually enjoying herself.

"Everybody having a good time out there?" Viper shouted into the microphone. "The party ain't over!"

The crowd responded with another loud roar, and he laughed, glancing over his shoulder, first at the band and then at Amanda. He reached up and pulled down his sunglasses just enough so that his blue eyes peered over the top. A mischievous gleam came to his eyes, and as the intro to the next song began, he pushed his sunglasses back up and began to dance toward her, his hips moving in rhythm with the beat.

The crowd saw the direction in which he was headed and went wild, the energy at a frenzied level. When he reached out and grabbed her hand, pulling her out of the shadows and into the spotlight, the noise from the audience drowned out the music from the speakers. As they ventured toward the front of the stage, he took a step back from Amanda, continuing to hold her hand. He stared at her, from head to toe, in an exaggerated leer that caused the color to flood to her cheeks but delighted the crowd of partygoers.

"Ay, mi madre!" he said into the microphone, a lustful tone to his voice. He pulled her into his arms, and not caring that the crowd was still screaming and shouting, he kissed her lips, dipping her backward ever so slightly so that she had to put her hand on his shoulder to steady herself.

When he gently released her, he turned to the crowd. "End of the night is going down!" he shouted into the microphone. "Let's make it a night you won't forget!" The crowd went crazy, and he stood back, laughing at their enthusiasm. When they quieted down enough to hear him, he placed his hand on his chest. "Everybody raise a drink, and let's make a toast!" As if on cue, a stagehand dressed in black crossed the stage with two fluted glasses filled with champagne. He took both glasses from him, handing one to Amanda.

"If you all are like me, it's been a year of ups and downs. Let's reach for the sky in the new year, because if there is one thing that I have learned . . . you can do anything that you set your mind to! And I have one person to thank for that." He took a step back and turned toward Amanda, lifting his champagne glass in the air. "To the heart of my heart and light of my soul," he said. "This toast is for you, Amanda."

He took a sip from the glass and encouraged her to do the same. Then he took the glass from her and handed it back to the stagehand before he wrapped his arm around her waist once again, the music playing. He leaned over and kissed her one more time, then released her, but kept holding her hand as he began to sing the next song, pulling her along with him across the stage as he sang. During the instrumental section, he danced with her, sometimes twirling her so that she spun around under his arm. He laughed and reached out to brush her cheek with his thumb before he turned back to the audience and continued singing.

When the song was over, the audience gave a final roar of approval, the electric energy of their adoration overflowing onto the stage. Alejandro took Amanda's hand, lifting it to his lips to plant a soft kiss on her skin before he gave a slight bow, allowing the crowd to cheer for her. She flushed and lowered her eyes until he encouraged her to wave to the crowd.

Laughing at her shyness, he grabbed the microphone one last time and shouted, "Happy New Year to you all! See you at eleven fifty-nine!" And with that, he gave a final wave before leading Amanda from the stage and through the black curtain that separated the public area from the private.

At the bottom of the steps, he turned to her and pulled her into his arms, lifting her from the ground as he spun her around. The joy on his face was contagious, and she found herself laughing, although she wasn't certain at what.

"¡Dios *mío,* Princesa*!*" He set her back down on the ground and placed both hands on either side of her face. "You are simply the most amazing woman!" He didn't wait for a response as he lowered his lips onto hers, ignoring the people who were nearby as he kissed her. "My Amanda," he murmured. "Happy New Year, Princesa."

"My Viper," she teased, oblivious to the people who were nearby, waiting for them.

"*¡Ay!*" He winced playfully. "There is no Viper with you!"

"Good," she said, reaching up to put her hand on the back of his neck. "I much prefer Alejandro."

He raised an eyebrow. "Always?"

She pursed her lips, trying not to smile at the insinuation behind what he said. "*Ja vell,*" she whispered. "Perhaps there are times when Viper is welcome . . ."

Tossing his head back, he laughed and pulled her into his arms for one more hug. "That's my *chica,*" he said.

Someone coughed behind them. They both turned. A young man stood there, a clipboard in his hand. "They are ready for you at the Countdown Stage," he said and motioned for them to follow him.

Holding her hand, Alejandro followed the man up the metal stairs to the elevated platform before the crowd in Times Square. When they emerged and joined the host of the countdown to midnight that was airing live on national television, they both waved to the crowd. When a general roar of approval came from those watching before them, Alejandro pulled Amanda into his arms and, in front of the millions of people watching, gently kissed her, the cameras zooming in on the happy couple.

The host laughed and waited until Alejandro released her, though he kept her at his side with his arm around her waist.

"The couple who needs no introduction," the host said into the microphone. "Viper and his leading lady, Amanda!"

The crowd roared, and Alejandro lifted his hand up in acknowledgment, pausing to correct the host. "My only lady," he said into the microphone, a mischievous smile on his face.

"We're just a few seconds away from the ball starting to drop. Any last words before we welcome the new year?"

Amanda remained silent, but Alejandro took the microphone and stared into the camera. "I wish everyone a year filled with good health, success, and lots of time for the things that really matter," he said, glancing at Amanda. She smiled and lowered her eyes. He turned back to the camera. "And with all of God's love and blessings," he continued. "May this year bless me with more happiness and, perhaps, even an expansion to my family!"

The crowd gave one last cheer as Alejandro handed the microphone back to the host, laughing as Amanda stared at him, her eyes wide and questioning him while her cheeks turned red.

The host laughed with him and said into the microphone, "Sounds like that's a new resolution for the both of you!" He pressed a finger to his ear and nodded his head, turning back to the camera. "I'm getting the word that we are just a minute away! You all ready for the countdown?"

With every eye trained to the sky, the crowd watched as the ball descended and a large clock ticked off the final seconds of the year. Alejandro pulled her into his arms, her back pressed against his chest as they, too, stared up at the Waterford Crystal Ball flashing brightly against the night sky. The crowd began to count backward as the numbers flashed on the clock:

Ten, nine, eight . . .

Amanda turned her head, and Alejandro bent down. "A family?" she repeated into his ear.

Six, five, four . . .

He laughed and nuzzled at her ear, waiting for the final three seconds to be counted down.

As the crowd erupted into cheers and song, Alejandro let his lips find hers once again, this time for a drawn-out kiss before he embraced her, rocking her gently in his arms as "Auld Lang Syne" played over the loudspeakers.

"Happy New Year, Princesa!" he whispered into her ear, feeling her tighten her hold on him.

As Alejandro and Amanda stood on the platform, the millions of people around them seemed to disappear. For them, the only thing that mattered was that they were together and that together they would face whatever the new year would bring, united in their commitment to supporting each other.

The cameras panned out, shifting from the Countdown Stage to the happy faces of the people in the crowd. The rest of Times Square celebrated the end of yet another year and the beginning of a new one, a year that many resolved would be filled with positive change and joy, peace and happiness. With God's blessing, it was something they all hoped to achieve.

"I love you," he whispered in her ear before releasing her from his embrace as the song ended.

She smiled and lowered her eyes. "I know that, Alejandro," she replied.

He leaned down to plant a soft kiss on the top of her head, a hint of a smile still playing on her lips as he did so.

That was the photograph that would be shown across the world, the famous Cuban hip-hop star and his famous wife, the former Amish woman from Lititz, Pennsylvania, sharing a private moment as they celebrated their first New Year's together with millions of people in Times Square.

Within minutes, the unlikely couple was quickly escorted down the steps of the Countdown Stage and to an SUV waiting in a cordoned-off area with a police car ready to lead the way. With lights blazing atop the police car, the vehicles whisked Alejandro and Amanda through the massive crowds and traffic, leaving the joyous celebration in Times Square so that they could retreat to the peace of their hotel, away from the crowds, the noise, and the paparazzi . . . at last.

Glossary

Pennsylvania Dutch

ach vell	an expression similar to *oh well*
Ausbund	Amish hymnal
bann	shunning
bruder	brother
Daed, or her *daed*	Father, or her father
danke	thank you
Englische	non-Amish people
Englischer	a non-Amish person
fraa	wife
Gelassenheit	yielding to the will of God
g'may	church district
grossdaadihaus	small house attached to the main dwelling
gut mariye	good morning
haus	house
ja	yes
kapp	cap
kinner	children
Mamm, or her *mamm*	Mother, or her mother
nee	no
schwester	sister
troovel	trouble
Wie gehts?	What's going on?
wunderbar	wonderful

Spanish

adiós	good-bye
ahora	now
Ay, Dios	an expression; literally: Oh, God
Ay, mi madre	an expression; literally: Oh, my mother
bueno	good
buenos días	a greeting; literally: good day
chica	young girl; also a term of endearment
chico	young boy
claro	of course
Dios *mío*	my God
escúchame	listen to me
gracias	thank you
la vida loca	the crazy life
listo	ready
mi amor	my love
mi hijo	my son
nada	nothing
permiso	permission/excuse me
por favor	please
por qué	why
qué linda	how pretty
salud	cheers
sí	yes
siempre	always
sueñas con los ángeles	an expression; literally: dream with the angels
te amo	I love you
vamos a la playa	let's go to the beach

Plain Return

Book Four of the Plain Fame Series

Sarah Price

Waterfall
PRESS

January 20

Dear Anna,

Christmas seems so long ago! Was it less than a month since I left Lancaster? With Alejandro's busy schedule, hours often seem like days and days like weeks.

While I miss all of you, I reckon the one thing I do not miss about Pennsylvania is the cold weather. For the most part, we have been fortunate to travel mostly to warmer climates during the past few weeks, and we even celebrated my birthday at a beach in Malibu. The water was too cool for swimming, at least for my taste. But it was nice to be outside during the day, even if most of the people who joined us were friends of Alejandro's.

In less than two months, we shall embark on the journey to South America for Alejandro's tour. And shortly after that tour, he has concerts scheduled in Europe. It's too much for me to keep track of, that's for sure and certain. I admit to being apprehensive about all of this travel. As I've shared with you before, there isn't much to see between the airports, appointments, arenas, and hotels. But it will be exciting anyway, I'm sure.

Please let me know how everyone is doing. I'm sure Jonas and Harvey are managing the farm just fine. From the weather reports that I've seen, I gather that you haven't had much snow in January. With February being such a short month, spring will be here before you know it. I can already see you and Mamm planning the garden at the kitchen table after supper and under the kerosene lantern.

I'm thankful to finally return to Miami. Even though it isn't Lancaster and there won't be any open fields or springtime crops, it is my home with Alejandro. It's certainly much nicer than Los Angeles! And the blue skies that drop into the sea are truly a gift from God to remind us of how he created this world with a plan for each creature, both great and small. While I hadn't expected his plan for me to take me so far away from my family, I pray each morning and each evening that I honor him in both word and deed.

I best post this letter now. We are ready to leave for the airport.

Blessings to you, Jonas, Mamm, and Daed.
Amanda Diaz

Chapter One

From somewhere in their home, a door shut, just loud enough to cause Amanda to stir from a not-so-deep slumber. Her loose hair hid part of her face until she rolled onto her back, the white satin sheet slipping from her shoulder and just barely covering her chest. As the quiet noises of morning woke her, she opened her eyes, just enough to see that it was almost eight o'clock. Filtered sun shone through a sliver of the drawn draperies, and she lifted her arm to shield her eyes. It felt too early to give up on sleep. After three weeks of travel, she wanted to absorb the comfort of being back in Miami at last.

It was morning and her body ached, every joint and muscle. With a soft, deep breath, she slowly moved her arm and let her eyes flutter open. Beside her, Alejandro slept, his head against the pillow. She smiled at how peaceful he looked, his dark hair draped over his forehead and his arm covering part of his face. She couldn't help herself and reached out her hand, hesitating just before her fingertips brushed against his bare shoulder. It quivered under her touch as he took a deep breath, a satisfied and sleepy groan escaping his throat as he exhaled. Despite the travel and the long days, his skin was so tanned compared to her pale complexion. She wanted to trace the muscle that ran down his arm, the one that wasn't tossed over the pillow. But she also knew that he needed his sleep.

Quietly, she slipped her legs from beneath the sheet and over the side of the bed. Her muscles ached from the past few weeks of travel. She wanted to stretch and work out the knots in her neck, but she feared waking him. With one last glance at Alejandro, hoping that her movements had not disturbed him, she finally let her feet touch the soft white carpet and forced herself to stand. Careful to make no noise, she padded over to the window.

The previous evening, they had returned late in the night. By the time they arrived back at the condominium, it was well after midnight and everything was dark. Now, with the break of dawn, she wanted to see it, the sky and the sun, the palm trees and the water. From the wall of windows in their second-floor bedroom that overlooked the terrace, she knew she would be able to see the ocean. She had missed that view, a realization that surprised her.

Careful to avoid letting in more light, Amanda peeked through the gap between the curtains, her eyes taking a moment to adjust to the sunlight that reflected off the pool's surface. The crystal-clear turquoise water shimmered as if a light breeze skimmed it. Someone had already swept the patio; not a leaf or flower lay astray. The cabana drapes were open, tied back to the wooden accordion-style doors that were only closed during storms, or so she had been told. During her brief stays in Miami, she had yet to experience anything less than pleasant weather.

In the distance, she could see the Atlantic Ocean. The rolling motion of the water looked calm and tranquil from her vantage point. She could barely make out a cruise ship on the horizon. It looked as if it was approaching the harbor located just a few miles north of their building.

Seeing the cruise ship, Amanda sighed, remembering the last time Alejandro had taken her on his yacht. Our yacht, she corrected herself, immediately feeling uneasy. The idea that all of this—the yacht, the cars, the money, and the fame—belonged to her now, too, simply seemed foreign and unnatural. It wasn't something that she wanted. No. All she wanted was his love. With that, her life was complete. The accessories that came with loving him meant nothing to her.

But she knew that these accessories were important to him.

During the past three weeks, she saw how Alejandro thrived on his professional life as an international sensation. When she had first accompanied him on the road, she hadn't paid as much attention to the little details. She had been too enthralled with all of the new places and experiences. Even more important, she had been enthralled with Alejandro. She had been quick to observe that there were two sides to him: one being Alejandro and the other Viper. It never ceased to amaze her how effortlessly he could switch between the two personalities.

When they were alone together, Alejandro pampered her with love and attention. But when he stood onstage, Viper emerged as he sang his songs, often with lyrics that caused her cheeks to flush, while dancing with the six dancers who accompanied him to each concert. Whether she observed his concert from the backstage greenroom or the wings of the stage, the dance troupe's suggestive gestures and dance moves were enough to make her more than mildly uncomfortable. And when Viper would grab one of the dancers by the hair or pull her close to him, the dancer placing her hands on his chest to steady herself, and his mouth less than an inch from hers, Amanda felt as though her heart would burst with humiliation.

Yet when she looked around, no one seemed to even notice. It was the same routine that Viper and the dancers had performed at all of the other cities, including the ones that Amanda had been to, prior to their marriage. But still, when she saw him gyrating with one of the female dancers, it made her feel unbearably tense and uncomfortable.

And then there were the reporters and the interviewers.

Despite her continuous exposure to the world of the media during the last few stops of his tour, Amanda still felt awkward interacting with them. Their intrusive questions always led back to one thing: Viper. Early on, she recognized that they took advantage of her shyness and inexperience when faced with the glamorous world of show business. Since she wasn't one to place herself on some sort of a pedestal as the wife of an international star, she had a hard time fitting into the glove they wanted her to wear. All that she wanted was to be herself, Amanda. But the more she met with the media, the more she learned another important lesson: no one seemed really interested in Amanda outside of the confines of being Viper's wife.

When Alejandro wasn't onstage during the preshow sound check or performing for his adoring fans, he was whisked from one appointment to the next. His new manager, Fernando, often accompanied him, ensuring that Alejandro arrived and left on time. Amanda watched all of this with a mixture of feelings. The logistics behind the life of Viper amazed her, but the intrusive idolization of the endless hordes of women who seemed to follow him wherever he went did not sit well with her. Still, he was always prepared and ready to smile and pose for photos. And the lack of sleep didn't seem to bother him at all. He slept when he could, even if it was only for an hour here and an hour there.

He reminded her of a young horse with enough energy to pull a buggy from Lancaster County, Pennsylvania, to Holmes County, Ohio. He had only one speed: on. And, privately, she admitted that she had a hard time keeping up with him, especially when his days often blended into nights.

So now that they were in Miami, having just six weeks to prepare for the start of the South American leg of his tour, Amanda was looking forward to helping him learn how to relax . . . if he let her. If there was anyplace where he might find that ability to catch up on his sleep and enjoy the sunshine, it was Miami, she thought.

She pressed her forehead against the cool glass of the window, pensively. How long had it been since she was last in Miami? Had it been since Thanksgiving? After all that had happened in the past few months, Thanksgiving felt like a lifetime ago. In fact, she realized that every day with Alejandro was like a lifetime.

Often, as daylight dwindled and gave way to the busy hours of nighttime, she was left with a fading recollection of what had happened during the early part of the day. It was a strange feeling indeed: as if they were going through separate episodes of their lives, immediately following one another but somewhat unrelated. And as one episode would ebb, another would flow, following the other as the earliest one was erased, falling into oblivion. It seemed like the twenty-four hours of their days kept stretching and expanding like a rubber band.

Unfortunately, she knew what happened when a rubber band was stretched too wide.

Even during the busiest seasons on her parents' farm, Amanda had never experienced a fraction of what Alejandro often had scheduled each day. And without complaining or looking weary, Alejandro bore it well. She had no idea from where his energy came. She only knew that it was consistent and contagious; he energized everyone around him with his engaging conversation and lively blue eyes that sparkled, especially when he spoke to his fans.

One time, many lifetimes ago in Las Vegas, Alejandro had commented that he lived a *fast life*. While he had praised her for adapting so well to it, in hindsight, Amanda knew how little she had been prepared for becoming a part of that fast life: the paparazzi, the fans, the commitments, and the travel. Always the constant travel. Why, since New Year's Eve, they had crossed the country at least three times! Just last night, she had teased him that their home should be aboard the jet, instead of in Miami.

Now, however, his immediate obligations were nil. After landing in Miami early in the morning, they were finally home.

Gazing back toward the ocean, she took a deep breath. The sun lingered above the horizon, and the drain on her body told her that she hadn't gotten enough sleep. Still, she couldn't lie in bed all day.

She needed to unpack their luggage, work outside in the garden, and help Señora Perez in the kitchen. After all, now that they were back in Miami, Amanda wanted Alejandro to have a nice home-cooked meal that evening. His eating habits on the road left a lot to be desired.

Just as she was about to drop her hand from the drapes, she felt him standing behind her. Without looking, she could just sense his body. She smiled to herself, waiting for him to wrap his arms around her, his bare chest pressed against her back. Even though she wore a nightdress, she could feel the heat from his skin through the silk. His fingers tugged at the thin strap of her gown as she felt him kiss the back of her neck.

"What are you doing up so early, Princesa?"

His voice sounded groggy, still thick with sleep. She could smell the faded scent of his day-old cologne, and she felt an intense wave of warmth course through her body that left her lightheaded and breathless. Just feeling his arms, so muscular and strong, holding her, made her feel safe. She leaned back so that her head pressed against the underside of his chin. His morning stubble tickled her skin, but she didn't mind.

"Come back to bed, *Aman-tha*," he purred into her ear, her name rolling off his tongue and his thick Cuban accent exaggerated. "For once, let's stay in bed until the sun sets. You and me. Alone with no interruptions, no cell phones, nowhere to go." He held her tighter, his embrace protective and strong.

"The sun has barely risen," she replied, her voice soft and innocent.

"All the more reason to stay together in bed. Just once, Princesa, *sí*?"

The invitation was enticing, and she knew that he needed his sleep.

She couldn't even remember the last time she had both gone to bed *and* arisen with him. No, on most nights, she either fell asleep first or awoke alone, sometimes both. After his concerts, there were always places for him to go and people for him to see. She knew that his obligation to interact with his public was the driving force behind his self-imposed sleep deprivation. Most of his concerts were back-to-back from Thursday to Sunday, and that permitted them time to fly to his Los Angeles apartment so that he could work with the recording studio and meet with other artists during the earlier part of the week. It had been a long time since she had seen him get a full night's sleep, perhaps even all the way back to when they were still at her parents' farm over Christmas.

Now, reluctantly, she pulled away from him and, taking him by his hand, led him back to the bed. He followed her willingly, a half smile on his lips.

"You need more rest," she said, helping him into bed as if he were a child. "And I am no longer tired." That wasn't entirely true, but she wanted him to rest, undisturbed, while she took on the duties of the house as a proper wife would do.

He shut his eyes and relaxed as she pulled the sheet over his chest, her hand purposefully grazing his skin. When her fingers lingered just a moment too long by his wrist, he wrapped his hand around hers and gently pulled her to his chest, shifting his weight just enough so that she was tucked against his body once again.

"I will sleep," he said, "but only if you stay."

With his arm holding her tight, she couldn't say no, even if she wanted to. And once she felt his tight grip on her, she realized that she wanted to stay. Relaxing, she listened to the softness of his breath as it slowed down. She gently stroked his arm, feeling each muscle that quivered beneath her touch. One of his legs was tossed across hers, another measure to ensure that she did not escape. With each breath that he took, she could feel his chest rise and fall against her back. She smiled to herself, shutting her eyes and allowing a light sleep to find her, once again.

When she awoke for the second time, she knew it was almost noon. Alejandro hadn't moved much, his arm still holding her and his leg now entwined with hers. Her body felt less weary, and she knew that, with great care, she could slip from his embrace and start the long list of chores that she had already mentally prepared. With a gentle, deliberate movement, she slid from under his arm and managed to escape his hold. For a long, quiet moment, she stood there, gazing down on this beautiful man that God had somehow placed in her life. He barely stirred, his chest rising and falling in a rhythm that told her just what she needed to know: he was finally catching up on those months of eighteen- to twenty-hour days.

And while she missed the farm and her family, she knew that her place was by Alejandro's side, a place where she longed to be and knew that she would never leave again.

Quietly, she made her way to the door that separated his bedroom from what had once been hers. She could change her clothes without risk of disturbing him, especially since she still kept her increasing wardrobe in that room's large walk-in closet. But as she turned the door handle to push the door open, she heard him whisper her name.

Looking over her shoulder, her long brown hair hanging in loose waves down her back, she saw that he was not asleep but watching her through hooded eyes. Those blue eyes! Always watching her with that look that made her feel so alive.

"*Ja*, Alejandro?"

"You are glad you are home, no?"

She smiled, letting her hand slide up the side of the door as she slowly slipped through the opening, pausing just long enough to answer him. "There is no place like home, Alejandro," she said softly. "But only if I am with you." She lifted her finger to her lips, indicating that he should speak no more and return to his sleep. With great care to remain noiseless, she backed through the doorway and softly shut the door behind her. His sleepy smile remained engraved in her mind as she set about creating a morning routine, since they would be home for a while now. Routine, she thought with a warm feeling of love and anticipation, would put everything on track, at last.

About the Author

The Preiss family emigrated from Europe in 1705, settling in Pennsylvania as part of the area's first wave of Mennonite families. Sarah Price has always respected and honored her ancestors through exploration of and research on her family's Anabaptist history and their religion. For over twenty-five years, she has been actively involved in an Amish community in Pennsylvania. The author of over thirty novels, Sarah is finally doing what she always wanted to do: writing about the religion and culture that she loves so dearly.

Contact the author at sarahprice.author@gmail.com.

Visit her blog at www.sarahpriceauthor.com or on Facebook at www.facebook.com/fansofsarahprice.